Return Fire

Barry Ozeroff

iBooks
Habent Sua Fata Libelli

iBooks
1230 Park Avenue
New York, New York 10128
Tel: 212-427-7139
bricktower@aol.com • www.BrickTowerPress.com

All rights reserved under the International and Pan-American Copyright Conventions. Printed in the United States by J. Boylston & Company, Publishers, New York. No part of this publication may be reproduced, stored in a retrieval system, or transmitted in any form or by any means, electronic, or otherwise, without the prior written permission of the copyright holder. The iBooks colophon is a pending trademark of J. Boylston & Company, Publishers.

Library of Congress Cataloging-in-Publication Data

Ozeroff, Barry.
Return Fire
p. cm.
1. Fiction. 2. Thriller—Fiction—Fiction, I. Title.

ISBN-13: 978-1-59687-936-2, Trade Paper

Copyright © 2012 by Barry Ozeroff

August 2012

Return Fire

Barry Ozeroff

www.ozeroffbooks.com

Praise for RETURN FIRE

"RETURN FIRE leaps off the page, and hits the reader between the eyes like a high-powered rifle bullet. Barry Ozeroff's writing is gritty, hard-edged, and utterly compelling.
This book has bestseller written all over it."
—Jeff Edwards, award-winning author of SEA OF SHADOWS and THE SEVENTH ANGEL

"Charged with adrenaline, RETURN FIRE is a high-speed police thriller that never lets you off the edge of your seat. Equal parts mystery and action thriller, RETURN FIRE is page-turning fiction at its very best."
—the American Author's Association

RETURN FIRE details the disturbingly realistic processes of a police sniper under intense pressure. It has enough action, sex, and violence to satisfy the most avid adrenaline junkie."
—Lisa Black, author of TAKEOVER

As a decorated SWAT sniper, Barry Ozeroff's aim as a storyteller is just as deadly accurate. RETURN FIRE is everything you could ever want in a thriller.
—Steve Hamilton, Edgar Award-winning author of NIGHT WORK.

Dedication

I would like to thank my family for all their patience and support during the writing and publication of this novel. A special thanks goes to my brother, fellow author Mark Ozeroff (DAYS OF SMOKE), for his professional assistance. The characters in this work who bear the names of friends and family have nothing in common with their namesakes.

This book is dedicated to my mother Sheila, and my late father Leonard, and to my grandchildren Abby, Rachel, and Leonard.

Also by Barry Ozeroff
SNIPER SHOT

Chapter 1

I stare at the computer in disbelief, wishing I had never decided to check my email. Nearly three months have passed since I got one of these, and I had begun to think it might be over.

But clearly, it is not. Jesus.

"Ben! Come on!" shouts my wife. I hear her put on Christmas music in the living room, and I am beginning to smell the first batch of cookies. Glancing at the screen again, I try to decide if I should show it to her.

Just as I'm about to call her in, the sound of sirens in the distance gives me pause. My ear, trained by nineteen years on the job, picks the sounds apart and identifies them individually. Two, maybe three, police cars, an ambulance, and the old-school mechanical windup of a fire truck, all going somewhere fast. Idly, I wonder what has ruined someone else's holiday. But as the sirens fade to the west, toward the tracks and their inevitable other side, I dismiss them. Not my problem, right?

Some questions are better left unasked.

"Ben?"

"Hang on, Sharon, I'll be right there," I yell. She has every right to know about the email. It is my responsibility to tell her, but on the other hand, I don't want to do that to her. I especially don't want anything to ruin tonight. Sharon wouldn't be able to hide the fact that something's wrong, and Leah, our eight-year-old, would pick up on it immediately.

No. Can't do it. I delete the email, close the program, and hit the power button. Not tonight. Not on Christmas Eve.

I go to the living room and pause, looking, before I enter. I am the worst kind of schmuck, and I do not deserve this, but here it is, and it's mine. Looking around the room, I take a mental picture of it all. Not just of the sights, but of the sounds and scents too. It's as if I have an instinctual knowledge that all this might change, and I want to preserve it forever in my mind as it is now.

Having already experienced just that, I tend to follow such instincts.

The lights of the tree cast a soft red and green glow about the living room, which smells strongly of natural pine. Beautifully wrapped presents are piled a little too high for a family of only three. Sharon has put on the *Charlie Brown* Christmas CD, and we listen to their version of the traditional carols. Seeing me at the door, Leah begins dancing the silly dance of the *Peanuts* characters to the tune of *Linus and Lucy*, and we all laugh.

Like roughly a third of American Jews, the Geller family celebrates Christmas, minus the Christ part. I just can't bring myself to deny Leah the experience of it all. It's Christmas Eve 2007, and all seems right with the world. Welcome to this side of Stratton, Oregon's proverbial tracks, where white, middle-class working stiffs thrive.

I am Officer Benjamin Geller, a veteran of the Stratton Police Department; a former corporate tax attorney who left the good life to fulfill a boyhood dream of becoming a police officer; one who has learned that we all live by the choices we make.

I am also a SWAT sniper. Originally, the Stratton SWAT team was known as SERT, or Special Emergency Response Team, but after a little incident involving me, the team was disbanded for a year, and when they brought it back six months ago, it came with the name change. Out with the old and in with the new, I guess.

I don't like to think about that little segment of my life, and though I am sure I'll have to recount it at some point, for now all I will say is that about a year and a half ago, I shot another cop during a SWAT incident. He was a fellow sniper, and I nailed him a total of four times with my .308 sniper rifle from a distance of about 120 yards, smashing his legs and hips like dry twigs. I guess I can't say it was an accidental discharge. He was my partner, and he shot himself in the mouth after I was done with him. 'Nuff said.

It is raining outside, and the forecast calls for snow. Snow is a rare treat in Stratton, which is only about fifteen miles east of Portland, but a white Christmas . . . Well, that's almost unheard of.

I am lucky to have the holiday off. My normal days off are Sunday and Monday, and Christmas happens to fall on Monday this year. This means I will also get New Year's Eve off.

It is going on 10:30 p.m., and Leah is fading fast. She doesn't believe in Santa Claus, or anything she can't see, touch, or otherwise experience—a characteristic she has learned from me. Nevertheless, she has made it a goal to stay up until midnight, just in case, but she will not make it.

Sharon is baking cookies. Not Christmas sugar cookies, but real, gooey chocolate chip ones. Is there another kind? The first batch is due out of the oven in four minutes.

And then, as if preordained by The Great Destroyer of Holiday Cheer, my department Nextel phone goes off, and I roll my eyes. Guys with families like to be with them on holidays, so there's almost always a last-minute outbreak of the flu on Christmas. The department has to maintain minimum shift staffing even on the major holidays, so when I happen to be off duty on Christmas, I get called first, because I'm the Stratton Police Department's token Jew, which is supposed to mean I won't mind coming in. Well, tonight they will be surely disappointed.

Sharon's eyes plead with me, and she says, "Ben, you're going to tell them no, aren't you?"

"Of course I am, honey," I say, opening the phone and revealing the little color screen.

But it's not a sergeant's pleading text for overtime. Not just my Christmas, but that of about twenty-five or thirty other families, has just been ruined. I look at the words and wish they simply weren't there. Not tonight.

SWAT callout. Domestic hostage/barricaded suspect. Attempted murder/kidnap/assault. Command post Rockledge Pizza Hut. Safe approach from the south.

"Christ," I mutter.

Sharon, who knows I'm not much of a praying man, looks at me and says, "Is it a SWAT callout?"

I can tell what's coming. Still, I can't just not go, simply because it's Christmas.

"Yes."

"Ben, it's—"

"Shar," I interrupt, cutting her off. "There are seventeen other guys on the team who really *do* celebrate this holiday. They have to leave their families and go, just like me. It's not like I have a choice."

Sharon slams the oven door open and proclaims, "You do have a choice, Ben. You can choose your family over your job."

I'm not doing this. I really don't want to do this. "Come on, Sharon. You know someone has to do it. You never complain about the overtime or the extra ten percent I get for being on SWAT."

"Yeah, but it's *Christmas,* Ben. Can't you just say you've been drinking? Paulson does it all the time!"

"Shar, you know I can't do that. I've got to go. You *know* this."

"But think of Leah. What about *her* holiday?"

"Sharon, do you really want me to say it?"

"Say what, Ben?" she retorts, the challenge plainly evident in her voice.

So I say it. "When you and Leah were being held hostage, what was I doing? Was I out there doing what I had to, or did I call in sick?" I start getting ready to leave, using exaggerated movements to let her know I mean business.

Sharon glares at me with an expression that looks capable of freezing water. "Well, I guess I should be thankful you weren't in what's-her-face's apartment getting laid! At least not that night."

I stop what I'm doing, and turn to confront her face-to-face. I'm so pissed, my body is as tense as steel, and for a moment, I consider slapping her. Instead, I grab her face roughly and kiss her, hard. "Sharon, I love you. It's *over* with Andrea. I think I've more than made up for that, don't you? Now let me get out of here, 'cause the sooner I leave, the sooner I'll be back, OK?"

She wipes a tear and exclaims, "Merry friggin' Christmas, world!" This is real profanity for her, a sign she is truly angry. It's also a compromise, and a temporary end to the hostilities.

It's too late, though. Leah is in tears now. She cries whenever Sharon and I fight, because the memory of when I moved out, back when *it* was going on, is so fresh.

"Daddy, are you going away again?" she asks. Before I can answer, her head jerks violently to the right, narrowly missing the wall.

She still suffers from residual effects of anoxic-ischemic encephalopathy—a form of brain damage—and undergoes occasional random spasmodic muscle contractions that make her jerk like a marionette at the hands of a drugged-out puppeteer. This, along with occasional holes in her memory, are the only reminders of the time when she and Sharon were kidnapped and buried alive without sufficient oxygen, and I had to use my .308 to torture their location out of the renegade officer who had kidnapped them. But as I said before, I really don't feel like talking about that.

"Yeah, baby, Daddy has to take off for a while."

I belatedly realize she interprets this as me going away to live in a trailer, which I did when her mother caught me screwing Andrea Fellotino, another Stratton cop, just before the aforementioned incident, and I hastily add, "But I'll be back before you get up in the morning, Princess, and we'll open all the presents together. I'm not moving out again."

She visibly relaxes, and I go into the bedroom to change. I keep a pair of camouflage BDUs and some cold-weather gear at home. Because I live close to the police station, I am usually among the first to arrive at the SWAT van when the team gets called out.

Ten minutes later, bearing a Tupperware container of steaming cookies for the team, I am racing toward the Stratton police station. There is no traffic, and I am able to make the two-mile trip in record time. After all, 'tis the night before Christmas, and all through the city, not a creature is stirring, except for a Rockledge shitbag who is holding his family hostage. Hell, that's not that big a deal for that part of town; around the precinct, we usually refer to it as Rockledge foreplay.

I arrive to find the parking lot empty and quiet. Buzzing myself into the portion of the building housing the fire department, I open the fourth bay, revealing the big, midnight blue SWAT van. I unplug the 220 umbilical, toss it into an exterior cabinet, and climb aboard. Removing the key from the ashtray, I start the big Caterpillar diesel and pull the rig out onto the tarmac. I then start the generator, and turn on the night vision-preserving red interior lighting. Next, I light up the rig's various computer systems, then go to the back and begin gathering my gear.

Within moments, my teammates begin to arrive. Carlos "Backflip" Vega is first, smelling a little like beer, which I pretend not to notice. Hugh "Baby Hughie" Wilkes is next, wearing a Santa cap, which he will likely try to wear in his place in the entry team "conga line." Next is Ray "Oy Vey" Schmeer, my new sniper partner. We are close friends, unlike my last sniper partner, Bob Slater, whom I shot to pieces.

"Happy Chanukah, Helen," says Ray.

"*Sieg heil!*" I bark in return. He knows I hate the nickname Helen, which stems from a day I shot so poorly someone remarked that my target looked as if Helen Keller had shot it. Helen Geller, get it? Ray's team-issued nickname is Pap—Pap Schmeer—but I call him Oy Vey, because coupled with his last name, it fits so closely to the Yiddish expression "*Oy vey iz mir*," which means, "Woe is me." There is nothing remotely Jewish about Ray, who is a Teutonic, blond-haired, blue-eyed German. I tell everyone we meet that he is Jewish, which used to piss him off, but now he just finds it funny.

He clicks his heels together, stands ramrod straight, and spews in flawless German, "*Kuchen meiner Muttis sind immer ausgezeichnet!*" The way he delivers it, it sounds like a phrase recorded from one of Hitler's speeches, but in fact means "My mommy's cake always taste great," and is the only thing he knows how to say in that guttural language.

It is team practice that the van will leave when the first five to respond are dressed out and fully prepared. That way, we have a ready-made IRT, or immediate reaction team, to conduct whatever type of immediate operation that might be called for—downed officer rescue, hostage extraction, emergency hot entry, or anything else that may be required. Even we snipers are cross-trained for such a possibility.

Most of the men (or the woman, as in the case of Ellen "Hairdo" Fitzsimmons, Stratton's first female SWAT member) keep their equipment in the van so they can respond from home and prepare while en-route to the scene. Quickly, the initial responders join me, and start getting ready.

Several folks show up, and Ellen Fitzsimmons is the last to arrive before we pull out. Not one to worry about modesty, she doffs her uniform and dons her BDUs without regard for being seen in her underwear. Too bad she's built like a Russian Olympian, but frankly, I'm glad of it. Not a month ago, I was attacked by a man whose wife I had just arrested for beating him up, and Ellen was my cover officer. She damn near wiped the floor with the guy. Not only is she willing to give one hundred percent in a fight, but she is more capable of laying a major hurtin' on someone than half the men in this outfit.

Fourteen minutes after my arrival, it is time to get under way. Carlos Vega gets on the computer and sends a page that the van is leaving. Hugh Wilkes, who has been our driver since he joined SWAT two years ago, gets the van rolling. Team leader Stan "Housing Authority" Hauser and Fitzsimmons drive the chase cars, one in front, and one behind the van. As we roll out the back gate, we slow briefly, and I extend an arm, hooking Brian "Armpit" Pole, the assistant team leader, into the van.

Surfing the floor against the motion of the van, I make my way to the weapons locker and carefully extract my rifle. It is a highly customized Remington 700 with a beautiful Dedal DayVision/NightVision interchangeable starlight scope. This rifle was once used to score third place in the National High-powered Shooting Competition at Camp Perry, Ohio. Its previous owner and the holder of that title was Bob Slater, my late former partner, of whom I spoke earlier.

After the matter of my little disagreement with Slater over the kidnapping of my family was adjudicated to my favor in court, Slater's parents donated the rifle to the police department for use on the SWAT team. Being the primary sniper, it fell to me. We share some significant history, this rifle and I, and we have grown rather fond of one another.

Lovingly, I load three .308 cartridges into the magazine. The second one is in case I have two bad guys to kill, and the third is in case one of the first two is a dud. It doesn't take more than one round to kill a man with this baby. Unless, of course, you're only torturing him.

Gustavo "Mini Me" Oronco, who has just come from the scene, fills us in on the call. Oronco is a jovial five-foot, three-inch Hispanic entry team member who is bald as a cue ball and is considered by all to be one of one toughest hombres on SWAT. He tells us that it is the Hicks family, and that Delray has stabbed his wife. He said the ambulance crew told him it doesn't look as if she's going to be celebrating Christmas this year, or ever again, for that matter.

I am well acquainted with Delray Hicks, his wife Denise, and their kids, as is just about every officer in Stratton. We have been dealing with them for years. They have two children, a teenage girl and a younger boy, neither of whom stand a chance of making it in the real world. Delray is a big, strapping man, but his wife is a whale, standing at least five-ten and weighing in at nearly four bucks.

Oronco tells us Christmas Eve got under way in the Hicks' trailer when, during an argument, Delray beat all but Jesus out of Denise in front of the children, and she returned the favor by smashing a beer bottle over his head. Either the nasty cut he received, the loss of the beer, or both, pissed him off, and he sank a ten-inch butcher knife into her right kidney

When the cops showed up, Delray answered through the door, threatening to "gut the first honkey-ass muthafucka'" who tried to take him out of there. Fortunately for us, Delray is more of a knife guy than a gun guy.

This is exactly the sort of thing our hostage negotiators live for. HNT, or the hostage negotiating team, loves to listen to the bad guy, kiss his ass, offer him milk and cookies or maybe a hug, then have him come out once they gain his trust. It generally works, but it can go on for hours, which doesn't bother them at all. Of course, HNT doesn't have to sit outside in thirty-five degree pouring rain, either.

I paint my face a frightening combination of green and black, hoping for a Navy-SEAL-in-a-foreign-jungle look. I hate the paint, but I like the look. I put on my fleece-lined Gore-Tex green jacket and my dirty, floppy boonie hat. Over my long underwear is a pair of lightweight rain pants, over which my BDU pants go. The idea is that my BDUs can get soaked, but my legs will stay dry. It rarely works like that.

After pulling on a pair of camouflage green hunting gloves with a slit for my trigger finger, my ensemble is complete. I attach a remote transmit button to the outside of my left index finger by means of a Velcro strip and don my radio headset. Switching over to the proper frequency on my portable, I do a radio check. Finally, I jump up and down, and hearing no jingling or other unusual noises, I pronounce myself fully prepared.

I have a backpack containing water, energy bars, fresh gloves, binoculars, wire cutters, waterproof waxed-paper notepad, space pen that can write on the moon, and a host of other equipment, which I throw across my back. I place my rifle into a woodland camo Gore-Tex drag bag, and wait for the van to stop rolling.

I know this trailer park well; particularly number eighteen, the Hicks' trailer. The park itself is situated on a main road, but number eighteen is in the back and faces railroad tracks, a wastewater treatment plant that smells suspiciously like a wastewater treatment plant, and a large, tree-covered hillside.

Ever since he got out of prison, we've all known that there would be a callout here. I first arrested Delray twelve years ago, when he was nineteen, for beating a neighbor with a metal pipe. The DA dropped the Assault I charge in exchange for his pleading guilty to an Assault IV with a minimum of six months, and which he did locally. He was just small-time then. His last stint was seventy-eight months for manslaughter. Delray Hicks has spent over half his adult life in either prison or jail.

Stan Hauser goes to a filing cabinet and removes a file marked "Hicks." It is a site survey of Hicks' trailer—a detailed plan for rapid deployment of the team if there is a callout there. It covers most of the logistical aspects of deployment and operation, such as the best routes of approach, the best staging areas for the command post and hostage negotiation team, and suggested locations for inner perimeter team members and snipers. Also covered in the site survey are detailed drawings and measurements of the trailer and its interior, evacuation routes, the gas plans, entry plans, LifeFlight landing zones, medical staging areas, the nearest schools, etc. There are similar plans for every hospital, school, government building, and trouble spot in our area of operations, which includes all of Multnomah County except the city of Portland, which has its own SERT team. Included in the packet are photographs of the entire family, and I take one of Delray for target identification. We update this file regularly, whenever new potential trouble spots are identified.

Studying the plan, I see that if I choose the predetermined side-one primary sniper location, I will have the cover of heavy brush, and a straight 105-yard shot into Hicks' front door and living room window. My partner will be lucky; his best position is from a neighbor's trailer directly behind Hicks'. While I'm freezing my ass off lying in a puddle and getting rained on, some old lady will be serving Ray Schmeer coffee and cake while bending his ear about her grandchildren. *Oy vey.*

The van slows, and the siren is silenced. As the cacophony around me quiets, it is time again to wonder if I will have to kill a man tonight. This time, though, my thoughts differ from before I joined the exclusive club whose members have taken human life. I still wonder if I will have to do it again; only I no longer experience dread at the thought. I have already bloodied my hands in this job, and whereas I don't *want* to do it again, I know that I can if I have to. Sometimes I am amazed at how I can so flippantly consider the very real prospect of killing again.

One thing that makes it easier in this case is that it is what we refer to as an "AVA NHI" situation, as are any problems between Delray Hicks and his wife. AVA NHI is cop-speak for asshole versus asshole, no humans involved. The only potential humans involved are the kids, maybe. At least, the youngest one. As shallow as that seems, it really does make considering his death much easier to stomach.

The van comes to a complete stop, and I throw the pack across my back and grab the drag bag containing my rifle. Shouldering past everyone, I position myself at the rear door, where I am joined by Ray. Since we're the first to be deployed, we like to be the first out of the van.

Our job is not so much to shoot the bad guy as it is to make detailed observations of everything going on at the target location, filter that information, and report it and its meaning to the command post. Our roles on the team are commonly referred to as primary and secondary sniper (primary on side one, or the front of the target location, and secondary on side three—the rear; the sides being numbered clockwise from the front of the building), but technically we are sniper/observers. Observing is by far the majority of what we do.

It was *all* we did until May 24, 2005. That was the night Hugo Route tried to kill his infant daughter, and I was forced to take him out as he placed a .357 Magnum to the baby's neck. My shot, which should have been taken by my then-partner Slater, passed through his wife's bicep on the way, severing her brachial artery and nearly causing her to bleed out. The wife, Pammi, later conspired with Slater to lie in her testimony to say her husband was not holding a gun at the time of the shooting. She was caught in her lie, but the police department still had to pay her $30,000 in an out-of-court settlement.

The ruling in favor of Pammi Route was not because I took the shot and she got hit, but rather because Slater *hadn't* taken the shot when he should have, which forced me to shoot from an impossible angle. The original ruling was for sixty thousand, but the jury ordered that thirty thousand of it had to be donated back to the police department, earmarked specifically for sniper training.

Because of that donation, I went to a Special Forces Advanced Urban Sniper School in Maryland. Additionally, the money allowed for a secondary sniper, and they brought Ray on the team, sending him to the beginner, intermediate and advanced sniper schools within six months of each other. The deal basically hosed Pammi Route, considering that her lawyer bills were about ten grand, leaving her with approximately $20,000 when the dust settled. I heard she bought a new car and went to Vegas with her share. Drive safely, Mrs. Route.

The van comes to a stop, and Ray and I jump out the back, ready to do Christmas battle.

Chapter 2

A patrol officer directs us to the temporary command post, which consists of a police car parked out of the line of fire, with a map and a hand-drawn diagram of Hicks' trailer on the hood.

For the first time I can remember, Lieutenant Vince Capelko, the team commander, is not on-scene when the team arrives. This means a patrol sergeant, Dolly Sector, is in temporary command of the incident until she is relieved by someone who outranks her. Sector is a tall, pretty woman of forty years with raven black hair. She's a new sergeant and is the most by-the-book supervisor I have ever worked with.

Sergeant Sector is a Christian, one of the really annoying ones. Even the other members of Stratton's "God Squad" call her Saint Sector, and the book she goes by is the Good Book. She has *WWJD* etched into the floor plates of her Sig Sauer magazines, and everything she does or doesn't do is based on her interpretation of the Bible. Nonetheless, she has always liked me, which I attribute to the fact that I am of the Chosen People, whom Christians seem to love boundlessly for no reason.

The only time I ever saw Dolly laugh at anything even remotely off-color was when I told her the old joke about Abraham arguing with God, and he said, "Now let me get this straight; the Arabs get all the oil, and we have to cut off the ends of our *what?*" I don't think anyone else in the department could have gotten away with that.

Anyway, in practical terms, even though Saint Sector is temporarily in charge, it will be tactical team leader Stan Hauser, a patrol officer, who will be calling the shots until he's relieved by a ranking SWAT sergeant or commander.

"Hi, Ben, Ray," Sector says, obviously relieved to see the team here. Patrol officers, who are ill-equipped and ill-trained to handle hostage or barricaded subject scenes, can do little more than contain the situation until SWAT arrives.

"Hey, Dol. What's Delray done this time?" I ask.

"He tried to mine one of his wife's kidneys. About twenty-five minutes ago, he threw her out of the trailer. She was able to crawl to some officers who evacuated her to paramedics, and they took her to Emanuel. Delray is still inside with his seventeen-year-old stepdaughter and his six-year-old son. We can hear a great deal of fighting; mostly the girl screaming to be let go, and him swearing and saying she's not going anywhere. It isn't good."

"What's he wearing?"

"Blue jogging suit."

"OK, well, Ray and I are ready to go, and we both know what he looks like. We'll be reporting to you until Capelko gets here."

"OK, well, if that's the way it works. Just so you know, though, I've never done this before."

"Don't worry. Hauser will be with you. Just do what he says."

"Thanks," she said, obviously happy to have someone telling her what to do. "Be careful, guys."

Ray and I separate and move out in different directions. His route will take him around the block to the next street over and through a door that has been left unlocked for him. Inside, it will be nice and toasty, with holiday music playing softly in the background, and the Christmas tree lights giving off a warm, happy glow. He will probably sit on a plush couch and aim his rifle through a window that is situated over a heating vent.

I, on the other hand, must hump across a muddy field in the dark, climb a rusty fence into a wastewater treatment plant, and then try to make my way back toward Hicks' trailer without falling into a vat of urine. I will lie in a puddle and get rained on, and the sight picture in my scope will jump around as I shiver in misery.

It is quite cold, and my gloves quickly soak through in the misty drizzle. My breath forms clouds of vapor around my head, and I begin to sweat from the exertion. In short order my face and head are steaming. I reach the fence and opt to snip my way through with wire cutters; at forty-two I already feel too old to climb fences if I can avoid it. There is sufficient ambient light to keep me from falling into the rancid holding tanks, but I quickly discover the light is unnecessary; I could avoid them by smell alone.

The trailer park materializes far off to my left. I make my way there and easily locate the Hicks trailer. As I approach, the yelling begins anew. It is a female voice, crying and saying things I cannot understand yet.

I find my spot, which is at the base of the only two fir trees in the area. They provide ample cover and even stop most of the drizzle from reaching me. Nonetheless, the sweat immediately begins to cool, making me one very uncomfortable sniper.

I withdraw the rifle from the drag bag and extend the forward-mounted bipod legs, adjusting their length so that the crosshairs are aligned perfectly straight. I always keep the scope set for one hundred yards, but I reset it for zero, then readjust it for a hundred yards just to make sure. Next, I check to make sure that a round is chambered and the safety is off. I know the chances of me taking a shot are very slim, but nonetheless, I know that I am capable and willing to do so if need be. Prior experience tells me I will sleep soundly if I do. The demons that once haunted me about my ability to kill with premeditation are now silent.

There are annoying branches in my field of view, which I cut away with as much economy of movement as I can manage. I place a beanbag butt-rest under the rifle's stock, and make my initial broadcast.

"Geller to CP."

"Uh, go ahead, Ben." It is Sergeant Sector, still sounding very nervous and insecure. Being in command of a SWAT operation for the first time must be a daunting undertaking for someone without a tactical background.

"Dolly, I'm going to tell you where I am. All you have to do is take notes, OK?"

"OK, Ben, go ahead."

"I'm in the predetermined primary sniper spot, one-hundred-five yards off the front door, under the twin fir trees. Target condition is as follows: the screen door is open, and the living room light is on. The blinds are closed in the one window I can see into. Nothing's moving, although I can hear both Delray and his teenage daughter yelling. OK?"

"Got it, Ben."

"Good. Just write down everything everyone tells you, and give it to Capelko when he gets there."

"OK. Uh, out."

I smile to myself at the hesitancy in her tone, and then settle into the business of being a sniper. I center the crosshairs on a spot three feet above the doorknob, leaving it set there for use in a moment's notice, and then scan the trailer and its immediate surroundings with a pair of high-resolution binoculars.

As teammates check in, arriving at positions around the house, the entry team waits in their conga line around the three-four corner of Hicks' trailer. From my perspective, that's the far right corner. Four men form the IRT, and position themselves along the number-two side of the trailer next to Delray's. They will handle any escapes from the trailer, the deployment of gas, and anything else that may need to be dealt with on a moment's notice, leaving the entry team to do only one thing—enter when the time comes.

There is a near-constant stream of shouted profanity coming from Delray Hicks. I have dealt with him for years, and have seen him in various stages of upset, but nothing like this. I hear him banging around the trailer yelling at himself and the boy, but mostly at the teenage stepdaughter.

"Look what yo' mama done to me, be-atch! Slap me upside the haid with a muthafuckin' forty! Now I be bleedin' all over the damn flo'! An' look at you; dress like a ho, be talkin' trash all the muthafuckin' time."

"Let me out dis trailer, Delray. You drunk, and nobody can talk to you when you drunk."

"You ain' got nowhere to go, girl. You wan' them police's to take my ass back to the joint? Ain' nobody goin' nowhere 'til dem muthafuckas is *gone*."

"They ain' goin' nowhere, Delray! You think they just gonna leave?"

All I hear in response is a resounding slap.

The argument is played out with the continual background music of the little boy's crying. I remember this child well from answering radio calls about Delray over the years. Built like a little tank, he will obviously be large and strong like his daddy, assuming the sperm donor was indeed Delray. But the similarities end there. The argument of environment versus heredity is settled when you look at his disposition.

I answered a call at the Hicks' trailer about a month ago in which the boy was playing alone out in the street while cars drove around him. Delray was gone, and the mother was sleeping off a hangover. Nothing happened as a result of the call, but I remember how scared the kid seems to be all the time. I simply cannot recall his name, other than that it is something ridiculous even by ethnic standards, but I do remember that the boy has a tendency to shake all the time. When the police come to the trailer on family beef calls, he is usually found cowering in the filthy shower stall. I don't think I've ever seen him without a snotty upper lip from crying.

I have only seen the daughter on one occasion. As I recall, she is a tiny thing, perhaps five three and a hundred pounds soaking wet. Given the size of her mother, I wonder how this is possible. Delray is a large man, maybe six one or two, and weighs at least 250. He's fat, but he's strong as an ox and as dumb as a box of rocks.

The argument continues for another ten minutes, mostly with name-calling and a variety of shouted epithets I cannot really understand.

Inner perimeter units staged closer to the trailer are giving Sergeant Sector regular updates on the arguing between Delray and his stepdaughter. I can't hear her as well as I can hear him, but it is clear she is trying to leave and he is threatening her if she does.

There is a large crash, as if something made of glass broke, or perhaps a tray of silverware has been dumped onto the floor, followed by a brief moment of silence except for the screaming of the six-year-old, then a hideous scream issues forth from Delray.

"Aaaaggghhh! You *cut* my ass, ho! Look what you done 'a my han! Gut-*damn!*"

Suddenly, the door bursts open, and the girl steps out onto the porch. In her hand is a long, wicked-looking carving knife. Her shirt is ripped open, revealing a small, tan breast that looks pale in comparison to the rest of her dark, satin skin.

Reflexively, my thumb mashes the transmit button against my finger. "Breakout, side one!" I announce in my calmest, most practiced sniper voice. "Black female with a knife, standing on the front porch!"

She stops short, as if she expected to see police everywhere. "Not moving from porch," I announce.

The IRT heads around the corner. I had been waiting for the door to close or the girl to decide which way she was going to go before having them move, but they do what they want to without waiting for me to give them direction. Normally, this is OK, but if I perceive it to be dangerous for them, I will advise them over the air not to move. Whether they will listen and take my advice is their choice, but normally they do. I am their eyes and ears, and they trust me implicitly in this.

The team doesn't run. They only move as fast as they can accurately shoot, which is a fast-paced, rolling gate. It takes several seconds for them to get around the corner, across a driveway, and move up alongside Hicks' trailer. It is during these fatal extra seconds while they are in transit that Delray's big form darkens the doorway. His face is streaked with blood, presumably from the forty-meets-haid encounter he described earlier.

Moving of their own volition, my crosshairs travel up to Delray's face. He is unarmed, or I would have already shot him. My thumb automatically mashes the transmit button as I advise that S-1 is now in the doorway.

He meets the reaction team face-to-face with his stepdaughter sandwiched between. Given the positioning of Hicks in relation to his stepdaughter, the IRT does not have a shot. I do, though.

But I cannot find sufficient justification for shooting him at this moment. He's not armed, threatening the girl directly, and is not a direct threat to the team.

If the IRT wasn't still ten feet away they'd have snatched the girl and face-planted Delray by now. As the distance between them closes, Delray' fist lashes out and punches the girl in the back of the head. Simultaneously, he grabs her knife hand and brings the blade to her throat.

There is a brief standoff during which I consider, then again discard the option of shooting Delray. Gustavo Oronco's head is now within inches of the bullet's trajectory to Delray' face, and he has already once moved directly into my line of fire. Oronco immediately engages Delray verbally, and it is my hope that he will be able to negotiate Hicks into custody. If it goes bad, I know I will rue the half-second during which I failed to pull the trigger.

"Geller to CP, no shot, no shot!" I say into my headset, stress now creeping into my voice. There is no response.

I can hear snippets of the conversation, and I realize Hicks is not giving up. Oronco is doing the talking, or shouting in this case, and I hear him ordering Delray to the ground.

Hicks yells something about us needing more than four SWAT muthafuckas to take him out of there, and then shoves the girl into the four-man element. Two of them instinctively sling their weapons to catch her. As he fades back into the trailer, my finger pulls the trigger to about five pounds, a half-pound shy of firing, but the girl and Oronco are still dangerously close to the line of fire, and my window of opportunity closes as surely as the trailer door which swallows Delray.

If not for the girl, the IRT would have followed him into the trailer and taken care of business, but she seems to hate them every bit as much as she does her stepfather, and is struggling like a woman possessed. She fights them with everything she has, and they finally knock her to the ground and literally drag her away.

"One in custody, proceeding to the HNT van," Oronco says over the radio, and Sector acknowledges. The girl is being taken to the hostage negotiating team for debriefing. Things quiet down, except for the boy's crying. Some time later, Sergeant Sector breaks squelch on the radio with an announcement.

"Um, CP to SWAT. Stan says we will now advance the rules of engagement to the level of . . . " She is off the air for a moment, during which time I am sure she forgot the term and is asking Stan Hauser. "We are now at compromised authority," she finishes. "HNT will attempt to open negotiations shortly. That is all. Uh, over."

Nobody says "over." I want to chuckle, but I'm too stressed from missing the opportunity to drop the hammer on Delray.

The elevation of the rules of engagement to compromised authority is pretty standard stuff. There are three different levels, the minimum of which is called standard rules of engagement, which are the same rules by which every officer in the field must play. The next highest is compromised authority, which means that all entry, gas, and other plans have been approved and are in place, and should anyone involved in the incident be compromised, the entry team can go in and execute their plans on their own authority without prior approval. The third and highest order of engagement—shot of opportunity—is an order for the sniper or anyone else on the team to take his or her first available shot to neutralize the suspect. Neutralize the suspect is a politically correct term which means blow the bastard's brains out.

For the first time since I've been here, things calm down inside the trailer. The boy's crying has dwindled to a quiet whimper, and for the moment, Delray seems to have no one to yell at.

Probably because things are now quiet, I become aware of how cold and uncomfortable I am. The drizzle has been steady, and though my legs and feet are still dry, they may as well be soaked because they are so clammy and cold under the rain gear.

My hat soaked through a long time ago, and my head is now wet as well. Small rivulets of cold water course down my face; the headwaters of streams which turn to rivers and snake their way under my clothes, soaking me from the inside out. My breath clouds up in front of me, and my teeth begin to chatter. I feel as if I've been here for hours; surely it must be 0300 or 0330 by now.

Just as I'm thinking this, the command post makes a brief broadcast. I am glad to hear that it is now the voice of Lieutenant Vince Capelko, the SWAT commander.

"CP to SWAT. It's zero hundred hours. Merry Christmas."

I think of what kind of Christmas I am giving my family this year by being here instead of there, and it doesn't seem as if the extra money is worth it. Then I think of the pitiful little boy inside the trailer who just watched his mother get stabbed with a butcher knife, and I wish I had never even heard of Delray Hicks. It is much better to be unaware of such things than to see the effect they have on the little ones.

Somehow, the Geller family Christmas seems joyous in comparison.

Chapter 3

Half an hour passes, during which the boy finally stops whimpering. While scanning with binoculars, I watch SWAT guys escorting a member of the hostage negotiating team with a bullhorn to the entry team's jump-off point.

"CP to SWAT, HNT will now initiate contact via loudhailer."

The negotiator raises the bullhorn to his lips and releases a piercing squeal of feedback that seems designed to grate the nerves. This is followed by an apologetic, "Delray? Delray Hicks?"

"God *damn*, y'all! Git dat muthafuckin' radio the hell away from my house! Y'all muthafuckas be wakin' up my boy, jus' when he fin'ly shut his sorry ass up!"

"Delray, we need you to step outside with your hands up. Will you do that for us?"

"Hell fuckin' no, I won'! Is you crazy, or jus' stupid? Come out wit my han's up? Sheee-it, you ain' gonna 'rest my ass cuz I cut my bitch, not when she done crack me upside the haid an' laid me open like a muthafucka 'fore I even touch her ass. I *ain'* goin' to jail, so ya'll might as well start shootin' now! First muthafucka try an' come in here's gettin' sliced 'fore he shoots my black ass, and that's a muthafuckin' *promise*! Which one y'all got the balls to come in firs'? Huh? Who gonna come get the nigga?"

"Delray, will you at least come to the door so we don't have to shout?"

"Muthafuckin' peckerwoods!"

"There's no need to be frightened, Delray, all we want to do is talk," says the negotiator condescendingly. "You have my promise that if you come to the door, we won't hurt you. Please don't be afraid."

I've got to hand it to these guys, they can be pretty creative. The negotiator is subtly challenging Delray's machismo, and I figure it will either piss him off and escalate things, or make him come out.

A moment later, the front door opens up, and Delray is standing there, now holding his crying son in front of him as if for protection. Other than the child, his hands are empty. The boy's eyes are so wide and white with fright they look like plates.

"Geller to CP, he's at the front door holding the child. He appears unarmed," I announce calmly.

"*What?*" screams Hicks. "Do I look afraid to you motha*fucka*? Here I is, right in my own gut-damn do'. What you gonna do about it? You gonna come get me? You wan' a piece of ol' Delray? Ai'ite den! Let's see if yo muthafuckin' snipers can shoot pas' my chil' befo' they gets to me!"

He holds the screaming child out in front of him, and in that moment, now frozen in my memory, I remember the boy's name. It is LaMonjello, pronounced LaMONjello, like a combination of Lamont, minus the T, and Angelo, minus the 'An.' I once asked the mother the origination of the name, and her explanation was that when she was pregnant, all she wanted to eat was lemon-flavored Jell-O. She said she liked the way it sounded so black.

Keeping the crosshairs focused on the little divot between Delray's nose and his upper lip, I adjust the magnification of my scope so I can see more, and watch the entry team disappear behind the trailer as the negotiator starts asking Hicks how old his son is. In a moment, they reappear next to the trailer, sneaking along the number-four side. It will now be over in a matter of seconds.

Just as they round the corner ten feet shy of the door, Delray is holding his son in front of him like a saucer-eyed offering when two things happen simultaneously. One, I both hear and feel the air above my head split as if opened by a zipper. The sound is like the buzzing of a giant wasp on crack; the feeling like a slight, but rapid increase of air pressure. Concurrent with that, Hicks' head explodes in a shimmering cloud of red mist. A fraction of a second later, a crack of thunder erupts all around me.

Hicks crumples to his knees in a kneeling position on the ground, and the boy, covered with ejecta from his father's skull, lands on his feet. Before his father is done falling down, the child hops off as if pulled by a string, and disappears into the trailer. Hicks bends forward at the waist and appears to settle as if praying toward Mecca for eternity, but he is too fat to come to rest in such a position. In slow motion, his upper body flops off to the right, finally settling into a half-sitting, half-reclining position; his left arm across his midsection and his right arm extended as if beckoning us in for coffee.

I have seen this before, and it is not something one gets used to. In fact, I am dazed into immobility; horrified, unable to even recall pulling the trigger. Someone is yelling "Compromise! Compromise! Compromise!" into the radio. As if this were all planned, the entry team, their stride unbroken, continues into the trailer, with two members remaining outside, standing a useless guard over the body.

I still do not fully comprehend how this has happened, but I am positive that I didn't shoot him. Someone did, though; another close-up magnified glance at the bloody pulp above Delray's shoulders confirms it. Just to make positively sure it wasn't me, I recheck my rifle, only to find there is a live round in the chamber and two in the magazine, as I knew there would be. Nodding to myself, I safe the weapon.

In a moment, Stan Hauser announces the trailer is secure. He then comes out, dragging the screaming boy with him, and calls for an ambulance. I cannot tell if LaMonjello is hurt or just covered with his father's blood, and this becomes my primary concern.

It had to have been someone on the perimeter team. Someone behind me. But I know the position of everyone on IP, and nobody is behind me.

But if it wasn't someone on IP, then . . . My stomach begins to cramp as realization dawns on me.

Capelko's voice comes tersely over the radio. "CP to SWAT... Who took the shot?"

There is no reply.

"CP to Geller."

"It wasn't me, Vince," I reply thankfully.

"Pap?"

"Negative," replies Schmeer.

"OK, then. CP to SWAT. Everyone remain in position. Acknowledge by roll call." I'm not religious by any stretch, but I pray that someone fesses up to it.

Starting with me, the entire team acknowledges. Nobody admits to it. If it is one of us, he will be lucky to just get fired. Ultimately, there's a good chance he'll face criminal charges.

If it was one of us.

In any case, this is going to be a nightmare for the team. An unarmed man who had been holding a child was shot and killed while surrounded by heavily armed SWAT personnel, and on Christmas morning too. The shitstorm that's coming will probably rival that of Ruby Ridge.

Hauser, Capelko and Brian Pole form a team, and go around confiscating weapons. When they get to me, they ask when I last cleaned my rifle. It was two weeks ago after range training and I have not fired it since, further proving I had not taken the shot. After they move on, my Nextel buzzes, and I see that it is Ray.

"Ben, tell me it wasn't you."

"It wasn't me. You either, I take it."

"Hell no. Someone's in deep shit. What IP guys are deployed on your side? It had to have come from somewhere on side one."

"I don't know. Terry Horner's seventy-five yards to my ten o'clock, but I know it wasn't him. Could it have been an AD?"

"That was no accidental discharge. It was way too accurate. You thinking what I'm thinking?"

Of course I had been; I just hadn't wanted to admit it to myself yet. I was still trying to avoid it. "Yeah, but God, I hope not. *Shit*, Ray, who else could it be? If he's here . . . "

"Ben, you'd better get out of there. If it was him, then you might be next. Your shadow—"

I don't hear anything else because I am already on the move.

There is a long story behind Ray's use of the term "my shadow."

It started after I repeatedly shot my former sniper partner, Bob Slater, a chapter of my life I didn't want to have to recount, but I suppose at this point, I will have to.

I was the primary sniper and Slater was still the secondary sniper when SWAT was called to a hostage-for-ransom siege at a place called

Northwest Healing. This was about a year and a half ago, in the summer of 2005.

To make a very long story short, the entire siege turned out to be staged, and by none other than Bob Slater. He and another guy named Tim Connors had prepped the building for an extended SWAT callout, and had dug a tunnel leading from a concealed entrance in the building to the city's main sewer line.

The whole point of the siege had been to hold selected hostages for a ransom of fifteen million dollars. One of the hostages was the Academy Award winning actress Loretta Epstein, who is the daughter of the infamous Pio Cantelli, one of the richest organized crime bosses west of the Mississippi. Epstein, who is plenty wealthy in her own right, had been the keynote speaker at the grand opening of Northwest Healing.

As I said, Slater and this Connors guy meticulously planned and carried out the whole Northwest Healing business venture for the sole purpose of inviting Epstein to speak, and then to hold her hostage, designing it to look like a random hostage-taking. Slater had ensured that he was the two-side sniper, and his preplanned position was by a sewer line that gave him access to the building during the call-out. He actually entered the building through the sewer and talked with the hostage negotiators himself.

But Slater wasn't satisfied with his half of the fifteen-million-dollar take. He double-crossed Connors, gunning him down during the siege and making it look as if a hostage had been killed when a deadline passed.

After hostages started dying, Cantelli paid the ransom with a snap of his fingers, and the money was delivered into Northwest Healing. Of course, Slater disappeared through the tunnel with it all.

Well, I figured out what he had done, but I couldn't convince anyone that it had really been Slater. However, I was able to convince *Slater* that I knew everything, and that I was bent on proving it to Capelko. In desperation, Slater kidnapped my wife and daughter, and buried them alive without sufficient oxygen. He then staged a second call-out in which he was supposedly holding my family in a motel room, but I knew they were buried alive somewhere else. Slater's intent on this second callout was to take both me and Lt. Capelko out, since we were the only ones who knew the whole Northwest Healing story.

In my own move of desperation, I broke into his house and stole the competition rifle he'd used to kill Connors during Northwest Healing, hoping ballistics would prove his guilt (incidentally, it is the same rifle I use on SWAT today), and started taking him apart with it until he told me where my family was.

In the process, he also gave a full confession to Northwest Healing. I left before giving him the coup de grâce I wanted to, and went to rescue my family. Slater took the coward's way out, and finished the job I had started by blowing his own head off with his backup weapon.

I barely made it in time to where he had my family buried, which was in the tunnel he'd dug at Northwest Healing. My daughter still suffers severe brain damage due to the lack of oxygen, but she is doing much better these days.

To wrap up that whole sordid story, only a hundred thousand of the fifteen-million-dollar ransom was ever recovered. The rest is still outstanding. I was tried on a variety of felony charges, but a mistrial was declared because someone tried to buy off the jury, using money that was later traced to the missing ransom, to get me convicted. Everyone, from the district attorney on down, realized that there was no way I was going to get convicted for anything, and they declined to try me a second time. The department backed me a hundred percent, offered me my job back, and here I am today.

What Ray meant when he referred to "my shadow" is this: During the investigation following Northwest Healing, it was discovered that there may have been another, silent, co-conspirator. His existence was never "officially" proven, but shortly after my trial, I found out he really does exist. I began getting threatening emails from him, telling me he was watching, that he had all the money, and that I couldn't hide from him. The department tried everything in its arsenal, including search warrants, to determine who the hell was emailing me, but was unable to figure out who it was.

Over time, he grew bolder. After a few weeks of emailing me every few days, he left a note on my police car while I was on a radio call. Not long after that, I found another note on my personal car when I had my family on an afternoon shopping trip at the mall.

Needless to say I was getting pretty scared. I began looking over my shoulder at everyone, wondering if it might be the guy. He'd told me straight out that he had what was left of the ransom, which was just under fifteen million dollars, so, given a little ingenuity, he could be capable of just about anything. We took to calling him my shadow, for lack of a better reference. Even he picked up the nickname, and began signing his emails "The Shadow."

Ultimately, the number of his contacts dwindled to one every couple of months, but the nature of the contacts got more intimate. For example, I took a rape report from a teenage girl whom I felt was lying to keep out of trouble with her parents for staying out all night long. That night, I got a detailed email in which he told me he didn't believe her story either, and mentioned the same faults in it that I had found, which included things I had not put into the report. I had talked to that girl in the privacy of her bedroom, alone, so I figure he had to have some damn sensitive and sophisticated listening equipment to pick up the conversation.

He told me once that my wife wasn't keeping the door locked when I was gone, and he was right. He described a piece of art Sharon got in Israel, which she keeps wrapped in a blanket in a closet and hasn't touched in three years.

And then, two weeks ago during sniper training, my target wound up with an extra hole for every shot I took. We never heard the shots, but I'd take one, and bingo, the next time we'd look, there would be two holes in the target. Ray actually saw the last one appear, within a second of mine. Each shot was incredibly close to my own, indicating that the shadow was a very, very good shot.

We scoured the area surrounding the range, but found no trace of another shooter anywhere. But off to either side are thick woods for a thousand yards in each direction, so he could have been anywhere. That night I got my last email from him, which simply said, "You weren't the only good shot out there today, were you?"

The point is, he was using a silenced, extremely accurate high-powered rifle, and he'd made it on and off the range without being detected. The intimidation factor has been ramped up significantly since that day.

Since the range, there has been no contact from him. Until tonight, of course. The email I found on my computer right before the call-out simply said, "Lot's of things can arrive by airmail on Christmas."

It would seem that Delray Hicks just got one of them.

Before moving too far out of my position, I take a long, hard look around me with my night scope. There are several small buildings associated with the water treatment plant capable of providing numerous places for my shadow to hide. There is also a copse of woods two hundred yards behind me, which would give him a three-hundred-yard shot. Three hundred yards is nothing for a decent shooter with a good weapon.

As I head back to the command post, I call Capelko privately via Nextel Direct Connect, and tell him I think this is the work of my shadow. He has already considered this, and has called in patrol officers and canines to cordon off the buildings and set a perimeter that will include the woods.

We both know that it is the proverbial closing of the barn doors after the horse has escaped, yet we must do it anyway. There's no way my shadow is still within a mile of here. But I know I will be hearing from him.

He has been in my home, he has followed me on radio calls, and he seems to stalk my every move. At any time he could have killed me, especially given his apparent marksmanship skills with a silenced sniper rifle. Or, he could do what I did to Slater, which is take me apart piece by piece, but he hasn't. He is merely there, watching, listening, and invading my privacy, which creeps me out more than if he were trying to kill me.

Detectives are already beginning to arrive when I reach the command post. They ask that everyone remain in his or her spot until they can document the positions. I am the understandable exception.

I ask Phil Mahoney, the detective sergeant, which Major Crimes Team is on call this week, and it is Team A. I nod, unsure whether I am glad, because Andrea Fellotino is on MCT-A.

Andrea is the female officer with whom I had a longstanding affair beginning a few months before the Northwest Healing incident, and lasting until . . . Well, let's just say we've ended it a few times already. She saw me through some of my toughest times. She also nearly cost me my relationship with Sharon. She is everything Sharon is not—young, pretty, vivacious, petite and horny.

I ended the affair shortly after I returned to work following the Slater thing, but as I have learned, ending an affair can be a relative thing. We saw each other sexually two times after it was positively over. By then, we were working graveyard shift together during the winter, and there was just too much dead time.

I would not have seen her again after the last "final" breakup if not for her persistence. Like a guy, all she wanted was an occasional sex partner, with no strings attached. But somewhere along the line we fell in love, sort of.

We share a lot, Andrea and me. We'd both been through more than our share of crap on the job. Andrea had been shot and wounded during a family disturbance in which another officer was killed, and during the ensuing SWAT action, I had shot and killed the assailant, a man named Hugo Route. My shot struck Route's wife Pammi before killing Hugo Route, but nonetheless, it was still determined to be a good shooting. And shortly after that incident came the Northwest Healing call-out.

Andrea was taken hostage at Northwest Healing—we later learned by my sniper partner, Bob Slater. As a condition of getting the ransom money, HNT made the hostage-taker promise to release Andrea unharmed first. He complied, but he made her strip naked before releasing her. As I found out later on, this was a personal insult, directly from Bob Slater to me.

That is how Andrea walked out of Northwest Healing, buck naked to the world. She was never quite the same after that. She put on a convincing facade of normality, but knowing her as well as I do, I could tell something was different. She became demanding and possessive, which I didn't like, but her appetite for sex increased exponentially, which I did. I had no explanation for this, but it was certainly fun in the beginning. After a while, though, it became too much, and I had to end to it. That was the *big* breakup.

Two more times she has seduced me, which, truth be told, isn't too hard to do. Andrea is very attractive on a variety of levels, and it is hard for me to stay away from her. Our last carnal stumble was several months ago, just before she went across the hall to detectives. Since then, we have hardly seen one another, as I have remained on night shift. I hate to say it, but I miss the sex, and have often thought about renewing the affair.

To do so, though, would pose too great a risk. Sharon was relatively forgiving the first time, probably because of everything I was going through. But she truly believes that I broke it off for good when I said I did, and she doesn't know about our last two dalliances. As horny as I am for Andrea, I adamantly do not want to lose Sharon and Leah. It would not be an even exchange by any standards.

I shake my head to clear these extemporaneous thoughts, and bring myself back to present. Stan Hauser is dropping the Hicks boy off with paramedics, and having nothing better to do, I make my way to the ambulance to check on him. When I get there, they are washing away blood, bits of bone, and pieces of his father's brain from him. For the first time tonight he is silent, and appears to be in a state of shock.

"His name's LaMonjello," I tell the ambulance crew who takes him from Hauser.

"Help me get him out of his clothes," the female paramedic asks her partner.

The male paramedic starts to unbutton his shirt, and LaMonjello bats his hands away saying, "No, no, no!" His eyes widen in fear, and he begins crying again.

"He won't let me."

"Well, you're the adult," she says with exasperation in her voice. "You're stronger than he is. Just take them off. I need to see if any of this blood is his."

LaMonjello fights him, trying to get off the gurney and out of the ambulance, further frustrating both paramedics. They physically hold him down, and he begins screaming.

I step inside and say, "Yo LaMonjello, what up, dog?"

He looks at me and his yelling quiets to a whimper, but he doesn't say anything.

"Check this out," I tell him. Though it is freezing, I peel off my woodland camo jacket and offer it to him. He is clearly taken with it.

"Want to try it on?"

His whimpering changes to hitching breathing, and he nods his head and says, "Y-yeah."

"First, you have to take that wet shirt off, though, so the jacket doesn't get all icky, OK?"

"OK," he says, and he takes the shirt off.

"Pants, too."

"I know."

I get an approving nod from the paramedics, who quickly pronounce him unhurt and clean him up. I then wrap him up in my jacket.

LaMonjello smiles tentatively, and says, "It warm."

I go to tousle his hair, and he flinches.

"Hey bud, I'm not gonna hurt you."

He looks at me with the eyes of an old man.

"You're name's LaMonjello, right? My name's Ben." I hold my hand out to him, and he places his hand in mine so gently I can barely feel it. I give it a warm squeeze, and his eyes open a little wider, but he doesn't try to let go. I count that as a victory.

A patrol unit shows up to take the boy into state custody. I open the trunk of the officer's patrol car, where I find a buddy bear, which is a donated teddy bear wrapped in sealed plastic.

"Hey LaMonjello, Merry Christmas," I say, offering him the bear.

His eyes narrow, and he says suspiciously, "Say what?"

"Merry Christmas."

His shakes his head and says, "You lyin.' It ain't no Chrismiss."

"Yes it is," I say defiantly, not really believing there's a kid alive who doesn't know it's Christmas.

"Then why I ain't got no Chrismiss tree?"

"You don't?" I say with disbelief. "Well, I bet you will later today."

He looks at me sideways and says, "It really Chrismiss?"

"Yep, it's really Christmas."

"Whoa," he mutters in genuine amazement.

It's Christmas morning, and there's a little boy who doesn't even know it? This tells me more about LaMonjello's parents than all my experiences with them combined. Now I'm glad his father is dead, and I find myself hoping his mother is too.

"Yeah. You really didn't know that?"

"Nope."

"And you don't have any Christmas presents?"

"Nope."

"Well, that's OK. I bet you get a bunch later."

He changes the topic without warning. "My daddy daid, ain't he?" he asks quietly, tears brimming in his eyes.

"I think so, LaMonjello."

The tears spill over the brim and make his cheeks glisten. He reaches out and holds my hand, and we just sit there like that for about three minutes without saying a word. Finally, I tell him to wait here, and I'll be right back.

I seek out the officer who is here to take custody of LaMonjello, and am told that the Oregon Department of Human Services is trying to find a bed for him in a foster home. They said it may take a while, since it is Christmas. They've got a file on LaMonjello from a previous case of suspected sex abuse, naming Delray Hicks as the suspect, and they already know there are no viable relatives with whom to place him. The only living grandfather is in prison and the grandmother is a junkie.

Suddenly, I want to take LaMonjello home with me. Feeling inspired, I call Sharon and explain the situation. She is excited about the idea, and I call DHS again, volunteering to be a temporary foster parent for him.

The caseworker calls a supervisor, and I am walked through the application process on the phone. The supervisor is willing to make an exception and lets me have him without the required home inspection, which they will do after the holidays if he is still there.

Now at least LaMonjello has a place for the night. I glance at my watch. 2:45 a.m. It's been one hell of a Christmas so far.

Chapter 4

It is 3:30 a.m. LaMonjello, exhausted from a long night of watching his mother getting stabbed, being held hostage, and having his father killed out from under him, is sleeping in the back of the ambulance. Merry Christmas, kid.

Crime scene techs crawl around the trailer and the surrounding woods like flies on a carcass. And speaking of carcasses, Delray Hicks' still lies in the doorway of his house, his right arm beckoning everyone in for a look-see.

Andrea Fellotino has been here for thirty minutes as part of the Major Crimes Team. Being the most inexperienced among them, she has been tasked with the job of interviewing witnesses. I am her first, since I had the best view of the shot and I have to leave with LaMonjello when I am done.

The interview is taking place in her car. We are finished with the official part, but since nobody is within earshot, we take a few minutes for the inevitable personal part.

Way back when, when we were lovers and I was going through all the trauma of the Route shooting, Andrea was the rock upon which I leaned to keep me sane. I could not open my soul to Sharon, since we weren't getting along at the time. I used Leah as much as I could, but she was more of a distraction from the trauma, and I needed someone to *talk* to about it.

On the flip side, Andrea had suffered tremendous emotional trauma of her own during her ordeal of being captured, held hostage, and ultimately being released naked in front of half the Stratton PD, and I had been *her* lifeline through all of that.

Tonight's shooting evokes memories of all of that mutual support. After all, we once loved each other, and it really does feel good to have her here. I suppose we have a tighter emotional bond than I would like to admit.

"I know we're not seeing each other any more, Ben," she says, "But I want you to know that I'm here for you. You know, to talk to, to get through all the shit."

"Thanks, but I'm really OK this time."

"Baloney. I know you too well. You watched that guy's face explode all over his kid, and now you're taking the kid home with you. I really admire you for that, but it also tells me what kind of impact it's having on you."

"Hey, I've seen this kid going through this shit since he was born. I'm glad he's out of this place, and I'm glad to have a hand in it, that's all."

"Don't get me wrong," she said, "I really admire you for it. I mean, it really shows what kind of man you are, but still, you don't fool me. What you've gone through, what you've had to watch, has been hard, and I hate to say this, but I *know* Sharon won't really understand. Not on the level you need, anyway."

She's right about that.

"I'll be OK."

"Bullshit. Come on, Ben. I'm the loser, I'll admit it, but that doesn't mean I haven't stopped caring about you. It doesn't mean I can't be there for you, as a *friend* at least." She lowers her voice, which has suddenly become husky, and adds, "It doesn't mean I haven't stopped loving you."

My heart does these little flutters when she talks like this. It evokes memories of her body's motion while straddling me—of what seems like hours of a rhythmic bouncing up and down we jokingly referred to as "plowin' the back forty," since it reminded us of the farmer on *Green Acres* riding his tractor.

"See?" she says triumphantly. "I know you so well I can tell exactly what you're thinking."

"Is that right?" I challenge. "By all means, Dr. Clairvoyance, please tell me what I'm thinking."

She starts humming the *Green Acres* theme song, and we both laugh.

"OK, so I'm transparent, what can I say? Let's just say I'm glad I have to take off with my new son, and you have other work to do. Otherwise, I'd be getting in trouble right about now."

"OK, well, call me sometime, and we'll, uh, discuss all this a little more privately, OK?"

I just give her this stupid, little boy grin. Dumb shit that I am, I probably will call her, but for now, it's time to take little LaMonjello home. What a stupid name, I think. Why couldn't they just call him Billy or something?

I pick him up, trying not to wake him, and am repulsed by his smell. The poor kid doesn't appear to have had a bath in weeks. His hair, way too long, is nappy and has pieces of fuzz and other debris tightly locked within it. His nose is plastered with dried snot, his fingernails are long and dirty, and his underwear, once white, are now gray and torn.

He does not waken as I seatbelt him into the back seat of the patrol car Ray has been given to take us back to the station. Ray has had nothing to do in the three-plus hours since the shooting, but that doesn't mean he hasn't been busy.

"I got a surprise for you back at the office," he tells me. I press him for details, he won't give me any.

When we get there, I am shocked to see nine beautifully wrapped Christmas presents waiting in the Records section.

Ray and the records clerks have called every officer they could think of with a kid about LaMonjello's age, and explained my situation. Every one of them was happy to donate a present intended for his or her own son from under the tree, and one of my night shift cohorts drove around the city collecting them like a Code-3 Santa.

Records clerks have made cards and tags for them in LaMonjello's name, and bingo—instant Christmas. I am damn near moved to tears.

While LaMonjello sleeps, we load the presents into my car, and Ray drives it home while I take LaMonjello in the police car, so we do not have to wake him up and can keep the presents a surprise. We bring the presents inside first, and once they are safely ensconced under the tree, I carry LaMonjello in.

Sharon covers the love seat with a sheet, and we lay LaMonjello down, giving him a pillow and covering him with an old blanket.

"I'm glad we're doing this, Ben," Sharon says. "He's going to be so cute once we get him cleaned up."

"You make him sound like some sort of plaything," I say.

"No," she answers playfully. "He's a boy. *This* is a plaything." She begins caressing my crotch. Her advances are a rare treat.

Feeling guilty, but at the same time manfully proud at my stable of willing women, I steal off with her to our bedroom where we make passionate love. I do not think of Andrea this time.

When we are done, I go back to the living room, where I go to sleep on the recliner next to LaMonjello, so that he can see a familiar face when he wakes. Sharon comes out a moment later, and lies down on the couch, and we all sleep in the warm glow of the Christmas tree.

LaMonjello sleeps well into the morning without waking from nightmares, which surprises me. Leah, rubbing sleep from her eyes, wakes us at six, which seems like mere minutes since I lay down. She does not notice LaMonjello asleep on the love seat.

"Leah, we have a real surprise for you this Christmas," I tell her.

Before she can say anything, I point to the couch. She turns expectantly, then stops and stares at him, dumfounded.

"A new brother," says Sharon. "A *temporary* new brother."

Leah neither moves nor speaks. She just looks at him. Finally, she pronounces, "He's dirty."

"Yes, he is. His father was killed last night, and he can't live with his mother right now, so they said he could stay here with us, for a few days. He's very poor, and didn't even know it was Christmas."

She regarded him a moment longer, then said, "He's African American, like Franklin Cornell at school. Only he's smaller, and has longer hair. I like Franklin. What's his name?"

"LaMonjello."

"That's a funny name. How long is he going to live here?"

"I don't think too long, baby. Maybe a few days. Just until they can find him a permanent place."

She approaches him, wrinkles her nose, and says, "Ugh. He really smells. Why's he so dirty?"

"Shh," I scold her. "You don't want to hurt his feelings. We got home very late, and he was sleeping, so he couldn't take a bath. He can take a bath after we open presents."

Leah considers the situation for a moment, then says, "If he didn't even know it was Christmas, and his mom and dad didn't take care of him, it's good that he's here. You guys are good parents, and after all, I *am* an only child. We have an extra bedroom, so there's plenty of room for him. He can stay."

Sharon and I look at one another, then laugh. "Well, Your Highness, if you say so," Sharon says.

"Yeah, it's OK." She looks under the tree, and says, "Where'd he get all the presents?"

"The police donated them for him, Sugar," I say. "I think he has more presents than you do."

Leah agrees to hold off on opening her presents until LaMonjello wakes up, and Sharon starts a big bacon-and-egg breakfast. The smell of it wakes LaMonjello, who looks around with huge, frightened eyes.

There is a period of recollection and panic, during which he cries very hard and tries to run out the door, but this passes quickly, and the smell of the food settles him down. We introduce him to Leah, who treats him with tenderness, as if he were a tiny, fragile baby, pointing out all the presents under the tree that have his name on them.

LaMonjello still cannot believe that it's Christmas, let alone that he has beautiful presents under a real Christmas tree. He regards the tree and the decorations around the house with awe, obviously never having lived in a place so nicely decorated for the holidays before.

Leah, who would normally not delay the opening of presents for anything, eyes LaMonjello and suggests we eat first. Sharon and I beam with pride at our little girl.

LaMonjello inhales his breakfast and asks for seconds. He gets all the leftovers, and scarfs down four pieces of cinnamon toast and two glasses or orange juice on top of everything else.

When he is done, he goes into the living room and looks at the pile of presents Leah has separated out for him. It is larger than the remaining pile of unsorted presents.

"Is all dem pres'nts really for me?" he asks incredulously.

"That's right, LaMonjello. "They're all for you."

"I ain't never had nuthin' like that befo'."

"Well, what are you waiting for?" I say. "Go ahead, open them."

He tears into them, and Leah, no longer able to restrain herself, does the same. In moments, the house is a wreck. Sharon digitally records the carnage for posterity.

LaMonjello gets a variety of toys and some clothes that will fit him perfectly. He is more excited about the clothes than the GI Joe, the remote-control car, the walkie-talkie set, and the book of punch-out paper airplanes. He immediately tries to dress in the new clothes.

"Whoa, hold on there, big guy," I say. "Why don't we get a bath first?"

I take him to the bathroom where he immodestly strips out of his underwear and goes to the toilet. To my amazement, he not only flushes, but washes his hands afterward. Sharon draws the bath, and LaMonjello doesn't seem to mind our presence at all.

The water turns black the moment he steps in the tub, but he luxuriates in it nonetheless. We change the water twice, scrub him down on the third tubful, and finish the job off with a shower.

LaMonjello doesn't mention his father, but does ask about his mother. I call the hospital and am told that she did not survive surgery. The knife sliced through her kidney, and the bleeding was too severe to control. She bled to death internally an hour after arriving at the hospital.

I decide to tell LaMonjello that she is hanging on, but is unable to take visitors today. I tell him that she has been injured very badly and may not survive. He accepts this without tears, and we take his mind off of it by driving him up Mount Hood to play in the snow, something he has never done before.

Dressed in Leah's underwear, his new clothes, and wrapped in my SWAT jacket, which he insists on wearing, LaMonjello spends most of Christmas Day in the mountains. We come home to the turkey dinner Sharon has had in the oven all day, and LaMonjello adapts quickly to life in a stable white middle-class home.

The following morning I tell him his mother has passed away. He cries for a long time, but eventually comes to accept it. Sharon goes to the store and rents an X-Box video game unit and two games, and by dinnertime, he has quieted and is absorbed in playing a game in which cartoon animals destroy everything they can find in heavily armed flying cars. This is sufficient to keep both Leah and LaMonjello wrapped up for days.

Two days after Christmas, LaMonjello is still with us. The Oregon Department of Human Services has informed us that they have arranged for a semi-permanent home for him, and Sharon, Leah and I all realize how attached to him we have become. The thought that he will have to move on to strangers is hard for us to swallow, regardless of whether they are black or not. LaMonjello has found a comfort zone at our house, and I am not anxious to take him away from that.

Nevertheless, tomorrow is our last day with him, and we are planning a party. In the meantime, tonight will be my first night back to work since the call-out.

I return to the streets looking over my shoulder the entire time, knowing that my shadow is still out there somewhere watching everything I do, as he has always done. Only now I am afraid it is from the scope of a high-powered rifle.

Chapter 5

It is a slow night, and there is no sign of my shadow. In the morning, I meet with Detective Sergeant Phil Mahoney about what they are now calling The Shadow Murder.

I learn that detectives found the spot where the shot came from. It was almost directly behind me by fifty yards, on a knoll with a three-foot elevation gain from my own position. This explains the sensation I had as Delray Hicks' head exploded. It was the bullet ripping the air only a few inches above my head on its way to him.

Mahoney tells me there was nothing between the shadow's position and my own but open space, which means he had *me* in his sights the whole time. Detectives believe that the shadow intentionally chose that position so that he would send me a personal message.

It could have been you.

This takes the game to an entirely new level.

They found a trail through the brush leading to a nearby road. On the trail were size-10 boot prints with a tread pattern common to many types of outdoor boots. The boot prints meandered through a small copse of woods before exiting at the dead end of a street that has a wooden barrier upon which a sign is posted saying there are plans for future construction. There are six houses within sight of the dead end. Of them, the residents of five were sleeping and heard nothing, but in the last, the one nearest the dead end, a little girl woke to the sound of a car door closing. She looked outside and saw the taillights of what she called a shiny black truck going down the street.

The girl is twelve, and had no idea what time it was. Detectives showed her pictures of taillight configurations from twenty different types of trucks and SUVs, and she had narrowed it down to a larger, newer SUV body style.

The caliber of the slug was a .308, just like what I shoot.

That's it. Considering these clues are all that we have for a man who presumably wants to kill me and has made the stalking of me his biggest hobby, it isn't very much.

As we are talking, Andrea comes in and goes to her cubicle. She catches my eye, and motions with her head for me to join her there.

When I finish with Mahoney, I do just that. We are alone, but still, we have no real privacy. I decide this is for the better.

"I take it you haven't heard any more from your friend," she says.

"No, but I've been checking my email every couple of hours. I know I'm going to hear from him."

"How are you doing?"

"I'm hanging in there. LaMonjello's been great. We've all grown really close to him over the past few days. It's going to be hard to let him go."

"When's he leave?"

"This morning. DHS is coming to get him at eleven."

"How's he feel about that?"

"It's hard to say. He's been hurt so often that nothing fazes him outwardly any more. He asked me if his father was dead, and when I said yes, he cried a little, but that was it. I took him home and told him this was going to be his new home for a while, and he just said OK. The day after Christmas, I told him his mother had died, and he cried for while, but then we rented him some video games, and that was the end of it. He's just so screwed up inside that his emotions are frazzled. The only thing he said when we told him he was moving to a more permanent foster home today was, "I hope they white.""

"God. It must be really hard on you."

"It is. We've all come to love him, sort of. He's just a tiny little kid. He's been beaten and abused his entire life. Even though it was never proven, we all know his father sexually molested him. He watched his father kill his mother, and some fuckin' wacko who's stalking me shoots his father out from underneath him. Christ, no wonder he's so screwed up."

"Ben, I see those wheels spinning. You want to keep him permanently, don't you?"

I do. I hadn't really realized it until she said it, but the truth is I do, and I bet Sharon does too. Leah would be excited as hell. She'd be the first kid on the block to have a little brother who is black.

"No. I mean . . . I don't know. I guess I do. Yeah, I do. I can't let them take him to someone else." I laugh sardonically. "Just what I need. Another kid."

"You better just forget it. It would be the *wrong* thing for you to do. Besides, I know what you *really* need." The twinkle in her eye makes my heart get all flippy.

Quietly, under my breath, I say, "I bet you do." Right there, the deal is set. There will be a fourth tryst for us, and soon.

"I checked the schedule for tomorrow," she says. "You're two over minimum on graveyards. Comp half the night off and be at my place at three thirty. I'll go to bed early for you."

"Andrea, I don't know. . . . I—"

"I'm a churnin' urn' o' burnin' funk," she says, quoting the James Taylor song that was playing the first time we ever made love.

"And I'm a *ce*-ment mixer, baby," I tell her with a sloppy grin on my face, knowing that it's wrong, but getting excited about it nonetheless. "I'll think about it."

"Good. Think hard, if you get my drift. I'll be ready."

We smile hesitantly at one another. Though I haven't really agreed, we both know I'll do it. The deal was struck with too little resistance, which tells her that I wanted it more than I had been letting on. Again, she is the victor.

"You're an evil little minx," I tell her.

"You have no idea, Ben. You have no idea."

I can't wait to get home and talk to Sharon and Leah about the idea of keeping LaMonjello, maybe even adopting him.

When I arrive, there is an atmosphere of sadness, despite the bright crepe paper ribbons and balloons Sharon has hung in the kitchen. She is already up, and has made a chocolate cake.

LaMonjello displays his usual take-whatever-comes-his-way attitude.

"Hey, bud," I say cheerfully when I walk in the door and see him. He is playing the video game. He pauses it like an expert, looks at me, and says, "Shairn make a cake, 'cuz I be leavin' today. It smell good."

"Smell*s*," I correct him, emphasizing the "s." "It *smells* good."

"Yeah, it do, don't it."

I smile to myself and give him a hug. *He* smell good, compared to when I first brought him home. Sharon has been giving him a daily bath. He looks good too. We took him to Kid's Cuts yesterday and got his hair cut. He really is a cute kid.

"Where's Sharon?" I ask.

"She in the bet'room. She be in there cryin'."

"Why?" I ask.

"'Cuz I be leavin', I guess."

"Does that make you sad?"

"Yeah, I like it here. Shairn an' y'all be nice. Lee nice, and I like her too."

"Leah," I say. "Lee-*ah*."

"Yeah."

"What else do you like about it here?"

"You and Shairn. Plus, my bed be clean, an' I ain' hungry no mo'. But ain't nothin' ever stay the same for me."

"We'll see about that," I tell him. LaMonjello shrugs his shoulders and goes back to the video game. I head into the bedroom.

Sharon looks up and sees me. The first thing she says is, "Ben, I don't want to give him up."

"Neither do I. But we'd better think about this. I'm not gonna keep him for a few weeks, then give him back to DHS. If we're gonna do this, we're gonna do it all the way."

"Like, adopt him?"

"That's what I'm thinking."

"What about Leah?"

"I think she'd like the idea."

"Well, what if she doesn't, Ben? What if it's a really bad decision?"

"There are a lot of what-ifs. What if he's got such bad psychological problems we can't handle him? What if he grows up like his father?"

"What's his medical history? Is there mental illness in the family?" she asks.

"Look at his father. But even beyond that stuff, Shar, what if he doesn't want to be raised by a bunch of lily-white honkies?"

"Do we have the right to do that?"

"Well, we love him."

"And, he loves us."

"He's too young to care about color or race right now. And if he's raised by us, then he probably never will."

"But do we have the *right* to take him away from his people?" she asks.

I get a little pissed, and say to her, "God damn it, yes, I think we do. Who the hell are 'his people?' Blacks? Look beyond that. He's a human being, a screwed-up little kid who needs real people to love him, care for him, and raise him to be a good person. What the hell difference does it matter what color they are? The bigger question is this. We have the ability, the means, and the heart to give him what he needs. Do we have a right *not* to?"

"OK, you've sold me. Do we have the right to do that to Leah?"

"We're her parents. We do what we feel is right."

"She loves him," Sharon points out.

"Yeah, but I'm afraid that right now it's like getting a new pet. Everybody loves him when you bring him home, but not when he keeps you up whining all night long, eats your slippers, and shits all over the house. The novelty will wear off, and we'll be stuck with all the problems associated with it."

"You know, she was teaching him to ride her bike this afternoon. You should have seen them, this lily-white girl teaching this young black boy to ride her My Little Pony bike with its basket and its pink and white streamers. He took to it like a natural. Let's just do it, Ben. Let's adopt him. I really want to."

"So do I."

Without further discussion, I head to the phone and call DHS asking to speak with a supervisor. After several minutes on hold, someone gets back on the line and tells me that the other family who was willing to take LaMonjello in is a black foster family who takes kids in as their main source of income. Theirs is one of those revolving-door foster homes, with kids coming and going all the time. That's what cinches it for me.

I'm told that we can keep him while we hire an attorney to look into the adoption. They will send people out to conduct a home inspection, which won't prove to be a problem. Our proposal to keep LaMonjello as a permanent foster child while we pull the necessary strings for an adoption is forwarded to the DHS headquarters in Salem. They will review all the data and make a ruling within a week, allowing for the New Year's holiday. In the meantime, he will stay here with us. It is the best we can hope for.

Next, we get to tell both Leah and LaMonjello that we were going to try to keep him permanently, so that things won't always have to change for him. Needless to say, they are both ecstatic.

Rather than going right to sleep, I take everyone to Walmart and let LaMonjello pick out a boy's bicycle of his very own. While I am helping him, Leah and Sharon go to buy him clothes. We pick up almost two hundred dollars worth of groceries, and I am exhausted by the time we finally get home, but it is well worth it.

LaMonjello runs directly into his room and starts trying on his new clothes. I make a beeline for the den and fire up the computer, dreading the prospect of contact by my shadow. As it is booting up, I look out the window at my family. Leah has dropped a bag of groceries and is picking them up from the driveway as Sharon, exasperated, looks on. Right now, it is just the three of us. With a little luck, in a week or maybe a month, there will be four of us. I find myself desperately hoping it will be so.

The computer has booted up, and I check my email. I have already checked it twice today.

Among the spam and refinancing offers, I find that which I have been waiting for. WatchinU@hotmail.com has left me a message. I knew he'd write me soon.

Well Ben, did you have a merry Christmas? Did you like my little SWAT surprise?

Were you able to feel the bullet as it passed your head? I have heard that sound before. It is a sound you will never forget.

I was taken by surprise with the compassion you've shown the niglet. You and Sharon had a very frank discussion about it, but you both forgot to mention me. Why is that, Ben? Do you not take me seriously?

You have to ask yourselves if it is really safe for him with your "shadow" out there. Is it safe for ANY of you with me out there watching, waiting . . .

Don't forget why I keep visiting you, Ben. What you did to Slater was . . . wrong. I will not go away, and you will not catch me. Think long and hard about whether you want to keep your pet boy. I never liked the mixing of the races.

Decide what you want, and do what you think is best. Just make sure you don't get complacent on me.

The Shadow

My shadow has made some very valid points. Even apart from his threats, it would not be fair to LaMonjello to have him live with us under these circumstances. Yet, the idea of him going to a revolving-door foster home sickens me.

I save the email to the hard drive along with all his others, and decide not to share it with Sharon right now.

In bed I lie awake for a long time before drifting off to a fitful sleep. All I can hope is that detectives will catch this guy soon. If they don't, I'm going to have to send my family away, and if that happens, I'll lose LaMonjello for certain.

Chapter 6

At roll call, everyone wants to know about the shadow. Word has spread about him since the Christmas shooting, and again, I find myself in the Stratton PD celebrity spotlight.

Up to this point, we had managed to keep the shadow thing under wraps, but like all the good gossip, it is now out in the open. The only thing I had managed to keep secret was my affair with Andrea, and that had been widely speculated about when it was in its prime, during the Northwest Healing and the Bob Slater thing.

People ask about the emails I've been receiving, and I give no details, but tell everyone that I think he's just a crackpot that gets kicks from screwing with me. I don't like being in the spotlight, and I came to graveyards mostly to avoid it.

True to the schedule, we are running two above minimums, and I spend the first couple hours of my shift agonizing over whether I want to visit Andrea. It will not be a problem for me to take comp time off at 3:00 a.m. if I want. I hate that I am considering breaking the shallow trust I've built with Sharon since she caught me cheating. I especially hate it now, when we are on the brink of adopting LaMonjello. Forcefully, I push him and our family out of my mind and concentrate on work.

The only significant thing to happen during my shift is arresting a drunk driver, and I have that paperwork wrapped up by 2:30. In the end, I decide to go. I am surprised at the ease with which I arrive at the decision. Sex with Andrea is too good, too alluring; the danger of it too enticing to pass up. Sharon still only sleeps with me once a month if that, and it's always the same, boring and repetitive, as if our only goal was to go forth and multiply. Andrea, on the other hand, is a bold, lights-on kind of lover.

Feeling scared and excited, yet already beginning to loathe myself, I secure my shift, and change clothes at precisely 0300. Fifteen minutes later, I cross the Glen Jackson Bridge into Vancouver, and park in front of her place. I still haven't contacted her to let her know I'm coming, just in case I decide to back out at the last minute.

Of course I don't, and before I can knock, Andrea opens the door, completely nude. With my heart ricocheting off my ribs like a high school kid's after the prom, I go inside, take her in my arms, and away we go.

My clothes are off faster than I can remember shedding them, and with almost no words, she and I spend the next hour writhing and pounding away at each other in bed. For me, the release is powerful, draining, and so very necessary. I do not think of Sharon, but I know that I will be awash in guilt afterwards. For now, though, I don't care.

Andrea seems to need this every bit as much as I. She has changed a lot since we were in love. I can see it in her actions and sense it in her attitude. She's somehow more carnal now than then. Almost feral. It used to be making love with us; now, it's raw animal sex. She makes me feel as if she's in complete control and I am just here, an insignificant part of the sexual experience except for what she makes me do; a living dildo. I don't like this feeling; more than using me, it's as if she is consuming me. The sex is great, perhaps the best I've ever had from a physical viewpoint, but I can't shake this feeling I get that she is in complete control. Separating myself from the physical reality of indescribably good sex, I find the experience distasteful, and resolve that this will truly be the final time.

After we are done, she confesses that she still loves me. I already know this, just as surely as I know I no longer love her. I was once torn between love for her and love for my wife, but that is no longer the case.

She looks at me, and tears form in her eyes. Andrea is very lovely, and she has been through a hell of a lot, but she is also an incredibly strong woman. It is odd to see her so vulnerable, so contradictory to how she was only a few minutes ago, and despite myself, I find that mostly what I feel for her is pity.

"Ben, I know you're married, and you have this family, and now you're taking on that little Hicks boy. I just look at you and wish that things had been different. I wish we could have gotten to know one another *before* you were married. I wish we could have gotten together then, without any baggage, and had a family of our own. Sometimes, I lie in bed before I go to sleep and fantasize about that. I see us marrying, and having a baby, and living together, and everything is so fine between us. . . . Do you ever think like that?"

Short answer? No. The reality of it is, if we would have met before I met Sharon, she would have been about thirteen years old. Sex like this would have amounted to first-degree rape. In truth, what I am thinking now is that I have risked too much in coming here. Good sex is not worth the loss of my wife and family, especially when I am trying to make a home for a troubled little boy who needs nothing more than stability. I'm thinking I'd like to get out of here and pretend I never came.

She is lying naked on the bed, her head across my chest, her legs splayed across mine. I casually massage her breast, and she caresses my now flaccid penis. Under these circumstances, I can hardly tell her what I am thinking. Since she has already said she knows it is not possible, what harm can it do for me to lie? If I tell her the truth, she would be devastated.

"Yeah," I say wistfully, as if lost in the fantasy, "I do think about that. We just seem so . . . right for each other. Doesn't it suck sometimes how reality gets in the way of what really should be?" This gives her what she wants, yet hits her in the face with the fact that she cannot have it. I am proud of the way I answer her.

"It does. I just don't think I could love anyone else."

"Andrea," I tell her, pulling her face up to mine and looking into her beautiful green, almost Asian eyes. "You need to look into a mirror and see how beautiful you are. You need to look inside yourself and see what a lovely human being you are. You need to imagine how you could be with me as your husband, and then put another man's face there, because trust me, I'm no peach. You are young and gorgeous and personable and intelligent and worth your weight in gold. Anyone who knows you wants you; you could have your pick of any available guy out there."

"I know all that stuff, Ben. It's just that it's not, you know, what I *want*. I know that someday I'll hook up with someone else, and we'll get married and have a family and be real happy, but I'll always think I'm settling for second best. I'll always have to live with that. Every time we make love, or every time I look at my child I'll always think it should be you, and I'll never be able to talk to my husband about it."

I am truly touched. I didn't think anyone could love me that much. But I am also getting antsy, and need to look for an out.

"Ben?" she says softly, sounding almost like a child. "I guess I just want to know, to hear it from you, that you would be with me if it were possible. You know, just an if-I-could-take-it-all-back-and-do-it-over-again kind of thing?"

I hate these scenes. Poor Andrea, I really do feel sorry for her. The truth is I wouldn't be with her, even if I could. Eighteen months ago maybe it would have been different, but not now. Now that I know her so intimately, I honestly don't find any attraction other than the physical with her.

Every guy instinctually knows what he's supposed to do in this situation. Lie your ass off, plain and simple. As if there were another choice. So, I let her have it. Before answering her, I squeeze her tight. "What do you think, honey?" I say. "If it weren't for Sharon and the kids, I'd be with you in a heartbeat, and I think we'd be the happiest couple in the world."

She sighs wistfully, and I cannot wait to leave. It is now five thirty, and she needs to shower to get ready for work. I shower with her but make sure not to use soap or shampoo so I don't smell like I took a shower, and as she's getting ready for work, she asks me to make her breakfast. What a nice little game of house we're playing, I think to myself as I scramble four eggs. We get to talking about my shadow as we eat.

She goes over essentially the same stuff Mahoney gave me earlier in the day, about the location from which he took the shot, and the SUV taillights.

I tell her that in my opinion, the suspect is obsessed with me because of what I did to his partner, Slater. I think his mimicry of the things I do is a sublime message to me. I'd bet that the rifle he used is a custom Remington 700 just like mine, and the ammo is Federal match-grade 168-grain boat-tail hollow points. About the boot prints, I'd guess they were a pair of Danners, the same kind I wear on SWAT.

She doesn't know anything about high-powered rifles or ammo, but tells me detectives are already looking into that aspect of it.

I tell her to have them check area gun clubs, too, since he would have needed a place to learn to shoot. Somebody had to have given him lessons recently. And he must have purchased a great deal of .308 ammo to gain the degree of accuracy he has achieved. Nobody shoots that well without dumping a veritable ton of lead downrange first.

At this point, Andrea gets a little offended and tells me they're not stupid in Detectives, and they've had people checking this stuff out already.

I'm glad for the sour note in our little game of house. This whole breakfast thing doesn't set well with me. We are acting like an old married couple, the stuff of her fantasies. She is calling me dear, and telling me that she has to leave for work, but I can stay as long as I like.

I have to time my arrival home as if I have just come off graveyard shift, which means I have to kill an hour or so before leaving. I hate it that I am so cunning in deceiving Sharon. I do not want to stay here, but I have nowhere else to go, so I do. On her way out the door, Andrea kisses me as if I'll be there waiting when she gets off work.

Sitting in her apartment, I get the heebie-jeebies, and decide I really don't want to be here. I leave and head to a nearby Denny's, where I sit and read the morning paper over coffee until it is time for me to go home. The papers are still running the story of the Hicks shooting. They come right out and say that the police don't know who took the shot, but the tone of the story is that maybe it was the police themselves who took it, and it has a strong subliminal hint of police cover-up. I do not like the way it sounds.

Allowing for rush-hour traffic, I time my return to the house perfectly, and walk in the front door the same time I do every other day. Sharon, loving the fact that we may get to keep LaMonjello, is in the best of moods. She greets me warmly; throwing her arms around my neck and giving me a big kiss, something almost unheard of since she took me back after Andrea. I haven't seen her so exuberant in a long time, and all it does is add to the crappy way I feel about myself.

After doing what I have just done, it is impossible for me to recall the reasons why I did it. I wish that Sharon could see into my heart and know that I really do love and value her above everything else in my life. Why I do not live by that canon is beyond me. I am so damn weak in the area of sex that I know it will someday be my downfall.

She wants to know if something is wrong, and I tell her only that I love her. I want her to come to bed with me, just to hold and not for sex, but she can't; she has to get up with the kids.

Not kid. Kids. With an "s." How odd that sounds.

What is even odder is to see them together, a pale, white girl with a pointed nose and long, straight blond hair, and a dark-skinned African American with his wide nose, large lips, and tight Afro.

They come chasing each other out of her bedroom, laughing. It is the first time I have seen LaMonjello laugh. They chase one another around a corner, and knock some books off a bookcase.

"Hey, guys! Slow it down or you'll wreck the whole house," I admonish.

"Sorry, Dad!" yells Leah as she disappears down the stairs with LaMonjello in hot pursuit.

"Yeah, sorry, Dad," echoes LaMonjello as the door to the family room closes on the sound of their laughter.

Chapter 7

Several weeks pass without incident. During this time, things progress wonderfully with LaMonjello. For the first week or so, it wasn't uncommon for him to wake up screaming and crying every couple of nights, but the intervals between the bad dreams are now getting longer. Every day he becomes a little more outgoing. He still sleeps with the light on and sucks his thumb for hours at a time during the day, but I believe those things will fall by the wayside. We take him to see a counselor every week, and we are quite pleased with the results. She is a specialist in the area of treating abused children, and she has established quite a rapport with LaMonjello.

He seems to be a good-natured, wonderful child of, and I don't know how this is possible, higher-than-average intelligence, and he loves our house. He and Sharon are growing quite close, and he's taken to Leah as if she were his biological sister.

The most negative thing about having him here is the fact that he is somewhat distrustful of me, which hurts my feelings more than I can express. The counselor says it is because he associates maleness with the cruelty of his father, and this makes sense. Not a day goes by that I don't silently thank my shadow for doing the world a favor by removing Delray from the equation. I have made gaining LaMonjello's trust my highest priority.

The adoption hearing is scheduled for the end of April, and we have shared with him what we are attempting to do. He understands adoption on a normal six-year-old level. We are trying to permanently bring him into our family as our own son, even though he really is not. He doesn't need to know anything more than that.

He speaks frequently about his mother, but he never mentions his father. Sharon tells him his parents are in heaven, but I can tell he doesn't buy it. I've tried telling her that the notion of God accepting his father into heaven with open arms must be ridiculous, maybe even offensive, to him. Why should a person as bad as his father be welcomed into God's good graces?

She stoically stands by her opinion that it would further traumatize LaMonjello to learn that because his father was a cruel, abusive child molester, his flesh is even now bubbling off his bones in the hottest furnace hell has to offer, but, I don't think it would hurt him at all. I think LaMonjello would cheer the devil on in his torment of his mother's sperm donor, since we know but a fraction of the hurt the poor boy has suffered at his father's hand in his short life, but Sharon is with him much more than I am and shares a special bond with him, so I try not to interfere.

During these weeks from late-winter to early spring, I hear nothing of my shadow. In fact, all through March and into April I begin to wonder if he may have been arrested, or even died. In a way, I hope not, because there wouldn't be any closure. It would be better to see him caught so I would never have to look over my shoulder again.

And look over my shoulder I do, every day, and will continue doing as long as he might still be here. Around the middle of April, I begin to get the feeling I am being watched on graveyard shift. I begin seeing suspicious cars hanging around on radio calls, and if someone looks at me sideways, I am sure it is my shadow. I am entirely unable to escape the feeling someone is following me around the city, though I have no proof of this whatsoever. I realize how ridiculous it sounds, but the feeling is overwhelmingly intense.

It is April 28, and I cannot shake the sensation that I am being watched. I realize it is most likely my imagination, but tonight, it is much stronger than usual. Perhaps it is because the adoption hearing is scheduled for Monday the thirtieth, two days hence, but the feeling haunts me relentlessly. The first call of the night is not mine, but I still go because of the nature of the call. It is a suspicious vehicle on Wooded Glen Avenue, parked on the northwest corner of Glacier, which is directly behind my house.

Mrs. Emery, my neighbor who called it in, didn't have her glasses on, and therefore had been unable to get the plate. All she said was that it was a "big, black, boxy truck." To me, that sounds like a newer SUV, like the one that left the scene of the Shadow Murder, and it is parked around the corner from *my* house. Obviously, I am concerned it might be him.

Officers flood the area, but nobody spots any possible matches. I immediately head around the corner to check my place, but nothing looks amiss, and everyone is sound asleep. I do not wake them.

Not much happens for the next few hours. I drive aimlessly around town with the radio on, not really looking for anything, yet at the same time, wishing something would happen to get my mind off my problems. At 3:30, it does. The call is a burglar alarm at a business complex. I am close, and arrive to find a rambling, single-story complex of nondescript offices and warehouses. After parking in a Burger King lot just west of the location, I listlessly begin circling the building looking for the proper suite number, but stop short when I find a broken window on the north side of the building.

Within minutes, my problems are forgotten. Other officers have arrived and established a perimeter around the building, and I can hear movement from within the suite with the broken window. Unfortunately, we do not have a canine on duty at the time, so I have the dispatcher call for a Portland dog, which takes twenty minutes to arrive. During this time, we can still hear the suspect inside breaking things open.

When the dog arrives, the handler makes his legally required announcement that a police dog is on scene, salivating in anticipation of tearing the guy a new asshole, while all the cops sit around and laugh at him. Of course, it comes out more like "Police canine! Come out or I'll send in the dog!" but that's what it means.

Upon completing the announcement, the point of which is driven home with the ferocious barking of the dog, the noises immediately cease, but the suspect does not respond.

"Come out with your hands up, or I'm sending in the dog!" yells the handler one last time.

Still nothing. The dog is now going nuts, growling and barking and straining on his leash. This reminds me of a stupid burglar years ago whom we caught hiding under a porch. When we made the announcement, he yelled back, "Send the fucking dog in!" I never heard a man change his tune so quickly once that dog commenced eating a femur sandwich. It's amazing how a fully grown career criminal can scream like a little girl while being eaten by an enthusiastic German shepherd.

"Last chance!" shouts the handler.

Still nothing. The handler grabs a handful of harness and hind-end fur, and tosses the huge snarling animal through the broken window.

"Find him! Find him, Rommel! Where's the bad guy?" The dog scampers off in search of a dirtbag to eat, and the handler and I go in while the other officers maintain the perimeter.

It takes all of thirty seconds for the dog to locate the suspect. As the dog corners him and we are headed across the room toward them both, the suspect knocks over a shelf of cardboard boxes, causing the dog to shy for a brief moment, which proves to be just enough. The handler and I are just getting our lights trained on him when he hits the panic bar on the closest emergency exit, setting off the alarm, and takes off.

I can hear the startled officer outside shouting something, and he begins to give chase as we charge out the still-closing emergency exit. Predictably, though, Rommel is faster than all of us.

The dog catches him thirty or so feet from the building in mid-leap, tackling him to the ground. Already keyed up, the suspect's instinctive reaction is to fight the dog—the worst thing he can do, especially with Rommel, who is a little crazy on his best days. His resistance is all the dog needs, and Rommel begins the splintering of the suspect's forearm. It is hard for the handler to pry the dog's jaws off, and like an idiot, I cannot stop laughing. From the suspect's crying, it seems as though the humor of the situation is lost on him.

And then comes the big surprise. Our suspect is a fourteen-year-old kid. I feel a momentary stab of sorrow for the poor kid, but I guess fourteen is as good an age as any to learn that you ought not run from the *po*-lice.

All in all, a call such as this provides us with our nightly dose of tension, fun, thrills and laughs. The only downside to it is I get stuck with all the paperwork while the other officers get their kicks and then leave. I am also saddled with the crime scene, but I don't mind this type of work. I've found that if you take the extra few minutes to put a good case together, you get a lot less crap from the DA's office, and things are that much easier in court.

I take photos of the point of entry, the smashed storage cabinets, the suspect, and his injuries before he is whisked away to the hospital. The arm is definitely broken, and I again feel bad for the kid. OK, maybe it's not as funny as it would have been had the suspect been a hardened dirtbag, but one thing I can predict with a fair amount of certainty—this kid probably won't be running from the police for a while. I take his boots to compare with tread patterns from other burglaries, then go in to the building and dust for fingerprints. There is a portable stereo and a locked metal box stacked up near the point of entry, and I get some decent latents from them. I finally clear the scene nearly two and a half hours after the original call came out.

I anticipate the paperwork will last me through the end of the shift, and figure that's it for my night. But then, the axe falls. When I am about halfway to the office, I get a call from the dispatcher.

It seems that moments after I pulled away, the manager of the complex saw a white male with a rifle step out of the bushes across the street from the crime scene. This suspect got into a dark green Ford Explorer, then drove away, heading west. The witness got the license plate, which came back "no registration on file," meaning that the registration is likely so new the owner's information has not yet been entered into the DMV computer.

By now, everyone is aware of my shadow and that he supposedly drives a brand-new dark-colored sport utility vehicle. All the cars in the city converge on the area.

Please let one of us find it, I pray, making a U-turn and heading back the way I just came.

When that faithless prayer to a God I don't believe in is completed, I hear one of our officers asking the dispatcher what the plate of the Explorer was.

"Oregon plate Sam John Victor 201," replies the dispatcher.

I hold my breath. Then, an octave higher than before, "One-fourteen, I am following that vehicle northbound on Eastwood Parkway approaching Burnsdale. Get me some cover up here!"

"Any available unit, start for one-fourteen's location, Eastwood south of Burnsdale, following a dark green Ford Explorer, Sam John Victor 201, possibly 'the shadow' homicide suspect."

There is a momentary jumble of radio confusion as each of the seven available units in the city responds. I know they are all changing directions and heading to likely convergence points, as I am. I am not far away, and can be in the area within two minutes. I floor it, and my car jumps forward like a rocket. But before I or anyone else can reach his position, the situation changes.

"One-fourteen, he's gonna rabbit! In pursuit, northbound Eastwood toward Lark!" The tone of the officer's voice and the sound of the siren ratchets up my own adrenaline level, making me drive twice as fast and half as carefully as I should.

Our senior nightshift supervisor, Sergeant O'Grady, is right on top of the pursuit. "Speeds and conditions?" he asks.

"Speeds are moderate, about fifty through a red light, and there's no traffic."

O'Grady was part of a growing cadre of officers who believe that the risks of a high-speed vehicle pursuit are usually not worth a night or two in jail for some petty bad guy, but I knew he'd never order the termination of this pursuit. This wasn't just a stolen car or some scrote with a chump-ass warrant. This was my shadow.

I put myself on autopilot. In such situations, my mind automatically functions like a geographical computer trying to predict the likely direction pursuit might take and where my closest point of convergence will be. I come up with a likely convergence point of the intersection of Lark and Toledo, and point my car in that direction. I will remain here in the hopes the pursuit will continue coming my way and I can get spike strips deployed in time. It's going to be close.

"Passing Tulare, approaching Lark," calls Jordan Mathewson, the pursuing officer.

I get the trunk open and grab the spike strip.

"Looks like he's setting up for a turn onto Lark!"

The chances are something like sixty-forty against me. The average fleeing subject makes a left, then two rights. I need this one to start with a right, and I just have a feeling he will.

I release the catch on the reel built into the spike strip's handle so the string will unspool as I toss the strips across the road. Then, grasping the handle in my left hand, I heave the three sections of spikes across Lark.

"Right turn!" yells Mathewson. "He's turning east on Lark!"

Yes! "One-twelve, I got spikes out at Lark and Toledo," I shout into the radio.

As I am making that broadcast, a pair of headlights comes into view heading right toward me. Not far behind them are the emergency lights and siren of Mathewson's patrol car. He is still alone in the chase.

I barely have enough time to lock the spool down, but my timing is perfect. I give the string a mighty yank, pulling the three segments of hollow detachable spikes across the eastbound lanes of Lark. The strips deploy magnificently, directly in the path of the speeding Explorer. The driver tries to swerve at the last second, but his efforts amount to too little too late.

I hear the satisfying *whump whump* of four hollow steel needles injecting themselves into each tire, followed by the hiss-hiss-hiss of the air rushing out through the hollow tubes as the tire rolls over them. It won't take long—the spikes are designed to quickly let the air escape without causing a blowout, and they work exactly as they were designed to.

Just as the Explorer passes over the spikes I shout, "Good spike!" on the radio, and yank on the handle again, pulling the strips out of the roadway. But Mathewson, inexperienced and too eager, is following his prey too closely. His right tires catch the strips as they are being pulled from the roadway.

There is another double *whump* and more hisses as Stratton police unit 575 hits the spikes and bites the dust. Realizing what he has done, Mathewson pulls his disabled vehicle off to the side, but the shadow apparently isn't as concerned about wheel damage. He accelerates and his tires begin to shred as he slides around the next corner.

The nearest unit is still half a mile away. Discarding the spike strips, I jump in the car and am already hitting the gas before I can get the door fully closed.

"One-twelve, I'm now lead in the pursuit!" I shout into the radio. "Fourteen is out, and we're turning north on Logan! He's going on shredded tires, speeds fifty-plus."

The irony of this is not lost on me. I am, to use a popular cliché, now chasing my own shadow.

But this is not a funny situation. I remind myself that he has a gun, and is wanted for the murder of Delray Hicks, not to mention the burglary of my own house and for stalking me and my family.

The pursuit is not wild as far as chases normally go. The rubber peels off the bad guy's tires, and soon, he is riding on rims, throwing sparks back at me like a mad Fourth of July display.

Finally, other units catch up and I relax some, knowing I have cover on-scene. All pursuits eventually end, and when they do, it usually goes one of three ways. Either there is a crash, which hopefully does not include the officer, or the suspect bails and runs on foot, or he is taken into custody, either with or without a fight. In this case, though, I fear there will be a shooting; he has way too much to lose. Any way you look at it, I'm glad I am no longer alone.

One of the vehicles to catch up with me is the Portland canine unit. When he joins us, I know the business of the shadow's stalking me is over, because he will never be able to outrun the dog.

It occurs to me that the fifteen million dollars my former partner stole from Northwest Healing may well be in that truck. I doubt it though, because my shadow is obviously smart, and has no doubt hidden it away where nobody can find it. I pray that isn't so, because if that's the case, he'll take his lumps, go to jail, and when he gets out, my nightmare will start all over.

But there is a way I can ensure that won't happen. Instantly, I decide that even if his hands go up in surrender, I will interpret it as him going for his weapon, and will beat him to the draw. I know I can make this into a justified shooting, no matter what he does. This guy killed Delray Hicks, and is trying to kill me, and he is armed. I will shoot him at the end of this pursuit, and I will make it appear justified, whether it is or not. The only way I can truly be done with him is if he is dead, and I will make him that way very shortly.

The vehicle is slowing now. I allow the car behind me to call the pursuit, so that I can concentrate on driving and watching the suspect. He looks shaken from the way he is driving. This heartens me, because I had been coming to view him as more than a man; almost like a malevolent, superhuman presence. But he is running now, just any common bad guy, and from the way he's driving, he looks scared. The Explorer is now weaving back and forth in the lane as if he might yet find a way out of this.

"There isn't any," I say aloud. I grit my teeth, thinking this man has been *in my home*, has terrorized me and my family, and he will pay for it. I am perfectly at ease with my decision to kill. He has terrorized my wife and me, made my daughter cry, and has put the pending adoption of my foster son at risk by stalking me, and now he will pay for it.

The Explorer has begun to smoke and is down to about thirty miles an hour. I am in a perfect position to PIT him, or to use the pursuit intervention technique of causing a controlled crash to bring this to a stop at a location of my choosing.

"One-twelve Nora, I'm in position to PIT," I say on the radio.

"Do it, Ben," answers O'Grady.

"Copy. For units in the pursuit, I'm gonna try to PIT once we get down the hill in front of the dog track."

As we go through the green light at the bottom of the hill, I goose my Dodge Charger and move up so that my front right fender is even with the left rear quarter panel of the Bronco. I match speeds with him, then drift gently to the right until our vehicles are touching, the wraparound PIT bumper of my police car catching his truck just aft of the rear tire. As I make contact, I wrench the wheel a hard quarter-turn to the right and punch it, displacing his rear end and causing him to spin out. Once his rear end is twenty-five percent off center, the spinout is unrecoverable, and he corkscrews around to my left. I cut to the right, pass him up, and hook a skidding U-turn.

The truck is rolling backwards now, and the engine stalls. I'm on the radio shouting "Successful PIT!" as I close in on the car's rear end, which is pointing toward me. At the same time, the next car in the pursuit approaches the Explorer from the front. He arrives first, and slams his front bumper into the center of the Ford's with a great deal of force, denting the Ford's hood and causing it to roll backwards even farther. As it does, I apply light brakes, and sail right into its rear bumper. I hit it hard enough that I briefly fear an airbag deployment, but it doesn't happen, and then I am out of the car, gun in hand, backing up to my rear bumper for cover and to avoid a crossfire with the car in front.

I don't have a shot yet, so I scream for him to come out of the vehicle with his hands up, but the shadow does nothing. There is no movement from within, and I interpret this as the suspect pointing a gun at me. I can see his head through the windshield, and am confident in my ability to hit it. Good enough.

I take a brief second to evaluate my line of fire, just to make sure there are no other officers or houses in the background, which there are not, then focus my vision on the shadow's head and begin to squeeze the trigger. Before I can get the shot off, the other officer rushes the car, entering my line of fire, and reaches through the open driver's window.

Shit! OK, if I can't kill him, then time for an ass-beating. I holster and rush to the driver's side. Together, we haul the suspect out through the open driver's window hair first, like a passenger sucked out of decompressing jet at forty thousand feet.

He is small and thin, the antithesis of the supervillain I had made him out to be in my mind. I roll him onto his back to get a look at him before breaking his nose, and that is when complete and utter dismay washes over me. This is no dark, malevolent shadow. The driver is a scared kid, and obviously not my nemesis. No more than fifteen years old, he has barely begun to grow peach fuzz on his upper lip. The kid bursts into tears with my fist cocked over his face.

I am completely dismayed. All pumped up and nobody to kill.

We hook him up and I throw him in the back of my car. The other officers are checking the Explorer now, and I go join them. Rather than finding a sophisticated sniper rifle, we discover a replica of an antique flintlock. They also find authentic looking Civil War uniforms, including a fife and drum set.

More confused than ever, I return to my car, read the kid his rights, and ask him what the hell is going on.

My disappointment is a physical thing as I confirm what I have already figured out. This is not my shadow. This is the partner of the kid we busted at the burglary scene. The business next to the one where I arrested the first kid houses costumes and civil war antiques, and this kid had been busy burglarizing it while his friend was in the other one. He had waited us out, and left only after the last police car, mine, was gone. Two teenage kids out on their first burglary spree.

The truck is an unreported stolen, taken from the other side of Stratton. One of my fellow officers goes to wake up the owner to tell them that the truck she didn't know was stolen has just been recovered half-destroyed.

The letdown I feel is indescribable. It means that my shadow is still out there, and I am no closer to finding him than I was before.

Chapter 8

The letdown is so great, and the dread of my shadow's continued existence, after I was so sure we had him, is so overwhelming, I feel like actually crying. I had been so sure it was the shadow! All I want to do now is go home and crawl into bed.

I do a rush job on the paperwork, and another officer transports my burglary suspect to juvenile hall. Finally, it's time to get off shift. I'm tired and let down, and have to drag myself out to my car. I put the key in the ignition and the engine turns over, but will not start. Swearing to myself, I grind away, but something is obviously wrong with it.

Then, a stab of fear hits me. Is my shadow screwing with me again? Is he aware that I thought we had him, and knowing me as well as he apparently does, is he now toying with me? Or worse, since I've had this premonition about him all night long, am I maybe right, and is this the beginning of a final showdown with him?

Suddenly, the car feels like a death trap. Fighting panic, I open the door and bail out.

Standing there outside my car and breathing heavily, I feel somewhat foolish. I take a look around, wondering if he is hiding somewhere nearby. What am I supposed to do now, I think to myself, run away? If he *is* here, there's nothing I can do. Then, I see how utterly ridiculously I am acting. If my shadow was here and he wanted me dead, I'd already be dead. Right?

Glad that nobody is around to see my Inspector Clouseau-like antics, I get back in the car and try the ignition again. It grinds away but will not start.

Like a jump scene in a cheap horror flick, a figure leaps at my driver's window and begins pounding on the glass. I nearly shit myself in fear.

"Hey Ben, something wrong with your wheels?"

It is Dave Powell, one of my fellow night-shifters. From the silly grin on his face, I know he has intentionally scared me. I surreptitiously flip him off by scratching the left side of my head with my middle finger and pretend to ignore him, but what I am really doing is buying time to get myself under control. A long moment passes before I trust myself to speak.

"Hey, don't knock my ride, Windy. This is a classic." Dave can be exceedingly flatulent at times, and has been given the appropriate nickname.

Everyone knows the pride I take in my cherry '68 Cougar. I like people to think I restored it myself, but in truth, I bought it in this condition. On a good day I might be able to change the oil without going to Jiffy Lube.

"Hey, I would never knock this ride. I *dig* this ride. But if it won't start, I can give you a lift."

I crank it over one more time, and nothing happens. Rather than deal with it, I decide to leave it in the lot and worry about it later.

"Fine," I say, locking it up and getting into his car.

"Bummer about that chase tonight. I mean, we all thought that that was your guy."

"Yeah." I don't feel like talking to Dave, or anyone else. All I want to do is go home. When I do, Sharon will want to talk, so I'll do what I normally do, which is tell her I'm tired and go lay in bed. But I know that sleep won't come easy today.

Dave pulls onto the main road, but when he should turn right on Burnsdale to take me home, he turns left instead.

"Hey, right turn, Dave. You know where I live."

"Hang on, Ben. Gotta make a stop first."

"Come on," I tell him. "I just want to get home today. Where're we going?"

"Won't take but a second, dude," he replies. Not feeling like arguing, I heave a sigh and settle in.

The next thing I know, we're pulling into Foxholes, a nasty little titty bar in Rockledge.

"Wait a sec," I protest, but Dave just gives me this big, dumb grin in return. "Dave, I don't feel like doing this . . . " I trail off, knowing that for the moment, anyway, I am his captive.

"One beer, man. One beer, and then you can go."

"Dave, Sharon will kick my ass if I come home with beer on my breath. You *know* this."

He makes a meow noise like a pussy cat, then a *whoosh-crack* sound like a whip, and I grin despite myself. Though I don't want to go in, I figure what the hell, there's nothing I can do about it anyway. It's only a beer.

We go inside, and I am surprised to see that there are others here. Usually, there might be only one derelict at this hour. As my eyes adjust to the dim light, I see that the others consist of everyone from the night shift, spread out along the first row of tables next to the stage. Two places in the middle are open, obviously left for Dave and me. At one of them is a spotless distributor cap that looks suspiciously like the one I usually keep under the hood of my Cougar.

I smile, and shake my head. Choir practice. OK, I can use this, I suppose. A naked waitress with five G's worth of prosthetic mams brings the first round, and I down it without coming up for air.

The curtain billows, and a dancer hits the stage. For a seven-o'clocker, she's not as bad as you might figure. I could do without the Harley wings tattooed across her abdomen, but at least it partially covers the cesarean scar. Dollar bills come out, beer goes down, and she gets more attractive.

By the fifth round, the shadow is all but forgotten.

Three hours and sixty-five bucks later, I am cruising home in the Cougar, singing along to Led Zeppelin's Black Dog on the radio. There are three messages on my cell phone, which I have decided are best left unheard.

At a red light, I look to my right and see a Stratton patrol car one lane over. The driver, a guy from my Academy named Jeff Jelderks, stares at me for a second, and then alternately covers his eyes, ears, and mouth in a parody of the "see no evil, hear no evil, speak no evil" monkey. I feel momentarily guilty about drinking and driving when I hate that crime and have a reputation of making a lot of arrests for it, but what can I say? I have to get home somehow.

When I let myself in the house, Sharon takes one look at me, and lets me have it with both barrels. She goes on for a while about how she was worried about me, how I could have called, how I should be more mature than this, and how I'm not some rookie who has to prove himself with his crazy party attitude. Blah blah blah. Suddenly, going to choir practice and driving home sloshed isn't as funny as it was a while ago.

"Come on, honey, I had a rough night," is all I tell her. It isn't enough.

"Ben, we're supposed to meet with the lawyer this afternoon about the adoption. Are you crazy, going out and drinking? What if you'd gotten in an accident? We'd never get to keep him! What's the matter with you?"

"God, I forgot," I mutter more to myself than to her. "I'll still be able to make it," I say, trying to sound reassuring. I'm sure I just sound drunk.

"God damn it Ben, go get in bed. You'd better be awake and sober in four hours; we have to be at his office at four thirty."

I glance at the clock and see that it is nearing noon. I'm tired as hell, and I already feel like shit. I can only imagine how much worse it will be in four hours. On top of that, I am sure that I look like shit, and I probably smell like shit too. Fortunately, Leah and LaMonjello are away at school (they go to the same school, where Leah is in second grade, and LaMonjello is in kindergarten), so at least they don't have to see me like this.

Muttering an apology, I stumble off to bed and hope I can get up at four.

"Daddy!"

The sound ricochets around my head like a bullet fired in the interior of a gigantic church bell. A pillow hits me in the face, and the feeling is the same as when, about two years ago, a guy named Laszlo Bowman pasted me in the face with a shovel, knocking me unconscious, on a radio call. I think my head might explode, and this is just a *pillow*.

It is everything I have within me to open my gummy eyes to the stabbing light of my darkened bedroom. I run my tongue over the sticky coating on my teeth, and taste the sour, stale-beer reek of my breath.

"Lee, lookit yo' daddy eyes," LaMonjello shouts excitedly. "They be all red and droopy an' shit. Why yo eyes all red and droopy, Daddy? Is you sick?"

"Yeah, LaMonjello, Daddy's sick," I mutter. The effort is so painful I wonder if I might be dying. I haven't had a hangover this bad in many years, and I have forgotten how much fun they can be.

LaMonjello has, along with his many other surprising and almost unbelievable characteristics, developed quite an advanced sense of humor. He rolls his eyes impossibly far to the right, so they nearly disappear, and his body follows them to the floor as if he has fainted. He pinches his nose and says, "Lee! Daddy breaf smell like a *gas station*. Run away from him 'fo he kill us all!"

Leah emits a wineglass-shattering screech that cleaves my head as thoroughly as a blow from an axe, and bolts from the room with LaMonjello hard on her heels. They continue running through the house screaming. Burying my head under the pillow does nothing to alleviate the pain.

I pry my eyes open again, and Sharon is there, bearing aspirin and a glass of water.

"I'm good to go," I manage to say. "Ready to roll . . ."

She hands me the aspirin, which I swallow without water. Her look is disapproving, and once again, I feel like a steaming pile left in my yard by a mangy stray.

"Sure you are, tiger," she says.

"I'm so sorry, Shar," I croak.

She sits down on the bed and says, "I feel too bad for you to be mad at you. I'd just go myself, but the adoption hearing is tomorrow, and we still need to go over some stuff with the attorney. We *both* need to be there."

Our attorney is a guy named B. Douglas Pasha, a senior partner with McMower, Pasha, Seagle, and Hall, one of Portland's better law firms. He doesn't come cheap, and we have our best shot at pushing the adoption through with him. I'm a registered attorney myself with the Oregon State Bar, but my area of specialty before I became a cop is corporate tax law. I don't know squat about adoption, but I have to admit, Pasha's done a hell of a job putting our case together. He's researched a great deal of case law that supports interracial adoptions and the ability of white people to keep their black children immersed in African-American culture, and his findings are pretty impressive.

But it has not come cheaply. Pasha's initial retainer of $7,000 is already gone, and the costs haven't shown signs of stopping. At our first meeting, Pasha's estimate was anywhere from twelve to fifteen thousand dollars, win or lose, and the only direction that estimate can go is up.

Paying for it isn't an insurmountable problem. Sharon and I have agreed to cash in our largest mutual fund and use that which we've saved so far for Leah's education. It will leave us mostly tapped out, but that's how committed we are to LaMonjello. In fact, we wouldn't have a problem with the adoption at all if it weren't for two things.

The first is LaMonjello's half-sister, now eighteen, who is also petitioning for custody with the representation of an NAACP pro bono lawyer. The second, of course, is the fact that my shadow is still out there.

The first impediment isn't really that significant. Sheila Jackson, who stabbed the late Delray in the hand with the same knife that killed her mother, turned eighteen last month, and is living with her thirty-year-old boyfriend Clifford Rosey, who is a pretty good guy, as it turns out. He left the air force two years ago as a certified jet mechanic, and works for United at the Portland International Airport. They are engaged, but apart from his "legitimization" of her, she wouldn't stand a chance.

We are willing to give her liberal visitation, but that's not good enough for her. I hate to say this, but there is state money involved if she gets full custody, and apart from that, she seems to have no desire to be a part of his life. Regardless, she's not a big worry.

Overcoming the second impediment is, though. The specter of the shadow hanging over me will no doubt greatly reduce my chances of a successful adoption. Pasha doesn't think a judge will cater to the idea of sending LaMonjello into a potentially dangerous environment. I can't say I blame him. The strategy is to minimize the shadow and the danger he represents. I know it is weak, but it's the best we can do.

I pull Sharon down onto the bed next to me and give her a kiss. She wrinkles her nose, and in a rare display of humor, she says, "Damn, he right! Yo breaf *do* smell like gasoline."

After getting cleaned up, Sharon and I pack the kids into the van and she drives us to the attorney's office. As we back out past the Cougar, I see that someone has parked it half on the grass and half on the driveway after taking out the mailbox.

The trip to the lawyer eats an hour of my time and another four hundred and fifty of my dollars, but after we are done, I feel that we have a better than average chance of winning full custody of LaMonjello. At the end of the session, time has restored me to a reasonable semblance of consciousness and awareness, and I feel at least somewhat human.

We have to be in court at one tomorrow afternoon, and I've already taken tonight off to ensure that I will be fresh by then. Now all we have to do is get through one more night without contact from the shadow.

Chapter 9

Judge Suzanne Payne scans the courtroom over the top of her brown reading glasses, her short hair, half gray, half blonde, framing her face in a boyish way. We've spent all day in court, and are now in closing arguments.

My attorney is just finishing up. "The benefits of having LaMonjello's residence and sole custody, both legal and physical, with the Geller family over that of Ms. Jackson and her current boyfriend, uh"—here Pasha pauses to check his notes—"Mr., ah, Rosey, are quite clear, Your Honor. On one hand, we have a loving, stable, well-adjusted and well-to-do nuclear family, and on the other hand, a transient, maladjusted, unstable teenaged girl with a drug habit and a criminal history. The fact that she—"

"Objection! Your Honor . . ."

"Facts well established through testimony and evidence, Your Honor. More than allowable in view of the circumstances."

"Prejudicial and argumentative, Judge," snaps the other lawyer.

Judge Payne fires off a quick "Overruled," and the trial continues.

The pro bono lawyer sits down heavily, and Pasha nods at the judge as if he were her equal. How this guy gets away with this arrogant, self-assured cocky manner is beyond me. He's all of five-five, and weighs maybe a buck thirty, has little-boy freckles, and is the embodiment of a "lawyer nerd."

"Thank you, Your Honor. As I was saying, I don't see how any court could sentence little LaMonjello to a life spent living on other people's couches, with no money, no supervision, and no one to help him with homework, let alone keep him in school, much less provide adequately for his most basic of needs—food, clothing and shelter—simply because the person with whom he would share this lifestyle shares his skin color and a common parent."

At this point in his little soliloquy, an aide to Judge Paine steps out from the door to her chambers and whispers something in her ear. Pasha sees this and politely takes a moment to gather his notes. The aide withdraws, and Pasha continues, without losing a beat.

"I'm sorry for Sheila Jackson; *truly* sorry for her recent losses, but a little blood and a little skin pigment doesn't go very far in providing for the needs of a very human, very *deserving* child like LaMonjello. Especially one with a background such as his, who will surely need advanced medical and psychiatric care. Which brings up another point, Your Honor. The Gellers have an excellent comprehensive health plan, whereas Sheila Jackson, at least for now, must rely on the limited capacity of the Oregon Health Plan. How could she possibly provide that which LaMonjello will require in terms of extended mental—and physical—health care?

"And as for the matter of his race, I think we've proven far beyond any reasonable certainty that the race of adoptive parents is of the least concern to the adoptee, and is virtually meaningless as to how the child grows up and views important things such as background, or race relations, etcetera. Personally, I find the very introduction of this . . . this *race card* offensive and racist to me in and of itself."

I nod right along with Pasha, but the judge's face remains passive.

Pasha continues, "Testimony has already established that if Ms. Jackson wins, she will apply for state aid through the welfare—"

"Objection!"

"Sustained."

Pasha is the picture of coolness, accepting the judge's ruling as if it were what he had wanted. "Thank you. Please strike the last sentence, and I will proceed. Now, as for this so-called shadow business, well, we have not tried to hide anything from the court. Yes, Ben Geller has a dangerous job. Yes, he has been what some would call 'stalked' in the past by a person dubiously nicknamed 'The Shadow.' But, what has this guy really done? He snuck into the house once, and looked at a picture in a closet. He listens to occasional conversations. He sends emails from time to time. I'm sorry, but this doesn't rise to the level of some dark, malevolent, lurking evil opposing counsel has been trying to paint. Far from it, I'd say. To me, *the shadow*"—Pasha reinforces his disdain for the villainous moniker by drawing air quotes with his fingers—"sounds more like a loser who could use a girlfriend, or should maybe get his TV fixed."

There are some snickers throughout the courtroom, and it looks as if Judge Payne struggles briefly with, but ultimately triumphs over, a smile.

To me, the shadow isn't a bored, lonely loser with a broken TV and an unsatisfactory love life. He is an infinitely financed, highly dangerous opponent who could end my life any time he pleased. A wolverine might look like a harmless little kitty cat to a curious child, but he'd better not back it into a corner.

"In short, Your Honor, this person, this *shadow*, amounts to a pain in the derrière; a minor, occasional worry, which is not the worry of anyone in the Geller household, but rather the combined forces of the Multnomah County Major Crimes Task Force, who will ultimately catch him, and see to it he gets the counseling and attention that he needs. In this room, he is below a minor player. Thank you."

Judge Payne nods her head. Her lips draw a tight, colorless line and she hums an elongated mmmmm-hmmmm. "A virtual nonentity, eh?" she says. "Well, I'm calling a recess, during which I will review testimony and make my decision. In the meantime, court is adjourned until 4:00 p.m."

She doesn't pound a gavel or anything. Rather, she simply stands up, turns around, and disappears. None of us in the courtroom move for a few moments, and then we all stand. The room is uncomfortable, since the only people present are opposing sides and their supporters.

We all try to avoid one another's eyes. Sheila Jackson confers with her attorney and her boyfriend *du jour*, and Sharon and I begin a stilted discussion of where to go for coffee.

As people begin filtering out of the room, the judge comes back in and says, "Wait a moment. Is everyone still here?"

Pasha looks around and says, "Yes, Your Honor."

"I would like to see Mr. and Mrs. Geller, alone, in chambers, please. It's two thirty now. Rather than resume at four, if the rest of you would take fifteen minutes, court will resume at two forty-five."

Pasha looks befuddled at not being invited. "Uh, Your Honor . . ."

"The Gellers only, Counselor."

He just nods. Even I know this is an unusual request. I take Sharon by the hand, and we follow the aide to Judge Payne's chambers.

Judge Payne closes the door behind us and invites us to sit down. Sensing something really bad, we sit, and look to her expectantly.

"Mr. and Mrs. Geller—Ben—normally, I would have no trouble making a decision about your case. You'd win. I'm just being honest with you. However, there has been a complication."

My heart is now racing, and I know that I will not get custody of LaMonjello. As bad as that is, though, I have a feeling that that is not the worst of it, and I know that my precautions about the shadow have all been for naught.

Sharon is stiff, her face pale and unmoving. She looks like a display in a wax museum.

Judge Payne gathers her wits and her voice strengthens. "Just a few minutes ago, this envelope was delivered to the deputies at the main entrance to the courthouse. We're talking with the deputy who took it now, and checking the surveillance cameras that monitor the sidewalk out front."

She hands me a large manila envelope, which I open. Sharon huddles next to me as I extract some photographs and a letter written in moderately legible hand.

The first photo I see has been taken through a door that is ajar. It is the bathroom door in the upstairs hallway of my house. Through the cracked door, I see Leah sitting on the toilet, oblivious to the camera's intrusion, wiping between her legs with a large wad of toilet paper.

A pitiful noise escapes Sharon's lips. The next photo is of LaMonjello in his bedroom. The angle is from inside his closet. He too is naked, and he is in the process of putting on a pair of pajama bottoms. One leg is in, one leg out. His back is to the camera; his butt smooth and lighter that the rest of his skin.

There is one last photo. It is of Leah, asleep in her bed. The covers have been pulled down, and she is clad in a Sponge Bob nightie. The camera angle is directly above her face, and the photographer's right hand is lightly covering her eyes, his fingertips gently caressing her forehead. The tip of his thumb is actually between her lips, and this molestation is the most offensive of them all.

Sharon covers her mouth, but an inhumanly painful cry escapes her fingers. Gingerly, touching only the edges of the photos, I replace them in the envelope and extract the letter.

Judge Payne,

Please think twice before you make your decision. The mixing of the races has always been something better left undone. Though you may have difficulty believing this, my concern lies solely with Leah.

The nigger may only be a fawn right now, but in a few short years, he will be a dangerous buck in rut. Though you can't see it in this shot, you should see the size of his dick already. Leah would not be safe there, and I want her to be safe.

I am,
"The Shadow."

Chapter 10

Judge Payne has agreed to a two-week delay in the case, without a detailed explanation to the attorneys, to allow the matter of the shadow to be investigated fully. It is actually a final opportunity for us to catch him so that she may have a clear conscience in awarding Sharon and me custody of LaMonjello.

At my request, with a promise that Sharon and the children leave the state for the duration, she has allowed us to retain temporary custody of LaMonjello, but there will be no further delays in the case. I know that, barring the capture of my shadow, I will not win.

I cannot live like this; it is too much. So, being a police officer, I formulate a stupid idea. The day after the disastrous appearance in court, I lay out my plan to Detective Sergeant Mahoney in a moving car so we cannot be eavesdropped upon. He tells me he will talk it over with the chief and get back to me. Before I leave for home that afternoon, I get an email from him. *Approved. Location and time as discussed.*

I breathe a sigh, but even I can't tell if it is relief or just nervous apprehension.

What I am doing is this: Tomorrow, I will be taking my family on a "surprise" camping trip to a remote site about forty miles away in the Cascade Mountains. Sharon will not know anything other than what I tell her, as will the children. What I will tell her is that I took two days off so we can go on a spur-of-the-moment camping trip in a little-known spot that is so remote the shadow will not have a chance to follow us. We will spend some last time together as a family for a while, and then she and the children will go to her grandmother's house in Herndon, Virginia to wait in safety and hope that the shadow matter is resolved before we go back to court.

That last part, at least is true. Unless we catch the shadow on the camping trip, they are going to go to her grandmother's in Herndon.

In the meantime, this is no camping vacation. Rather, it will be a well-laid trap, with my unwitting family and me as bait.

Even now, select members of the SWAT team are heading out to the campsite, which is a little-known area near Trillium Lake on Mt. Hood, to scout the place out and set the ambush. The rest of the team is being paged and will join the scouts and other snipers at 0500.

The plan is for me to bring the camping trip up to Sharon this afternoon, and head out late tomorrow morning. Once we get there, I am on the clock as usual, since I am now part of a sting operation aimed at catching a man wanted for murder.

My job will be to stay close to my family and protect them. Since they will have no idea that this is anything other than a normal camping trip, they cannot give anything away. The idea, of course, is that the shadow has nothing better to do than to sit around eavesdropping on me and my family, and that he will hear about our plans and follow us out to the mountain to screw with us.

Somehow, I know in my bones he will do this. It is like I am getting to know him, as he has obviously gotten to know me, and my only worry is that he will somehow discover this is a trick. I don't believe he will try to molest us in any way, but I will be armed and ready, and actually hope he does.

Anyway, undercover detectives will be staking out my house starting tonight, and will be on hand at various locations along the way to look for anyone following us up the mountain. I will have a portable "bird dog" tracking device with me at all times, and an Oregon State Police helicopter will be on standby for aerial support.

The way I figure it, this is our best—if not our only—chance to catch him. If we do, that will solve my biggest problem, but that won't be the end of trouble for me; after the shadow, I'll have Sharon to deal with. I won't even allow myself to consider how pissed she will be with me when she finds out I have used her and the children as bait. If my plan fails, then she will never have to know, but I'll still have the shadow to deal with. It seems I can't win for losing.

I walk in the front door and find Sharon on the floor playing a video game with the kids. While I was gone, we had a security company install a sophisticated home alarm system. I have no faith in it whatsoever.

"Honey, I have something I want to talk to you about."

"Can't it wait? I want to get LaMonjello back for beating me three games in a row." I am constantly amazed at LaMonjello's progress in adapting to the average life of a middle-income suburban child. He even beats Leah at these games.

"No, this is really important." She locks eyes with me for two heartbeats, then immediately puts the controller down and follows me.

I take her into the bedroom where I know other conversations have been heard before. There, I lower my voice conspiratorially, and lay out the plan, telling her only that we're going on a spur-of-the-moment camping trip before she and the kids go to Tucson to visit my mother until the adoption hearing. The Arizona part is a lie, just in case the trap doesn't work. In that case, detectives in Tucson will stake out the Tucson International Airport for the shadow on the date and time of the arrival of the fictitious flight, while my family will actually be safe in Virginia, visiting her grandmother. It is a last-ditch fail-safe.

Sharon is amenable to the idea of both the camping trip and the Tucson visit, but I know that when she finds out that I have used her and the kids as bait, her head will rotate and she will spit green pea soup at me. Dejectedly, I mentally calculate all the ways she will kick my ass when this is over.

Together, we tell the kids we are going on a surprise camping trip tomorrow. We tell them not to talk about it to anyone; that it is just our own little secret. They are excited enough. We try to make it a regular night, but after the kids are in bed and Sharon is asleep, I lay awake wondering what kind of man would intentionally use his family as bait.

It is incredibly difficult for me to act normal as we load the car for the camping trip the following morning. My urge is to look around and see if I can spot the cops, but I don't want to give them away.

Uneventful is the word that best describes the only on-duty camping trip which I've ever heard of. Other than my being armed and looking at every tree as if it is about to start yelling and throwing apples, this little excursion proves to be fruitless. I have deliberately chosen a spot that can be easily watched on all sides; one in which there is only one easy way in and out. We don't hike, but we fish from the banks of a pleasant mountain creek near where I park the camper, which I have borrowed from Ray Schmeer. LaMonjello catches the first rainbow trout, a thirteen-inch keeper which he insists on holding until long after it ceases movement. The fishing is good, and we dine on our catch.

For a long time, while catching and cleaning the fish with the children, I almost forget that I am working and that there are armed officers surrounding our trailer and watching our every move. The barrel of a .40 cal in my back is a constant reminder, though.

The sun sets and we sit around the fire roasting marshmallows and making s'mores. By now, I am feeling very sorry for the officers in the woods around us. I am growing increasingly disappointed as it becomes apparent that the sting operation is going to be a failure.

As always seems to happen when we are in the woods after dark, we grow tired quickly, and go to bed early. By nine thirty, the children are both asleep and I am getting outright depressed. I had not thought my shadow would try to contact me, but I had been certain he would at least follow me up here, and optimistic that the perimeter guys would nab him.

At ten thirty, Sharon and I go to bed.

Shortly after two, something wakes me up. I am momentarily befuddled, trying to remember where I am. Then it comes to me and I try to figure out what woke me.

"Ben, did you hear that?" Sharon asks; the fear in her voice accompanied by a death grip on my arm.

"No. What was it?"

"I don't know! I thought I heard voices, and something moving around outside."

I keep the light off, and as I reach for my gun, someone begins pounding on the camper door.

"Ben! Wake up!"

It is Ray. I get the door open. Somehow, Leah is still sleeping, though LaMonjello is awake and had crawled into her bunk with her at the first sign of trouble. My fear melts into something akin to joy. There is only one reason why they would wake me in the middle of the night.

"Tell me you got him, Ray."

He looks at me, and I immediately deflate.

"No, Ben. *We* didn't get *him*."

"Oh, Christ. Who? How bad?"

"Gus," he says gravely. "And, pretty bad."

Gustavo Oronco, the smallest man on the entry team, is still alive. He had been placed in the most remote spot on the perimeter, watching the most unlikely point of infiltration, which is the creek bed west of our campsite. He was fine at 11:00 p.m. when he last checked in. He failed to check in at one, and it took forty-five minutes for the team to find him.

Gus had been diligently scanning the woods around him with night-vision goggles when he was accosted from the rear. He had been garroted, but not fatally, stripped naked, and tied over a fallen tree with his hands bound to his ankles.

The worst of it is Gus had been raped; sodomized like Ned Beatty's character in *Deliverance.* As a final indignity, a peanut butter and jelly sandwich from his cooler had been smeared on him from his feet to his crotch, providing an insect highway to his genitals and anus. His radio was taken, but his weapon left with him along with all his other equipment.

Gus was found ten minutes ago, covered with bugs and bites, and is currently being loaded into a patrol car for immediate transport to the nearest hospital, which is in Stratton.

Sharon doesn't say a word to me all the way down the mountain. I don't blame her. Leah has remained asleep, but LaMonjello has been clinging to her since Ray knocked on the door. Though he has no idea what has happened, or why, instinct has told him danger is afoot.

When we get home, I carry Leah inside and put her to bed. I go to our room to change, and find LaMonjello sleeping on Sharon's shoulder. I retire to the couch, where I have been silently banished.

Sergeant Mahoney stops by at nine the next morning. He has secured a reservation change, and Sharon and the kids are leaving for Herndon at noon today. I breathe a little easier knowing they will be gone. Gus is still in the hospital, but he will make a full recovery. Physically, at least.

Still hoping the second sting might work, I tell her about the schedule change. She is all business, and the shoulder I get is colder than when she caught me sleeping with Andrea. She still thinks she is going to Arizona.

We get to the ticket counter at the airport, which is where she discovers she's going to Virginia instead of Arizona, and accepts it as if it were an expected change. I get warm hugs mingled with tears from both children, but Sharon won't even say goodbye, let alone give me a kiss.

I think maybe I've finally given her more than she can take.

The two weeks have passed faster than I would have thought possible, and they have been bad on all fronts—Gus, Andrea, Sharon, and the adoption.

What happened to Gus eats at me night and day. The ultimate responsibility for it is mine and mine alone, since it was my idea to stage the camping sting operation. Gus apparently isn't doing so well; he has kept entirely to himself following his release from the hospital, refusing to take visitors or to come back to work. I tried calling the day after he was released, but the phone went right to voicemail. He didn't answer when I knocked on his door, despite that his truck was in the driveway. I will give him the time he needs, but I hope he can recover from this.

In addition, I've had nary a word from Sharon, who will return with the children tomorrow evening, which is Sunday. I've talked to the children, who are having a good time, but they say their mother gets angry every time they ask about me. Who can blame her? I had put her and the children in jeopardy during the sting, and didn't even give them the courtesy of telling them. As I had suspected, this is more of an affront to her than having the affair with Andrea.

I am the worst sort of man imaginable, and I am beginning to hate myself.

The adoption hearing resumes Monday morning, day after tomorrow, no matter the status of the shadow case. Sadly, there has been no progress whatsoever in the investigation. I stand a zero chance of getting custody of LaMonjello due to the shadow's photos and letter, let alone what happened on the camping sting. Apart from the psychological damage to Gus, the incident in the woods only serves to demonstrate the shadow's propensity for violence. I can no longer claim that the shadow is merely a pesky bother, and I now find myself reluctantly agreeing with Judge Payne. As much as we love him, LaMonjello would not be safe in my house with the shadow out there.

There has been no further communication from him since the failed sting, and I believe the reason behind the lack of contact is the rape. My gut instinct tells me that he did not intend to do that; that he lost control of himself and is ashamed of it. Ultimately, if that is indeed the case, it is the one good thing to come of all this. If he lost control, then he has exposed himself as vulnerable. He made a mistake, and if he made one, he will make others, and that is how we will catch him.

On the other hand, if he disappears and makes no further contact, even if for a *good* reason like his death, then I will never know, and will have to live looking over my shoulder for the rest of my life. We would never catch him, and if we don't catch him, I will never get custody of LaMonjello. Things couldn't be much worse, and my mood tonight is black and foul.

I should not have come to work, but the last thing I wanted to do was sit in the house all by myself again. Still, I am relieved it has been a slow night. All I have done is drive aimlessly around the city, answering radio calls like an automaton when dispatched, thinking about the past two weeks.

With all the stress we'd been through with Andrea, the shadow, and the adoption, Sharon hadn't exactly had sex at the top of her mind. Then, after the photos, and particularly after I had used the family as bait on the camping trip, she has completely frozen me out of her life.

A little sex with Sharon would have alleviated at least some of the pressures I was facing. However, she has been cool and distant in that regard for a long time. Since the affair with Andrea, sex had been terribly unpredictable in our marriage. Mostly, there was none, and then without warning she would be all over me. After maybe two days we would be back in the desert for another several weeks.

Every time I broached the subject, it was like stabbing her with the Andrea knife again. Knowing this, I have stoically born my pent-up sexual frustration, but that has left Ben one unhappy and tense middle-aged man.

It goes without mentioning I was in quite a state after Sharon left. Not surprisingly, Andrea somehow or another knew that. She was there and willing whereas Sharon was not. Truth be told, there wasn't really much resistance in me. She called me the night after they left town and I allowed her to come right over, having her park down the street and sneaking her in the back door like a teenager, just in case there were nosy neighbors watching.

That made us think about something else to stress over. The shadow was probably watching, and he could take photos of us and give them to Sharon.

In the temporary post-sex stress relief, I gave the whole matter a great deal of thought, and concluded that I don't think the shadow means me any harm. Obviously, he could kill me any time he wanted, but he has never moved to harm me personally, and I don't think he has any intention to. I think in his own twisted way, he is trying to look out for me, as stupid and senseless as that sounds. Why, I don't know. I suspect that it is a cruel way of showing me how benevolent he really was, by controlling my life—the same way a cat might toy with a mouse, carrying it around in her mouth, batting it silly, tossing it in the air, but never killing or doing any real harm to it. Apart from the Oronco incident in the woods, he has done nothing overtly threatening, if you considered the photos of the kids to be his way of steering me away from the adoption rather than an overt threat to my family. His defeat of us in the woods was a message designed to tell us exactly how stupid we were to think we might outfox him.

An hour after Andrea left, the physical and mental relief provided by the sex was wholly overshadowed by my guilt, and the idea that instead of fucking Andrea, I should be concentrating on healing my relationship with Sharon and keeping my family intact. I became morose and depressed.

Sharon's silence toward me continued throughout her trip. Last night, I tried calling her again, but when Leah gave her the phone, she hung up without talking to me. Feeling self-destructive, I surrendered to my ultimate weakness, figuring with everything as bad as it is, I might as well at least fuck my brains out one final time, so I called Andrea again. After we screwed like dogs on the floor of her kitchen, she told me she wants me to leave Sharon and move in with her. That was the final brick.

Andrea simply doesn't get it, and I've been fooling myself hoping that she did. I don't love her, and I don't want her for anything other than sex. I can't even have that now, because she wants the whole enchilada. I guess I somehow believed that, like me, Andrea knew deep inside that what we had was purely physical and nothing more, but I've been fooling myself. She really does believe that we were meant to be together, and finally, she has made me see the light.

If she hadn't suggested that I leave Sharon and the kids for her, I would probably have continued seeing her, even if Sharon took me back.

But her words made me see things differently. Sex with her isn't worth the emotional baggage of knowing that I'm encouraging her love for me when I cannot return it. I just don't need that.

So, we had a fight and I left her naked on the floor, using the shadow as an excuse to stop seeing her for good. In retrospect, I should have told her she was only a sexual relief valve for me and nothing else, and that I wanted to heal my marriage; that the only woman I had room for in my life was my wife, but I saw no reason to destroy her. Even though I spared her that, and used the shadow as an excuse to permanently break up with her, she still did not take it well. She started crying, and as I left, she threw a spoon at me and called me a lying bastard. She looked like a little kid, sitting naked on the floor with snot running down her nose, and I felt nothing but relief that our affair was finally over.

So, tonight I am here at work, but not really here. I am pissed, depressed, worried and terrified, all at the same time. I cannot face life without my family, and I am too much of a shallow, foolish asshole to keep them. I am driving around in my patrol car pondering these things when somewhere in the back of my mind, I hear Sergeant Sector's voice on the radio, calling unit one-twenty-eight to tac one.

"One-two-eight?" echoes the dispatcher.

Is there any way at all to heal my family and get Sharon to trust me again? How did I get myself involved in this situation?

"One-two-eight, switch to tac one for the sergeant."

Someone isn't answering the radio, but that knowledge isn't strong enough to pull me out of my reverie. The fact that I am unit one-twenty-eight hasn't registered with me yet.

The problem is multifaceted; I don't want to make an enemy of Andrea, since she's on the Major Crimes Team investigating the shadow case. I can't continue existing under the pressure of having the shadow still out there, and, I have no idea how to fix the damage I've caused my family.

"What was his most recent status?" asks Sergeant Sector on the radio.

"He's been clear since zero-zero-forty hours, when he finished a traffic stop at Second and Market," the dispatcher says.

Second and Market? That's where I made my last traffic stop. The realization that they're talking about me on the radio slaps me in the face. How did it start? Dolly had asked me to go to tac one.

"One-two-eight, I'm Code Four, and I copy I'm wanted on tac one. Switching over now," I advise quickly. I change frequencies to the tactical net, which, when not being used for something tactical, is a free conversation net.

"Go ahead, Dolly."

"Wake up, Ben. I'd like to stop and grab a cup with you."

"No thanks, Sarge. I'll take a rain check, though."

"Come on, Ben, I'm dyin' out here. Let's make it Expresso's."

"I just had some," I lied.

"I insist, Ben."

"Insist like, as in it's an order?"

"Ben, meet me at Expresso's in five."

I know everyone is eavesdropping, and I hate that. I try to overcome my irritation and save a little face. "You buyin'?"

"It was my invite."

"OK, seeya there in a few."

I do *not* want to go to coffee with anyone, especially Saint Sector. She's going to ask me if I'm OK, and tell me that if I need time off, it's a slow night anyway, and screw minimum shift requirements, they'll manage without me. She'll be concerned that I have to face Judge Payne in the adoption in just under thirty-six hours, and that I will lose LaMonjello for certain. She may even order me to go home, which would mean I wouldn't have to burn sick time or vacation hours, because the department would have to pay my salary. But I don't want to do that, either. If I give any open door at all, there will no doubt be an invitation to attend church or give my burdens to Christ, or something. With Saint Sector, that's where all conversations end up.

I hook a U-turn and point my black-and-white in the direction of Expresso's, where, at this time of night, the employees sport lots of exposed ink and metal, and blast music with four-letter words at decibel levels that violate the city's noise ordinance. But at this hour, they are the only game in town. They're not close to any dwellings, and have great coffee, which comes with a fifty-percent police discount because they like cops keeping riffraff away. Which is kinda funny, because we tend to view the employees as such. But, good, cheap coffee keeps us coming in.

I pull into the lot, but Dolly isn't there yet, so I wait for her in the car.

"Thirty-one Sam, traffic," Dolly tells the dispatcher.

Good. Maybe her traffic stop will turn into a drunk driver or something, and she won't be able to make it to coffee.

"Go ahead."

"Oregon X-ray Willie Ocean Seven Four Two. We're gonna land at NE Seventeenth and Crane."

"Copy. Time is zero-two-thirty-eight."

I suppose that since I was supposed to meet her, the friendly thing to do would be to drive to Seventeenth and Crane to cover her, so I start the car and head over there, hoping something will happen that will prevent us from having coffee.

You'd think I'd have learned by now to be careful what I hope for.

Chapter 11

I'm just about there when Dolly gets back on the radio and asks for a Code 1 cover car, which means non-urgent backup.

"One-twenty-eight is with her," I advise, killing the lights and rolling up behind her unit. Dolly is standing at the right rear corner of her patrol car with a driver's license in her hand.

"Whatcha got, Sarge?"

"Two guys, both Baker brothers. Driver gave me an ID card, passenger gives me a generic name and DOB; says he has no ID. The driver's gonna be suspended no doubt, and the passenger is obviously lying about his name."

"Baker brothers" is a reference to David Baker, the phonetic alphabet for the letters DB, which, in police lingo means dirtbag. When we're dealing with more than one dirtbag at a time, this has evolved into David Baker and his brother, or the Baker brothers.

On any other night, I would be pissed off, because Sector is one of those sergeants who, upon finding a big bucket of shit, will dump it onto her cover officer rather than clean it up herself. Me, I've always had a "you catch 'em, you clean 'em" philosophy, but that doesn't prevent me from having to do other people's police work. However, right now this is exactly what I was hoping for, to get me out of meeting her for coffee.

Dolly is busy on the inquiry net running the driver and passenger, using only the name and date of birth the passenger gave her. I switch my radio to the inquiry net to listen.

"Thirty-one Sam?"

"Go ahead."

"Your first subject, Andrew Joseph, is clear and suspended with fifty-one info. Your second subject, Williams, is clear and UTL." Fifty-one info means something you don't want the bad guy to hear, and UTL means unable to locate any record of him.

"Go ahead with the fifty-one info."

"Joseph is suspended. He's also a corrections client, on parole for Robbery II, and is flagged 'armed career criminal.'"

"Got it. Start me a hook for NE Crane, just north of Seventeenth."

"Copy, your tow will be Stratton Better Wrecker, your case number is 08-10543."

"Thanks."

Dolly begins writing the ticket and tow report, and I am glad she's in a mood to do her own work. I keep my eye on the car, which is lit up with Dolly's spotlight and the two bright takedown lights mounted on the front of her light bar. Her overheads are pulsing bright blue and red. The two dirtbags are sitting quietly in the car. I can only imagine the conversation, since they must have guessed by now that the car is getting impounded.

This is where I watch real closely to see if they toss contraband out the window so we don't find it on the inevitable inventory search. People—and I use the term lightly—also have a tendency to get pissed off when you take their wheels. It's one of the more common forms of job satisfaction, especially when I'm in the kind of mood that I'm in now. If I didn't mention it earlier, I'm in an ugly, black mood, and my give-a-shit factor is at an all-time low.

A few minutes later, Dolly is done with the report and the citation, and is ready to spread the good news to the occupants of the car that it is getting towed.

"Let's approach," she says.

She goes to the driver's side and I approach from the passenger side, staying a step or two behind her. Both of us stand behind the driver's and passenger's window, so if they were to take a chump shot, they would first have to telegraph their intentions and screw up their aim by twisting unnaturally in their seats to do so. We also get a little bit of cover from the car's B-pillar from this position.

Dolly lights up the interior as she arrives, and I wait until the passenger's attention is on her before I do the same. In the meantime, I can see that everyone's hands are empty. Dolly glances up at me, and I give a slight nod.

She is now presenting the driver with his ticket and the happy news about the car. It's going to cost him about two bills to get it back, and my guess is the tow company will soon own this fine ride.

The passenger gets pissed off when he hears the ride is getting towed, but the driver accepts the news without comment. Just as the passenger, who still doesn't know I am here, starts to smart off to Sector, I rap harshly on the window with the butt of my light, scaring the snot out of him. He twists around, opening his eyes wide into the darkness, and I hit him with the intensely bright beam from my Streamlight, directly into his shit-brown eyes. He winces in pain and curses, and I have to suppress a chuckle. I love this kind of stuff, and am starting to feel better.

"What!" he demands impolitely.

"Get out of the car."

He turns his back to me, crosses his arms, and leans against the door, which makes me cranky. It seems I have lost his attention, but I think I know how to get it back.

Without warning, I yank the door open, and my new friend tumbles out onto the pavement. Now, he's really pissed, which makes two of us. He gets up, and for the first time I can see that he's a bigger guy, maybe six-one and over two hundred pounds. He's got long hair and a spiderweb tattoo on his neck. He's also wearing long sleeves, and I'm guessing the rest of him is covered with prison tats. He has one of those hard, lined faces with creases beyond his years. This guy's been around, and I remind myself not to underestimate him.

I hear Dolly asking for another car, and I feel a little better because of it.

"Hey man, what's your problem?" he asks.

"I don't like being ignored," I tell him.

"Oh well. I got the right to ignore you. Am I under arrest?" he replies.

"Not yet," I retort. "What's your name?"

"Ask her," he says, nodding at Dolly without taking his eyes off me. His stare is hard—mean, and full of hate. I decide to go slow until the next unit arrives.

"I'm asking you. She forgot."

"Williamson. Harry Williamson."

"And, what was that date of birth again, Mr. Williamson?"

"Look, run me in your system. I'm clear, man. Why are you taking the car?"

He wants to draw me away from the ID questions. How many times have I heard this? Next, he'll tell me he never had a license, never had an ID, never had a ticket, has never been contacted by the police, and never reported a crime. Any one of those things, and I could find him in the computer system. Hell, he's even used the terms "run me," and "I'm clear." Like he's never been around the block before. A blind man could tell this guy's done time in the can. I may be dumb, but I'm not *that* dumb.

"Just give me your birthday, Spike. And, keep your hands out of your pockets." I want so badly to pat this guy down, but right now, it is not safe. Dolly's moved her guy around to the sidewalk on my side, but if he gets squirrelly on me, it would be a two-on-two fight, and we don't do things like that. If it's two suspects, it's gonna be four officers. If he throws a punch, I hit him with fifty thousand volts of Taser. If he pulls a knife, I pull a gun. Hey, it's only fair.

"What's this 'Spike' shit, man? Am I disrespecting you? Why are you on me?"

My patience is running out. "Date. Of. Birth," I annunciate slowly, pantomiming American Sign Language with a great deal of exaggerated hand flapping in the air. This causes his eyes to narrow and his expression to darken.

"March 13th. Happy?"

"Thank you. What year?"

"Uh, '68. Look, I gotta be somewhere, and I'm gonna be late now if you're taking the car. I need to go."

"You're gonna wait. How old are you?"

He mumbles something unintelligible.

"What?"

"Thirty-six," he says pantomiming ASL. I smile.

"And, what was the number on your ID card?"

"Never had an ID card."

"No kiddin'? How about your Social Security number."

"I don't know, man. You see this scar? I had a bad accident and I can't do numbers any more. I can't remember a lot of shit."

"Really. Well, when was the last time you were arrested?"
"I never been arrested."
"Yeah? Where'd you get those tats?"
"Friend."
"Butt buddy, more likely."
"Hey, fuck you! You got no right to treat me like this."
"Chill out, hombre. Let's start again, only this time we'll be nice to each other, OK? I'll say something, and you respond. I'll start. Now, it is my belief that you are lying to me because you have warrants for your arrest. Your turn."

He shakes his head and clams up. I nod and take the time to do the mental math, seeing that he just passed the date he gave me as his birthday.

Dipshit. He should be thirty-nine. I decide I'm going to hook him, because now I'm getting pretty uncomfortable, but again, not until cover gets here. It's my guess he's got a wallet with ID in it.

Just then, another car arrives, and I breathe a sigh of relief. It is one-forty-eight, John Buchanan, who likes to fight. Buchanan takes a look at the Baker brothers and sees who's going to be the problem. He faces my guy off at a right angle, so there's no crossfire.

"Guess what, Spike. Turn around and put your hands behind your back. I'm hooking you up for your safety and mine. Don't worry, you're not under arrest. . . . Yet. Right now, I'm just detaining you." Whenever I do this on shaky ground—i.e. arrest a guy without probable cause, I always tell him he's being detained, which is the truth. If I cannot determine his true identity, or if there's no warrant, I will ultimately have to let him go.

The moment I put my hands on him, his partner lunges at Dolly. Nobody is really watching them, and he has a moment before we cover the short distance. He clamps a hand on the butt of her gun and gets it half out of the holster before she gets both her hands over his to hold it in.

This is not going well. Dolly is tall and lanky, but he is bigger and has her by fifty pounds. Out of the corner of my eye, I see Buchanan racing toward her, his pistol already in his hand. My full attention is on her as well, which means nobody is watching my other new friend, Spike.

Faster than I can recall, I get my Taser out, flip the safety to OFF, and put the laser dot on the guy who's fighting Dolly, right in the center of his back. I hear a loud *PFFTTT*, followed by the buzz of an angry swarm, and suddenly he is doing the chicken dance right there on the side of the road. Then his whole body stiffens and falls to the ground, trailing the two wires connecting the darts with the still-live Taser. Those darts have little fishhook barbs on them and penetrate the skin a quarter of an inch. The bottom one has nailed him just above his ass, the top in the center of his left scapula. Dolly dives down to cuff him up, and out of the corner of my eye, I see that Buchanan has placed himself between the action and Spike, who has thankfully chosen not to be a problem right now.

The five-second electrical burst cuts off, and hotshot immediately tries to pull the dart out of his back, which is a no-no. Another squeeze on the trigger and he's a body boner again, riding the lightning for a second time. These are five-second bursts of fifty thousand volts, and they hurt like hell. I can light him up about eight more times before the Taser runs out of juice.

This time, when it's over, he is a lamb to the slaughter. "No more!" he whimpers.

Dolly ratchets the cuffs down hard, and we both glance up to see where Mr. Williamson is.

He is standing there with his hands up, the red laser dot of Buchanan's Taser bright on his chest. Dolly cuffs him up also, and pats him down, immediately finding his wallet, *with* his ID.

Barry Williams, Jr., not Harry Williamson, date of birth April 20, 1969. He is actually thirty-nine. Dolly gives the records clerk the guy's true ID, and surprise surprise, he has multiple warrants for his arrest. Buchanan stuffs him into my car while Dolly rolls the driver over and pats him down. Both he and Williams, I can now see, are covered with Aryan Nation and other white supremacist prison gang tats.

Andrew Joseph, the driver, looks right at me and starts yammering, "You chickenshit pussy. What's the matter, can't face someone alone, one on one? You gotta have your pals come back you up? Can't fight a fair fight, can you? You ain't shit without your friends backin' you up, and all your fuckin' toys! Hey, you're a kike, aren't you? I can tell by your rat-bastard nose. Guess what? My uncle was a cook in the German army. I got an oven reserved for you, you Christ-killin' sheenie clipcock—"

PFT-buzzzzzzzz

Ooops, did I do that? It seems as if he's riding the lightning again. It makes me feel good to see him spazzing on the sidewalk. "Phaser's on stun, Cap'n," I hear myself say in a Scottish accent.

"Shut it down, Ben!" says Dolly sharply. In a flash, I realize I'm breaking a cardinal rule with the Taser, which is using it to punish someone. No longer a less-lethal method of control, it is now a punishment tool, which is a nice way of saying torture device. Such misuse, incidentally, has been the number-one source of lawsuits against police for using them, and is the also the number-one reason police departments have lost the right to use them. It was also something they hammered into us for half of the allotted four-hour training block we had to go through in order to be certified to use them.

Now I'm thinking to myself maybe I shouldn't be lighting him up. I realize that he's still laying there doing the chicken dance.

"I said, shut it down, Ben. Now!" Sector yells.

My hand goes to the safety, which is the only way to turn it off when you're jump-starting someone. But I move slowly, and as was my obvious intention, the five seconds run out and the Taser shuts itself down.

"Damn it, Ben! That's it, you're over the line. Put this guy in my car, then give me that Taser!" I can't believe my ears; nobody's *ever* heard Dolly swear before. She must really be pissed, but right now, I couldn't care less. Because of all the crap going on in my life at this moment, I'm in as black a mood as I can remember.

Buchanan's calling for firemen/paramedics, which is standard procedure after someone gets tased. They will remove the darts and give Joseph a quick medical check. I pull the cartridge out of the Taser and throw it as hard as I can. It goes to the extent of the wires, which pull taught against the barbs in Joseph's skin and make him grimace, then falls to the ground.

We get him stuffed into Dolly's car on his stomach. As we do so, I grab the dart embedded in is shirt and "accidentally" yank it down and out. Joseph screams in pain, and I crinkle my nose, squint my eyes, and say in my old bubbe's Yiddish voice, "Oy, I'm such a *meshuggeneh klutz*! Vot have I done?" Then I slam the door on him.

Dolly joins me on my side, and physically shoves me out of the way. She reaches down to my left thigh and yanks the Taser from its drop holster strapped there, then gets her light on the guy, which reveals the Taser dart. No longer embedded in Joseph's shirt, it is now dangling, its barbed end red.

She dons a pair of rubber gloves, opens the door, and raises Joseph's T-shirt. There is a shallow one-inch jagged slash in the center of his shoulder blade. It is little more than a deep scratch, but it's pretty bloody.

"You gonna let him get away with that, you fuckin' cunt?" yells Joseph. Dolly slams the door on him, turns to me, and says, "Get back to the precinct, Ben. Go to my office and wait for me there." She then walks several feet away and stands there with her back to me and her head bowed, breathing hard.

I look at Buchanan, and he just stares back at me quizzically. "My office" is a lot worse than "coffee." I've really stepped on my dick this time, but I'm so pissed off I don't care. I shrug it off, get in my car, and head on back to the office. What're they gonna do, send me to graveyard shift and give me crappy days off?

Chapter 12

I get back to the office and check the computer to see what kind of calls are holding before getting out of the car. Nothing, which doesn't surprise me. I was kind of hoping there would be some big bucket of crap in my beat so I could take it and be tied up for a while. That way, Dolly might forget how mad she is at me.

I go inside and sit down in the sergeant's office. Sitting in there alone makes me feel like a little kid who's been sent to the principal's office for shooting rubber bands at the girls. She's already arrived and is busy helping Buchanan get the prisoners in the holding cells; something I should be doing, leaving the sergeants free to do whatever it is they do during sleepy time.

With all this time to myself, I'm starting to think about what could happen to me. I mean, when we first got the Tasers, there was a lot of talk about not screwing around with them, or using them inappropriately. I'm thinking Dolly might view my last burst on Joseph as inappropriate.

As much as I don't want to admit it to myself, *I* view my last burst on Joseph as inappropriate.

Shit. This may not go very well. Now I'm thinking that the DA's office, if presented with my actions, may view them as inappropriate. Criminally inappropriate. It's a given that an Internal Affairs board will view my actions as inappropriate.

The thing that really sucks about this is this; we shouldn't *have* to eat the kind of crow Joseph was giving me. You shouldn't be able to say that kind of stuff to the police without getting your ass beat to a bloody pulp. But, this is the twenty-first century. That guy has the constitutionally protected right to say what he said. The other thing that sucks about this particular situation is that if it were anyone other than Dolly Sector, this would be a non-incident. I can't think of another sergeant who, under the circumstances, wouldn't have seen a damn thing, but Saint Sector's conscience won't allow her to look the other way.

When I was a brand new rookie, the first drunk driver I ever arrested resisted my efforts to put the cuffs on him. We struggled, and he ended up facedown on a gravel lot, replete with (appropriately) bloody lips. Well, when I asked him if he understood his Miranda rights and would he like to make a statement, he said, "Yeah," then spit a big old bloody goober right into my face.

I flat-out lost it. The only thing I remember is the drunk cowering in the back seat, cringing and trying to get his hands, which were cuffed, up in front of his face. That's when I realized that I had my fist cocked back, just ready to drill him. Without even lowering my fist, I looked over at my sergeant, who was also my cover unit, and had seen the whole thing. Now bear in mind, this was back in 1988, and my sergeant was a twenty-five-year veteran.

He was staring at me, and as I watched, he calmly gave me a little nod, and slowly and deliberately turned his back. Back when he started, if you did something like spit on the cops, you'd end up in the hospital, and even the judges would tell you that you got what you asked for.

So I drilled him, lacerating his lower lip on a tooth, and it felt good. The cut I received on my knuckle taught me to use an open palm strike instead of a fist when it's going to be flesh-on-flesh, but it was worth it. I assume his lip eventually healed. I know my knuckle did.

And here I am, nineteen years later, at the mercy of a sergeant who has less seniority than I do, sitting like a little kid in the principal's office.

Dolly finally struts in and sits on the corner of her desk. "Ben, what did I see out there? What happened?"

I don't know what to say. I assume she saw and heard everything. If I say I taught him a lesson, I'm in trouble. It's funny; I taught my old sniper partner a really *big* lesson, and wound up being a hero. How ironic if I bite the dust for something like this.

"Ben?"

"Look, Dolly, what are you planning on doing? How about you tell *me* what you saw?"

"OK. I saw you use that Taser to punish Joseph for mouthing off at you. And, I saw you use the dart to cut him."

Oy vey iz mir.

"Not everything is as it appears, Dolly."

"Don't give me that, Ben. I saw it, and I don't like it. My gosh, it was *criminal*, for goodness sake."

Gosh? Goodness? "Criminal? It was . . ."

"What?"

I had nearly said "justice."

"Nothing. Look, I'm here in the sergeant's office, and you're telling me you witnessed criminal behavior on my part. I want a union rep." I am hoping that Dolly can see past her religious conscience and tell me to just go home and cool off or something. Because if she doesn't, I could actually lose my job over this.

"I think you're going to need one."

"What were you going to see me about at coffee before all this crap got started?"

"I was going to see how you are doing. I know this shadow business has you upset, and I know that you're going to court tomorrow for little LaMonjello. By the way, I can't say how much I admire you for doing that."

"Thanks," I say dejectedly.

"How's all that going, by the way?"

"Not good. According to detectives, there's no progress whatsoever in finding him, and the judge said no more delays. The day after tomorrow I have to go into court and tell them that this guy's still out there. And, she's not going to be able to grant me custody because of that."

"If it means anything, I've prayed about that, and I will some more."

I looked her in the eyes, and put my cards on the table. "Dolly, I don't even know if God can help me if my job is in jeopardy. I don't know what will happen to LaMonjello then. Look, how about I take the rest of the night off, and if that hemorrhoid Joseph doesn't complain, we all forget about the Taser? I don't think I can hack the added stress of worrying about my job."

"God works in mysterious ways, Ben. Sometimes bad things happen to good people, and when they do, we don't understand why. Sometimes, it takes terrible trials and tribulations to burn resistance to God's calling out of us. He has plans for you, Ben, and this might be what it takes for you to look to Him."

My eyes inadvertently roll, and I just want to hit her.

"Look," she continues, "I know you don't want to hear it, but the Bible says to trust in God and lean not unto your own understanding. You're asking me to look the other way, and I can't do that. This job is all about trust, Ben. But even beyond that, I know that God is in control, and I have to trust in Him, and that this is all part of His plan. I don't like doing this, but I'm going to have to place you on suspension. I'll pray over it, believe me, but I feel led to do the right thing, and to trust that the Lord has everything under control. I know it's not how you feel or what you want, but it's something I need to do."

"Come on, Dolly. You heard what Joseph said. He was resisting, verbally if nothing else. Look, you *know* I could get fired over this. If he complains, then yeah, do what you have to, but come on, don't *initiate* it."

"Ben, I'm not saying that what he said didn't get me angry as well, but that doesn't give us the right to . . . to do what you did. I'm sending you home, and I'll pray about what to do."

"You're suspending me. That means there will be an IA. How am I supposed to deal with that, the shadow, the adoption, and my marriage?"

"Are there problems at home, Ben? I mean, it's none of my business, but I've heard rumors about . . . well, never mind. It's none of my business. Just know that I'm praying for you."

This is the last thing I need on top of everything else, people talking about me. "Rumors about what?" I ask.

"Well, about Andrea."

Just then, as if on cue, a loud, warbling alert tone interrupts us. It means there is a high priority in-progress call about to be broadcast, usually something like a bank robbery or something. We rarely get the alert tone on nights.

"All available units, start for 3153 SE Deer Creek Way. Residential burglary, in progress. Neighbor reports that a male dressed in all black removed a window in the back of the house and went inside. Stand by . . ." She is silent for a moment but does not stop cueing the mike, and then continues. "OK, I have an update. There is now a fight in progress in the house, lots of things breaking; we're trying to get more info."

I looked at Dolly, and I could see her weighing the pros and cons. "I'm on SWAT," I said weakly. "And I've got the car," referring to the SWAT car with its night vision gear, MP-5 submachine gun, and assortment of other special equipment that can be invaluable on this sort of call. Only SWAT members were authorized to drive it.

I could read the uncertainty in her eyes, and I pushed on. "Plus, we're at minimums. If I go home, we're below minimums. This call's in my beat, and Ralph's got that drunk driver crash, which is gonna tie him up for the rest of the night. Come on, Sarge."

"All right, Ben, go. But when this call is over, you come back and see me. I'm sorry, but I have to do what I have to do."

I leave without another word. As I am getting into my car, the next update comes out.

"Units en route to Deer Creek, we have a witness on the line who thinks this could be a homicide in progress. She can't see anything, but heard screaming, which was suddenly cut off. Nothing from the residence in the last minute or so. Suspect is described only as thin and wearing all black."

I am racing toward the house with lights but no siren. A siren is not necessary at this time of the night, and I do not want to alert the bad guy that we are coming. I'm still a half-mile from the house when units start arriving.

"One-sixty-eight, staging at the corner of Deer Creek and Durango Canyon on the north."

"One-eighteen, arriving on the south, off Buttonhollow. I'll stage at Deer Creek and Buttonhollow."

I get on the radio. "One-twenty-eight, I'll join one-eighteen on the south in less than one. Let's get a dispatcher and have everyone go to tac one for this."

"Copy. All units on the Deer Creek call, go to tac one."

Another unit arrives on the south as I change channels on my portable radio. Buchanan has left the puke from Andrea's stop in a holding cell and is now here, answering for the south side guys.

"This is one-twenty-eight. Who all is on the north?"

"One-five-eight, one-eighteen, and one-sixty-eight. You guys have three on the south?"

"A-firm."

"How do you want to handle it, Ben?"

"The house should be about mid-block on the east side of the street. Let's just close in on it together."

"OK."

I am in charge of this incident, for several reasons. One, I'm the senior officer tonight; two, I'm the only SWAT guy out on duty; and three, I want Dolly to see how indispensable I am.

"You guys have a dispatcher over here now," says the radio. Since we are on a tac net, normal radio formality isn't necessary, and we can talk more casually. "There are no further updates. We're off line with the original reporting party who is now hiding in her closet next door. We got one other call from 3172 SE Deer Creek, across the street, who heard lots of screaming from the house across the road. He hasn't heard anything for about two or three minutes."

"OK."

Rich Calhoun, John Cable and I begin sneaking through flowerbeds and shrubbery, heading south and hugging the houses in the east side of the street. I lead the way with my SWAT-issued MP-5, which, unlike our patrol weapons, is fully automatic. Being a sniper, it is not my primary weapon, but I am cross-trained and qualified on it. The cross-qualification only goes one way—it takes too much to qualify anyone else as a sniper.

Glancing down the street, I see the south side team coming toward us, mirroring our own movements. We leave a trampled wake of crushed spring flowers across the front yards of the houses we use to cover our movements. This is an extremely affluent neighborhood, and tomorrow the police will likely get more calls from people concerned about their petunias getting trampled than about whatever trouble happened at their neighbor's house.

I look at the house numbers as we approach. I am at 3133, and the house next door to the north is dark. The other team has stopped one house south of the dark one, so I am sure we have 3153 boxed in. To confirm, I cover my flashlight with cupped hand, leaving only a tiny beam, which I direct at the large, brick, two-story.

There it is—the number 3153, written in nice gold script by the front door. I key my mike. "Buch, take one guy and go to the back on your side. I'll take the back on this side. You other guys, get on the front corners so you can see both the front and your respective sides."

Silently, we fan out. I head to the back, which is enclosed by a wooden fence. I motion to Cable to kneel down, and using his back as a stepping stool, I step up, and my rifle barrel and my eyes clear the fence at the same time as I take a peek over the top.

The house is dark, and I cannot see the windows clearly. "Buch," I whisper, "can you see anything from your side?"

"No, all dark. I can get over this fence though."

"Stand by," I say. "I'm going over now. Wait for me, and I'll cover you when you come over."

"Copy."

I step up on Cable's back. Using upper-body strength only, without hopping up or kicking the fence, I silently slide over, flattening out as softly as possible on the ground in the backyard. There is no response from the house, so I have Buchanan come over. He is considerably noisier, but there is still no response from the house.

Now there is no hard cover, only the concealment of the shadows. Buchanan and I join up on his side, and I have two other officers get a perch on the fence to cover us as we approach. One of them has an AR-15, which makes me feel better. A pistol is next to useless for this kind of long cover, but it is better than nothing.

Slowly, we approach the house, and when we are about twenty feet away, I see that one of the ground floor windows has been removed, and is now leaning up against the wall under an open rectangular hole.

My troubles are now temporarily forgotten in the developing tactical situation, and I am all business. "One-twenty-eight, the three-one window's been completely removed from the frame; ah, that's the first one on the left as you face the back of the house. Dispatch, can we get more units here? We got any canines?"

"Negative on canines for the entire county, but your office has already paged one out. As for other units, we now have five units on the perimeter, plus you two in the yard."

"OK, let me have one more in the yard. Is thirty-one Sam here?"

Dolly answered up for herself. "I'm here, Ben."

"Dolly, given the info we have, I don't want to wait for a canine. I'd like to do an entry with four guys. That OK with you?"

"You're the tactical man here. You call it."

"OK then. Cable, you and Calhoun join us in the back, and we'll announce and enter. You guys OK with that?"

"Affirm," said Calhoun, the excitement in his voice evident. I wouldn't play it like this if these weren't the best guys we have on nights. Next to SWAT, Cable and Buchanan are about the best we have. Calhoun told me the other night that he's putting in for SWAT the next time there's an opening.

In a moment, there are four of us huddled in the shadow near the window. "Is the perimeter completely buttoned down?" I ask nobody in particular.

The dispatcher answers, "Yes. You now have four additional county units plus a Salmon Creek unit on the perimeter, and the three initial Stratton cars."

"Copy. Do I have two long guns on the back?"

"One-sixty-eight, both me and County five-five are on the back fence with long guns."

"Copy. Then we'll begin approaching the house."

I look at my team, and we all share a nod. I then begin creeping toward the open window.

I have a bad feeling about this call. I remember hoping Dolly would find some shit to get into so I wouldn't have to have coffee with her. Well, it seems I got what I hoped for.

Chapter 13

As we near the back window, my growing feeling of dread becomes impossible to shake or ignore. I steel myself for what we may find in there. Fortunately, I see no toys or other evidence of kids that might live here, and I am glad of that.

I raise a fist when I get to the window, figuring that my team, though they're not on SWAT, will nonetheless know that means stop. Instinctively, they all hunker down and cover the windows with their weapons. I stick my head in the open window, and listen intently.

Silence. Nothing but a sepulcher-like silence. Not even the ticking of a clock to give some depth to the blackness in front of me.

Now comes a moment I dread. I have to give up our advantage. I hit the interior of the house with my flashlight. It reveals nothing out of place. I shout, "Stratton Police, we know you're in there! Come out with your hands up!" There is no answer. My words are swallowed in the black space past my light, and as they fade away, the house reverts to stillness and silence. It's like looking in Tutankhamun's tomb for the first time.

Scrutinizing the floor in front of the window, I see wet footprints and bark dust on the carpet. There's not much, but it goes in the direction of the stairs. I back my face out of the window and get on the radio.

"One-twenty-eight to thirty-one Sam, there's definite entry, footprints going toward the stairs, no sign of any exit from my vantage point. Given the nature of what we have, you might want to think about activating SWAT before we make entry."

Dolly may be a new sergeant, but she's still a fifteen-year police veteran. Her answer surprises and impresses me.

"Thirty-one Sam, negative, *because* of the nature of what we have. Hopefully, this is not what it appears, but if it is, someone inside may need the police, and we're the police. Nobody said this job is safe. Make the entry."

"One-two-eight, copy." Secretly, I am glad. I doubt someone stole into this house, slaughtered the occupants, and is still in here drinking coffee. If it is some kind of violent crime, the suspect is likely long gone by now.

I try to tell myself that it is nothing more than a drunken homeowner who came home late, forgot his keys, and went in through the window, only to get bitched out by a pissed-off wife. That her yelling and screaming is what made the nosy neighbor think someone was dying. If that's the case, they're no doubt now sound asleep and about to get the surprise of their lives. Ninety-nine percent of these calls turn out innocuous, no matter how bad they look in the beginning, and my brain tells me this is one of those ninety-nine.

My gut, however, begs to disagree. The gut feeling I have tells me that something very, very bad has happened here tonight.

I turn to my team and say, "Me first, then on my signal, one by one."

They nod and behind me, Cable raises his pistol, pointed into the house. I sling my emper and climb in the window. I gain a foothold just inside, using a couch as cover, and signal for Cable to come in. Once he is safely in and on the other side of the room covering the kitchen, he signals for Buchanan, who is immediately followed by Calhoun.

I keep the stairs covered while the others check the main ground floor areas such as kitchen and bedrooms. I'm not worried about these; the footprints lead directly to the stairs, and I know that we will find what we are looking for at the top of them. Nevertheless, it has to be done.

Three minutes after making entry, we have declared the ground floor clear, and the others are lined up behind me at the bottom of the stairs. Only then, when we are holding at the base of the stairs, do I smell it.

Copper. It is as if someone is holding wet pennies under my nose, and my heart begins to race. I cannot control the tap dance my right foot is doing, and I know my hands are shaking.

John Cable taps me on the shoulder and whispers in my ear, "You smell it?"

I nod, not really trusting my voice. It is the smell of violence—of opened flesh, and of blood. I take a moment, which seems like an eternity, to gather my wits. Now is not the time to wimp out, and I force my voice to work, my limbs to comply.

"I'm gonna announce again," I tell the men behind me.

"We're ready," says Buchanan, raising his long gun so that the barrel extends over my right shoulder just in front of my face.

"Stratton Police Department!" I yell. "Come to the top of the stairs with your hands up!"

My voice is consumed by the darkness and silence around the corner, and the house becomes deathly silent again. "Stratton Police! We're sending up a dog! Come out now, and you won't get bit!"

"Want me to growl?" asks Buchanan, trying unsuccessfully to use humor to alleviate the tension we are now all feeling.

"We're gonna have to go up there," I say in return.

"Yeah, I guess we are," he replies dully, with no more pretenses at humor.

I hit my mike button and say, "One-twenty-eight. No response to announcement. We're going upstairs."

I don't even know why I said that; it was completely unnecessary. My nerves are shaky, because now I know without a doubt this is going to be bad. Contrary to popular belief, cops are not "hardened" to homicidal violence, to the sight of brutalized, lifeless bodies, to the stench of gore. At least here in Stratton, we don't face it every day, and when we do, it exacts a heavy price.

I peek around the corner and shine my light up the stairs. The first things I see are a pair of men's boots—Danners, like my own—on the top stair. One is lying on its side with the sole exposed to the harsh glare of my Streamlight. It is red and shiny.

"Christ," says Buchanan behind me.

All of us begin advancing up the stairs, guns trained on the landing above. When I get to the top, I turn on a hallway light, which reveals bloody boot prints all over the floor. There are at least two bedrooms, a couple of closets, and a bathroom. There is an overturned table on the floor at the end of the hallway, with a potted plant that has spilled dirt on the cream-colored carpet. Boot prints in blood mixed with potting soil are everywhere, concentrating on the last open door on the left, and it is obvious that that is where we will find what we are looking for. I say nothing, but Cable utters a nervous "Oh, shit" as he rounds the corner.

I am now praying there are no kids here. I am not a squeamish man, but I have serious reservations about my ability to hold it together if faced with slaughtered children.

"OK, guys, we gotta do this," I say. "I'm gonna provide long cover down the hall and I want you two to start with the bedrooms. We'll save the murder room for last."

"Fuck," breathes Buchanan at my use of "murder room." I hadn't even realized that I'd said it.

"John, you OK for this?" I ask, not taking my eyes off the hallway as seen above the front sight of my MP-5.

I can hear him breathing hard, but that's all. "Buch, man, come on. We're gonna do this together, OK? Piece of cake. Be done in five minutes, right?"

"Yeah, no problem. I got it. I'm fine, Ben. Come on, Jeff, let's take the first room."

All the doors leading up to the murder room are closed. They check them one by one. The first, a guest room, seems undisturbed. The second is an office of some sort, and nothing looks out of place. The next, another bedroom, is being used as storage, and is clear as well. Then, we are at the murder room.

"OK," I say, "let's do it."

I turn the corner and flood the room with light. That it is a horrific scene is immediately apparent. Everything has been knocked over, bloody bedcovers are twisted on the floor, and blood is everywhere, even on the ceiling and walls. The amount of blood soaking into the carpet is indescribable, and it seems like ten people must have been required to provide it all. A Mansonian masterpiece.

I have seen scenes like this before, though none quite as horrific. I have learned that blood with this type of spray pattern and in this quantity can only come from arterial spurting. Brachial, femoral, carotid; it makes no difference which artery. Flay one open and it sprays like a hose. Couple that with the victim's death throes and this is the result.

The body is halfway between the bedroom and the bathroom. It is naked, an adult male in his mid-thirties or so, and has suffered major trauma from an edged weapon. I see defensive wounds on both forearms, no doubt received when he put his arms up to protect his face from the blade. There is a large slash across the left side of his head and face, as if the killer tried to cut his head off and missed. A second attempt has bitten deeply into the right shoulder, which now hangs open with a gaping red crevice exposing the trapezoid muscle, which has been flayed to the bone.

The third attempt at this was more successful. The victim's head is still attached, but the third blow caught him on the left side of the neck and sliced more than three-quarters the way through.

I hear heavy panting, as if someone is out of breath, and I am about to check to make sure my team is OK when I realize it is coming from me.

"Oh my Christ," says Cable, sounding like a little kid.

"Almost done, Jeff, just the two bathrooms," I say. "Stay focused until we finish those, then go out and get some air."

"I'm good," he says, now sounding better. We make for the first bathroom, and I half expect some character from a slasher movie to be cowering naked in the shower.

Both bathrooms are clear, but the killer has left his murder weapon behind in the hallway bathroom. A razor-sharp, wicked-looking scimitar with a two-foot blade, wrapped in a bloody towel, is lying in the bathtub.

"Ah, one-twenty-eight, we got one fifty-five-Adam victim, white male adult, in master bedroom. We're gonna need suits and the M.E. out here."

"Copy."

I give the murder room another glance. It is now a crime scene, and must be protected as one. As such, access to it is now limited to a need-to-be-here basis. None of the officers outside, including Sergeant Sector, will be allowed in.

The scene truly is horrendous, and has the appearance of a display of horrors in a wax museum. It is not the first time I have noticed that dead bodies do not look human, no matter how "fresh" they may be. When the life is gone, so is the person, and what is left is so much waxy meat.

"Ben, you'd better come in here," says Buchanan from the bedroom that serves as an office. I back out of the room, careful to keep out of the blood and boot prints—a nearly impossible task—and go into the office.

Buchanan has not touched anything, but directs his light to the computer desk. My eyes follow the beam, and when they see what it illuminates, my life changes forever.

Chapter 14

"What the hell . . ."

Laid out neatly on the desk are photographs, several rolls of film's worth, in neat, evenly spaced rows. All the pictures are of my house, my family, and me. Most, like those delivered to Judge Payne two weeks ago, are of my children, have been taken from inside, and all without our knowledge.

Though it is still too early to be positive, it would appear that the murder victim is my shadow, and that he has finally met his match.

I look out the east-facing window of the murder room almost two hours after I arrived at the house. Through the bloody spray on the glass I see the beginnings of what promises to be a magnificent sunrise. It is already an excellent day.

Detectives from MCT-A have been here for an hour. I am the only patrol officer who has been allowed to remain within the crime scene. Once it became apparent that the victim of this murder is my shadow, I was given special permission from Sergeant Sector, who appears to have had second thoughts about suspending me in lieu of the circumstances, and Detective Sergeant Phil Mahoney, in charge of the Major Crimes Team, to be temporarily assigned to MCT-A for this investigation. For lack of anything better to do, I have been detailed the responsibilities of inner-crime-scene security, which means not letting anyone upstairs until ordered to do so.

I have no real official duties, and am told I will be used as part of the search team once the warrant comes through. This scene is being treated differently than most murder scenes. Besides the crime of murder, we are now investigating the shadow case as well. There is always the outside chance that the murder victim is an accomplice of the shadow's, leaving the real villain still out there, but I know this is not the case. Proof positive will come with the results of tests comparing DNA from the piece of shit lying a few feet away from me with semen recovered from the sexual assault of Gus Oronco.

There is no doubt in my mind that the dead guy, over whose body I am watching the sun rise with joy and gladness in my heart, is the shadow. My theory is that somebody figured out that he was sitting on a pile of cash, came here, and did him for it. Perhaps I need to reevaluate my disbelief in karma.

No longer am I repulsed by the graphic horror of this scene. I am certain that the world, *my* world anyway, has just undergone a vast improvement, now that the former occupant of this husk over which I am gazing is gone.

There is a photo of him on the wall above the desk. In it, he is standing at the lip of a great canyon somewhere. So that is what he looked like in life, eh? I like the way he looks now better. I can yet barely come to grips with the fact that it's over now, and on the day before the adoption hearing too. I look down at the body one more time.

This corpse was my shadow. I want to urinate on it.

A detective is sitting in his car on the phone with a judge, arranging a telephonic search warrant. The search that I and the other officers conducted when we got here was perfectly legal since we were looking for a murder suspect, but we had the wisdom and experience to stop when we found the photos of my house. Now, with a warrant, we will be able to search the entire premises for anything that could be remotely related to not just the shadow case, but also the Northwest Healing case from nearly two years ago.

I am excited beyond imagination, for nothing has had a greater affect my life than that case. My family was nearly killed, my daughter has suffered permanent brain damage, I have undergone emotional duress that has left me seriously scarred, and I have had to do things most people can't even have nightmares about. And, as a direct spinoff of that terrible chapter in my life, I have undergone twenty-two months of intense stalking, culminating with the molestation of my own daughter without her knowledge as she slept, believing herself to be safe in her own home and bed.

Rage overcomes me, and I suck back snot from the deepest, nastiest recess of my nasal passages and collect it in my mouth. Just as I am about to expectorate it into the tortured expression on the face of my nemesis, it occurs to me that this body will be minutely examined during the autopsy, and any alteration of it will be seen as manipulation of the crime scene. That could lead to allegations that evidence has been altered, and I could create more trouble than the momentary joy of desecrating the corpse would give me, so I am forced to swallow it.

There is a buzz of activity below, and a group of detectives, including Andrea, enter the house. "Ben, come on down here," shouts Sergeant Mahoney. I head downstairs to the living room where they have all gathered.

"OK, folks, listen up. We just got a carte blanche warrant for the house, the computers, all closed containers, the body, the premises, and all associated vehicles and alternate locations, which will include rented storage units or anything else. Ben, you'll never guess who the on-call judge was."

I am about to say her name, but he doesn't give me the chance. "Yep. Suzanne Payne, and she sends along her best wishes. Says she'll see you tomorrow morning at the hearing."

Maybe Dolly is right. Apparently, God *does* work in mysterious ways.

The first rays of sunlight penetrate the windows, and the effect is as if God Himself is blessing me and the LaMonjello adoption. Hey, I'll take all the help I can get.

Mahoney reminds us that there is a strong likelihood that fifteen million dollars in cash is hidden somewhere in this house, and tells us that the officer standing crime scene watch outside the house will have to search each of us when we leave. This doesn't bother anyone, because we all know it is designed to protect us. He then breaks the team up into two-man search cells, and assigns each a different part of the house to search. He will float, keeping track of any evidence the searchers find. I don't know if it is because he knows, suspects, or is ignorant, but he assigns Andrea and me as a team, and gives us our choice of where to search. I think about protesting the partnership, but this would complicate things, so I remain silent.

Of course, I choose the office. The master bedroom will have to wait until the inner crime scene has been secured, which the most senior

MCT guys are doing. The ME has arrived, and is standing by, but nobody will be touching the body for hours.

Andrea is no longer mad at me. In fact, she is excited at the discovery that the dead guy is my shadow, meaning my troubles are over, at least in that regard. She's acting like we never had a fight. I can't stand it when women flip-flop like that, and I keep a professional air between us.

She and I go up to the office. She first peeks in on the murder room, and stares long and hard at the body. "So, that's your shadow, eh?" she says. "He's not so scary looking now, is he?"

"Nope. I kinda like him this way."

"No wonder he was jealous of LaMonjello," she says. "Look at the size of his willie."

"Hey, *I'm* jealous of LaMonjello. This guy wasn't kidding."

Andrea makes a little frame with her hands and aims it at the dead man. "Hell, you got him by at least an inch. If all this was just a contest to see who has the bigger dick, he could have saved himself a lot of trouble."

I just smile—glad, I suppose, that we can be friends now. Andrea always had a great sense of humor. "Come on," she says, "let's get started."

The first thing we do is start cataloging the photographs. Right away I see that this guy has chosen the shots he sent Judge Payne with great consideration. Among the many violating photographs, there are naked shots of all of us, including several of Sharon and me making love. Andrea glances at each. I am somewhat dismayed to see that he was there the one night in the last six months that she went down on me.

I'm waiting for Andrea to say something, because I told her that Sharon never does that. How can I explain that the photo is of literally the one time in months?

"Andrea—"

"Don't, babe," she says. "Don't worry about it. I'm just glad this prick is dead."

We search the desk next. There is a file in the bottom right drawer marked "Geller." I open it, and there are photocopies of my vehicle registration, the deed to my house, my last will and testament, which I am reminded to update, my birth certificate, and numerous other documents. Other files contain letters he never sent. Still others contain information on my relatives, but this is mostly limited to their addresses and MapQuest directions to their homes. Information on Sharon's parents in Virginia is there as well.

We search the rest of the room without finding much else, and then it is time to get into the computer, which is on and connected to the Internet. I know enough about computer searches to unplug the computer with the screen on, just as it is. It is easier for the computer forensics guys to reconstruct the last thing the suspect was doing that way.

I am about to unplug it, but then I give in to temptation, and move the mouse. The screen saver disappears, revealing his desktop. His internet browser is open, and it is open to his hotmail account. At the top of the page is the greeting, "Welcome WatchinU," which tells me that this is no silent partner, but the shadow himself. I already knew this, but the confirmation elates me.

Resisting the temptation to open his sent mail folder, I instead move the cursor down to the bottom of the screen to see what other programs might be open. Internet Explorer has another open window, which has been minimized. Knowing that I shouldn't look at it, I click on it nonetheless. A web page opens, and on it is a line of thumbnail photographs of two men having anal intercourse.

"Sick!" says Andrea. "Ben, put it back just like it was, and let's not touch anything else," she adds.

"No kidding. I don't think I want to see more." I minimize the porn and the screen returns to the hotmail account. I leave the computer plugged in, just in case our computer forensic guys want to look at it here in the house.

The porn site and the shadow's violation of Gustavo Oronco makes me wonder if he ever had a sexual interest in me. The implications make me shudder. With his financial backing, he could have easily kidnapped me and . . . well, in my nineteen years as cop, I've investigated a great deal of rapes, but not until recently have I ever really thought of what it would be like to be a rape *victim*. The thought of it happening to me chills my blood.

Then I get an idea. I sit down and bring up the start menu.

"Ben, what are you doing? Leave it for the experts," Andrea chides.

"Hang on, I just had an idea," I counter. I go to the start menu, click on search, and enter the following criteria: *.jpg. That's when I hit pay dirt.

There are hundreds of photos and videos of this guy, whose name we'd already established as Reginald Karch, age thirty-four, having sex with another man. Only one other man. And when I realize that I know his partner, I am shocked into utter speechlessness.

It is my late nemesis, my former sniper partner Bob Slater, architect of Northwest Healing.

"Oh holy mother of God . . . "

Andrea stands next to me and simply stares openmouthed at the screen in shocked silence. I wonder what she might be thinking, since it was Slater who had held her hostage at Northwest Healing, and therefore Slater who had released her naked in front of the entire police department and numerous television camera crews.

Slater, gay? Bob Slater? I'd worked with him for years, and had no idea. Nobody did; I had never heard one whispered word of gossip or speculation. And he was lovers with this Karch guy. This explains a lot. Karch, the silent partner in Northwest Healing. I'll bet even Tim Connor, who was until this moment Slater's only known partner in Northwest Healing, whom Slater shot down in cold blood to double his share of the take, wasn't aware that Slater was gay and had some kind of sick, twisted relationship with Karch. Or that Karch even existed, for that matter.

Karch was no doubt in on the planning of Northwest Healing from the beginning, and I suspect the original plan called for the elimination of Tim Connor from its inception.

Christ, no wonder Karch had it in for me after what I did to Slater. I can't imagine why he had ever allowed me to live.

"Oh my frickin' God. Ben, the money's got to be somewhere in the house," Andrea breathes.

We call Sergeant Mahoney upstairs to show him what we've found. He tells us they've already found evidence downstairs that linked Karch to the remodeling of the Northwest Healing building to allow for Slater's escape after the ransom money was delivered.

I check my watch and see that it is after nine. In Herndon, Virginia it is just after noon. Sharon will be busy packing for her 4:00 p.m. flight home, dejected, no doubt, because of the impossibility of winning custody of LaMonjello tomorrow. She will no doubt still be pissed at me, but now I can hope that the news I will impart to her will be sufficient to alleviate both problems.

Chapter 15

Late that afternoon, after only three hours of sleep, I greet Sharon at the airport. At least she is now speaking to me, a significant improvement over the past two weeks of silence. Still, I sense a change in her. Andrea, it seems, she could at least handle, but using her and the kids as bait, this I am not sure of, and I desperately hope I haven't gone too far.

There are no more tears; no more harsh words. I receive a desultory peck on the cheek from Sharon and warm, wonderful hugs and kisses from the children.

LaMonjello's acceptance of us as his parents appears to be complete. Besides some bed-wetting, night terrors, and the tendency to hide whenever he senses trouble, I see no signs of the overwhelming traumatic stresses he has gone through. Sharon and I have arranged for regular psychiatric treatment along with the counseling he is already receiving, and appointments have been scheduled. Conversation with the kids is animated, but between Sharon and me, it is wooden and businesslike.

I have alluded to the Karch investigation, telling Sharon that we now have nothing to fear about tomorrow's hearing. Hearing the news seemed to revive her somewhat, and she puts the kids to bed early so that we can talk about it. I crack a bottle of white Zinfandel, and by the time we finish it, she knows as much as I know with regard to Karch, Slater and Northwest Healing. Some of her personality seems to filter back into her with the wine and the story, and I have reason to hope that we are not finished yet as a couple. As we prepare for bed, she allows me to kiss her, and even kisses me back, albeit on the cheek. Her kiss and her smile, as well as her muttered "I love you" in response to my enthusiastic one, are saccharine, yes, but encouraging nonetheless.

We sleep in the same bed tonight, and I am surprised to see that she is not wearing heavy flannel pajamas. She normally sleeps in her panties and a T-shirt, and that is exactly what she is wearing. We've been married a long time, and I know that if I ask her, she will probably sleep with me, but she knows me well enough to know that I won't ask. She does not ask me about Andrea, which is a relief. I wasn't sure if she would or not, but I had already decided to lie to her if she did.

Again, I solemnly resolve never to sleep with Andrea ever again—or any other woman for that matter. From the way Andrea treated me at the crime scene, she appears to have forgotten that I left her naked on the floor after picking a fight with her when we last saw each other. Now I can see her for what she is, and more than anything else, I pity her. There will be no more trysts between us.

With the pending successful adoption of LaMonjello tomorrow, I cannot further risk it. Besides, I can now see Sharon for what she is, and that is a wonderful person whom I had selfishly grown tired of. I double my resolve to make her feel like the number-one priority in my life. As we head toward court in the morning I notice that her mood is brightening considerably.

Knowing that Judge Payne was roused at oh-dark-thirty yesterday to grant the telephonic search warrant of Karch's house, I feel supremely confident in the outcome of this morning's proceeding. Needless to say, the hearing does not last long.

Opposing counsel has nothing new to add. He has been briefed that the shadow is dead, and knows that his case has suffered the same fate. Judge Payne dismisses Pasha's opening statements with a wave of her hand.

"Counsel, this court is well aware of all the developments of the past day," she says. She then turns toward Sheila Jackson and her lawyer. "Is the respondent willing to stipulate to the facts surrounding the so-called 'shadow' case?"

The NAACP pro bono lawyer stands and dejectedly acknowledges his willingness.

"Good. Does respondent have anything else to bring to the attention of the court?"

"No, ma'am."

"Excellent. In that case, the court finds in favor of the petitioner. Sole custody, both legal and physical, to the Gellers. Surname change to be included if they so desire. Visitation by respondent shall be the third Saturday afternoon of every month from noon to 4:00 p.m. if she so desires. Mr. Geller?"

Pasha raises himself to his full five-three and says, "My client would like his son's name changed from LaMonjello Hicks to LaMonjello Geller, Your Honor."

"Granted. Ms. Jackson?

The NAACP attorney and Sheila Jackson confer for a moment, during which I can hear Sheila swearing. I hear the words "Uncle Tom" and "honkey-ass bitch," and then she stands and storms out of the courtroom.

The lawyer stands and says, "Ms. Jackson abdicates, Your Honor. I, uh, well, I apologize for her behavior."

"Fine. In view of Ms. Jackson's nonverbal response, there will be no visitation. Congratulations, Mr. and Mrs. Geller. This case is closed."

LaMonjello Geller. Just like that.

Two days later, we get the bill from Pasha's office. Eleven five. Leah's education fund and our mutual fund cover it in full, but leave us with nothing. With my check alone as income, we are able to bank about a hundred fifty dollars a month. We already have a savings account for Leah. That afternoon we go to the bank and open another account in LaMonjello's name. Every payday we can afford to, we will put seventy-five dollars in each account. When we get home, it is time for me to try to catch a few hours' sleep before returning to work.

The list of my earth-shattering problems is dwindling. The shadow—gone. LaMonjello—ours. My marriage—a ray of hope. Dolly Sector—still pending.

I am more than apprehensive about going into work tonight because of Dolly's somewhat vague threats before the Karch murder. I hit the locker room and change without incident, and time my arrival in roll call to just after it starts.

When I make my way into the roll call room two minutes after 11:00 p.m., a couple of things hit me right away. One, Sergeant Sector is not here, and I know she is supposed to be. A swing shift sergeant is conducting roll call in her place. The other thing I notice is that Lieutenant Jered Scott, the lieutenant in charge of the Investigations Division, *is* here tonight. This generally portends some kind of major announcement, good or bad. Tonight, it can only mean bad.

Scott sits through the roll call briefing with no explanation offered why he is here. The sergeant explains away Dolly's absence by saying that she's come in early and has already hit the street. Since I am the senior officer, I am entitled to the first choice of beat assignments, and I choose my usual, district one-twenty-eight. Nobody says anything, and I feel I have passed my first hurtle.

After roll call, everyone shuffles to the door. I take my time to ensure that I am last out. The lieutenant jockeys into position to intercept me at the door, and I know I'm not going to clear my second hurdle. The lieutenant shanghais me on the way out the door.

"Ben, uh, I need to see you in my office," he says.

I just nod. *Shit.*

I am taller than the lieutenant, and just as old, but again, I feel like a kid in trouble, an experience that is happening all too often of late. How I am getting to hate this feeling.

I stand before his desk as he shuts the door and sits down. "Ben, Dolly came to see me yesterday. She's leveling a relatively serious charge against you."

"Exactly what charge, Jered?"

Scott's eyes went to the floor, and he said, "Assault III."

A cop turning in another cop. Man.

"Dolly's leveling this charge, not the bad guy, right?"

"Yeah. Well, both of them, actually. He filed a formal complaint after he bailed out."

"And what about the DA's office?"

"This afternoon, the DA said his office would most likely proceed with the charge. They want us to do interviews, and then, if they think there's a case, it will go to grand jury. Uh, Ben, he also said he was going to confer with a federal prosecutor about charging you with Assault Under Color of Authority too. I'm really sorry."

I just nod and don't say anything. A federal charge carries the weight of ten charges filed at the state level. If I am convicted of Assault III on the state level, I wouldn't conceivably do any longer than six months, or perhaps a year at most. Most likely, they would offer me a plea bargain to Assault IV, and I could skate with probation and never even go to jail. But I could go to prison for a long, long time under a federal charge.

"OK, Jered. What's the procedure from here?"

"Mahoney's here now. He'll be conducting the investigation, and will be doing most of the interviews tonight. He started to interview Dolly, but she got called away to an officer-involved accident. One of the rookies, Olson, backed over some old lady's dog as she was walking him. Squashed poor little Dioge like a pancake, and nearly hit the old lady. Anyway, she's pitching a major bitch, and the swing shift sergeant was tied up, so Dolly had to go take the call. Mahoney doesn't want to be here all night doing interviews, so he's going to interview you first, then finish with Dolly when she's done calming down the old lady. Ross Chamberlain is here for you as your union rep. You'll see him after we're done, before you talk to Mahoney. I don't have to tell you that you shouldn't answer any of Mahoney's questions."

"I know. I've been here before, LT."

"I remember. Buchanan's tied up with Joseph tonight, but Mahoney's planning to pull an all-nighter on this. He'll talk to John tomorrow morning before he goes home, then he'll go to the jail and interview those pubes you and Dolly arrested. All interviews should be done by noon tomorrow. Then Mahoney'll gather all the other evidence—forensics report from the hospital, the fireman's and paramedic's statements, photos of the injuries, the downloaded Taser report, the Taser darts and spent cartridge—and get the whole thing wrapped up and sent to the DA's office by five."

"Jesus. How come they're fast-tracking this, Jered?"

"Ben, I didn't say this, OK? But there are people—very influential people, some of whom are upstairs in this department—who disagree with the way you conducted yourself during the Slater incident. They also disagree with the way the city and the DA's office handled their end of it. Those people have been waiting for a long time for this."

"Yeah, but Dolly's not one of them. She can't be; I've talked with her a lot about that after it all happened." I am now feeling trapped and desperate, and it's hard to keep the quiver out of my voice. I bite the inside of my lip until I taste the tang of blood, and it helps to keep me focused.

I just won custody of LaMonjello, and now I'm facing criminal charges? *Federal* criminal charges? Obviously, I'm going to lose my job if this thing flies, but that'll be the least of my worries. I'll be in freaking *jail*. Or, better put, I'll be freaking, in jail. Losing my job is inconsequential compared to that.

"Ben, Dolly's just doing what Jesus tells her to. You know, WWJD? You already know that. Christ, we've all meted out a little street justice from time to time, Saint Sector included. I saw her knee a manacled guy in the balls about ten years ago BC, just for calling her a dyke."

BC, in reference to Saint Sector, means Before Christ; when she was an unsaved heathen like the rest of us. Before she was part of the God Squad.

"Jesus wants to get me fired? Christ," I reply dejectedly.

"You ready for Chamberlain?"

"Yeah."

Scott nods, then gets up to vacate the office. He claps me on the shoulder as he leaves. A moment later Ross Chamberlain, the union president, walks in and takes Scott's place.

"I'm not even going to ask you what happened," he tells me without preamble. "All I want you to do when Mahoney questions you is to refuse to make a statement. You know the drill."

I do know the drill. It has only been eighteen months or so since I faced my last prosecution on federal charges. That one ended up in a hung jury with no retrial. Somehow, I doubt I'll be as lucky this time.

"I've read the initial report," continues Chamberlain. "Any idea what John Buchanan will have to say?"

I have a good idea what Buchanan will say. He's an old school cop's cop who will swear he didn't see anything illegal. Buchanan's a good man to have in your corner. Thin blue line, code of silence, us versus them, and all. Hell, that's the way it should be.

"I'm not worried about John," I say.

Ross smiles. "Me, either. That'll make it two against two, with no dashboard video or other corroborating evidence. If that's the case, the DA's office, even the federal prosecutor, will probably think twice about prosecuting you, and even if they do, you shouldn't have any problem in court."

I think he's being a little over-optimistic, but even if he's right, there's still a very large other component to this whole deal, the impact of which is only slightly less devastating than going to jail.

"What about the department's internal affairs case?" I ask.

Ross sighs. "You know they went to bat for you the first time, with that whole Northwest Healing thing. I just don't have a clue what they'll do with this one. My best guess is they'll go with Dolly's allegations, and fire you. There are those, both upstairs and across the street, who think you should have been fired after Northwest Healing, and they'll be calling for blood after this hits the news."

"OK. Anything else for my interview with Mahoney?"

"Nah, since it's a criminal case, he'll Mirandize you. Just invoke, and then he'll place you on leave. Go home and enjoy your beach days. He'll order you to be available for questioning, which means keep your department phone on, and that's the end of it until court. They'll hold off on the internal affairs investigation until after the trial, if you're found not guilty. If you're found guilty, there won't be an IA. They'll just fire you."

"So basically, I'm fucked either way?"

"You never know, my friend. Like Saint Sector herself has said, God moves in mysterious ways."

Ross steps out of the room, and returns in five minutes with Detective Sergeant Phil Mahoney who, without preamble, sets a large black cassette recorder on the table.

He attaches a little standup microphone and says, "This interview is being audio-recorded. It is Tuesday, the 29th of May 2008, at 0005 hours. Present are Officer Benjamin Geller, Officer Ross Chamberlain, and myself, Sergeant Phillip Mahoney. This is the initial interview of Officer Geller regarding the arrest of Andrew Joseph on May 26th of this year.

"Ben, this is a criminal investigation, not a departmental internal affairs investigation. Do you understand that?"

Mahoney is acting like a jerk. Last time, he was a hundred percent on my side. I don't understand what his problem is now, and it annoys the hell out of me.

I lean forward to the little microphone, putting my mouth right next to it so my voice will be annoyingly loud when it is played back, and say, "Uh, yes, Sergeant, I understand."

Mahoney looks pissed. Chamberlain fights a smile. Mahoney says, "I will now read you your Miranda rights. You have—"

"I understand," I say, interrupting him. Returning his assholic attitude is the only pleasure I am likely to derive from this whole sad affair. "Oh, sorry."

He reads my rights and asks me if I understand them. Face to the mike, I say, "I understand."

"And, having in mind and understanding your rights, will you make a statement?"

"No. I am invoking my right to an attorney."

"OK," he says, "Then for now, this interview is concluded, and I am turning off the recorder."

As he reaches for the switch, I lean in close and say, "I understand."

Mahoney switches it off, then says, "Look, Ben, this isn't funny. You could be looking at your job, and a whole lot more."

"I understand."

"Despite what Ross says, you should talk to me, Ben."

"Not today. Am I suspended, fired, going on leave, or can I go hit the street?"

"You're on admin leave as of this minute. You can't come into the building without an escort. Turn in your gun and your badge, then go home. I'm ordering you to remain available by Department Nextel until further notice. Do you understand?"

I lean forward, look him in the eye, and say, "I understand."

Chapter 16

Glum and dejected, I enter the lieutenant's office and face Jered Scott.

"I'm sorry, Ben."

"Me too, LT," I say, unsnapping my holster. He looks as sad as I do as I draw my Sig Sauer .40 and thumb the mag release button. The magazine slides out and I catch it and place it on the desk. I then rack the slide, ejecting the round in the chamber, which bounces off the desk. The lieutenant captures it in his meaty hand before it hits the floor.

I lock the slide open and place the pistol in front of him. I then unhook the badge on my shirt, secure the pin, and place it next to my gun.

"This doesn't mean you won't put them back on, Ben."

"I know." We both know I'll never put them back on, but some things are better left unsaid.

Scott stands up and offers me his hand. I shake it and give it back, and he says, "Just so you know, I disagree with all this. If the dirtbag wants to complain, then we look into it. If it needs an IA, then we do it. If he can prove some lame-ass violation, then we deal with it. But the buck stops there. This bullshit about a cop turning in another cop for not taking some asshole's shit is just that—bullshit. Like I always say, if they can't respect us when we get there, then by God they should fear us when we leave."

I digest all he has said. Basically, it's useless, since that which is happening is happening. Nonetheless, I am grateful for his support.

"Thanks, Jered."

There is nothing else to say, so I turn and leave. It is probably the last time I leave this building as an employee, and I feel like crying.

I drive home, trying to figure out what I'm going to do when I get there. I am now a parent of two children; I have a house, a wife, more debt than I care to admit, and a very limited-duration income. As if I haven't already given my wife enough reason to hate me.

It is 1:15 a.m. and raining when I get home. Being on a graveyard schedule, I am going to be up most of the night. It will take me several days to acclimate to human being hours.

It's been a hell of a night so far. I am glad that Sharon and I are starting to get along, because I really need her now. After turning in my badge and gun, I need nothing more than someone I love to lean on for support, and I am glad that it is Sharon, and not Andrea.

We live in a split-level home, and I climb the short flight of stairs to the kitchen. There is a six-pack in the fridge calling out to me. Turning on the light, I immediately see something out of place, and that's when my night starts getting *really* bad.

Chapter 17

There are watery shoe prints on the floor coming in from the rear slider. The door is unlocked and ajar, with no sign of forced entry. My heart rate doubles, and my head pounds with an adrenaline dump. My hand goes for my gun, but of course, it is not there.

Somebody killed Reginald Karch. Is that person here, in my house, right now?

I lock the door and head straight to the kid's bedrooms. LaMonjello's is empty, making my heart pound even harder. I find him asleep in a little nest of blankets on Leah's floor. Leah is curled up in a question mark around her blanket on her bed, sleeping soundly. The TV is on, and I turn it off.

Quietly, I open the master bedroom door and peek inside. Sharon is sound asleep. Normally, she hears me pull into the driveway and would be awake, waiting for me in bed. I search the rest of the house, only to find nothing out of place, and no intruder.

Going back to the kitchen, I turn on the outside light illuminating the deck and backyard, but there is nothing to see. Looking down, I place my foot over the prints on the linoleum, and see that they are larger than my own size 10s. My heart begins to hammer in my chest.

Another explanation occurs to me, and I try to force it from my mind, but I cannot. I am supposed to be at work. I am not expected to be home until after seven. The children are asleep for the night.

My wife is alienated from me, and I have hurt her deeply. But she is an attractive woman; someone who craves companionship and closeness, both of which I have denied her.

The footprints in the kitchen are those of a *man*.

I head back to my bedroom, but Sharon is still asleep. "Sharon," I say firmly, but quietly. There is no response. "Sharon!"

Sleepily, her eyes open up. "Huh," she murmurs, sounding suspiciously like someone feigning sleep. "Ben? What are you doing home?"

A million things are going through my mind, and I can't say anything.

"Ben?"

"What's going on, Shar?"

"Huh? Why are you home? What time is it?"

I turn on the light, and that's when I see them, right on the night table next to my side of the bed. A pair of gold-rimmed glasses.

I don't wear glasses.

I yank the covers off of Sharon. She is wearing a T-shirt and panties, just like normal.

"Ben, what the hell are you doing?" she demands, fully awake now. Rather than answer her, I strip the covers off the bed. Down over the edge of the mattress, where the sheets get tucked in, are two things. A pair of sheer, black crotchless panties I have never seen before, and an open condom wrapper.

I am in the car, just driving. I have no idea where I am going. Sharon and I have had a terrible fight. She would not reveal her lover's identity to me, and I don't suppose it makes any real difference.

Leah involved herself in our fight, jumping up on the bed to separate us. It was heartbreaking to watch her head snap jerkily to and fro, a reaction that seems to only happen when she undergoes great stress any more. LaMonjello, sensing trouble, disappeared from the first angry words. I could hear him sobbing somewhere when I left, but I don't know where he was hiding, and I didn't bother to check.

I have never felt suicidal in my life, but for the first time, the pros and cons of it run through my mind as I drive aimlessly around the city. I am in the same boat I was during Northwest Healing—facing the loss of my family—only now it is infinitely worse.

I have done irreparable damage to my marriage, so much so that my wife is now having an affair behind my back while I am at work. She will most certainly leave me, and with her will go Leah. As for poor little LaMonjello . . . Like he so aptly once stated, nothing ever stays the same for him. I have given him just enough hope and stability so that he will no doubt be broken beyond repair when I yank it all out from under him.

But the final destruction of my marriage and the loss of my family is not all I face. I have also ensured the loss of our sole source of income, our savings, and our retirement, but still, that's not all. I very well may have secured myself a few years in a federal penitentiary to boot.

Cops don't do well in prison.

I had lost hope before, and had my life restored to me. I had lost my family before, and had them restored to me. When they were buried alive under Northwest Healing, I didn't think I had a chance of ever being together with them again, but it was granted to me. So why should I now expect *another* chance at redemption, after blowing the first one so badly? No man gets two chances like that, and that is why suicide seems like such a logical choice to me.

It's the middle of the night and I have no place to go. For now, I am quite satisfied to drive aimlessly in circles. I consider calling Ray, who has the night off and would no doubt be happy to go out and get drunk with me, but the truth is, I don't want to be around anyone right now. I just need time to think.

I cannot help but wonder how Sharon could do this to me. But even as I think this, I realize how hypocritical it is, given the fact that I have done it to her first.

The difference, as I see it from a male perspective, is that I slept with Andrea merely for the sex. At least, that's how it began. That is also certainly how it ended. And it's more than fair to say I have wanted out of that relationship with her for a very long time. The real feelings I had once developed for her seem to have melted away at the same rate as her possessiveness of me has increased, and the only reason I have ever gone back and slept with her since then have been purely physical. That should stand for something, shouldn't it?

Sharon, on the other hand, is a woman, and women generally don't have sexual affairs for purely physical reasons. Following that logic, I can't help but fear she may have already fallen in love with someone. And that is the most devastating of all possibilities, because the truth that I have known for a long time—even through the affair with Andrea—is that I have always wanted my marriage with Sharon to work out; to be happy and successful, until death do us part. Perhaps that's why I am thinking about death right now.

I'm not actually suicidal; I simply note that the topic is at the forefront of my mind. I do not fear death, and never have; instead, what I do fear is the idea of pain, suffering, or having a lot of time to think about it as it is happening. Therefore, I could eat my barrel without a problem, but I could not, say, drive my car into the river and ride it to the bottom.

I shake these thoughts out of my head, and stifle a yawn. It is nearly 3:00 a.m., and I am finally starting to get tired. My mind is blessedly blank for the first time since I left the house, and I have to force myself to think of a plan. Should I go back home? Should I go to a motel? Sleep in the car? I cannot decide, and I don't feel like I have the mental energy to try to work it out.

Feeling like a man who has come to the end of his rope, I decide on a motel and steer toward the cheapest one in town that is at least somewhat habitable. That, I decide, is the Motel 6 on the edge of the freeway in Salmon Creek, just north of Stratton.

I am on the western edge of Rockledge, close to the Portland city border, and am making my way northward on SE 162nd Avenue, a main route. The area is jam-packed with high-density, low-income, federally subsidized apartment complexes, and is a hotbed of gang, drug and vice activity of all sorts. In my younger years, I used to hunger for this district. Now, I stay the hell away from it whenever I can. Even as I think this, I notice a helicopter maintaining a low hover over Rockledge a short distance in front of me, somewhere in the heart of the worst area, near 162 and Burnsdale. This too is highly unusual, since there are no police agencies with rotary-wing aircraft in the metro region. It must be a news chopper, which means something big has happened. To have drawn a news helicopter at this hour, it must be something *really* big.

As I get closer to a particularly nasty gang-infested apartment complex, I see the reflection of police lights flashing off fog, drizzle and flare smoke up ahead. There are a lot of lights, way more than from one patrol car. I crest the hill, and can finally see the scene. The entire intersection is closed off, and from the large piles of cold white flare bones, I can tell it has been for some time.

I count eight patrol cars from Stratton, Portland, and Salmon Creek, all scattered about the intersection. There are two fire trucks, and a large white van with county plates, which I recognize as belonging to the Medical Examiner. The Portland Police Bureau's Mobile Command Unit is here, along with numerous unmarked police vehicles and civilian cars, indicating that whatever crime has been committed has drawn the response of the Major Crimes Team.

A sullen officer stands in the intersection, shoulders drooping, and tries to direct me around the scene. I ignore his gesticulations, and drive right up to him.

It is Dave Powell, who took me on my ill-fated trip to Foxholes. I roll the window down, allowing in the rotor slap of the chopper and the sound of the mobile command post's generator, as well as the cold drizzle, which instantly coats my face.

Dave recognizes me and says, "Ben? I heard you got suspended. They call you back for this?"

"No, I'm apparently out for the long count. Called me back for what?"

"Oh shit, you mean you haven't heard?"

"Heard what? What the hell happened?"

"It's Dolly, Ben. God, this is fucked up."

"What, Dave? What's fucked up?"

"Ben, she's dead," he says sullenly. "She was killed on a traffic stop. A single shot to the head."

Chapter 18

I have been here at the scene for a half hour, and have spoken with the lieutenant, Jered Scott, who has filled me in on the details.

It seems that shortly after I left the office, Dolly called and said she was coming in for her interview with Mahoney, giving an ETA of ten to fifteen minutes. That, according to dispatching records, was at 0043 hours.

At 0051 hours, Dolly put herself on a traffic stop via her Mobile Data Computer terminal, which means she entered the vehicle plate and the location into the police dispatching records herself from her car's computer rather than doing it by voice on the radio. She gave her location only as "162/Burnsdale." To make a traffic stop without advising the dispatcher verbally is virtually unheard of, for basic officer safety considerations. We always want the other cops to know where we are and what we are doing, and besides, radio traffic is usually at its lowest during these hours. Doing it via the computer means that no other officers would know what she was doing, or where, unless they manually checked her status on their own MDCs.

At 0052 hours, the computer, which automatically runs the license plate of a car on a traffic stop, sent her a message that the vehicle was a recent Portland stolen. The same message was simultaneously sent to the dispatcher, but apparently went unnoticed. It was later determined that the dispatcher didn't see it because she was chatting with another dispatcher on their computers about their boyfriends.

At 0054 hours, the Bureau of Emergency Communications, BOEC, received a solitary 911 call of shots fired at 162nd and Burnsdale. The call was anonymous, and came from a pay phone located at the blood plasma donation center located there.

For reasons yet unknown, the call was not dispatched by BOEC for another two minutes, and then went out to units one-six-eight and one-six-nine, which acknowledged and began heading for the area at 0056 hours. Shots fired calls in that neighborhood are such a common occurrence that it is not considered much of a priority any longer unless there are numerous reports at one time.

At 0059 hours, the dispatcher on net eight did a routine check of the status of all units and saw that thirty-one Sam, Sergeant Dolly Sector, had placed herself on a traffic stop eight minutes earlier, at the same location as the shots-fired call, but before the call came out. She then saw the computer's notation that the car was stolen, and made a frantic call for Sgt. Sector on the radio, but received no response. Too late, she advised one-six-eight and one-six-nine that the sergeant had made a traffic stop on a stolen vehicle at the same location as the shots-fired call, and was now not responding to the radio. She requested that they both step up their response to Code 3 until they could make contact with the sergeant. She also directed all available units to start for the area.

One-six-nine, Officer Zack Rattray, was first on the scene. Six seconds after his arrival, Rattray put out a desperate call of Code 0, officer down—the highest order of cover call that an officer can broadcast.

Cars responded from everywhere. Stratton, Portland, Salmon Creek and Multnomah County Sheriff's units all converged on the scene, setting up a wide perimeter and closing down the entire Rockledge area. All Stratton units have been out of service since the shooting, combing all of Rockledge for the suspect, but it's been to no avail. The suspect was long gone by the time Rattray arrived.

Portland is covering priority 1 and 2 calls for service in Stratton, and will probably do so at least until tomorrow. Dayshift is being called in even now, to continue the search door-to-door if necessary. And that's where things stand now, two-and-a-half hours after the shooting.

Once he finishes telling me the details as we know them, I forget that my life has fallen apart and that I am exhausted. After a couple of hours, the lieutenant allows me to go through the police line to the inner perimeter, where the actual scene is. Even though so much time has passed, the scene remains frozen in time, and is still exactly as it was the moment the echoes of the fatal gunshot faded into night like so many before it.

As I walk in from the south, I see Dolly's patrol car parked askew against the east curb line of NE 162nd, a block north of Burnsdale. The stolen car is parked two car lengths in front of it, and both vehicles still have exhaust plumes jetting out of their tailpipes. The door of the stolen, a mid-eighties Toyota Corolla, is open. Dolly's door is closed.

Dolly is lying on the pavement next to the driver's door of her car, face down in a large pool of pink rainwater. Her gun is still strapped into its holster. I see no medical debris lying around, which tells me she was already gone by the time Rattray and other first responders arrived. A red traffic cone has been positioned about three feet from the suspect vehicle's left front fender. I don't need anyone to tell me it is marking the location of a spent shell casing, meaning the shooter has used a semiautomatic weapon as opposed to a revolver.

You can sometimes get latent fingerprints from a spent shell casing.

My eyes, reluctant thus far, now have nothing to do now but go to Dolly's body. I am struck by how alone she looks, lying there on the pavement. I am the closest person to her, and I am still thirty feet away.

Saint Sector . . . Sarge . . . Dolly. She had been on her way into the office to give a statement that would sink my career as surely as the iceberg that killed the *Titanic*. And now look at her. Despite what she was doing, she did not deserve this.

Where she was going and why she was going there matters not one iota to me now as I gaze at her body, face down on the wet pavement. Her religious convictions were annoying, but despite them, I have always liked her. Hell, in a way, I loved her. She was a cop, a sister in blue, and it shatters me to see her lying like this, face down on the street, in the cold rain.

From where I stand, I can tell that she voided bowels and bladder upon her death, something that happens quite often when a person dies suddenly and violently, though you rarely hear about it.

I look at her and bear no malice whatsoever. What she was on her way to do, she was doing out of a sense of duty, of conscience. Skewed as it was, she was just trying to do the right thing, and I admire her for that.

As I gaze upon her, I do not yet see a dead body with a mane of black hair matted down from blood and rain. Perhaps it is because she is face down and I cannot see much of her flesh, but I don't see the waxy lifelessness that death brings to people. Not yet. Instead, I still see Dolly Sector, whom

I love as I do all other police officers out here, regardless of whether I like them or not.

Though I know she is dead, it is hard to process that in my mind. I am cold and wet, and she is lying on the pavement, and therefore she must be colder and wetter than I am. I am lonely, but I can move to a knot of people and talk to them if I want. She cannot. She is a police officer, and she shouldn't be allowed to lie alone on the cold ground getting wet like this; she should be covered up, kept warm, kept *company*. I hate it most that she is alone. It just does not seem right.

Sudden, hot tears sting my nose from the inside. I cannot keep them in, and they spill out to mingle with the rain already soaking my face. I bark out a sob, startling myself. Dave Powell, who has come up behind me, wraps his arms around me, and I lean on him for support. I feel his body shaking along with my own.

Handlers with canines, who have been out trying to track the suspect, return in defeat. It is extremely difficult for a dog to track someone on concrete in decent weather, let alone in conditions such as we have here tonight.

The door to the mobile command post opens up, and I see detectives of the Major Crimes Team come out. Andrea Fellotino is among them. She does not see me, and I turn aside so that she will not.

I am not needed here. There is nothing for me to do, and I am on admin leave, so I head back to my car, but I cannot bring myself to go anywhere. Instead, I turn and walk back to the inner perimeter. The detectives have gathered in a knot with the M.E., the CSI people, and Lieutenant Scott. I know they are going to go to Dolly and begin the exhausting process of documenting the scene immediately around her and searching for trace evidence before moving her out of the weather.

I also know that between the police and the paramedics, there have been probably five to ten people who have already walked around the scene, contaminating it with their presence. One more will not do any more damage.

I ask Scott's permission to have a moment with Dolly before they disturb her. He confers with Phil Mahoney, who gives a curt nod of the head. I have already explained why I am out here, and I think Mahoney feels he owes me one.

Ducking under a lazy smile of yellow police tape, I approach Dolly and slowly kneel down next to her, taking care not to disturb a thing. If there is an exit wound on the back of her head, it is concealed by her hair. I cannot see her face.

"Oh Dolly," I say, my tears falling into the matted red tangle of her hair. "Dolly, Dolly, Dolly. You were only doing what you thought was right. I'm so sorry. So, so sorry. Don't you worry about me, honey. I'll be fine. Don't you feel bad about what you were doing. It's OK; I—I forgive you."

I am now balling like a little girl, but I don't care. Gingerly, I reach my hand out to her. My hand hovers near the top of her head, where the hair appears to be wet only with rain, and is still black. Gently, my fingers caress her head. "I hope you were right, Dol. I hope you ended up where you always wanted to go."

Hands lightly touch my shoulders, and I yield to their gentle pull. Tenderly, lovingly, Andrea leads me back to my car, where I sit alone and cry until I fall asleep.

Chapter 19

I awaken with the weight of the world on my shoulders. The first thing I see is all the police lights, and only then do I recall that Dolly has been killed in the line of duty. I glance at my watch, and see that it is 0430. I have been sleeping for perhaps a half hour.

Then, as I come fully awake, I recall that I stormed out of the house after discovering that Sharon had another man over, in my bed of all places, while I was away at work. This she has done with the children asleep in the house.

I am then reminded of why I was home in the first place, which is because I was placed on admin leave pending criminal charges and an IA that will surely result in the loss of my job. It is as if I have been falling off a succession of cliffs, each higher than the one before it.

The next step on my road down memory lane is the recollection of suicidal thoughts.

I dismiss the idea of eating my barrel and move back to Sharon's betrayal. How can I call it betrayal? Had I not put her through the selfsame thing, several times over? Hadn't I expected her to live with it, to forgive and forget, and to take me back as if nothing had ever happened?

Yet the betrayal that I feel is not so easily dismissed. How had Sharon forgiven me? Can I be as forgiving as her? Do I *want* to be that forgiving?

Looking into my own heart, I realize I do, but I don't know if I can. The thought of her lying naked with him, displaying herself through a pair of crotchless panties, which she wouldn't dream of wearing for me, is more than I can handle. I cannot drive away images of another man, faceless except for a pair of gold-rimmed glasses, touching her, making love to her, performing cunnilingus on her, receiving fellatio from her.

Funny how, when I think of me and Andrea doing the same things instead of Sharon and her mystery lover, it is not the same. Men have different needs; it is almost to be expected, I tell myself.

Of course, following that train of thought was it not a man Sharon was with when I came home tonight? Was he then blameless, because after all, he is only a man, with manly needs?

I shake myself, and look out the window to take my mind off the situation. The M.E. and his body snatchers are rolling a gurney toward the crime scene, and my mind goes back to the sight of Dolly face down in the rain, the water pink around her head, lying on a sidewalk that has been spat upon by countless dirtbags.

I begin to cry, and all the reasons merge together into a hopeless, overwhelming, suffocating blackness. My job, my wife, my sergeant . . . Have I been evil? Is there some orchestrater of bad karma who decides to fuck with people past their point of tolerance just for the fun of it? If so, what have I done to deserve his wrath?

I stare vacantly at my hands in my lap for a long period of time. When I look up next, the M.E.'s body snatchers are rolling the now covered gurney back toward the county M.E. van. I do not want to see this.

I slip the car into gear and begin driving. I am back to where I was before, not knowing where to go. I decide to stick with the original plan, and I head to the Motel 6 in Salmon Creek.

It is after 5:00 a.m. when I finally check in. The room is Spartan but clean, and I climb into bed. Now, after one of the most stressful nights of my life, I find I cannot sleep. Every time I close my eyes, I get a double feature of Sharon happily and slurpily doing things with another man which she will no longer do with me, and then of Dolly Sector, one of the most annoyingly sincere and nicest humans I know, lying face down on a rainy street; cold, alone, and wet through and through, with people standing around looking at her but making no attempt to comfort her, to warm her, to *be* with her.

The sky lightens the window around the heavy drapes like the corona of the sun during an eclipse, and sometime after sunrise I drift into a fitful sleep.

My pager wakes me at ten. I see that I slept through a department-wide email informing officers of Sergeant Sector's death. I skip that and look at the second message, which is from my house. It is Leah, paging me from Nextel's website, something I showed her how to do last month.

daddy dont move out come home and be with us lamojelo wants u to come home to please daddy come home

The innocence of her message, the childlike sincerity of it reminds me that she has seen this once before, and it is one of the few stressors that bring out the symptoms of her anoxic brain damage. My heart aches in a way I've never experienced for my family. The vision of Dolly lying in the street, which will stay with me for the rest of my life, reminds me that life is worth living. Through her death, I see a reason to live, and the need to make my life all it can be for my children.

Child*ren*. As in more than just one child. What their lives will be like, how they will grow up, is largely my responsibility. If I ever wanted to dump Sharon, if I ever wanted to get together with Andrea, now would be the time, but the price my children would pay for it is not worth it. Good T and A is one thing, but I don't have the right to sacrifice the family for it. And if I really think about it, there's nothing really all that wrong with Sharon's Ts, or her A either, for that matter. They may droop a little farther than Andrea's, but they are also fifteen years older than hers. Fifteen years of drooping that we have shared together.

But what if Sharon no longer wants me? What if she feels she has tried hard enough, and has given up on me? What if she no longer loves me because of all that which I have done to her? That would certainly explain her ability to become attracted to another man. Might it be too late to keep my family together? Now, for the first time, I notice Leah makes no mention of her mother in this email.

The thought that Sharon may no longer want me galvanizes me into action. I get up to take a quick shower, and see in the mirror my face red and splotchy, my eyes swollen from crying. Good Christ, what a roller coaster I am on.

I call home, almost praying that Leah will answer the phone. Thankfully, she does.

"Daddy!" she screams, sounding more relieved than excited.

"Punkin, didn't Daddy tell you that we'll always be a family? Huh?"

"You did, Daddy, you promised! Will we?"

Leah doesn't mince words, and I have learned to cut right to the chase when talking to her about something important. She has been a bottom-liner since she could first conceptualize progressive thought.

"Of course we will. I've got to stay at work just a little longer, baby, and then I'm going to come home in a couple of hours, and I'm not going to go back into work for a long time. I think I'm going to be taking some vacation time so we can all be together. Is that OK with you?"

"Oh Daddy! Can we go to Sunriver?"

"No, sweetie, I think we'll just stay home and spend a lot of time with each other. Now listen. Daddy's got to go for now, but will you do me a favor?"

"Well, I don't know . . . "

"You stinker!"

"Say please!"

"Please?"

"OK."

"You go tell Mommy that I'll be home in about two hours, OK? Tell her I love her and I can't wait until we're all together, because being with my family is the best thing in my life. And, you go give LaMonjello a big hug and kiss for me, and tell him I'm coming home to see him. OK, Princess?"

"OK, Daddy. I love you."

Glad to have Leah pass my message on to Sharon, I hang up, hoping for the best. I can't wait to get home, but first I have to stop by the department, which must be a madhouse after what happened last night.

They haven't made enough Kleenex to satisfy the needs of the Stratton Police Department today. Almost all officers, staff, and support personnel are here when I arrive at eleven, as well as numerous representatives of the various media. An edition of the Oregonian is floating around, and someone places it in my hand.

The headline is *STRATTON POLICE OFFICER KILLED*, and immediately below it is a photo of me kneeling next to Dolly's body, reaching out to stroke her head. The shot was taken from behind me, so my body is blocking all of her except for her legs. It is a very moving photo.

Everyone is commiserating with one another, but the most sought-out are those who responded to the call when she was killed. There are no detectives here, as they are all busy working the case. The city has hired a caterer, and there is food aplenty, but nobody is eating.

Many people ask me about my status with the department, and I tell them I am on admin leave pending an IA. Everyone knows it is about a complaint involving Dolly, but people are too respectful to ask specifics.

After I've been here for a half hour, Phil Mahoney comes out to address the crowd with an update. The stolen car is being processed for microscopic forensic evidence, but the results won't be in for a while. The immediate good news is that a great deal of latent fingerprint evidence has already been taken from the car, and there has been a match on a suspect who has an unrelated outstanding felony warrant for his arrest.

He passes out a wanted bulletin listing a thirty-one-year-old suspect named Enrique Payala Aceves, better known as Chango. Most cops, and all EMGET officers (East Metro Gang Enforcement Team) are familiar with Chango, who has a long record, most of it shared between Stratton and Portland police.

Chango's photo is familiar to me, but I do not remember if it's from other wanted bulletins or whether I've arrested him before. As if he wasn't ugly enough, his most blatant feature is a hideous tattoo plastered across his bald head and forehead.

In Spanish, Chango means monkey. Payala Aceves has a tat of a fearsome, screaming chimp's face with an open mouth and sharp teeth prominently displayed across the middle of his forehead. They say he loves the reaction he gets from most people when they first see it. The work is very well done, and must have cost a lot of money. Chango keeps his head shaved, and the monkey's body crawls back across his scalp. It is holding a .45 automatic, which is down by the back of his neck.

I think I have arrested him years ago, but I do not remember the tattoo. My arrest must have been when he was younger, before he got it. Mahoney tells us he is a bad dude, which we already know, and that he is a longstanding OG, or original gangster; a member of the Rollin' 60's, a spinoff of a notoriously violent LA street gang. Portland police EMGET officers will be visiting roll calls to educate us about the 60's and where we might be likely to find Chango.

Chango's record includes arrests for assault, unlawful possession of a firearm, manufacture of a controlled substance, menacing, auto theft, and a host of other charges. He is on parole, and failed to show up at a scheduled meeting with his parole officer at ten this morning. A nationwide NCIC felony warrant for his arrest has been issued, and police departments and highway patrols from the Canadian to the Mexican borders have been notified. It is believed that Chango is still in the area, but he has many contacts in Mexico, and he is expected to make his run for the border very soon.

Chief Moody addresses the crowd of assembled officers, and offers overtime for anyone who wants to put in four hours for triple-strength patrols. He wants every patrol car in Stratton on the streets continuously for the next forty-eight hours.

A seniority-based sign up sheet has been posted, and the crowd thins as officers get in line to sign up. I know I will not be counted among them, but if my life was different this morning, I would be.

Before he goes back to the investigations department, Mahoney catches my eye. I approach him and he tells me that Dolly's death doesn't change anything regarding the department's IA or the criminal case against me. He says it will now be delayed for at least a week, but even if Chango isn't caught, they will have to free up at least one detective to investigate my case, since I am still on full salary for the duration of my administrative leave.

"Come on, Phil," I tell him, "let me come back to work. I can help with this investigation. No field work—just let me help with admin stuff, or computer searches, or even to man the frickin' tip line or something. I can *help*!"

"Ben, you're not even allowed in the building. Still, we need all the help we can get. I'll tell you what. Let me talk to Moody about it, and I'll get back to you. That's the best I can do."

It's better than I had hoped for. I look at my watch, and it is now nearly noon. I told Leah I'd be home in two hours, and I intend to be.

I'm leaving the frying pan and heading for the fire. What if Sharon doesn't want me to come back? So far, she doesn't even know I've been placed on leave, let alone that I'm facing an IA and criminal charges. Normally, she doesn't listen to the news, and probably doesn't know about Dolly, either. All she knows is that I caught her fucking another man.

I just hope that she did it to get back at me, and not because she's fallen in love with this schmuck. Christ, I don't even know who he is.

I drive home, not knowing if I am headed toward a place of future memories, or one where the only memories lie in the past.

Chapter 20

It would seem that my message to Sharon through Leah has been not only received, but welcomed. The first thing I see as I pull up in front of the house is a large yellow ribbon tied around the fir tree that stands as a lone sentinel in my front yard. It is, I suppose, the Pacific Northwest's version of Tony Orlando's old oak tree. The second thing I see are my children, Leah and LaMonjello, waiting for me on the front porch.

As if on cue, they rise and run toward the car as I pull up the drive, and I can hear them yelling "Daddy!" in unison like twins might. No longer do they look like a little black boy and a little white girl to me. Now, they just look like my kids. They are all over me the moment I get out of the car, and it would appear that the fighting and my hasty departure of last night are all but forgotten.

"C'mon, Daddy," LaMonjello screeches, grabbing me by the hand and leading me to the backyard. "Les' go back an' play us some football!" I have been teaching him the rudiments of the game, and he already shows surprising speed and packs an amazingly powerful punch on the tackle—his favorite part of the game—despite his age and little-kid size. I grab the ball and make a run for the goal line, which consists of two garbage cans set up ten feet from the patio. I let him catch me, but I am not ready for his tackle. He launches himself at me like a cannonball and catches me full-on in the solar plexus, knocking me down and sucking the wind from my lungs.

"Lookitchoo Daddy. You all tired! Ain't even breathin' an' shit!"

"Le . . . LeMon . . . Watch . . . your . . . mouth . . . "

Leah seems to enjoy anything LaMonjello does, and we have a quick pickup game after I take a few minutes to recover. LaMonjello is surprisingly gentle with Leah, and once again, I wonder at his innate ability to read the world around him. We play for a few minutes, and then I get what I want; out of the corner of my eye, I can see Sharon watching us in the living room window. I whoop it up with the kids, whipping them into a family frenzy in the hopes Sharon will see the value of having us all together. I can be a devious son of a bitch when I have to.

When I finally do make it inside, Sharon is as meek as a lamb. Her demeanor is pure contriteness, and it would seem that she wants us to remain together every bit as much as I do. She has cleaned the house as if George Bush were stopping by for dinner, and the kitchen smells like heaven itself.

Obviously, we have a lot of stuff to work through, but on the surface at least, my worst fears—that she has fallen in love with someone else and wants to break up the family to be with him—appear to be groundless.

After I take a moment to gawk at how nice the house looks, I approach her. She stands in the kitchen waiting for me, head bowed, contritely, silent. I sense her desire for my forgiveness exuding from her every pore. I look at her, thinking of my own indiscretions, which far outweigh hers. She, in turn, silently implores me to accept her back. Her eyes are bright and wet, her demeanor entirely submissive. I see her body's quivers transmitted through the hem of her pants.

Sharon is past forty and slightly overweight; almost, but not quite dumpy, but not what most would call an eye-catcher, either. Andrea, as I have previously described, is athletic and cute, petite, shapely and perky. Yet somehow, the wife I see standing before me makes Andrea pale in comparison, and I do not feel worthy of her. The concept that *she* would need *my* forgiveness just doesn't compute. What I see before me is, at this moment, the epitome of beauty, both inward and out; the most desirous woman alive; someone whose love I could only dream of having.

She stands there, quaking, in the hopes that I will take her back; that somehow I can find it within me to forgive her, when the truth is, she doesn't realize she has it all backwards.

I approach her and kneel down at her feet, wrapping my arms around her knees. "Sharon, I, I'm sorry. I'm so sorry."

"You? No, Ben, *I'm* sorry," she says, with tears in her eyes. "I am so sorry. I—" She breaks down sobbing, and kneels down with me. "Oh Ben, how could I? I'm sorry, I'm sorry . . . " She trails off into more sobs.

"It's not your fault, baby. Just tell me it's over. Tell me you want to be with me. Because I've learned something. I want to be with you. More than anything in the world, I want to be with you."

We cling to one another in a desperate, loving, death grip. Unable to overcome the pent-up emotions of all that has transpired, I break into large sobs, crying in front of her for the first time in years. The moment is broken by the sound of little voices.

"Lee, check out Mommy and Daddy! Ooooh, dey's *kissin'* and lovin' on each other like dey never fight befo'! Ain't nobody leavin' nobody. I done tol' you you was wrong!" He sings his taunts to her, and they jump on us, which results in a group hug/wrestling match on the kitchen floor.

We have much to work out, Sharon and I, but at least now I know we won't be back before Judge Payne, fighting one another for custody of our kids.

We take some time alone to talk while the kids play video games and watch TV. She wants to discuss her affair, but I hush her. I'm not ready to go there yet, and besides, I have some important things to talk about myself. The only thing I wanted to know about her affair was whether it's over, and she assures me endlessly that it is.

I produce an Oregonian and show her the story about Dolly. As she reads it and views the photograph of me touching Dolly's hair, she gloms onto me as if she were a conjoined twin. I fill her in on the details about getting placed on admin leave, facing an IA, and the potential criminal charges. Rather than getting mad at me or becoming upset, she is all the more sympathetic.

She also becomes horny as hell, but I am not ready for that. Her desire stems from her desperation to stay together, but the timing is all wrong. God only knows when it will be right for me, for I cannot get the image of another man on top of her out of my mind. For the moment, she will have to suffice with that which women say they want most, to simply be held.

That I *can* do, and I do it with gusto.

My admin leave is a paid vacation, and my only restriction is that I remain available by phone. It does not ring, and we spend the first two days hanging around our favorite spots in Portland. The weather has turned nice, which is normal for late May to early June, and we decide to keep the kids out of school for a day or so.

After the first few days we load up the kids and all of our bikes and drive to downtown Portland, where we ride along the Willamette River and eat ice cream at the riverfront shops. We have lunch and snacks and spend more money than we can afford.

On the third day, there is a Celebration of Life gathering for Dolly at her church. Before we get there, Sharon and I stop at an ATM for coffee money. When we try to take out twenty dollars, we find that there is only eighteen-fifty left in our account. Our bills are current until the first of the month, and then we have to pay everything. I'll have my paycheck by then, but without any overtime. And, I don't expect the checks will last long. Despite that Dolly died before giving her statement, I don't see any way I'll be able to keep my job considering the IA and pending charges. Not with that shitbag Joseph out there spewing his venom, trying to get me in trouble.

In a worsening frame of mind, we head to the Celebration of Life. Completely separate from the coming funeral, this is almost a purely religious ceremony, ostensibly designed to commemorate her life, but in reality it is a thinly veiled attempt to win over the souls of the lost and worldly mourners. Most of the department is here, and additional tears fall by the bucketful. Andrea comes in about halfway through the service, and after many attempts which I intentionally ignore, she finally succeeds in catching my eye.

Hers is one chapter of my life which is definitely closed for good. I look at her and it is like looking back at a nightmare from which I had to struggle to finally awaken. On the other hand, I look at my wife, and it is like looking at the most desirous thing one can dream of, only to awaken to the bitter disappointment of realizing it was only a dream. But I only have to squeeze Sharon's hand to assure myself that she is no ephemeral and fading memory from a dream, but rather my newly rediscovered dream-come-true in the flesh.

Andrea and I lock eyes for a moment, and her eyebrows raise, a hint of a smile playing at the edges of her mouth. Barely perceptibly, she slowly bounces up and down in her pew, and her eyes narrow seductively.

It is an invitation to plow the back forty, and it holds no temptation for me whatsoever. I feel my own features darken, and I deliberately place my arm around my wife, drawing her close to me. At the same time, I slowly shake my head negatively. The sky of her face darkens, and I am sure she gets my message. Women are natural experts at deciphering these things, and I am glad that I (and Sharon too, I hope) are at last rid of our extramarital affairs for good. It strikes me odd that after so many attempts to end this affair, after having remained up at night thinking of the perfect combination of words to do it, it takes nothing more than a facial expression and an overt display of affection for my wife to better accomplish what couldn't be accurately expressed with words at all.

The morning after the Celebration of Life service, my department Nextel rings. It is an email from Lieutenant Scott to come into the office regarding the IA and pending criminal charges against me. Ross Chamberlain, the union president, has already been notified and will be there as well.

The time to face the piper, it would seem, has finally come.

The mood in the police station is still somber. The flag out front is at half-mast, and badges are covered with black elastic mourning bands.

My mood is a perfect match. I've worked out of this building for nearly twenty years, striving for a nice PERS retirement, for which I'll qualify in five short years. For which, I should say, I *would* have qualified, before I let a man like Andrew Joseph ruin it for me by allowing him to get my goat in front of the wrong person.

This makes me think of Dolly again, and I really feel like shit as I open the door to Scott's office and face my final act as a police officer.

Chapter 21

Stepping into the lieutenant's office, I can immediately feel that the mood in here is not somber, but light. Chamberlain, Lieutenant Scott and Sergeant Levin, the other graveyard patrol sergeant, are all waiting for me, joking around and laughing about something. From their demeanor, I know I am not the butt of their jokes. Given the situations going on around here, the lighthearted mood is hardly appropriate.

"Come on in and close the door, Ben," says Scott.

Suspicious and wary, and not at all knowing how to act, I do as instructed. It is then that I notice my badge and gun on the lieutenant's desk.

"Got some good news for you, Ben," Scott says. "As of this moment, you're fully reinstated. You can remain on paid leave tonight, but tomorrow night you're due back on patrol. I don't know what kind of karma you have going for you, but I'm tempted to ask you to buy me a lottery ticket."

"I don't get it," I say, sounding as puzzled as I feel.

"It's all gone. The IA, the criminal investigation, everything. Just . . . gone," says Chamberlain.

I sit down and say, "Somebody want to let me in on it? I mean, I know Dolly's the one who instigated this, but isn't Joseph saying I Rodney-Kinged him or something?"

"Uh, Ben, there is no Joseph, at least not any more," says Levin. "He was killed in a pedestrian hit-and-run yesterday afternoon. The Vehicular Crimes Team was called out on it just before that church service for Dolly."

"What? Holy shit! Wasn't he in jail? I mean, we took him for a warrant. He get OR'ed?" OR means released on his own recognizance.

"Yep. OR'ed at six yesterday morning. Hell, he was probably home before you were. Then last night, he was crossing Lark to get to the stop-and-rob in the 17200 block—you know, that little market across from his apartment—and a stolen Nissan Maxima doing sixty took him right in the center grille. Lights out, baby, DRT."

DRT means dead right there. In this case, I would imagine it means more like fifty to a hundred feet away from right there.

I am a little too flabbergasted to say anything. Now there are no remaining witnesses against me. There is, however, one last witness, though I doubt he is against me.

"What about John?"

"What about him?" Scott asks. "He was interviewed yesterday, and his testimony basically exonerates you. According to Buchanan, after you tased Joseph the first time, he said something about kicking your Jew-fuck ass and got up to fight you again, so you tased him again. Which sounds perfectly appropriate to me. Also, he told us how Joseph deliberately hooked the dart on the door frame of your car when you were putting him in the backseat, then told Dolly you used it to cut him. Of course, we never got Dolly's statement, and because you were at one point facing criminal charges and you invoked your rights, by contract, the department can no longer compel you to make a statement. So, the only witness they have is Buchanan, and his statement clears you. Welcome back."

I don't know what to say. My entire life has been handed back to me, just like that. I feel incredibly relieved that it's all over, but at what cost? Dolly's life? How am I supposed to feel about that?

Regarding the death of Andrew Joseph, anal pore extraordinaire, well, at least he died for a good cause.

"I know what you're thinking, Ben," says Chamberlain, but it's not your fault she died. As for the shitbag, oh, well. I guess Dolly was right. There really is a God."

"I know, but man, I feel *guilty* somehow that she's dead, because it helps me out."

"Well, don't," says Scott. "Dolly's Dolly. Her death and your investigation were two separate things. Mourn her death and celebrate your clearance. Hey, you know what they say—the good Lord works in mysterious ways. God giveth and God taketh away and all."

Yeah, I'd heard that before. From Dolly.

I walk out of the office scarcely believing this turn of events. The wound carved in my soul by kneeling at Dolly's body the other night is still open and raw, yet at the same time, her death has set me free and given me back my future. I cannot properly process this information right now, and wonder if I will ever be able to.

Now that I have my life back, and am allowed in the building, I decide to head to investigations to see what kind of progress they're making with the various major investigations they have going on there now.

With everything going on, it is not surprising that almost nobody is here. Mahoney is seated in his office staring at papers. He does not see me come in, and I am not about to get his attention. The only other person around is Terry Horner, our lead juvenile detective, who is also a member of the inner perimeter team on SWAT.

Horner sees me and says, "Ben! Hey, great to have you back. I couldn't believe it when I heard about that slimebag Joseph. Who'da thunk?"

"Yeah, it's kind of weird, though. I'm happy, but how can I be happy? Dolly's dead."

Horner just shrugs his shoulders. "Gift horse, I guess. I don't know what to say."

"What's Mahoney got to say about it?"

Horner looks around conspiratorially, and lowers his voice. "I heard he was checking into what you were doing when Joseph bit the dust. You believe that? Like you murdered him or something."

I do a cartoonish-looking double-take, not believing I heard correctly. This really pisses me off. I've been a cop here for damn near twenty years, and now they're thinking I'm killing the people that are going to testify against me?

"He think I shot Dolly too, the prick?"

"Well, they can't pin *that* one on you. But what if they ask what you were doing when Joseph got splashed?"

An hour ago, I would have told them to go fuck themselves, but that was before I got my job back. Now, I suppose I'd cooperate as best I can. I think back to what I was doing, and then it comes to me. I was just finding out how poor I really was at the ATM. There would be both a video and electronic record that I was there, and that ATM is miles from where Joseph got hit across town. Plus, I'd been with the family every moment of the day from waking up to going to bed. There was no way they'd be able to pin it on me.

"I guess I'll cooperate. It won't be hard to establish where I was. I was with my family all day, and we stopped at an ATM in Stratton on the way to Dolly's little church service thing. When was he killed in relation to the service?"

"Just around the time it was getting started."

"Good; I was miles away. So that's my story, and I'm stickin' to it! Like I said, I have an alibi."

Horner laughs at my use of the word "alibi," but I hadn't meant it to be funny. I laugh with him as if I had meant it to be a joke all along.

"By the way," he says a moment later. "You hear about the DNA match we got on Karch?"

"No."

"Ninety-nine point nine percent match, which means Karch raped Gus, which confirms that Karch was your shadow."

"I had no doubt," I hear myself say, but secretly, I am awash with relief. In the back of my mind was the fear that it wouldn't be a match, but now I am just about positive I actually am out of the woods.

"What about the Northwest Healing ransom money?"

Horner snorts. "We have nothing on that at all. Nobody thinks anyone's going to see any of that money again."

I shake my head. "Fifteen million bucks. Can you imagine that? Somewhere out there is a suitcase full of money. Probably some doper will eventually find it."

"Either that, or the dude that killed Karch found out that crime really does pay."

"Yeah, well, if I suddenly retire, you'll know where to look."

"You and me both."

Horner has nothing more to tell me about Dolly's death, other than that everyone's working on it. Even he is chasing down leads from the anonymous tip line, between working an active case of two juveniles doing armed robberies in Stratton and East Portland, and a month-old high school rape. He thinks Mahoney will put him on Dolly's case full-time pretty soon, since the number of tips on the line is up to two hundred, and they're still coming in at the rate of five or six per day.

Feeling good about myself despite Dolly's death, I pat Horner on the back and head for the door. Sharon's not going to believe what I have to tell her. On my way out, Mahoney steps out of the office and we come face to face.

"Glad to be back, Ben?" His tone is ice cold.

"Never thought I'd live to say it, but yeah, I'm glad to be here. It's better than the alternative."

"Well, we all mourn in our own ways, don't we?"

Where the hell does he get off? We were once friends. Aren't we all supposed to be on the same team?

"Look, Phil, if you have something to say to me, then I'd appreciate if you just say it. You're acting like I'm some kind of rogue cop gone bad."

"You know, Ben, the first time, with Slater—it was a little more understandable. When it comes to family, a man's got to do what a man's got to do. But I'm a firm believer that lightning doesn't strike twice in the same place. Not this kind of lightning, anyway. I see a pattern developing here, and I don't like it. And now you're skating away, happy as a lark and Dolly's not even in her grave yet."

I can feel my face getting hot, and I know I'm turning red with anger. "I'm not even going to respond to that, Phil. If that's how you think, then you're more full of shit than I thought."

"You wanna know how I think? I think patterns don't lie. I think you're a rogue. I think if somebody wrongs you, you "handle it." Your way, with force. I think you like to operate *outside* the norm."

"Don't give me that shit, Phil. I've seen you go off on people before. I remember you breaking your little finger on a shitbag's skull not five years ago."

Mahoney's shaking his head vigorously back and forth. "Not the same thing, Studley. That guy *hit* me, for Christ's sake."

"Yeah, and then we got him cuffed and stuffed. It was during the stuffing, *after* he was cuffed, that you cold-cocked him. I was there, remember?"

"You remember things differently than I do. You seem to remember it the way *you* would have done it, not me. You ever see a complaint come out of that? No. So don't pop off to me about me abusing people. That's your bailiwick, not mine."

"You squirrelly bastard, I remember going out to Smutty's that night, and you bragging to half the shift about teaching that guy a lesson. And now you're too righteous to even admit it!"

"Watch yourself, Geller. Don't take that tone with me, or I'll do you for insubordination."

"Oh, fuck you, Phil. Don't talk to me like I'm some fuzz-nutted rookie. You don't scare me, and now I don't respect you any more. You're pissed at me because one aspect of Dolly's death was beneficial to me. You think you have some sort of monopoly of affection for her? You think *I* didn't like her? *Love* her? Well, I did! You don't think I'd rather she was alive? Do you think I'm *glad* she was killed?"

"Yeah, Ben, I do." His tone was quiet and mocking.

"Go to hell, Phil."

He opens his mouth to say something, but turning my back, I close the Investigations Section door and walk out on him.

Chapter 22

I stuff the anger I feel over Mahoney's idiotic accusations, and walk into the house to tell my wife that our worries about losing my job are finally over. I refuse to let Mahoney get me down, though I cannot believe the colossal prick he is being.

"Honey, guess what?" Sharon and I exclaim at the same time. This makes us laugh together.

"You first," she tells me.

"OK. I'm not in trouble at work any more."

"What?"

"You're never gonna believe this, but the guy who was bringing those charges against me, Joseph? He's dead."

"What? How? When?"

"The other day. He got mashed by someone driving a stolen car."

"He's dead? So, he can't complain about you?"

"That's right. He never had a chance to make a statement to Mahoney, so now there's no 'victim' in my case. The only other witness was John, and his statement exonerated me. So now, they have no case whatsoever. They gave me my badge and gun back, and I'm back on the schedule. It's over. Period."

"I can't believe it. And now, there's no way you can get into trouble over that business with the Taser?"

"That's right," I say with a smile.

"And he got hit by a stolen car, like Dolly?"

"Yep. And some say vehicle theft is a problem."

"Not this time. I can't believe you're really, totally off the hook. I mean, it's horrible about Dolly, but *everything's* over?" She breaks into a grin. "What are we supposed to say?"

I just shrug, and she gets up and throws her arms around me. Then she steps back and says, "Well, that's not the only good news, Ben. It looks like our luck is changing on every front. Guess what happened while you were gone?"

"I don't know. Tell me."

"Oh, not much. I just got the mail is all."

"I'm using my finely honed powers of police perception here, and I am quickly deducing that there was good news in the mail."

"Um, maybe. You know that savings bond someone gave you when you were born? Your grandparents, maybe?"

I wrack my brain, but I just don't remember anyone ever telling me about it. "Uh, no, not really."

"You never mentioned it to me, either. Well, anyway, look at this."

She is grinning from ear to ear, and is now standing up in excitement. I find myself on my feet too, putting my hands on her shoulders to settle her down, but her elation is contagious.

She picks up an envelope I hadn't seen and hands it to me.

"What is it?" I ask.

"Just read it."

Inside is a letter from the San Diego Savings Bank of La Mesa, California, which is where I grew up. It tells me that after serving the citizens of La Mesa for sixty years, the bank must now regrettably close its doors. My savings bond, which matured in 1968 and has been accruing interest ever since, has been converted to a bank check from their parent institution and is enclosed. Looking at Sharon, I slip open the inner envelope, and see a bank check from Bank One.

It is in the amount of ten thousand dollars.

Sharon and I break ice of a different kind later that night. After taking the kids out to dinner and a movie to celebrate, we come home and discuss our good fortune. The amount of stress relieved by the DNA confirmation that Karch was indeed my shadow is immeasurable. I truly hadn't realized just how afraid I was that it would not prove to be him—that the DNA would not match, meaning that there was still another out there.

Sharon too had the same fear, and tonight, with the triple whammy of finding out it really was Karch, my entire future being handed back to me, and finally receiving the check for ten grand, we are feeling like the old Ben and Sharon from years ago.

Our union is like a Mozart symphony—wholly complete in its sense of pace, rise and fall, ebb and flow, and we reach the crescendo in perfect timing and harmony. We both feel a special closeness, a deep abiding love for one another that neither of us has felt in a long, long time. We make actual love, instead of just having sex. Now, having experienced both, I can testify that real love is indescribably better.

As we lay basking in our post-lovemaking serenity, my mind wanders to the sense of fulfillment I had once thought I found with Andrea. The affair had peaked just about the time of the Northwest Healing incident. It is amazing how much I have matured since then. I see my need for Andrea as purely juvenile, the yearnings of a young, immature man. Have I changed that much in just two short years? It is incredible what time and life and experience can do for a man.

Painfully, I hope Sharon has learned the same lesson. Her extramarital experience may have been more recent than my own, but at least it was shorter-lived. I do not care to know her partner's identity. What matters is, whatever he did for her, I know in my heart of hearts that it cannot match what we now feel for one another. Biologically, we share Leah, and now LaMonjello has joined us and fits in as if he were designed to be our child.

"We have a family," I hear myself say out of the blue. I am thinking aloud, but she is on the same track, and carries my thought process through.

"A *real* family. He's every bit a member as Leah. You know, he doesn't see himself as different."

"I know. It's amazing, and I'm not sure how he gets past the fact that he is a different color, his hair is so different, his background is so different, the way he talks is so different, and the list goes on, yet he sees himself as her brother and our son."

"I think it's us. We love him like a son, so, especially at his age and given his background, he can't help but see himself as ours."

"I love you, Sharon." I mean this. My eyes stare into hers and my voice betrays my emotions.

She wraps herself around me, and we hold each other so closely we are nearly one being. "I do too, Ben. I always will."

And this is how we fall asleep.

I cannot decide if I can bring myself to attend Dolly's funeral. There is nothing I hate more than police funerals. Two years ago, shortly before that whole sordid Northwest Healing affair began, the Stratton Police Department buried its first member, a good friend of mine named Dan Hollister. After that, I don't think I can take another police funeral.

The kids are in school and Sharon, who hadn't known Dolly very well, is babysitting the children of another officer. I don't want to be around the house, and I have already paid my respects to Dolly and made my peace with her as she lay on pavement in the hours following her death. I do not think I can bring myself to go through it all again.

Nonetheless, I put on the same black suit I wore to Dan's, just in case I end up there, and I get in the car. I still haven't decided whether or not to go, and about the time the service is getting under way at her church, I find myself pulling into the police station parking lot. I know there will be only a skeleton crew on, maybe a records clerk and one or two support personnel. I doubt any officers will be there.

The building is like a ghost town. I stay away from the business office because I don't really want to explain to anyone there why I can't bring myself to go to the funeral. Instead, I go to the Investigations Section, where I know they keep a large status board for major cases. Maybe I can learn something about Dolly's case.

The tomblike quality of the empty building is depressing enough. I am so very glad I did not go to the funeral.

I am intently studying the board when I sense someone behind me. I turn, and see that it is Lieutenant Scott.

"Hi Ben."

"Hey, Jered. How come you're not there?"

"Ah, you know. Someone needs to man the phones and be here in case something comes up. A lot of the guys back here were closer to her than me, so I volunteered."

He does not ask why I am not there.

"Yeah," I mutter. "I couldn't bring myself to go, either." He just nods as if he understands. No further explanation is necessary.

After a moment's silence, I ask, "So, what's the deal on Joseph's hit-and-run?"

"Not much to say. It happened right in front of his apartment. Joseph was crossing north to south at an angle, and this mid-nineties Maxima comes barreling down the street at sixty and just center-punches him. Damn near totaled the Nissan, and did total Joseph. Knocked him seventy-eight feet, and left his Nikes at the point of impact."

"Was he all gooey?"

"They say he was busted up pretty bad. Not much in the way of skin left on him once he was done skidding, but there wasn't that much spaghetti. Wanna see the pictures?"

"Naw."

"Anyway, Scavelli found the car on 190th north of Lanhill. It wasn't hard, all the fluids had leaked out and he just followed the trail. Joseph really put a hurtin' on that little car."

"Anything to ID the driver?"

"Not yet, but get this. Scav cut the airbag out of it and sent it to the lab. They were able to get some DNA off it, where it scraped some skin from the driver's face. There wasn't much, but they got enough for a match. All we need now is a suspect to match it up with. The dog couldn't find anything when it tried tracking; you know what kind of people live around there. It's no surprise that nobody saw anything."

"Yeah, you could open up with an AK-47 in the middle of street in broad daylight, and nobody would see anything. What a toilet that place is. Hey, I've never heard of taking DNA off an airbag before. That something new?"

"Not really. They've been doing it for a couple years now, and it's a great tool. But first, we gotta find the suspect."

"What kind of injuries we lookin' at?"

"Not much. Those airbags deploy at, like, two hundred miles an hour, and like I said, there's some skin tissue on it, so he'll have some facial abrasions. There wasn't any hair or whiskers on it, but definitely enough tissue for DNA. No prints this time."

"Hey, at least we got prints from the car that got Dolly. I'd rather have them from Dolly's than Joseph's."

"Oh yeah, me too. We're gonna get that Chango prick; it's just a matter of time."

"I'll drink to that."

"Yeah, well, while you're at it, toss a few for her. She wouldn't mind."

We are both quiet for a moment, then without warning, I burst out laughing.

"The hell she wouldn't," I say.

Scott nods, then falls apart himself. Our laughter trails off, leaving us both with unshed tears which have nothing to do with laughing, and we ease into a companionable silence, broken only by an occasional sniffle.

A moment later, Scott's phone rings, interrupting the mood. He disappears into his office, and from the one-sided conversation I hear, I know something big is afoot.

I glance in, and he is taking notes. He looks up, and, seeing me in the doorway, he motions for me to come in.

"Uh, that's Terminal Six, right? And the ship is the *Aristelle N? M*, like Mary? OK. We'll get that all figured out. I guess you'll handle it unless we can figure out where he went in. But I'm going to have my people in on it, if that's OK with you. OK, thanks, Don. Right. We'll be there in driving time. OK, bye."

"This sounds good," I say.

"I'm not sure," he said thoughtfully, "but the timing's sure bad, what with the funeral and all."

"Well, what is it?" I ask impatiently.

"We found Chango."

"Where?"

"Caught in the anchor chain of a Croatian container ship in the middle of the Columbia River. Damn, and I don't have a single detective available."

Then he looks at me with a little twinkle in his eye. "How'd you like to make a little overtime, Ben?"

Chapter 23

I've always loved the drive along NE Marine in Portland. The roadway parallels the Columbia River and is absolutely beautiful, regardless of the weather conditions. In the summertime, Sharon and I like to ride our bikes along the paved pathway, only feet above the majestic river's rocky banks.

As I pass Portland International Airport, a lumbering 747 appears out of the steady drizzle, floats briefly alongside my car before passing me up, and settles lazily down to the runway, where it appears to hesitate for a moment as if considering whether to actually land before smoothly touching down. The sheer size and grace of it astounds me.

I would be enjoying this trip if not for the fact that that it is about the death of a police officer. And the only reason I am here is because everyone else is at that officer's funeral.

It is very rare that I travel west of I-5 on Marine Drive. Here, it becomes a largely industrial area, and I know I am reaching the Port of Portland when I see the huge cranes rising up like titans in the distance.

The guard at the shack hesitates, then waves me through as I flash him my badge without slowing. I have to dodge forklifts the size of Freightliners, which lumber to and fro stacking forty-foot containers several stories high, but I finally make my way toward the docks where I am supposed to meet a tugboat.

It would seem that the crew of the *Aristelle M* landed an unexpected catch while weighing anchor as they prepared to get under way in the river. A body—well, a *part* of a body—was hoisted aboard as the anchor chain was raised. The crew managed to get the mechanism stopped before the body was ground to pieces as the chain passed into the ship, and as I understand it, it is now supposedly just hanging over the side while the ship is being held by the other anchor. Every minute their departure is delayed costs the ship and its operators a lot of money.

Apparently, the body isn't in the best of shape, but the one thing that was immediately apparent to the ship's officer who discovered it was a large, frightening tattoo of a screaming monkey on the dead guy's forehead.

The captain, who is Ukrainian like the rest of his officers (the men are all Croatian), called his stevedore company, who called the Coast Guard, who called the Port of Portland police, who called the city police, who called the sheriff's department, where someone happened to remember that Stratton was looking for a guy with a monkey tattoo on his forehead. The commander of the S.O. dive team, who had gone to the Academy with Dolly, called Stratton PD. And here I am.

The Sheriff's Office has dispatched a boat for the recovery, but their ETA is still an hour away. In the meantime, I am to board the ship and take charge of the situation. The lieutenant said a tugboat has been arranged to take me to the ship. Once there, I am to keep an eye on the body, supervise the recovery, and remain with the body until relieved by a Stratton detective.

The drizzle mixes with fog and makes it difficult to see. There is a large ship tied up at the dock, the *Maria Evan*, and behind it (her?) is a tugboat that looks like a bath toy in comparison. Across the river, closer to the far shore, is an incredibly huge ship. Letters that must be twenty feet tall clearly spell *Aristelle M* across the stern.

A narrow metal gangplank leads down to the deck of the tug at an impossibly steep angle. Somehow, I manage to negotiate it without falling, or even more importantly, scuffing my only pair of decent shoes.

"Hello! Anyone here?" There is no response. "Uh, ahoy?"

An extremely dirty, longhaired man of half my age leans out of the pilothouse. "Ahoy?" he says with a smirk. "Avast, and shiver me timbers, bucko! Aaaaarrr!"

I nod my head, acknowledging my idiocy. "Very funny, Matey. I'm Officer Geller. You must be Captain Ridley."

"Aye, Frank Ridley, that be I."

OK, enough pirate talk, for God's sake. This guy obviously thinks he's funny.

My hands go up in surrender. "OK, OK. Well, Cap'n, how about you give me a ride out to that boat out there?"

"I can do that," he says amiably. "You wanna ship that hawser for me? Then, go ahead and make yourself comfortable." He disappears before I can ask him what the hell he just asked me to do.

I'm standing on a floating piece of dirty steel in my nicest suit, getting soaked; how am I supposed to make myself comfortable? He disappears inside, and I can feel the deck beneath my feet begin to rumble. While I am trying to figure out what a hawser is, and how or where I am supposed to ship it, a deckhand emerges, gives the mooring line a yank, and coils the heavy rope around a pylon on the deck.

The deckhand looks at me like I'm stupid, then points at the rope and says, "Hawser." He points at the pylon on the deck and says, "Davit."

"Aye aye," I reply, and he smirks and disappears. I'm starting to remember all the nautical terminology I've ever learned, and I create a quick mental picture of myself at the helm of a triple-masted sailing ship squinting into an oncoming gale while fighting thirty-foot seas and loving every second of it.

The engines roar, black smoke belches, and with surprising speed, the tug pulls away from the dock and heads out across the rain-dimpled river, which looks to be nearly a mile wide at this point.

The *Aristelle M* begins to grow rapidly before my eyes as we approach her. I am reminded of how poorly equipped I am for this trip, as I stand there in the wind-driven rain, so I make my way into the pilothouse with Captain Ridley. It is very warm and comfortable in there, although it reeks of diesel and oil, and the chatter of the marine radio is very soothing to me.

"They say the body is afoul the portside anchor chain," Ridley shouts above the roaring diesels. "You want to make a bow approach to have a look before we come abeam?"

I think I know what he's saying, but I pretend to give it intense thought just in case, then say, "Yeah, I think that'd be best."

Ridley wheels the little boat around so that we pass along the tremendous length of the ship, then swings around to approach from the front, which I am savvy enough to know is the bow. The roar of the engines lessens sharply, and the boat immediately slows and settles, pushing a veritable wall of water loudly before it.

The gigantic vessel in front of us is visibly straining against an impossibly huge, comic book-looking, rusted iron chain protruding from the right, or starboard, side of the hull. The links are each the size of a Volkswagen Beetle, and weigh even more. As we swing around the bow, I can see the port-side anchor hanging several feet below the hull. Just where the anchor meets the chain, a comparative tiny pink and green thing is dangling, caught up in it.

Permission to come aboard is denied, Chango.

Ridley is on the radio, talking with the captain of the *Aristelle M*, and as he maneuvers the tug around the huge vessel, I begin snapping digital photos of the body hanging off the anchor. Ridley finesses the tug alongside the ship, and slowly moves in until the rubber tires lining the prow bump hard against her. The captain keeps enough headway against the large ship so that it is as if the two vessels are magnetically affixed together. A steep metal ladder descends from the rail high above me, and Ridley bids me goodbye.

The wet ladder is covered with grease and is filthy. It is so narrow that I cannot keep my suit jacket and pant legs from touching it, and halfway up the suit is all but ruined. By the time rough hands haul me over the railing, my shiny black leather shoes look like a pair of well-worn but sissified-looking Army boots. By now, I don't care. This is the first time I have ever been aboard a ship, and I find myself gazing around like a tourist at Merchant Marine World.

A man who I initially believe to be a machinist or a mechanic by the greasy and unkempt look of him approaches me, sticks out his hand, and says in heavily accented English, "Hello, I am Captain Vasiliy Asterov. Welcome aboard the *Aristelle M*."

Giving up any last attempt to remain clean, I take the dirty hand and shake it. "Officer Ben Geller, Stratton Police," I say, showing him my shield.

"I like police. You want to see body now? Yes?"

"Yes."

"Good, good. We have sufficient crew, have no need of another. Yes?"

"Ah, yes. I get it. Good one."

"Yes! Officer of deck, Ivan Nevchenko, discover passenger hanging around anchor chain. Hanging around . . . Ha! Is American slang, no?"

"Yes." Yes, no; no, yes . . . God, this guy is confusing. Do all captains double as comedians, regardless of their country of origin?

"Yes! Come, see passenger. Monkey is what you want, no? Monkey?" he said, pointing at his own forehead.

I just nod and say yes. Along the way, we are joined by another non-uniformed officer, whom I assume to be Nevchenko.

"Are you the officer who initially discovered the body?" I ask the newcomer.

He looks at me vacantly, then beams me a broad, toothy smile and says, "Amereeca! Baze-boll!"

"Yes," I reply sullenly.

"Ivan loves America, but he does not speak English," advises the Captain. I have already deduced this.

We walk nearly two hundred yards to the bow of the ship. As I mentioned there are two anchors, one on each side, and it is the port side that has reeled in today's catch.

The anchor chain, which is stored deep within the ship in a locker the size of a small airplane hangar, emerges from below through a gigantic tube, and is wound over a tremendous gear, which sends it forward to where it eventually exits the ship through a large hole in the prow. This hole is cut at a sharp downward angle, and when fully hoisted and locked in place, the anchor rests partially within and partially without the hull of the ship, well above the waterline.

The chain and anchor are connected by an immense iron ring. It is in this ring that the body has been snagged. I snap more photos, zooming in on the screaming monkey and its sharp fangs positioned over the empty holes of Chango's eye sockets.

The heavy anchor seems exceedingly large to me like everything else aboard this vessel, and sways ponderously to and fro like the pendulum of a gigantic grandfather's clock. The pink and green cargo lodged within it appears to be keeping time with a dangling, handless arm.

"You see? Unwanted passenger. Stowaway! Ha ha!"

I'm beginning to like Asterov. I take another look at the body, and see that Señor Payala Aceves has certainly seen better days. His left arm, shoulder and half of his torso are stuck within the ring. The legs are ripped to shreds, the left one is gone from the knee down, and the right hand is missing. I count at least five small crabs clinging to their dinner, mostly on the ragged lower half of the body.

Apart from the eyes, the head is quite intact and not too discolored. The screaming monkey tattoo can be easily seen from our vantage point.

I drop back on the deck and face a small gathering of dirty crewmen. There is nothing that I can see that distinguishes the captain or officers from the men. I am surprised; I would have thought the officers would at least be wearing uniforms or something. Everyone is whispering in spy-movie language.

The captain, grinning, says, "Hey, maybe you hungry, want food. We have great chef. Make good crab cakes."

"I don't like seafood," I say. "Got any monkey meat?" The captain quickly translates, and everyone cracks up. He slaps me on the back and says, "I like American police! Make good joke. Not like Russian police, who are joke."

"Da."

We all move to the interior of the ship to escape the elements. Along the way, I Nextel Lieutenant Scott.

"Well, Jered, I'm here. And so is Chango. Or what's left of him, anyway."

"What's he look like?" Scott asks.

"He's soaked up a lot of the river. I can't tell if he just drifted into the anchor chain or if it snagged him while dragging along the bottom, but unless there's another dude with that ugly tattoo, it's gonna be our boy."

"Is he aboard the ship yet?"

"Naw, he's still hanging off the chain. The S.O.'s not here yet. I don't even know how they're gonna get him down."

"There's an M.E. aboard the river patrol boat," Scott says. "I just talked to their lieutenant, and they're about ten out."

"OK. You got any detectives coming?"

"Working on it. Just stick with that body until they get there though."

"I know."

"Later."

A few minutes later, the river patrol boat arrives.

Chapter 24

Three deputies, a Portland detective, and the Medical Examiner are in the patrol craft. They circle around to the bow of the ship, and position the little vessel so that it is almost directly beneath the swaying anchor.

It takes a great deal of maneuvering on the part of the deputy at the controls of the patrol boat, but he maintains his position in the confluence of currents and eddies forming around the bow of the giant freighter. I am watching all of this from my perch on the prow, leaning as far over the high rail as I possibly can.

I recognize one of the deputies aboard. He is Vince Morgan, and we used to occasionally cross paths on swing shift many years ago.

"Ben," he yells. "That you up there?"

"'Sup, Vince?"

"Tell those guys to start lowering the anchor, but real slow, OK?"

"Hang on."

I hop down and face the captain. "Can you lower the anchor very slowly?"

"Is easy. You tell when to stop." He speaks Russian into a portable radio, then says, "Can lower any time."

I lean back over the prow, and Morgan gives me the high sign. I reach backward with my arm and make a lowering motion. After a moment, the chain next to me jerks, and I can feel a vibration beneath me as the giant gears belowdecks grind into life. The chain begins to spool outward, and the anchor and its passenger creep lower toward the water.

"Doing fine," yells Morgan. Everyone's face is turned up expectantly. Curious Russians join me along the prow. Slowly, Chango nears the surface.

"Hold it!" screams Morgan, and I instantly motion for the captain to stop the anchor. It takes a moment for the communication to reach the officer operating the gear, and Chango slips beneath the swirling, brackish water. When the gear stops, the anchor and Chango are several feet beneath the surface.

I motion for the anchor to rise up, and it begins its ascent. When the body materializes in the murky gloom underwater, I motion for him to stop. By the time the message is conveyed to the control room, the body is coming back out of the water. When the gear grinds to a halt, the upper part of the body is above, and the ragged legs are hanging in the water like a grotesque impersonation of a kid sitting on the side of a pool dangling his legs.

Rubber-gloved deputies reach up and begin untangling Chango's arm from the giant rusted ring. Even from where I am observing, I can see the waterlogged skin of the forearm peel off against the rough iron surface. One of the deputies attaches a line around the torso, and then the body is free. They never lose it back to the water, and manage to get Chango pulled into the boat without difficulty.

"Got him," shouts Morgan, giving me a thumbs-up.

"Wait there! OK? Hang on a minute," I shout back. Morgan nods. I see the M.E. already performing a cursory examination of the body as I hop back onto the deck of the ship.

"I need to get on that boat," I tell the captain.

"Tug boat get called away," he says. "Take long time to get another. Best way to get off ship is ride anchor down. Yes? Stand on anchor and ride to police wessel."

"What? Are you kidding? I'm not doing that!"

The captain shrugs. "We must depart. Ship lose money sitting in river. You can depart downriver when other tug is available. In Astoria."

I'm not going to Astoria with this ship. Who the hell knows if another tug will be free there? I feel like I'm aboard another country here, like I could just disappear and nobody would know where to look.

"I'll ride the anchor," I tell him.

"Yes! No problem. Will be fun," he says.

I go back to the prow, where the patrol boat is now standing farther off than it was for the recovery. I motion to it to move in, which it does.

"I'm coming aboard," I shout. "I'm going to ride the anchor down."

Everyone nods, and the anchor rises to its berth half in, half out of the ship. Crew members bring a rope that they have fashioned into a self-tightening circular knot big enough for me to slip under my arms. Once I am secure, I climb over the side and they slowly lower me to the anchor. The greasy rope bites hard into my chest and armpits, my back slides down the dirty, rusted side of the ship, and any intact portion of my suit is ruined in the process. It is not far to the anchor, and I step out onto the right-side spar, clinging to the main shaft, all the while being careful to avoid the tatters of pale meat left in the iron ring above me.

The pressure around my chest is instantly relieved, but I am still very high above the water, and I decide to keep the rope around me as a safety measure.

I look up, and Captain Asterov is looking over the prow waving at me. "You have good time aboard my ship, no?" he yells. "And now is time to drop anchor, very fast. Straight to bottom! Ha!"

"Very funny," I shout back. "I'm ready!"

The captain says something into his radio, and the anchor jerks, then slowly begins its descent. The patrol boat is beneath, standing off to the side so that if the anchor drops suddenly, it will not be crushed.

I am very secure standing here, and when I am only a few feet above the boat, I wiggle out of the line.

Just before I hop onto the deck of the patrol boat, I look back up at Asterov and his crew. They are waving at me.

"We beat your ass to the moon, you red bastards!" I shout, and hop off the anchor safely onto the patrol boat.

The captain's response is lost in the sound of the patrol boat's engine as it turns and heads away. I wave at the crew, who are waving amiably back. Both anchors are now on the way back up. Once we are clear, the gigantic *Aristelle M* begins making way down the river faster than I would have thought possible for such a great ship.

We speed away heading east, and I give a final wave before turning to examine for myself the strange cargo we have taken aboard.

Chango is unclad, though I suspect that he was wearing clothes when he went into the river. The trauma to the lower part of his body, including the severed leg, is the most blatant, with ripped skin and torn flesh hanging exposed. Yet it is not gross. There are no fluids left in the body, and the river has washed him cleaner than he has probably been in quite a while.

I turn to face the men, and realize that I know the Medical Examiner from previous death calls in Stratton. I imagine he knows most of the cops in the greater Portland area.

"Ben Geller," I tell him, not offering my hand. His is gloved and wet.

"Stan Kowalski," he said. "I know we've met before. The, uh . . . Oh wait, I know! It was that guy who fell across a steam-heated radiator when he had the big one a couple years ago. The neighbor smelled him slow-cooking two weeks later, right after Valentine's Day. That was your call, wasn't it?"

"Yeah. He was cooked through."

"Hey, I thought he smelled good. But I was hungry that day. This guy was murdered, you know that?" he said, pointing to Chango.

"How you figure?"

"Oh, the gunshot wound to the temple had something to do with it." Kowalski separates the hair on the right side of Chango's head, and clearly visible is a medium-caliber gunshot entry wound.

"No exit wound," he says.

"Good. Means we'll get the bullet back."

"Another thing. His right hand has been severed."

"I see that. His left leg, too."

"No, the left leg has been ripped away, probably by the anchor dragging over it. But the right hand has been cut off, intentionally, with a sharp blade. See the difference in the stumps?"

I take a close look at the ragged stump around the left leg. Torn flesh, the sharp splinters of white bone, and pink, washed-out muscle tissue, all hanging in uneven shreds. Then, I look at the right wrist, which Kowalski is holding up for my inspection. Clean, even edge, white bone sharply shaved off, and no hanging or torn flesh. Very smooth.

"Damn. You're right. Any idea how long he's been dead?"

"I won't know for sure until I get a chance for a detailed examination, but I can tell you it's longer than a week. I'd say he's been in the water at least nine, ten days."

"Are you sure?" I ask. That can't be right. Dolly was killed only five days ago, and Chango had to be alive to do that.

"Oh, there's no doubt about it. I can give you an immersion window that is highly accurate, say, seven to ten days underwater, just based on the deterioration, color, and condition of the skins and tissues. Not less than seven days under water, not more than ten."

"You're positive?"

"Not a doubt. Why?"

"No reason." I pull my Nextel from by belt and call Lieutenant Scott. I am using the telephone mode rather than the direct-connect mode, so the conversation will be more private.

"Hey, Ben. What's going on?"

"We've got the body. I'm on the sheriff's boat heading in to the River Patrol office. The M.E.'s here, Kowalski, and we've already made some significant discoveries."

"Talk to me."

"He was murdered. Gunshot wound to the right side of the head, no exit wound."

"So we'll get the bullet."

"Yeah."

"Good. What else?"

"Two things. One, his right hand was cut off, Kowalski says with a sharp blade, as in intentionally. And two, he's been in the water not less than—get this—seven days."

I can hear the wheels turning inside Scott's head. "Ben," he says, "is he sure about that? Because how could he have killed Dolly five days ago if he was been dead in the water two days before that?"

"I asked him the same question, Jered. He's positive. He can't narrow it down any more than seven to ten days before he actually gets inside Chango, but he's positive on the seven. Minimum."

"Holy shit. Look, I've got two detectives on the way to the River Patrol office right now. If they're not there when you get back, they will be shortly thereafter. Stay with that body until you can hand it over to them."

"I know. I will."

"And Ben, keep what you just told me to yourself. I don't want you to talk to anyone else about it, you understand? No leaks."

"Don't worry, Jered. But what do you make of it?"

"I don't know, but something isn't right. Just stay with the body, and don't say anything to anyone about what the M.E. said."

"OK."

We hang up, and everyone falls into silence. I am wet through and through, and the motion of the boat is beginning to make me queasy. My suit is completely ruined, and the Department is going to have to buy me another one. They're not going to like that, but oh well.

I close my eyes and allow the boat to rock me. Time seems to pass incredibly slowly, and soon I am in danger of puking. After what seems like an interminable length of time, I open my eyes. We are headed across the river directly toward the Multnomah County Sheriff's River Patrol office, and I feel like I could cry with relief.

Detectives from Stratton are waiting on the dock, which means my job here is finished. I am very relieved to see that Andrea is not among them.

Chapter 25

Steve Staley, our most experienced detective, is leading the investigation into Dolly's death. Both he and Kimball have been pulled from her funeral for this. I brief them on what we have so far. I have recorded the names of the pertinent people aboard the *Aristelle M*, and have kept a log of the times they arrived at Terminal Six, weighed anchor to leave, my arrival, and the recovery of the body. I have the number of the stevedore company, who can get hold of the ship by radio if necessary.

I give them the information Kowalski has given me, and they both make the same connection Scott and I have. If Chango has been dead for seven days, he could not possibly have killed Dolly.

Kimball voices the first theory.

"I'd say we need to start looking at some of Chango's closest associates. Maybe *he* stole the car, but it was one of his buddies who shot Dolly."

"But then, why would Chango end up dead?" Staley asks.

"Who knows?" answers Kimball. "Maybe Chango was gonna drop a dime on his buddy, so the guy whacked him? Problem is, all we got was *Chango's* prints from the car, not the buddy's."

"Maybe Chango stole the car, and some rival banger took it from him, killing him in the process, and that dude shot Dolly," I volunteer.

"Still, where are the other prints? Why just Chango's in the car?" counters a deputy.

"Gloves?" says Kimball. "But bangers don't wear gloves," he muses to himself more than to us.

In the meantime, a big white Ford van pulls up to the dock, and the body snatchers get out. These are contracted people whose job it is to transport remains to the morgue. They wear shirts and ties, which I could never figure out. If I had that job, I'd wear level III biological containment gear.

The body snatchers are making jokes about the corpse. They are not even funny—he looks like he could use a hand, he's a foot shorter than he looks on TV, he's been monkeying around with too many anchors, etcetera. It takes them no time to get Chango all packaged up and loaded into the van. It is decided that Kimball will ride to the M.E.'s office with them. Staley will drive me back to my car, then meet Kimball at the M.E.'s office.

An hour later, I walk into the office to document my activities aboard the *Aristelle M* in a police report and to fill out a time sheet to ensure that I get my overtime for being called into work on a day off.

Dolly's funeral is over, and many officers have congregated at the PD. Word is already out that I have been reinstated, and everyone gathers around me. My trashed suit is quite the conversation piece, and I bring them up to date on the recovery of Chango's body, minus all the details that would make it a really good story. I just say that many parts of his body were missing due to the anchor getting dragged over it.

Everyone moves on to the business office of the PD, where a great deal of food has appeared, and I place the camera's digital card into evidence. As I am doing so, Ray Schmeer walks in.

"*Oy vey*," I say when he appears.

"Jesus, Ben, you look like shit."

"Thank you. You're looking mighty dapper yourself," I tell him. I don't think I've ever seen Schmeer in a suit before, and he looks different. It's not just the clothes, though, and I'm wondering if his hair is cut differently or what.

"How was the funeral?" I ask.

He begins telling me about it. It was mostly a rhetorical question. I do not really want to hear the details, but Ray is bent on telling me anyway.

As he talks, my mind wanders and it comes to me. It's his glasses. Ray is sporting a pair of new, frameless glasses that are smaller than his old ones. They make his face look larger, and change his appearance a great deal.

As he rambles on about how sad the funeral was, a terrible revelation comes to me, and I feel like vomiting.

He is talking about trying to hold it together during the playing of Taps when I rudely interrupt him. "You goddamned fucking son of a *bitch*," I yell.

"What?" he says, bewildered.

"Prick!" I get up and give him a shove, sending him across the room into a computer on a desk behind him. The monitor teeters, then crashes to the floor but does not shatter. I am nearly blind with rage.

People watch with mouths agape, not quite knowing how to react. Some stand up and approach me. "What the hell's the matter with you, Ben?" Ray says, picking himself up and straightening his new glasses.

I cock my fist back behind my head and am about ready to loose a roundhouse right to his Teutonic face when I am restrained from behind. My outburst has brought half the department into the report room. I struggle against the hands holding me, and all I can manage is, "Fuck you, Schmeer! Fuck you!"

I break free of the officers restraining me, and storm out of the office, leaving my report unfinished on the desk. I go straight to the parking lot and get into my car. Not knowing where I am going, I squeal out of the parking lot to the bewilderment of an audience of officers who have followed me out to watch.

It was the glasses, you see. Ray's new ones. I last saw his old ones on the night table next to my bed the night I caught Sharon sleeping with another man.

I have been tortured day and night ever since I discovered that Sharon had been with someone else. I don't think I would have been able to handle it at all had not my own affair with Andrea precipitated hers. Still, that did not lessen the pain; it only made me more able to endure it.

The good thing about her affair was it caused me to see how much I truly loved her and wanted her, more clearly than any other circumstances would have. So I endured the pain. In a way, I *welcomed* the pain, because it was the ultimate payback for my own sins.

My biggest struggle had been dealing with the possibility that Sharon had fallen in love with her mystery man. I could only hope that he was some dumb, good looking twenty-year-old boy toy with a hairy chest and a big dick; a human vibrator she had used to dull the pain I had inflicted upon her. That her affair was an unconscious method of getting me back for my own.

Therefore, the identity of her lover was of no major concern to me. Some kid at the grocery store. A UPS driver who made a "special" delivery. Her fucking therapist for all I care. The point is, she promised me it was over, which meant that it was over. Sharon would not, nor could not, lie about such a thing.

Nor could she lie if I had asked her who it was, either. I am a hundred-percent certain about this, so I resolved not to ask. After all, it was part of my punishment to never know. To always wonder if every fitness instructor at the gym who smiled at her may have once known so intimately the places on her that only *I* had known. Had seen her only as *I* was supposed to see her.

That was my hell—to never know. It was an unspoken punishment between us, that I would never ask and she would never tell, a secret pact which we would both have honored forever. And we did. I only found out by accident.

But, dear God, Ray? *Ray*, my best friend? How could she? How the hell could *he*?

Tears blur the view as I aimlessly drive. Ray . . . It is the ultimate betrayal. Yet, is this somehow going to change things between Sharon and me? I mean, I have forgiven her for having sex with another man. Should it matter who the man was?

It shouldn't, but it does now. Anyone but Ray. Jesus Christ, even my own affair was not with my wife's best friend. Her best friend is a stone fox, and I'd be lying if I said I had never spilled my seed in the bathroom while thinking about her, but I would never actually touch her, *because* she is Sharon's best friend. Andrea is a coworker, someone with whom I work closely and have developed a bond of friendship. It is different, having a close friend that is of the opposite sex. You tend to open up much more intimately than you would with your best pal of the same sex. And, obviously, therein lies the danger. Unless she is a disgusting blowpig, there will be a chemical reaction that can become virtually unstoppable. The boy-girl thing.

So, my affair was at least somewhat understandable, but Sharon. . . She and Ray only knew one another through me. She didn't work with him, didn't get to know him, and never underwent tremendously stressful situations with him as I had with Andrea. Therefore, that she took up an affair with him is a double betrayal.

And, as for Schmeer . . . Well, you just don't do that. What else can I say? There are some things one simply doesn't do. One doesn't lust after children. One doesn't disrespect a man of the cloth. And one doesn't fuck his best friend's wife.

I look around and see that I have driven myself into the Columbia Gorge. I am perhaps twenty-five miles east down the same river I was on a few hours ago on the *Aristelle M*. The road twists and turns, gaining elevation as I travel into the gorge.

I pull over briefly at Vista House, which offers a breathtaking panoramic view both east down the river gorge and west toward Portland. This spot was depicted in the movies *Bandits* and *Short Circuit*. The views are indeed spectacular. East is full of majesty, with lush mountains rising up on the south on the Oregon side, and green fields and rolling hills on the north in Washington. West is not so pretty, looking over Stratton and the city of Portland. The wide Columbia snakes to and fro between them like a swath of silver paint from the brush of an artistic god.

To my right, the view is pristine—the river gorge, untouched and pure. To my left, the views are soiled and marred by industry. All I see are cities: Stratton, Salmon Creek, Portland. The paper mill in Camas, Washington stains the view with a smudge of ugly pollution, which I find appropriate for my mood. Interstate 84, buzzing with noisome traffic, is wide and busy. Signs of humanity everywhere spoil the otherwise beautiful panorama.

Somewhere down there among the pollution and corruption is Ray Schmeer, with knowledge of my wife that I was only reluctantly willing to share with a grocery boy or a deliveryman. Sharon is also down there, somewhere within my view. How will I face her?

For the moment, I will not. I decide to head east, where it is still pristine and beautiful. The road snakes downward now, down to the level of the river, with the gorge walls rising up on my right like green, living walls of rock. I pass waterfall after waterfall, but the beauty of them fails to stir me.

When I get to Multnomah Falls, I stop to gaze up at the water cascading down from six hundred feet up. I wonder what it would be like to be up there and to jump in, to mingle with the water in an exhilarating plunge that will end the pain. Not that it matters; I would much rather live with the pain than end it with my death.

Still, I need to work it all out—how I will deal with the knowledge I have been given, but my mind is a blank. It all seems like too much to deal with, and I would rather just drive away than try to work it out. Just then my pager goes off.

I don't want any contact with anyone. I want to ignore it, but because I am on SWAT I cannot. Reluctantly, I pull out my Nextel and check it. It is email, from Sharon.

Ben where are you? Dinner in 1 hour. Love, Shar

She does not know that I know. I am not supposed to know. I was *never* supposed to know.
Sharon has fulfilled her part, in that she has let the matter go and renewed her love for me. I thought I had done the same, but now I am not so sure.

I have an hour before dinner. With my Nextel already in hand, I direct connect a number from memory.

"Ben? What's up?"

"Are you fifty-one?"

"Yeah. I'm in the car, alone."

"Can you meet me in Starbucks in Salmon Creek? I'm in the Gorge."

"I can be there in ten minutes. Oh Ben, I knew you'd eventually call me."

"It doesn't mean we're back on, Andrea."

Chapter 26

The drive to Salmon Creek takes almost exactly fifteen minutes. While en route, I wonder just what the hell I am doing. I justify this to myself with the idea that Andrea may be my former lover, but she is still a friend. She's the only friend I have who really knows me—not just my innermost thoughts, but the way I actually think. Plus, she knows just about all the details surrounding my marriage. She's the only one I can talk to about this. Who else could I turn to? Ray Schmeer?

So she's a girl. I recognize the danger, but we have already gotten that boy-girl thing out of the way. The sexual part is over. That has been made unquestioningly clear. But that doesn't mean the friendship has to end, and friendship and advice is what I need now.

It nags at the back of my mind what Sharon might think of this meeting. But it is not a betrayal. I will never sleep with Andrea, or any woman other than Sharon, ever again. If Sharon wouldn't like me meeting with Andrea, then maybe she should have fucked a fitness instructor or a delivery boy instead of my best friend.

Andrea's car is already there when I arrive at Starbucks. She is at a table with two drinks, a foo-foo one for her, and a black coffee with no sugar for me. The double takes she and everyone else in the coffee shop give me reminds me of what my suit looks like. As if I could care right now.

"Uh, nice suit, Ben. Men's Wearhouse?"

"Yeah. It was on sale."

She stands up and approaches me, but stops short. It is not because of my appearance, but because of the message I sent to her at Dolly's Celebration of Life. Neither of us says anything for a moment, and then she brushes off my shoulders and says, "Ben, thank you for calling. I can't think of a better ending to a stressful day. How are you doing? I, uh, I heard about what happened at the office."

"That's probably all big gossip now, isn't it? What are they saying?"

"That for no reason, you picked a fight with Ray. What the hell happened?"

"Is anyone speculating why?"

She looks down into her drink, and takes a moment to reply. "There's a rumor that he slept with your wife."

"Christ."

"I'm just glad you came to me about it. I knew you would. I *knew* it!"

She has a victorious note in her voice that unsettles me. Like she controls me, or at least can predict me so well that somehow I'm not in control of my own self. I hate that feeling, and am instantly reminded why I ended it with her in the first place.

"Is it true?"

I look at her and hesitate. Well, hell, I came here for a reason, didn't I?

"Yes."

"That son of a bitch! Oh Ben, I'm so sorry."

"Thank you." She does make me feel better. Just knowing there's someone to "feel my pain" as it were, helps immensely.

"Will you leave her?"

Her directness startles me. But it also makes me think.

"No," I say after taking a moment to think. "I can't. I really do love her, and I've accepted her affair as punishment for . . ."

"For us."

"Yes."

"But you didn't know it was with Ray, and that changes things."

"Yes!"

"Ben, listen to me. This is coming from a woman, OK? An extramarital affair is not something a woman takes lightly. You can't imagine the amount of thought and angst that goes into it. OK? It's not like a man, where you get a hard-on and find a warm place to put it. So, when a woman cheats, there's a lot of consideration that goes into it. She had to *think* about who to cheat with. She had to *decide* to do it with Ray."

"I don't know," I counter. "Maybe it was a spur-of-the-moment kind of thing."

"Get your head out of the sand, Ben. She knows who Ray is to you. It's why she chose him. I can tell you with absolute certainty she knew you'd eventually find out. I think she *wanted* you to find out."

"Why? To hurt me? Hell, just screwing around hurt me."

"More than to just hurt you. She wants to leave you, but she doesn't have the guts to do it herself. It's like suicide by cop. You don't have the guts to kill yourself, so you point an unloaded weapon at the cops, and they do it for you. *That's* what she's doing. Divorce by forced hand. She doesn't have what it takes to divorce you, so she wants you to do it for her. And, don't be an idiot. You should."

I take a moment to digest this. It does not set well with me.

"Not Sharon. If she wanted a divorce, she'd just go out and do it. She wouldn't get all devious and under the table, hoping I'd find out it was Ray. She'd simply walk into a lawyer's office and they'd come serve me papers the next day."

"No she wouldn't. Trust me, I'm a woman. I know what she'd do, and this is it. And like I said, you should do what she wants. Her affair with Ray is just telling you one thing. She's going to do it again. And again, and again, and again. Trust me. Women can be devious little bitches, and I can see right through that one."

Andrea is spewing female venom like a snake spitting poison into its victim's eyes. Trust her because she's a woman? How about *don't* trust her because she's a woman? And a devious little bitch.

Why the hell did I do this? I look at my watch. Half an hour until dinner. I have no idea what I am doing, or what I am supposed to do.

"Ben, listen to me. Leave her. She's gonna take you to the cleaners. You've seen this before. Now you have *two* children you'll have to pay for. Child support for what, eleven more years? Plus alimony. Plus your PERS. God, Ben, don't be blind. Don't let her rip you off!"

"So what you're saying is just because I found out the affair she had was with my best friend, I'm supposed to forget all about us forgiving each other, and moving on with our lives, and healing our marriage, and raising our children. Just like that," I say, snapping my fingers in front of her face.

"Yes, that's exactly what I'm saying. God, Ben, don't let yourself be such a pussy-whipped, naive little idiot! She's not some angel who took an emotional hit and innocently sought out an understanding hand to hold.

She's a devious little bitch who aggressively fucked your best friend dry and laughed at you while she rode him! She—"

"Andrea, shut the hell up!" I interrupted her. "Good God, listen to yourself! You're like, obsessed with this or something. Christ, you need to lay off. I *hurt* her. She hurt me. But the thing you don't understand is Sharon and I still love each other. No, you're wrong. We *can* work this out. We are *supposed* to work this out, and we will. We just adopted LaMonjello, for God's sake. We're not going to tear his life apart all over again because we're acting like little kids who fight at recess. I'm not about to put Leah through a divorce and rip her little heart out of her chest because you think I should leave Sharon."

"No, I'm only thinking of *you*, Ben."

"And in your opinion, what should I do after I do leave Sharon? Have you got to that point yet?"

She remains silent, afraid of the vitriol in my voice. After a moment, she speaks, but softly, like a child.

"I have thought of that, Ben. I love you, you know that. And I really believe that in your heart, you love me too. Why else would you have called? I think we're right for each other. I think Sharon knows it, and that's why she slept with Ray. I think you and I should be together, and I think the gods agree."

"Do the gods know that I just adopted a little boy who needs a stable family?"

Her countenance begins to change, to get dark and almost ugly. "Come on, Ben, grow up! Quit hiding behind LaMonjello. I think you just adopted him because you're too much of a pussy to leave the little cunt . . . " A shocked expression comes across her face.

"Oh Ben, I'm sorry. I didn't mean to say that. It's just that you have no idea . . . "

"Goodbye, Andrea," I say, shocked and disappointed. I had suspected for some time that Andrea had somehow been damaged at Northwest Healing. Hell, how could she not? First she was involved in an officer-involved shooting, then she was held hostage and released naked, and then there's the whole Sharon-beat-her-out thing, as if it were some kind of competition. I don't think she has the mental or emotional capabilities of putting the cumulative stress of it all in perspective. I think it must have somehow screwed her all up.

It would appear that I am right. She reminds me an awful lot of Glenn Close in *Fatal Attraction*.

I stand up to leave. I still have plenty of time to make it home before dinner. Now I can't wait to see Sharon and the kids. It's amazing, but I really did make the right choice in meeting Andrea here, although I could never in a million years have thought it would turn out like this.

"No, Ben, wait! Please, sit down. Give me a chance! There's . . . there's something I need to tell you. Ben, please."

"I'm leaving. I'm going back to Sharon, and I'm going to hold her in my arms and tell her how much I love her. I'm never going to mention a word to her about Ray. I'm going to take my children out for ice cream, and then I'm going to rent their favorite movie and fall asleep with them watching it on my lap in my easy chair. Thank you for meeting with me, Andrea. I don't know if I could have come to the same conclusions without you."

Her face clouds over with rage. I shake my head. She needs help. I should have seen it a long time ago.

"You have no idea what I've done for you, Benjamin Geller. I've saved your fucking life! I've given you my *all*. I've done things for you you'll never in your wildest imagination ever dream of! I've handed you your life on a silver platter, and all you can do is shit on me in the name of your slut wife and your snotty little kids. Fuck you, Ben! I *hate* you!"

I show her my back and storm out the door. Never in my life have I ever wanted to strike a woman as much as I want to bury my fist in her face right now. I actually have to pull over down the street to cool down, I am so pissed.

I cannot wait to get home and see my family. Sharon is truly the greatest woman I know, and I am no longer angry with her in the slightest. To think that I once thought I was falling in love with Andrea. Sharon has the right, in my opinion, to cheat with *all* my friends. She could fuck my goddamn *brother* for all I care, after what I put her through, so long as she comes back and wants to be with me.

I head home, anxious to be with her after what has turned out to be an emotionally stressful day. When I arrive, the smell of homemade spaghetti sauce makes me realize that apart from coffee, I have had nothing to eat all day long.

Sharon greets me with a kiss, which quickly turns passionate. I let the kids tackle me, and romp with them for a short time on the floor until Sharon signals me from the bedroom door. Then, they go back to their video while Sharon and I disappear into the bedroom.

The knowledge I have brought home with me does not affect my performance with her in bed. My forgiveness of her is complete, as is hers of me. We are in love like we have not been for many, many years.

There may truly be something wrong with Andrea, or maybe she's just unable to deal with her jealousy. Who knows? Who cares?

We eat a wonderful dinner together as a family. The sauce is heavy on the spices and garlic, just the way I like it. Afterwards, I take the children to Dairy Queen and Blockbuster, just like I said I would.

On the way back, armed with *Kung Fu Panda*, we stop at the bank. Sharon wants to deposit our ten thousand dollar check, which is fine by me. She has already decided the best way to divvy it up.

After losing everything, then gaining it all back with interest, like a modern-day Job, things are finally as together as they ever have been for me. I pull the wrong way up to the ATM so she can access it through the passenger window. The kids are occupying themselves in the backseat and I am patiently waiting.

And that's when things start falling apart all over again.

Chapter 27

"What the hell?" Sharon says, staring at the screen.

"What's up?"

"This is weird. Check this out. I'm trying to pay off the Visa bill, but it shows a zero balance."

"What do you mean, a zero balance?"

"Just that. We don't owe anything."

"Uh, that'd be nice, but we owe like, eleven thousand dollars."

"I know. But look at this. It shows a zero balance."

I lean over and take a look. She's not mistaken; our Visa account shows that we owe nothing.

"Well, we'll straighten it out in the morning. I want to get a little rest before going in to work tonight, so let's get going."

"Hang on a sec. Ben, something is screwed up. Everything is showing zero balance. Look, our mortgage, second mortgage, the car, everything. Zero balance."

"Well obviously the system's down or something. If it was just our Visa, I'd be worried, but if everything is off, it must mean the bank's computers are screwed up. Let's just go."

She gets her card back and we go home. It is 7:00 p.m. when we get back, and I lie down to catch some rest before going in for graveyard shift.

I've already blackened out the windows, and I turn on the bedside fan for white noise. Even if I don't get any sleep, just lying down and resting will help. But given all that I've been through today, I'm pretty exhausted, and the last time I remember looking at the clock, it was seven forty-five.

At eight thirty, Sharon wakes me up. "Ben," she says, now sounding worried. "Something's going on."

"Huh?" I was actually sleeping pretty hard, and I resent having to get up now. "Sharon, I was really sleeping. Come on, can't it wait?"

"No, listen. I called the toll-free numbers for our mortgage company and Visa. Ben, our accounts really are at zero. They were paid off yesterday. *All* of them. With cash."

"What?"

"They either wouldn't or couldn't say who did it. Ben, someone spent almost two hundred and fifty thousand dollars on us yesterday. More, if you consider everything else we owed. No car payment, no loan, no house, no second, no lawyer, nothing. And, that ten-thousand-dollar check? There was no bond, Ben. I checked. That bank doesn't even exist! Someone just sent us money, for no reason, and tried to make it look legitimate with a fake bank letter."

"Jesus Christ."

"But I've been thinking, Ben. It's a lot more than that. Don't you see? Everything bad that has happened to us has been taken care of. All of our troubles are gone now. *All* of them."

I am going from sleep mode to oh-shit mode real fast. I think I know where Sharon is going with this. It's been trying to coalesce somewhere in the back of my own mind for a while now, but I've been making an almost conscious effort to keep it buried back there. "And?"

"Well, there are just too many coincidences. Don't you see?"

I sit up and allow the cobwebs to clear. I want to hear it from her, so I say, "No. Make me see."

"Look, first, you had the shadow. That was a legitimate problem. Someone was stalking you, ever since Northwest Healing. Some malevolent, unseen person, terrorizing us, getting into our minds, our lives, our house. And what happened? He was brutally killed."

"Yeah. That was the beginning of the good times. That's when we got LaMonjello."

"Right. And since then, just about everything has gone in our favor. But how? How have all these things gone in our favor, Ben?"

I thought I was supposed to be the policeman here, but she is thinking more like a detective than I am.

"Well, the shadow was killed, but then there was Joseph's excessive-force complaint. But Dolly got killed, which made the I.A go away, and gave me my job back."

"But Joseph was still complaining to the D.A.'s office," she says, goading me on.

"Right, but he got . . . My God, Sharon, you're right! It's death. More specifically, it's homicide. Everyone who was in my way was murdered. It's like it was designed to keep me in the clear."

"And now our finances are all taken care of."

"Sharon, what are you getting at? Exactly what is your theory?"

"Ben, I think you're being stalked again. Only this time, rather than some malevolent intent, it's like, some twisted kind of *benevolent* intent. I think whoever's doing it is the person who killed Karch. I think when he did it, he got the money, and now he's doing everything he thinks is necessary to protect you, or benefit you or something."

The final vestiges of sleep melt away, and suddenly I can feel the color in my face doing the same. I actually feel myself growing weak.

"Ben? My God, Ben, what's wrong? You look like you're going to throw up."

That's apropos, because I feel like I'm going to throw up. "Oh my God, honey, not *he* did it to protect me, *she* did it to protect me!"

"What? Who?"

Andrea's parting words slice through my brain like the scimitar through Karch's neck: "You have no idea what I've done for you. I've handed you your life on a silver platter. I've done things for you that you could never imagine."

"Oh, Christ," I moan.

"Ben, you're scaring me. What is it?"

"It's Andrea Fellotino. Oh dear God, she even told me as much."

I tell Sharon how the death of Chango didn't fit with the fact that he was the driver of the stolen car that Dolly stopped, which meant that he couldn't have killed Dolly. Then another little revelation comes to me. How is it that I couldn't see it earlier?

"Honey, Chango's fingerprints were all over that car. But Chango was already dead by then. When we found Chango's body, his right hand was missing! Don't you see? I'll bet my left nut that all of Chango's prints in that car came from that right hand."

She says, "Ben, are you suggesting that Andrea killed Chango, then cut off his hand, stole the car, used the hand to put his fingerprints all over it, *and then shot Dolly?* You're suggesting that Andrea killed Dolly?"

"No . . . maybe . . . I don't know! Yeah, I guess I am. Sharon, it fits. It *all* fits. Listen, Andrea is one of the detectives that's investigating Karch's murder. Hell, I even told her a bunch of stuff that might have helped her. I told her that I thought Karch was mimicking me, imitating everything about me. I told her that if I was the investigating officer, I would start checking stores that sell Danner boots, which are the kind I wear, and I'd be checking gun clubs and stuff to see who taught him to shoot . . . "

Something else dawned on me at that point. "God! The suspect who killed Karch was wearing Danners, and left them behind. Big ones, like size ten or twelve."

"But couldn't that have been, you know, a false lead, something she did to make you think it was a man that killed Karch?"

"I guess so. But wait a second here. We're talking about Andrea. She's a cop! She *liked* Dolly. We need to take a step back here, and look at what we're saying. I mean, this is almost the exact same thing as Bob Slater. A cop who has gone bad and is going around killing everyone. I can't go to the department and say, "Hey, remember me, the guy you were going to fire yesterday? Guess what? Andrea killed like, four people last week, and I cracked the case again. Next time you get a murderous rogue cop, call me, and I'll figure it all out for you.' My career is just about on the rocks as it is."

"Tell me this, then. A minute ago, you looked like you were about to die. And you said Andrea nearly told you as much. What did you mean? What did she say?"

"She said I have no idea all the stuff she's done for me—that she's saved my life, and given it back to me on a silver platter. That she's done stuff for me that I could never dream of."

"That's pretty vague."

"Yeah, but still, you should have seen her. It's like she's become this whole other person. It was really creepy. She was just plain scary, and that's no shit."

"Look, Ben, let's just run with this for a second, OK? Just you and me, because I don't think it's as crazy as it sounds, and it might really all fit. Let's say that Andrea is crazy in love with you, and completely off her rocker. She's a detective assigned full-time to trying to figure out who's stalking you, so she knows all the facts. And . . . you're having an affair with her, so you're probably giving her intimate details and your own thoughts that you wouldn't give another investigator. Now you take it from here."

She holds my hand, which tells me volumes, and gives me the last bit of encouragement I'll need to do this, and I continue her thoughts.

"I tell her to check out stores that sell Danners. I tell her that the shadow would have needed to learn how to shoot somewhere, so she should check out gun clubs within fifty miles or so. I tell her he would have needed to buy lots of .308 caliber ammo, so check out that angle. But she tells me I'm not the first one to think of all that, that they've already run those leads down. But what if they hadn't? Let's just say they haven't thought of all that. She does all that stuff, and who knows what else, and develops information that points to Karch as the suspect."

Sharon picks up the thought. "Maybe she doesn't have what it's going to take to arrest and convict him. Maybe she figured out who he is and where he lives, and she goes and breaks into his house to get more evidence. He wakes up to find her in the house and she winds up killing him."

"No," I tell her. "That doesn't fit. The killer wore size-ten Danners, which he left at the scene. Andrea's feet are tiny; real slender and petite. . . . Shit, this is a detail I wouldn't have mentioned if I wasn't sleeping with her, and I realize only too late what I've done by saying it.

Sharon has always bemoaned the fact that she has large hands and feet. She knows that I find small, slender hands and feet as attractive on a woman as her hair or face, and it's always bothered her. But to her credit, she just squeezes my hand and says, "It's OK, Ben. Just go on."

My mind does a little flip-flop, and it occurs to me that Ray Schmeer's dick makes my own manhood, of which I am relatively proud, look like it belongs on a twelve-year-old boy. What goes around comes around, Benny boy.

I blink myself back to the here and now. "OK, I'm sorry. Let's just keep going. We'll say, for purposes of this wild theory, that Andrea's crazy. She's got, like, PTSD or something. Something's snapped in her head, and she's now a twisted, psycho killer. She knows Karch is the man, my shadow, and she doesn't care about arresting and convicting him. She wants to protect me from him, to *avenge* me for all the shit he's put me through. Why, I don't know, but it doesn't really matter.

"So, what's she do? She goes out and gets large size men's boots to throw us off. She makes sure they're Danners, to like, send a subconscious message to me or something. Then she goes to his house, breaks in, and kills him. She knows the cops are going to go over every inch of the murder scene, but it doesn't matter. Hell, she knows that in a matter of hours, she'll be *part* of the Major Crime Scenes team that will be going over the scene. She knows everything about crime scenes. Maybe she's even like, naked or something, so she doesn't leave trace evidence.

"Anyway, she kills Karch, but first, she gets him to tell her where the money is. Maybe that was all she intended to do, but she can't stop there because I tased that dude Joseph. Now, my job's in jeopardy, because Dolly's going to turn me in.

"So, she devises the plan of killing Dolly and making it look like Chango did it. I mean, she's got access to Chango's info. She finds him, kills him, cuts off his right hand and prints up the car with it, then dumps his body in the Columbia River. Eventually, it gets carried downstream and is picked up by the *Aristelle M's* anchor. In the meantime, she somehow contacts Dolly that night, and fakes the traffic stop."

"How?"

"Damn! Check this out, Shar! Dolly has never, not *ever*, made a traffic stop on her MDC. Nobody does. But she did that night. I think Andrea flagged her down, shot her, then set the cars up to make it look like a traffic stop, and got on Dolly's MDC and put her out on traffic."

"So, Andrea's fingerprints would be on the inside of Dolly's car, wouldn't they?"

"No way. Andrea's smarter than that. She would have been wearing gloves when she was in the stolen car, but not when she contacted Dolly. I bet she would have put the gloves back on for when she moved Dolly's car."

Sharon takes it from here. "But there's still another witness, isn't there? Joseph, who is also going to make a statement against you. So, she steals another car, waits for him to go out of his apartment, and runs him down."

"Exactly. And check this out! Chango was killed at the same time as that church service for Dolly."

"So?"

"Andrea got there late! She came in when the service was about halfway over."

"You're right! But again, there's no evidence because she's wearing gloves."

"Yeah."

And then it hit me. "Holy shit, Sharon! There *is* evidence!"

"What?"

"The traffic investigators did something in this case I've never heard of before. They cut the airbag out of the stolen car that hit Joseph, sent it to the lab, and they were able to get DNA off it. The only DNA that could possibly be on it would have to belong to the person driving it. It would be proof positive if there was a match!"

"But what would you compare it to? How would you get DNA from Andrea?"

"A warrant. If they believed our theory, they could get a warrant to take a DNA swab from her mouth. That's how it's normally done. Saliva is full of DNA, and it's the least intrusive method of getting it. But I guarantee you, Shar, they'll never even *listen* to this theory, let alone accept it. Especially not from me. I mean, I don't even know if *I* believe it."

"But everything fits, Ben. Especially with what she told you about giving you your life back on a silver platter."

"I know, but that's hardly a confession to what, four murders? I'm telling you, even if I went to Lieutenant Scott and he believed me, it's going to wind up on Mahoney's desk, and he's got it in for me. This is no different from what happened with Slater. Nobody's going to believe me."

"Ben, if she's got fifteen million dollars, and even gets an inkling that they're looking at her for this, nobody'll ever see her again."

"No shit. And if they swab her for her DNA, she'll know why, believe me. By the time the match comes back from the lab, she'll be in South America. So, we're pretty much screwed."

Sharon remains quiet for a moment, then, her voice actually lower as if someone might be listening, she says, "What if you got DNA evidence of your own, and it came back as a match? Then they'd *have* to listen to you, wouldn't they?"

"Yeah, I suppose they would, but how am I supposed to get it?"

"Come on, Ben, you're not stupid. She wouldn't even know you're getting DNA."

"I'd have to get a saliva sample from her. I'd have to be alone with her. How could I do that? I don't *want* to do that."

"I don't blame you. But other than saliva, what other kinds of DNA are there that would work?"

"Well, hair, but it has to be the root. Blood. Semen. Maybe fingernails, but I don't know about that."

"Well, I'm assuming she couldn't give semen."

"Any bodily fluids work, hon. Snot, tears, vaginal secretions, anything you can think of."

"Gross. Ben, I think she did it. I really, really think she did. And I think you can prove it."

"Are you saying what I think you're saying?"

"I think you should get her DNA."

"How? You want me to see her again?"

"Ben, if what we think is really the case, she's *murdered* to make you happy. More than once. And probably more than to just make you happy, she probably wants to make you hers. And what happens when she finally gets the idea that you're not going to live happily ever after with her? Then *you're* next! So, yeah, I want you to see her again if that's what it takes. I'm not saying to sleep with her, but maybe you could get some of her hair or something. Look around her bathroom. God knows what you might find in a woman's bathroom. Kleenex, fingernail clippings, hair off the floor, underwear in the laundry, even."

I'm kind of warming up to the idea, although when I last saw Andrea, she was more than a little scary. What if she really was a stone-hearted killer, and she figured out what I was doing?

God, I am giving myself the heebie jeebies. I can't believe what's going on here. My wife is telling me to go to Andrea's apartment.

"What if I can't get any? I've got to tell you, Sharon, I don't want to go over there. Andrea's a little, uh, shall we say, possessive? She wants me to get a divorce and marry her. I fought with her when I last saw her, and she's really pissed at me. I think I could go over there under the pretense of making up, but she's going to want to sleep with me. I'm sorry, but I'm just telling you the way it is."

"Ben, listen. I truly, truly believe that she's the killer. From the first time I set eyes on her, I've known that she's messed up. A woman can see that in another woman. You've already slept with her. If worse came to worst, I'll bet you could do whatever you had to in order to get DNA from her."

"Jesus, Sharon. You're practically telling me to sleep with her."

"No, I'm not. I'm just telling you that that woman needs to be in prison. Nobody is in the kind of position that you are to prove it. I know you could get it without sleeping with her, but if you had to, the end would justify the means."

"Honey, I'd have to testify about how I got the DNA in court. Would you want me to do that?"

"Ben, do what you have to, but prove that it's her. This madness has to end. She killed a police officer! If you had to sleep with her and then testify about it later to put her in prison for that, then so be it. I'll stand right beside you."

"Jesus, Sharon, I don't even know if it would fly in court."

"I'll bet it would."

"God."

"Think about it, Ben. If there's another way, do that. If not, do this."

Sweet Jesus. All I feel is cold and scared inside. It's like two years ago, all over again. I don't know if I can do it again.

Chapter 28

I go to work tonight wondering how in the world I am to pull this off. I do *not* want to sleep with Andrea. I don't even want to see her, but I cannot think of another way.

In my heart I am convinced she is guilty, although my head tells me it simply cannot be so. What is the likelihood that there have been two renegade officers from the same department going around killing people, and I am the only one who ever knew about it? To even think about it makes me feel as if I am crazy. But that's how I felt when I first suspected Bob Slater two years ago.

It defies the laws of probabilities that such a thing could happen again within the Stratton PD, much less that I would be privy to it before anyone else. Yet, four people are dead—Dolly Sector, Reginald Karch, Andrew Joseph, Enrique Payala Aceves, aka Chango.

Jesus.

No matter how I try to punch holes in it, my theory stands. The pieces all fit, yet still, there must be some other explanation I haven't thought of, one that could make Andrea's seeming complicity all just a horrible coincidence.

I go to work as usual, and as my night wears routinely on, I am almost able to talk myself out of my theory. It just can't possibly be. It would be a horrible mistake to contact Andrea tonight. In trying to collect evidence of a crime she almost certainly didn't commit, I would stir up that whole hornet's nest of our affair. But Sharon wants me to do it. She is even willing to allow me to sleep with her for this cause. Why would she allow that?

Because logically, it must be so.

Still, nagging doubts persist. I simply don't want to believe it. Yet I think I should believe it. If Andrea has done these things and I don't do something about it, when will it ever stop? *Will* it ever stop? Who might be next?

A cold chill shakes me from my spine outward as a horrible revelation comes to me. Suddenly, I know who will be next. Dear God, I hope I am not right because if I am, if there really was a pattern of victims consisting of people who had hurt me, then who is the next logical victim?

I don't need to struggle to recall exactly what Andrea and I had been discussing when I last saw her. I was complaining to her that my wife slept with my best friend. If Andrea sees herself as some sort of avenging angel bent on easing my pain by murdering those who inflict it, then . . .

Sharon.

Now I don't have a choice. Now I have to see Andrea. I cannot risk Sharon, Leah or LaMonjello. I simply cannot.

How will I do it, though? She lives in Vancouver, Washington. By whatever means, I know now that I need to do it, and it has to be tonight. The faster I can get DNA to the crime lab, the faster I will know. But, after the way Andrea and I argued this afternoon, I'm not sure she'll even see me.

The more I think about it, though, the more I believe in my heart she will. I think she would love it if I sought her forgiveness and wanted to renew our affair. Yes, she will see me.

I have to be careful, though, because I cannot afford to get caught by the department. A lot of folks in city management would like nothing better than to see me get fired, and if I took a trip across state lines to see my girlfriend on duty in a patrol car, I would certainly be fired.

I think of, then dismiss, the idea of doing it tomorrow. Tomorrow is a weekday, and Andrea will be at work. I could go to her apartment while she's at work and break in, but that would taint the evidence to the point that it would be inadmissible in court.

I could try to meet with her in the morning, after I go off duty and she gets to work, and try to get some DNA somehow here, but how? I doubt I could get enough saliva from a coffee cup to test. I doubt that I could get strands of her hair with roots attached by running my fingers through it while kissing her. I couldn't take her saliva from my own mouth, as it would be mixed with my own.

In the back of my mind is the knowledge that her other bodily secretions, those of her nether regions, are swimming with DNA, and I could obtain some with my fingers, but I desperately do not want to have sex with her of any kind if I can avoid it.

The only thing I feel about Andrea at this point is fear. She seriously scares me. If she did *half* of what I think she did, I could be in some deep shit if she gets an inkling of what I'm trying to do.

Finally, I set my jaw and decide that I have to see her tonight, no matter what the risk. Should I call her first? I suppose I should, but I don't want to call her too far in advance. I'd rather call her after I'm in Washington and nearing her home on Vancouver's east side.

There is a quiet time nearly every weeknight between 4:00 a.m. and 6:00 a.m. It is during this time that I would have my best shot. Also, I almost never take a lunch break on graveyards, even though I am entitled by contract to two fifteen-minute coffee breaks and one thirty-minute lunch break.

I will take my breaks tonight. Once I am over the bridge into Washington, I will put myself out on lunch. Nobody monitors break times on graveyards, and I can stay out for an hour. It shouldn't take longer than that. If I get a radio call while on the freeway en route to her place, I can always say that I was following a vehicle while waiting for the registration to come back. That wouldn't fly once I was across the state line, but until then I should be OK.

Now with my plan in mind and the decision to execute it made, I feel much better. My only job for the next few hours is to hope that it is a slow night.

It turns out to be just that. I spend the time thinking about the lines I will use on Andrea.

It is my intention to leave precisely at four o'clock. But as it turns out, I inadvertently stumble across a drunk driver at 0345. It is a routine case, but I still have to transport the bad guy to jail. I process him and do the paperwork necessary to book him into jail, then make the drive to downtown Portland. It's a slow night at jail and I get him lodged faster than normal. As it turns out, the timing is relatively good, because I'll have to take I-84 back to Stratton, and I can just grab the 205 north on the way. Her place is off Mill Plain, just east of the freeway. Though it's later than I had planned, I'll be there about the time she is up and getting ready for work, which means we'll have neither the time nor the opportunity to have sex.

I have second thoughts all the way back. I can think of a lot more reasons why I shouldn't do this than why I should, but the clincher is, Sharon's right. If this is Andrea, then she's a lot crazier than I could have possibly imagined, and she really is a threat to Sharon. I've just discovered I'm in love with Sharon; I don't want to risk losing her, let alone place my family in further jeopardy.

When I get to I-205, which leads north into Washington State, I find myself taking the exit. Screw it, I tell myself; I don't care if I get caught. This may be my only opportunity, and I simply cannot allow it to pass me by.

Eight minutes later, I am standing on Andrea's porch ringing her doorbell. Glancing at my watch, I see it is just after six. I know her schedules. She'll be up already, getting ready for work.

"Ben? Ben, what the hell are you doing here? On duty, too. Are you crazy?"

"Hi Andrea. Sorry to bug you at home, but can I come in for a sec? I won't stay long, I promise."

Looking as if she can't believe I'm here, she says nothing else and steps aside. I take it for the invitation it is, and follow her.

"I've been driving around all night thinking about our conversation yesterday. Look, Andrea—honey—I'm really sorry. The last thing I want is for us to be mad at one another. We've been through a hell of a lot together, and I think you know you will always occupy a huge portion of my heart. Maybe the largest part. I don't know if I'm making the wrong decision or the right one, but I just had to come here and tell you that, no matter what happens, I . . . I still love you."

"What are you saying, Ben?"

I take her hands and gaze into her eyes. I block out all thoughts and suspicions that she may be a murderer so that she cannot read it in my eyes and say, "I'm not really sure. I think I'm saying that I've got too much tied up with Sharon to just flat-out leave her, what with the kids and all, but I also have a history with you that I can't just walk away from, either."

"Are you saying you want to keep seeing me?"

"Yeah, I think I am."

I see her entire countenance change. She brightens so much and so quickly that it is almost frightening. This, more than anything, makes me think I am right. "Oh, Ben, I've never stopped loving you. I've . . . I'd do anything for you!"

She steps in to me, wraps her arms around me, and kisses me deeply. I close my eyes, and while her tongue explores my mouth all I can see is the Reginald Karch crime scene. Dancing across the stage of my mind are images of his wounds. Deep, horrifying slices through his neck and the side of his head, much worse than any Hollywood director could come up with for a Halloween movie.

He had been mutilated with that scimitar, and his assailant must have been covered in hot blood. I'm not squeamish, but if I had that much of someone else's blood all over me, I'd probably throw up.

Andrea's hands wander to my butt, and I have to force myself not to withdraw from her. Kissing her requires more force than I have within me, and I hope she doesn't grope me, because I couldn't get an erection if my life depended on it.

"Ben, what's wrong?"

"I don't feel well," I say honestly, pulling back. I really do feel like I might puke. I'm scared, I'm creeped out, and now the images of Karch's corpse are replaced with those of Dolly's body lying empty and lifeless on the wet pavement in a pouring rain. Andrea's touch feels like ice, and I have this insane desire to run to the bathroom for a shower rather than evidence-gathering.

"My God, Ben, you're pale and sweating! You look sick."

"I need to use your bathroom."

My stomach actually is heaving, and I spend the first few minutes on the floor in front of the john. She knocks on the door to ask if I'm OK.

"Yeah. I'm so sorry, I just feel like shit."

"I wish you could stay," she says. "I'd call in sick just to take care of you."

"Me, too. Just give me a sec, OK, babe?" Once I'm sure I'm not going to vomit, I stand up and look around. I've been in here before, and I know my way around the place. Quietly, I open the top drawer. All of her brushes and combs are there right where they belong.

A red brush with white plastic bristles is her favorite and has been used the most. A thick tangle of hair carpets the bottom of it. Using a nail file I find in a little dish on the counter, I dig it out, and having nothing else to do with it, I wrap it in toilet paper and place it in my wallet.

"How are you doing, honey?" Andrea asks from the bedroom. Our fight of the previous afternoon is completely over, and she's back to playing house just like she used to. Her switch is complete.

"I'm OK. I'm just gonna sit here for a second and see if anything wants to come out. Of either end," I joke lamely.

"Yuk!" she says playfully. I wonder what she would do if she knew what I was really doing.

Next, I check out the trash, and that's where I strike gold. There is a small but heavy cylindrical wad of toilet paper in the trash. Having spent nearly twenty years living with a woman, I recognize the casket of a used tampon when I see one. I wrap it in a thick cocoon of toilet paper and put it in my pocket.

Lastly, I fish out a dirty pair of underwear from the laundry basket in the corner. A quick inspection shows at least one of her familiar well-trimmed black pubic hairs inside along with the usual female stain. I fold it inward into a little ball and stuff it into my back pocket. Then I flush the toilet and go out.

"You look better. How do you feel?"

"Not so great. I wonder if I'm coming down with something."

"I hope not. Look, Ben, I swear to God I wish you could stay here. Maybe sometime soon, but I understand it if you have to leave. Of course, you're welcome to stay as long as you like, but you're on duty, and you have to get the car back. And I have to get ready for work too; it's nearly six thirty. You should get going. You'll be lucky if nobody figures out that you're missing in action."

"I know, but I had to come see you." I force myself to take her into my arms and kiss her goodbye.

She crushes herself happily against me and says, "I love you, Ben."

"I love you too, Andrea. Thanks for being here."

And that's it. Feeling like I've narrowly escaped something really bad, I get back into my patrol car and drive back to Stratton.

Everyone is hanging around the report room getting ready to go off duty. Nobody comments that I've taken forty minutes longer to get home from jail than usual, and I'm sure nobody even noticed.

I pull out my notebook and begin writing up the drunk-driving case. I don't have to do it now, but I want to wait until everyone is out of the report room. At seven, everyone goes home, and once I have the place to myself, sneak an evidence form from the report writing room. I call the records department and get the case number for Dolly's shooting, which will be required to get evidence into the lab.

I carefully extract the thatch of hair from my wallet and place it into a clean, self-sealing paper envelope. I then place the panties in a paper bag, which I seal with red evidence tape. Finally, I package the tampon in the same manner. I place all three items into cardboard box, seal it with more evidence tape, and put the case number and my name on it, listing myself as Detective Geller. On the lab request sheet, I mark all three items as "Samples of DNA From Known Suspect," and request they be tested for DNA and matched to the other DNA evidence listed in this case, i.e., the DNA from the stolen vehicle's airbag.

Finally, it is time to leave. Nobody is around as I walk out of the building to my personal car carrying an evidence box, and I'll bet nobody would have said anything anyway.

Twenty-five minutes later, I walk into the Oregon State Police crime lab in Portland with the box. A lab tech checks it in.

"I need you to check these items against a DNA sample we've already submitted on the same case number. It's a hit-and-run, but it might very well be the same suspect in the case of the Stratton sergeant who was killed in the line of duty last week," I tell her somberly.

"No kidding? You guys develop a suspect already?"

"There's a good chance. But you can imagine the confidential nature of this one, so I'd rather you not talk about it, even to the other techs here, OK?"

"Hey, I understand. I'll give this top priority and strict confidentiality. Don't worry about that."

"Good. Trust me, if this suspect pans out, the shit will hit the fan soon enough. But if it doesn't, and word of it gets out, it could seriously compromise the case. So please, remember the confidentiality. Here," I said, giving her my business card. "I've put my own personal cell phone number on the back. Give me a call the moment the results come in, OK?"

"You got it. I really hope it pans out."

"I don't," I say before I realize it. She looks at me quizzically and says, "Wow. The plot thickens. This normally takes a few days, but I'll step it up as fast as I can. I knew Sergeant Sector from coming in here when she was the detective supervisor. I always liked her."

"Thanks. Call me the moment you get the results, no matter what they are. And keep this totally fifty-one."

"I'm already working on it, and my lips are sealed."

It's nearly 1:00 p.m. when I get home. Sharon, nervous, greets me at the door. "I was afraid to call because I thought you may be at her house. Well?"

I tell her about my night, and my success at getting the evidence out of Andrea's bathroom. Hesitantly, she asks, "Did you have to, you know . . . "

"No, don't worry about that. She kissed me, and I had to kiss her back, but the way it worked out, we couldn't have done any more even if she wanted to. There wasn't any time, and besides, she creeped me out so bad I doubt I'll be able to get it up for a month. Being there actually made me get physically ill. It worked out as a perfect excuse to spend some quality time digging around her bathroom, but I spent the first few minutes on the floor in front of the toilet."

She puts her arms around me and leads me to the bedroom. The kids are in school, and I'm afraid she's going to want to make love. In an ironic role reversal, all I want is to be held. The sexual irony nearly makes me smile, but I feel too drained even for that.

"Ben, I'm so sorry about everything that's happened between us. I hate myself for cheating on you. It was, like, a revenge thing."

"Sharon, don't. First of all, I deserved it."

"That's never an excuse, especially the way I did it. There's something you should know . . . Ben—"

"Stop! Don't say a word; I don't care. You know why? I hate myself for starting it all. I think I went through some kind of midlife crisis or something. You're the best woman in the world, and I did something horrible to you that you didn't deserve. OK, maybe you shouldn't have cheated to get me back, but what choice did I leave you? You weren't feeling loved or appreciated here; no wonder you sought it elsewhere. Who you sought it with means nothing, *nothing*."

"Oh, but Ben . . . "

"No, Shar, don't say anything. Look, I swear to God this is true, and I'm only going to say it once, so listen carefully. I've thought this completely through, and don't say a word when I tell you this, because after I say it, this conversation is over. I wouldn't care if you had slept with my *best friend*, and I mean it. All of that is over now, for both of us, and that's all there is to it. I mean that literally. Now, don't say anything. Just put your arms around me and lay down next to me until I go to sleep. I'm so tired. I'm so fucking tired . . . "

When I wake, it is dark outside. The clock on the night table tells me it is eight forty-five. The first thing I do is check my Nextel, but I haven't missed any calls from the crime lab.

I want to get up, but I am still exhausted. Normally I would be in great shape, rested and ready for work, but I cannot fathom the idea of going in tonight. I can't even get out of bed. Sharon comes in at nine thirty to wake me, but I still don't feel that I can even move, let alone go to work. It's like I haven't slept in days.

"Ben, you can't go to work like this. Why don't you call in?"

I'm not a sick time abuser like so many guys at work, but I don't feel capable of working tonight. I don't even put up an argument. I call in sick and have Sharon bring the kids in to see me.

They jump on me and frolic for a few minutes, and I force myself out of bed to read them stories. We do this in Leah's room. She is wearing a pink nightgown with little moons and stars on it, and is warmly enveloped in her Dora the Explorer sheets. LaMonjello is lying next to her. His skin is dark, his eyes impossibly black, and his hair, two inches long, is braided into tight cornrows. Sharon did that the other day after LaMonjello saw a singer with cornrows on TV. How she learned is beyond me. He's wearing a basketball jersey and boxer shorts.

For a moment, I see these kids through the eyes of a stranger, and the contrast between them is shocking. Then, I just see them as my kids, and I wonder at how we have come together as a family in so short a time.

Barely half a year ago, LaMonjello had almost no chance whatsoever of making it in this world. What an unimaginably bizarre and unpredictable set of circumstances it is that has changed all that for him.

They both fall asleep, and I carry LaMonjello back to his room. More than once we have woken to find him in Leah's bed in the morning.

Sharon is tired, and so am I. She sits with me for a few minutes while I catch the news at ten and have a leftover veal cutlet, and then we go to bed.

As we lay down, Sharon snuggles me close. "Ben, thanks for going to Andrea's. I know you didn't want to, and that it was a risk. I'm just so afraid she really did do it. What's next?"

"If the crime lab shows it's a match, the first thing I'm going to do is take it right to Lieutenant Scott. He's not going to want to believe it, and it's going to take a lot of convincing, but he won't be able to argue in the face of the evidence. Once he comes around, he'll want to meet with Mahoney. They'll call Andrea into the office and arrest her, I guess."

"What if they don't believe you?"

"They *can't* not believe me. I'll have the lab report and the DNA. They'll want to get another sample to test against the airbag on their own. Andrea will either allow it, or they'll get a search warrant and take it without her permission."

"Will you have to testify about your affair at her trial?"

"There's not going to be any trial. There's no way she's gonna go to trial. She'll plead to whatever they offer her, and it will all just fade away."

"Could they give her the death penalty?"

"Yeah. But like I said, they'll deal. She'll plead guilty without a trial in exchange for life in prison, and that will be it, I suppose."

"Make love to me, and let's go to sleep."

We do both. I pop awake at 2:30 a.m. feeling scared about the coming day. I don't know what I fear most—that the evidence will condemn Andrea or that it will exonerate her. When it's dark outside and you can't sleep, you question everything.

Is it crazy, this theory that Andrea killed Dolly? Do I still love her? Will Sharon ever sleep with Ray or anyone else again? Assailed by doubts and fears, I drop back into a fitful sleep.

My nightmare is a bad one. In it, Dolly is lying on an autopsy table. She has been flayed open, but there is no doctor around. I am there to collect evidence, but I cannot remember what kind of evidence I am supposed to collect. I know if I don't get it, I will blow the entire case.

I approach the table, and it begins to rain in the autopsy room. My only thought is to cover Dolly; the rain filling the open red cavity of her chest with pink water is too much of a violation. As I get to her, her eyes suddenly open impossibly wide, and she begins to sit up. That's when I scream and Sharon shakes me awake.

I am soaked with sweat, and I cling to my wife and cry like a small child.

When I next awaken, it is light outside, and Sharon is not in bed. I look at the clock and see that it is almost ten.

Still tired, I get out of bed. The kids have gone to school and Sharon is on the phone with her best friend. I check my Nextel, but there is no message from the lab.

I know there will be later today. God, I cannot wait for this day to be over.

Chapter 29

At noon, Sharon and I go out for lunch. I am no longer nervous. My fears and worries have been replaced by a sort of grim resignation. I cannot win. If the test comes back as a positive match, everybody loses. If it comes back as a negative match, whoever is now stalking me, whoever killed at least four people, is still out there, free to continue.

Sharon and I keep clear of the subject during our lunch at Red Lobster. Our waitress looks like a shorter, older, pregnant version of Andrea, and I wonder whether Sharon notices. If she does, she doesn't mention it.

Halfway through lunch, my Nextel buzzes against my hip. This will be it.

"Geller."

"Hi, Detective, this is Dixie from the crime lab."

Glad to know your name Dixie, now get to the fuckin' point. I struggle keep my tone pleasant and casual. "Hi, Dixie, thanks for calling."

"Those DNA samples you sent in, for the match to the Joseph case? They're all from the same person, and that person is a 99.99-percent match to the DNA we got from the airbag of the car that killed Joseph. So, if the guy, well, I guess the *woman*, who killed Joseph also killed Sergeant Sector, then you have your suspect. Ninety-nine-point-nine-nine is as high as we can go with a positive match."

"Christ."

"Is this good news, or bad?"

I take a moment to collect my thoughts, and give her a non-answer. "Both, and neither. Listen, Dixie, hang on to those results, and don't say anything to anyone. I'll be there to pick them up in half an hour."

"Oh, you don't have to worry about that. They're already on their way back to your police department."

It's an odd feeling when your heart stops in your chest, yet your arms and head pulse with an adrenalin dump that feels like electricity. "What do you mean?" I manage to ask. Sharon is now looking at me with a concerned expression on her face.

"Just after the results came back, not more than ten minutes ago, a couple of Stratton detectives showed up for another matter, so I gave it to them."

"Who were the detectives?" I ask, not so successful this time in keeping my voice neutral.

"One was Robert Joelle, and the other said she was your partner. Andrea something."

I can't say anything for maybe twenty seconds.

"Officer? Are you there?"

"Tell me what you said when you gave it to them," I snap at her.

"I didn't tell them anything, just like you said. I just thought that since they were going back to Strat—"

"Just tell me what you said!"

"I . . . I just said you dropped this evidence off for testing, and to take it directly to you. I didn't even tell them what it was for. It was all sealed up in an envelope and everything."

"OK. What time was that? Ten minutes ago?"

"Yeah, if that, even."

"God damn it, I told you . . . Oh, never mind. Thanks, Dixie. Bye."

I hang up before she has a chance to say anything. Sharon has already figured it out.

"Somehow or another, she was there and got the results, right?"

"Yeah. Come on, we're going to the police station."

Red Lobster is just around the corner from the police station, and we get there in about a minute. I never carry a weapon off duty any longer, but I wish I had one now. I don't fool myself into thinking there's a possibility that Andrea would assume the evidence was for some legitimate case. She even told the lab tech that she was my partner.

When we pull into the office, Sharon says, "Ben, I'm going to drop you off here, and go pick the kids up from school. I'll take them to Monica's house, then come pick you up. I'd just feel better about them not being where they should be right now, you know, just in case. Besides, they love going to Monica's."

"Honey, I don't think you have to worry about that. Well, maybe it's not a bad idea. Give me a call when you get to Monica's and I'll let your know if I need a ride or not."

"God, I can't believe it's true. She did do it; all of it. At least it will all be over now," she says, squeezing my hand and giving me a quick kiss as I get out. I tell her I love her and close the door. She heads off to the school while I go inside to figure out what to do now.

Everywhere I turn, it is business as usual. People say hi to me, and as I head to the Investigations Division, I pass a detective who mentions nothing.

I go right to Lieutenant Scott's office, but to my dismay, he is not there. I try to Nextel him, but all I get is the beeping noise that says his phone is either off, busy, or out of range.

Predictably, both Robert Joelle's and Andrea's desks are empty. There is a dry-erase status board on the wall outside Sergeant Mahoney's office. Next to Joelle's and Andrea's name the word "Lab" is written in Andrea's smooth script.

Mahoney is at his desk. I remember the last time I talked with him. He told me straight up he thought I was happy about Dolly's death because it got me off the IA hook I was on in the Andrew Joseph matter. And, he hinted he thought I might have had something to do with Joseph's death. Now, he was the only one to go to with this.

I walk into his office without knocking.

"What do *you* want?" he asks accusatorially.

"Listen, Phil. You may not like me anymore, and the feeling may be mutual, but I have something to tell you, and you have to listen."

"No, I don't. I'm busy; come back later." He seems to forget I'm here and goes back to the report on his desk. I hate it that I have to deal with him. God, I wish Scott were here.

"Phil, listen to me. Trust me, it's important."

"Get out, Ben. I'm busy."

Angrily, I sweep the contents of his desk onto the floor. "There. Now you're not busy any more. God damn it, Phil, this is important."

"Are you *trying* to get fired?"

"Shut up, Phil. Robert Joelle is in trouble."

This gets his attention, and he says, "What do you mean?"

I heave an incredibly huge sigh. Where to begin? "I want you to listen to this whole story before you tell me I'm crazy and to get the fuck out of your office. Joelle is in trouble because he's with Andrea, and Andrea knows she can't come back here. Ever."

"Get to the point, Ben. I'm listening."

His rage is gone, and I read in his body language that what I've just said is consistent with something he knows already. This encourages me to go on.

"Andrea and I were having an affair, and she started getting weird on me. Possessive, like we were married, or even more, like I was her property. This was going on for the past two years. She was working my "shadow" case, before we knew who Karch was."

Mahoney was all ears now, and it occurred to me that he might have had suspicions of his own about Andrea. "Well, I gave her some of my own thoughts on ways she could work the case. I told her to check places that sell Danner boots, because I felt that the shadow was mimicking me. I told her to go to sporting good stores, and look for large sales of .308 match-grade ammo, since he would have to put a lot of rounds downrange in training to take that shot on Delray Hicks. I told her to check gun clubs, because he'd have to be a member of one to get that much long-distance range time in, unless he had a place of his own with enough room to train out to a couple hundred yards.

"Anyway, I think she did those things, and figured out that the shadow was Karch. I think she did it on her own without telling anyone, and when she was sure it was him, she killed him."

I paused a moment, waiting for Mahoney's fury, but it didn't come. All he did was tell me to go on.

"I think she did it to protect me, and when she did, she came into the rest of the stolen money from Northwest Healing."

"Why?"

"In a matter of two days, my debts were all taken care of. I got a fictitious letter from a bank along with a counter check for ten thousand dollars, telling me an old investment matured. The adoption of LaMonjello, the little Hicks boy, just about broke me, but suddenly, that debt, my first mortgage, my second mortgage, and all my other bills were anonymously paid off, in cash. It was as if my life was becoming perfect. And then, I got into trouble over Joseph.

"You know the rest of that story. All the witnesses against me turned up dead except Buchanan, whose testimony was supportive. If he would have corroborated Joseph's story, he'd be dead now too. Because to help me, she killed them all. Karch, Dolly, Joseph, Chango . . . Dolly, Phil. She killed *Dolly*."

"Ben, you are seriously fucked up, you know that, don't you? But I'm gonna humor you a moment longer. For now, let's just assume it's all true. Why would Joelle be in trouble?"

"I ended my affair with Andrea, and she got really dark on me. She made innuendos that support my theory. So much so that I practically *knew* it was true. So, the other night on the way home from jail, I stopped by her place in Vancouver. I pretended that I wanted to renew the affair. While I was there, I went into her bathroom and collected evidence. DNA evidence. I got hair from her brush, a used tampon from the trash, and a pair of her underwear from the dirty laundry. I took it to the crime lab to match against the DNA from the car that killed Joseph. I told the stupid lab tech to call me directly the moment the results came in. Well, she just called. Ninety-nine-point-nine-nine percent match. Andrea was driving the car that killed Joseph."

Mahoney got up, stepped outside his office and looked at the status board. "But when Robert and Andrea got to the lab, your lab tech gave the results to Andrea, not knowing she was the suspect," he finished for me.

"Yeah."

"I sent them down there with evidence from a rape that happened last night on graveyards," he mused. "How much time since they picked up the evidence?"

"Twenty minutes, half hour tops. You believe me, don't you?"

"Yes. I was starting to suspect her, not for *murder* for Christ's sake, but for hiding her actions into the Karch investigation. I've discovered that she knew his identity two days before his murder, but didn't say anything to anyone. I started suspecting her of other things too, and people have been coming to me with her personality changes. Asking what the hell's going on."

"What do we do?"

"I'll try calling them in on something else."

Mahoney dials Joelle's Nextel direct number, and gets an immediate connection. "Robert, you there?"

There is no response.

"Robert? Answer up, your wife called. There's some kind of problem at home. Answer up, Robert. You there?"

Silence. Next he dials Andrea's.

"Andrea? You there?"

No response. "Andrea, Robert's Nextel is dead. I need to talk to him, some problem at home. Answer up."

No response.

Mahoney picks up a radio and depresses the transmit key. "Sixty-one-oh-nine, can I have either sixty-one-fifty-one or sixty-one-oh-five on detective's tac one please?"

"Sixty-one-fifty-one or sixty-one-oh-five, go to detective's tac one for the sergeant," the dispatcher replies laconically.

Silence.

"Sixty-one-fifty-one? Sixty-one-oh-five? Detective's tac one." After another pause, she says, "Sixty-one-oh-nine, there's no response."

"Copy." He puts the radio down and says, "Fuck!" He leans out of the office toward the detective secretary. "Becky, what car does Robert Joelle have?"

It takes her a minute to find it, and she says, "Two-fourteen, the blue Buick."

"Find me the reg info on that car, now."

Without blinking an eye, she starts digging through papers in a file cabinet. "God, the shit is gonna hit the fan now," he says.

"What are you going to do?"

"Get a statewide BOLO for this car to be sent via MDC only. The Buick doesn't have an MDC. I'll have to name Andrea, and say that she's an armed and dangerous on-duty police detective who is wanted for murder, and that Joelle may be a kidnap victim. Christ, I'd better go right to the chief with this. Come on, Ben, you're going to tell your story to Moody."

He grabs his radio and we head down the hall toward Chief Moody's office at a fast clip.

We never make it.

A flood of officers comes stampeding out of the report room, nearly knocking us down. They hit the back door, and immediately we hear sirens as a wave of police cars takes off out of the lot.

Mahoney turns on the radio, jacking the volume level up.

"Copy, shots fired! SWAT is being activated. All units clear and respond Code 3 to the active shooter at Poway Valley Elementary School! Multiple callers say at least one adult and one student are down."

I close my eyes and lean on the wall for support. Poway Valley is where Leah and LaMonjello go. Where Sharon just went to pick them up.

Chapter 30

Mahoney is driving Code 3 to the school, and I am beside myself in the passenger seat. I can only half concentrate on the radio chatter about students in a panic and reports of people down inside the building.

It requires a conscious effort for me to stay in the here-and-now, to keep my mind from regressing back to when Bob Slater had kidnapped Sharon and Leah, and reliving the feeling of doom that overcame me then.

I did not think I would see them alive again. And here I am one more time, right back in the same predicament. Only this time, it is not because I solved a puzzle that I am here; it is because I was too weak and shallow to overcome my lust for a younger woman. And, it would seem that I couldn't have chosen a crazier woman.

Officers are arriving, and from the radio traffic, it sounds like pure pandemonium at the school.

"One-two-one, on scene, there are kids running around everywhere!"

"One-forty-one, I got a teacher telling me there's a class being held hostage, I'm trying for more!"

"One-six-one, I'm being flagged down on the southwest side of the building. Stand by . . ."

We are southbound on Crane approaching Poway Valley; the school is about a mile east of that intersection. Mahoney kills the siren and takes the corner wide. A minivan full of crying children escaping the school swerves to avoid our fishtailing police car, and hits a pickup truck. Mahoney taps the brakes, but I yell, "Forget them; just get me to the school!" He floors it and a moment later, we round a bend and the school comes into sight.

Pandemonium is a good word. There are literally hundreds of kids running around in a blind panic. Adults, both teachers and neighbors, are chasing them down and corralling them in a large yard just east of the building.

"One-six-one, I have the principal on the south lawn. She's saying the shooter is a female and is holed up in a kindergarten class on the west side, near the office. Safe approach from the east on Poway Valley!" At the same time as this transmission is broadcast, my pager goes off.

"Over there, on the grass," I shout, pointing to the school's front yard. Carlos Vega is standing on the lawn next to a crying female whom I recognize as Penny Logan, the principal. Mahoney taps the siren, scattering children, and drives right up on the lawn. He grabs the radio, finds a clear spot in the near-constant string of mostly useless transmissions, and says, "Forty-one-oh-one, let's get a temporary command post set up in the southeast corner parking lot. All officers not in a perimeter position meet there."

"Copy, temporary command post, southeast parking lot," echoes the dispatcher.

I get out of the car, pulling my Nextel from my belt and looking at the message. It is the active shooter SWAT callout. Deep in the back of my mind, I had been hoping it was Sharon telling me she and the children were fine. I don't expect to get such a page.

As I approach the confusion on the schoolyard, the sound of crying and screaming children reminds me of the scene in *Titanic* where the people are still alive in the water after the ship goes down. If I wasn't in a blind panic before, I am now. My children are here somewhere. My wife is here somewhere. Why couldn't I have come to the school with her?

I add my own panicked voice to cacophony. "Sharon! Leah! LaMonjello!" I am running around now, looking at the faces of individual kids, searching out my own. I am no longer able to hear the radio. Instinctively, I head for the open doors of the building when I am grabbed from behind. My arm is roughly twisted, and when I fight, enough pressure is applied to bring me to my toes.

"Ben! Stop!"

It is one of the defensive tactics instructors, and she has me in a pain-compliance come-along hold.

"Colleen, my kids . . ."

"We're doing everything we can, Ben. Come on, they're asking for you back at the command post." Gently now, she leads me back to the command post, where Mahoney is talking with Vince Capelko on a tactical net.

"Vince, this is Phil. Listen, I have good information on your active shooter suspect. Don't question it, just listen to me."

"OK, Phil, just go ahead."

"Your shooter is Andrea Fellotino. She is on duty, armed, and probably has her radio with her. As of forty-five minutes ago she's wanted for the deaths of Reginald Karch, Dolly Sector, Andrew Joseph and Enrique Payala Aceves. She was last seen with Robert Joelle, who is now officially missing and not answering up. Ben Geller's wife Sharon is also probably in there. She went to get their two kids, and we think Andrea went there to . . . Uh, for the same kids, with uh, unknown, but nefarious, intentions."

By this time, radio etiquette was a thing of the past. "Are you shitting me?"

"No, God damn it. It's Andrea, and she's probably listening to us right now!"

"Jesus Christ. OK, get the word out to anyone who's not eavesdropping. Are you in charge out there?"

"Yeah, it would appear so."

"OK, well, you'd better think twice about sending in an active shooter team, Phil. She knows how all that works and like you say, she's probably listening to us now."

"Good point."

"Is this thing still contained in a room on the west side?"

"As best as we can figure, yes."

"OK. Put a team together, but don't have them try to get into the hostage room. Have 'em establish a foothold and do any person-down rescues they can, but have them hold *outside* the hostage room door."

"OK, got it. What's your ETA?"

"The van should be arriving in about ten or so minutes. As soon as you see anyone from HNT, have them try to get ahold of her. Unless . . . Andrea? Are you on this side?"

There was a brief moment of radio silence, and then, "You're goddamn right I am." I squeeze my eyes shut and try not to panic at the ice in her voice. "Now listen carefully, everyone. The only cop I want to see coming through my door is Ben Geller. Anyone else, and there will be dead kids. I'm sorry it's come down to this, but I hope you don't underestimate me. Ben obviously did."

There was a moment's pause, then Mahoney voice.

"OK, Andrea, whatever you say, but think twice about this. It's not too early to call it quits with minimal damage."

There was no response, and I tried to grab the radio from his hand. "Let me talk to her! Phil, I can talk her out!"

He slaps my hands away, and tries a different tack. "Andrea, do you need medics in there? Or is there anything we can do for you? Andrea? Andrea, answer up, OK?"

"Dispatch to sixty-one-oh-nine, I show her radio switched off."

Mrs. Logan sees me and recognizes me. "Ben," she says, coming to me and giving me a hug. "Oh my God, I am so sorry," she babbles. "This woman, she came here looking for your kids. She asked for them by name, and said she was a police officer. She showed me Stratton PD identification. It looked real enough, but how could I know? She wasn't mentioned on your emergency contact list. I didn't know what to do, and I told her what classrooms they were in, but told her I'd have to call either you or Sharon before she could go there. And then, she just left. I tried stopping her, but she just headed out and went to Leah's room, so I called the police. And then your wife, Sharon, she came in right after that. I told her what was happening, about that lady, and she ran down to the classroom. I . . . I sent Marty Spaulding—he's the gym teacher—down there, and then went to call the police, and that's when we heard the gunshots. It was down the main hallway, where the second, third, and fourth grade classrooms are. And, that's when everyone came running out. People were screaming and . . . "

"My wife? The kids?"

"I don't know, Ben, nobody knows! Look at all the children! Oh God . . . Nobody knows anything. We're trying to account for all of them now, but everyone's saying that there was one, a little girl, who was hurt. And an adult, too. They were shot, but nobody knows anything! Lots of people are still missing! I haven't seen them! Ben, I . . . "

She's obviously fighting for control, but I'm the wrong person to help her with that. It's hard enough for me as it is. I turn away from her and begin heading to the lot where they are corralling the children.

In the back of my head, I hear Capelko saying, "Ben, I'll send someone over there. HNT is on the way. I want you to wait here, then join up with them when they get here. You got it?"

"Huh? Yeah, Vince . . . Sharon, and the children—"

"I'll send someone over there to look for them," he assures me. "Right now, I want you to be available to me, understand?"

They want me out of the way. That much I understand. Mahoney immediately is caught up in a conversation with Sergeant Vanderkeeffe, the day shift patrol sergeant. Officers responding to his call to gather at the south lawn are arriving, and I join up with them.

There is a momentary lull in the action, and everyone is talking about Andrea. The consensus sounds like disbelief; but, as one officer pointed out, you can't argue with the fact that Andrea herself confirmed it on the air.

I am spotted, and the focus immediately turns to me.

"What's going on, Ben?"

"Mahoney said Andrea came after your kids!"

"We'll find them, Ben; it's all gonna turn out OK."

They are swarming me so intently I don't really have a chance to answer anyone. Vanderkeeffe, who has been with Stratton PD for thirty-one years and is the department's most senior officer, sees us and immediately starts issuing orders.

"Everybody shut the hell up and listen! Carlos, pick four guys and form an entry team," he says to Vega, the only other SWAT officer here. "Not you, Ben. HNT will be here shortly, and you're to meet with them the moment they get here. The rest of you, fan out along the east and west sides of the building and head south. Gather every kid you find and take 'em over there to that yard. Teachers will be there taking roll, and we'll give kids back to the parents at the intersection of Airy Creek and Poway Valley. Any witnesses who can add anything at all, keep somewhere else.

"Obviously, be careful around the west side. The room she's in faces the playground, and they're saying the blinds are all down in her classroom. Try to stay in a position of cover and call the kids on the west side over to you if you can, but if not, go out there and grab 'em. And I don't want to hear any whining about exposing yourself to the windows. I'd rather she shoot you than a bunch of little kids while we stand around in a position of cover with our thumbs up our asses. This is what they pay you the big bucks for. Now get the hell out of here!"

I have only been here maybe three to five minutes, and there is still no word about Sharon and the kids. For lack of anything better to do until HNT gets here, I join a group of officers sweeping the east side of the school, and begin herding crying children toward the processing area. Anyone who looks near Leah or LaMonjello's age, I question, but all I get is blank looks and tears.

"Have you seen my daughter, Leah Geller?"

"Have you seen a little black boy, kindergarten age?"

I shepherd a group of five blank-faced children to the processing area and give up. Fighting the temptation to enter the building, or to walk around to the west side and start knocking on the windows, I instead make my way back to the command post.

Vega and his makeshift team are positioned at the west doors of the school, preparing for their first foray into the building. Capelko is in contact with the van, which is en route and only a few minutes out. American Medical Response ambulances have begun arriving and are standing by.

A large, dark blue truck sporting numerous antennae pulls up to the school and drives up to the command post. It is the hostage negotiating team's van, and Bo Pinter, the lead negotiator, steps out. Taking a quick look around, he spots me and calls me to the van.

"Ben, I was told to look you up. Come on in. We're gonna be pretty busy here getting things set up, but while we do that, I want you to talk with Sam Pruitt. Tell him everything you can think of regarding Andrea. *Everything*, OK? I know it's not going to be easy, but face it, everyone knows you guys were having an affair, so *talk* to him about it. OK?"

"Don't worry, Bo. My wife and kids are in there somewhere."

"All right then."

He steps out and I go in. The interior of the truck consists of two separate rooms, each with a bevy of computer monitors and sophisticated electronic gadgetry. Sam Pruitt, the team's intelligence officer, is waiting for me.

"Ben," Pruitt says, "Man, let me tell you how sorry I am that all this crap is going on. I would have never thought Andrea could pull something like this. Anyway, I'm going to need you to tell me everything you can about your relationship with her. This thing is obviously connected with you and your wife and kids. I mean, it looks like she's actually *targeting* them."

"She is."

"Why?"

"In her mind, she and I are supposed to be together. She thinks that if it wasn't for Sharon, my wife, we'd be a couple."

"Ben, sorry, but I gotta get into this. Pretty much everyone thinks you two were sleeping together. I'm gonna need you to—"

"Don't worry about it, Sam," I interrupt him. "I've got nothing to hide. Sharon and I have made our peace. She knows everything."

Sam pauses for the briefest moment. In it, I could see that he wanted to tell me something, and it occurs to me that he knows about the affair between Sharon and Ray Schmeer. Do I have *any* dirty laundry that hasn't been aired in front of this Wisteria Lane of a department?

He skips it and says, "OK. Good. Now, tell me."

I give him a barebones rundown of my history with Andrea, and the changes that have come over her, beginning with her release from Northwest Healing. As I tell him the story, I can't imagine how I couldn't have seen the bell curve of her personality changes as the shadow case impacted my life. It is now clear to me, given the ups and downs of our relationship and the impact the shadow case had on me and my family, that the totality of the circumstances sent her over the edge. In recalling it all, I wonder at how I *hadn't* seen from the beginning that it was Andrea that killed Karch. And that opens the doors to the guilt. If I had cared more about my own family than my own selfish desires . . . If I could have been strong enough to end it when I knew I should . . . If I had been savvy enough to recognize the personality changes in Andrea . . .

If. If any of those things had happened, Dolly would be alive today. There wouldn't be an active shooter incident at school. My family would be safe.

As I am talking, I see a sniper/observer team heading off between two houses west of the school, where they will no doubt have their choice of several good sniper positions offering excellent views of the classroom windows.

Suddenly, for the first time, the realization hits me that it will be Andrea in their scopes. *Andrea.* There is no way I could possibly work this call-out, even if my family wasn't in there. I could shoot a bad guy; that much I had already proven. But Andrea? No way.

Jesus . . . Whether it is entry, snipers or inner perimeter, *somebody's* going to take a shot today. Someone who was with Andrea at morning roll call a few hours ago.

No. Stratton SWAT cannot be handling this.

Interrupting my story to Pruitt, I step out of the van and look around. Stratton cops are everywhere, but not Stratton SWAT. It is the Portland SWAT van that is parked down the street, and it was a Portland sniper/observer team I had seen going between the houses. Our guys were first responders, but they are not handling the callout. Clearly, though, it will be Stratton on the phone, which makes sense to me.

Though the scene is still mass confusion, there appears to be some order to it now. Police officers are now stationed at the door to the building, and adults and children are still coming out in groups of two or three. It would seem that I stepped out at the right time, because as I watch, one such group, consisting of a couple civilian adults and several children looking shell-shocked, comes out. Watching them, I sit down on the ground and begin crying.

One of the adults is Sharon, and one of the children is Leah.

Chapter 31

A smattering of applause breaks out from the HNT team and those officers around us as Sharon, Leah and I embrace one another in tears of happiness. After allowing us a few moments without interruption, Pruitt says, "I hate to break this up, but let's take it in the van, OK? We need to talk with you guys, find out what's going on inside."

All I can do is nod. Sharon is laughing and crying at the same time. Leah is simply crying and has welded herself to me, her arms squeezing my neck and her legs locked around my waist. Both appear to be completely uninjured. Physically, at least.

I give Sharon a questioning look, and her tears change from joy to sorrow. "LeMonjello?" I ask hesitantly.

"I don't know, Ben, I just don't know."

We go into the van, where everyone tries not to look at us. Apart from the initial radio contact with Andrea, no one has been able to reach room number two, the kindergarten room where she has apparently decided to make her last stand.

"The most important thing we have to do right now is find out from you anything pertinent that we'll be able to use to help the rest of those kids in there. I promise you we'll try to get you guys out of here as soon as possible, OK?" Pinter says.

"I understand," Sharon replies, clamping onto my hand with surprising strength.

"OK, well, what can you tell us? Describe what happened for us in as much detail as you can, all right?"

"She killed Mr. Spaulding! I saw him, and he was dead!" Leah sobs.

Sharon puts her face in Leah's, and says, "Don't think about that, OK baby? Mommy and Daddy need to talk to the officers, and tell them what we know about that lady so they can arrest her and keep everyone else safe."

"You don't have to pretend, Mom," she spits. "Dad and the SWAT team are going to kill her. I hope they do! I hope they kill her before she hurts LaMonjello!"

"Oh sweetie, don't say that. Try not to think about that. Everything's going to be OK, I promise. LaMonjello's going to be just fine. We'll all be together, safe at home, later tonight. I just know it."

"Do you promise?"

"Yes, I promise," she says.

I want to believe her, but I'm not so sure. Sharon holds Leah's face in her hands and says, "Now, one of these officers is going to get you out of here for a while until all this is over. Is that all right with you, baby?"

"I guess. Will I see you at home tonight?"

"Of course."

"And you'll be there too, right Daddy?"

"You know I will baby, and like Mommy said, LaMonjello, too," I say with a desperation I hope sounds more reassuring than it feels.

"Do *you* promise?"

"I promise," I say, praying that it was true.

"OK then."

Someone finds Leah's teacher, who agrees to take her for the duration. After another family hug, they leave, and Sharon starts her story.

"I came here to pick up my children," she begins without preamble. "Because Ben figured out that Andrea was off her rocker, and had killed Dolly and everyone else who was causing him problems. She was stalking him because . . . because she loves him in some kind of weird, twisted way. Anyway, she must have come into all of the money from Northwest Healing after she killed Reginald Karch, because she paid off all our debts with it. She was trying to fix all of Ben's problems, so she could have him to herself, I guess. Anyway, once Ben discovered that Andrea figured out that he was on to her, it only seemed reasonable that she might see me or my children as another one of Ben's problems that needed to be eliminated. So I came here to take them where she couldn't find them.

"Apparently, Andrea got here just before I did. The principal told me that a female Stratton cop was here trying to get to my kids, but they weren't going to release them to her. She said that Andrea had gone off looking for the kids, but she had walked right past LaMonjello's room. The gym teacher had already gone off looking for her. I ran down to Leah's room, but she hadn't been there. The door was closed, and Mrs. Rody was reading to the class.

"I ran in and closed the door. I grabbed Leah, and we started to head out, but when I opened the door, Andrea was there. She pulled out her gun and pointed it at Leah, but then a man—the gym teacher—came up and tackled her from behind.

"I grabbed Leah and ran, and that's when I heard the first gunshot. Everyone in the classroom started screaming, and I turned around to have a look. Mrs. Rody had closed the door, and now the window was shattered, so I knew the shot had gone into the room. Andrea was still fighting with the gym teacher for control of the gun, and it went off again. There was a lot of blood, and I couldn't tell who was hit, Andrea or the teacher. I pushed Leah into the closet, and we buried ourselves under all the mops and stuff. Nothing happened for a long time, and then Carlos and the others came and rescued us."

"Did you have any conversation or any kind of interaction with Andrea at all?"

"No, there wasn't any time. As soon as she saw us, she just pulled the gun out and pointed it at Leah; then she got tackled from behind. How is that gym teacher? Was he killed?"

I am curious about this myself, since I have heard nothing of casualties as of yet.

Capelko answered. "I'm afraid he didn't make it," was all he said.

"Any kids?" I ask hesitantly. Please let there be none.

Capelko looks around as if to see who might be listening, then says, "Yeah, a little girl got shot in the stomach with that first shot. Medics are with her now at the dead end of Airy Creek, which is what we're using as the LifeFlight landing zone. The chopper's on the way to pick her up."

"Do you have a name?" I ask.

"No, not yet."

Pruitt pumps Sharon and me for more information, and I answer as best I can, but my mind is on LaMonjello, holed up in the kindergarten room with Andrea. One thing's for sure; that boy isn't stupid. By now, he must know exactly why she is there. The thought of him staring down the wrong end of her pistol makes me wish I were staring at her from the right end of my .308. I can't imagine what might have snapped in her mind to bring all this on, and I can't help but wonder how much I had to do with it. Again, I wonder why I didn't see all this coming somehow, and if I had, whether I might have been able to do something to prevent it.

To say that LaMonjello is in grave danger is a serious understatement. Andrea is up to—what? Her fifth kill? I tick them off in my mind. Karch. Chango. Dolly. Joseph. And now, the gym teacher.

Andrea knows there's no way she's going to walk out of that room and see the light of day ever again. She'll be lucky if she can plead her way into a sentence of life without the possibility of parole. She's already got plenty of special circumstances that makes hers a capital case.

Suddenly, I recall something that fills me with dread. I remember a conversation Andrea and I had one night about a year ago. We'd just finished making love, and were talking about an Internal Affairs investigation the Major Crimes Team had done into a crooked cop in Portland. She'd interviewed the officer after his arrest for stealing property and drugs from the evidence room, and selling them from his patrol car.

It was a strange topic for the afterglow of lovemaking, but we often talked about bizarre things at such times. It was a follow-up interview conducted in jail, a month after the arrest. Andrea said he was like a caged animal, and he started crying when talking to her about it. The officer's life was in jeopardy in there, and he had been placed in isolation. He told her it was much worse than he'd ever imagined on the inside, and this was still just county jail. The officer was looking at a minimum of two years in the pen, and didn't think he'd be able to hack it.

Andrea told me quite seriously that she would rather die than ever go to prison, and I believed her. When I think about the way she said it, it was almost as if she knew she would face such a situation someday.

This brought out recollections of other pertinent conversations we had. Andrea is a staunch atheist, and therefore has no fear of death or of going to hell. We talked a *lot* about that after her rescue of Dan Hollister, in which she won the departmental Medal of Valor. Andrea had thought she was going to die, especially when she got hit during the exchange of gunfire. And then, after Dan died, we discussed it again.

"Sam," I say suddenly to the negotiator, "I just thought of something you need to know." I tell him about Andrea's statement that she would rather die than go to prison, and Pruitt makes sure Bo Pinter comes to hear what I have to say. I tell them about her lack of belief in any form of afterlife or God, and therefore, she has no moral compass by which to steer her life, other than that which she finds within herself.

I know Sharon finds this difficult to hear, because she knows the information I have must have come from pillow talk. Still, classy lady that she is, she grabs my hand as I impart it, and gives me three quick successive squeezes. This is our little code for "I love you." I return them without breaking the rhythm of my story.

The hostage negotiators find this information to be significant, and in the minutes before Capelko instructs them to attempt contact with Andrea, they get together to discuss strategy.

"What can we use as a positive?" asks Dick Meyers, one of the negotiators.

"Not a hell of a lot," answers Pinter. "You all know Andrea; she's not going to buy a damn thing we have to say. You can't tell a cop who has committed multiple capital offenses that she should stop before she does something *really* serious."

"How about family repercussions?"

Again, they turn to me.

"Ben?"

It is embarrassing to know so much. The way they question me, and the speed with which I reply, makes it seem as if I were her husband, and it is painfully obvious that we were lovers.

"Her father died when she was young, and her mother lives with a guy she can't stand. In, like, Detroit or Chicago, or somewhere around there. She does have a younger brother, though; he's in college back east somewhere. He wants to be a cop, and they're pretty close."

"You know his name?"

"She calls him Skip, but I don't know his real name."

Pinter turns to Pruitt and says, "Sam?"

Pruitt, who is reaching for a phone, says, "I'm on it."

Another negotiator enters the van with a list of all the children the school believes are holed up in the kindergarten class. Included on his list are four kids who don't belong in that class, but who are still missing. I take a look at the list, and of course, LaMonjello is on it.

I had been harboring a secret hope that LaMonjello's predilection for smelling trouble may have warned him to get away before all this started, but they are now almost done gathering stray students, and everyone else has been accounted for. Other than the missing four, all of those not accounted for belong in LaMonjello's class.

One of the negotiators is a liaison officer between the tactical team and HNT, and he is monitoring the deployment of Portland SWAT. "They're just about in place," he said. "They're going to want us to make contact any minute."

Pinter said, "Dick, grab the bullhorn and test it out. Since there's no phone in the kindergarten room, we're going to try her on the radio first. If we can't get her there, then I'm going to have you move into the building and loudhail her. If we need you, all you'll do is try to make contact and tell her we'll call her on her Nextel."

"Probably the only positive we're going to have with her is her intelligence," Pinter says. "I'm going to go at her as an equal; straight up from the first, with no attempts to bullshit her. What do you guys think?"

Before the rest of the negotiators can answer, I say, "You're right. If you talk down to her, you'll lose her. Don't do any HNT bullshit with her. Talk to her as if she knows every one of your tricks, because even if she doesn't, she'd recognize them, and then she'll be done."

"Thanks, Ben. I thought as much."

Just then, someone tries the door, but it is locked.

"Goddamn it, open the door," yells Vince Capelko. Someone lets him in, and he says, "OK, the Portland SWAT commander says they're ready for you to make contact."

Pinter calls the dispatching center. When he hangs up, he says, "They say she turned her radio on fifteen minutes ago, and has been switching between SWAT, the main net, and tac one ever since. She's on the main net now."

Pinter heaves a huge sigh, closes his eyes, and just sits there for a moment. The he picks up a radio and hits the transmit button.

Chapter 32

"HNT One, can I have forty-one-oh-five on tac one?"

Without hesitation, Andrea's voice comes over sounding completely unstressed.

"Forty-one-oh-five, copy." If I didn't know what was going on, I'd think this conversation was nothing more than perfectly normal radio traffic.

Pinter switches frequencies, and says, "Andrea, it's Bo. You OK in there?"

"Yeah, I'm fine. Listen, Bo, I'm sorry this thing's fallen in your lap."

"Hey, don't worry. Gets me off patrol. I'd rather talk to you than take all that day shift paper. Andrea, is everyone in there OK? I mean, do you guys need, like, medics or anything?"

"No, everyone's OK."

"OK then. You got your Nextel on you?"

"Yeah."

"How's your battery?"

"About half."

"OK, I'm gonna give you a call on that. There're too many eavesdroppers over here."

"OK. And, to all the eavesdroppers, I just want to say I'm sorry about all of this. I've really loved working with you all."

"OK. I want you to know everyone's pulling for you, Andrea. You got a lot of good friends out here. Go ahead and turn off your radio, and I'll call your Nextel."

"OK."

I'm appalled at how *normal* she sounds. Depressed, maybe resigned even, but normal. I guess I thought she would sound like a raving lunatic or something. It just seems so incongruous for her to sound like plain old Andrea.

There's a pang of emotion somewhere deep under the surface inside me. I once loved her. But I remind myself of how LaMonjello must be feeling now, and the pang of regret over Andrea instantly turns to rage.

Pinter and the other negotiators have a brief discussion of tactics. They refer to me as a "TPI," which I know to mean a third party intermediary. It is decided that the phones will be kept on speaker so everyone can listen to the negotiations, and I get the feeling from them that this is somewhat unusual. But, why not? This is an unusual case.

Normally, Pinter's secondary negotiator, a child abuse investigator from the sheriff's department, is the only other person who listens in on both sides of the conversation. I can't recall her name, but I do remember a mutual dislike, although for the life of me I don't remember why. Besides filtering everything that goes to the primary negotiator, one of her jobs as secondary is to add her input by making written suggestions and observations, which she passes to him in the form of handwritten sticky notes.

"Just keep doing what you're doing, Bo," she says. "She seems to want to talk like this is some kind of normal day. I say go with it—whatever she wants."

"Yeah, that's the plan so far. OK, I'm calling," Pinter says, dialing the keypad of a phone unit set in a complex, heavy box with a great deal of switches and knobs on it. I know this to be the base unit of the throw phone, but it is obviously much more than that as well. He is speaking over a large headset with a hand control and a mouthpiece that reminds me of the type used by aircraft pilots.

The phone rings, and Andrea answers it immediately.

"Hello?"

"Hey, Andrea."

"Listen, Bo, I just want to say I didn't want any of this to go down like it this. I really am sorry. I swear to God I didn't want any gunshots or panic here today. I know I shot that guy who attacked me. I think he's a teacher or something. Is he . . . Is he going to be OK?"

The coach writes furiously on the top sheet of a pad of sticky notes, rips it off, and hands it to Pinter. He glances at it and nods. "Yeah, the guy's a teacher. Medics took him away, so he's still alive at least. That's all I know."

"There were two shots. Did I hit anyone else?"

The coach writes again, and this time, I see her note says, 'lie.' Pinter, however, shakes his head and says, "Yeah, a little girl. I'm told she's gonna make it, though."

"Oh my God. Oh shit. Bo, I swear to God I don't want any kids hurt. It's important that you believe me about this."

"Of course I do. Hell, we've known each other for what, three years? I know you didn't mean for anyone to get hurt."

"Thanks, Bo."

"Andrea, the only thing is, I'm just flat-out baffled by this whole thing. I mean, none of us know very much about how this could have happened."

"Come on, Bo, don't snow me. You know a hell of a lot more than you're going to tell me."

"Listen, Andrea. The only thing I know for sure is that you're not stupid. I'm not going to bullshit you or play you like some shitbag like we usually deal with. I mean, this is all tragic, but I *know* you. You're one of *us*, not them. And if it's OK with you, I'd like that to be how we treat one another. Does that work for you?"

"Thanks, Bo. I appreciate that. But I think that 'one of us' status may have ended a little while ago. I mean, once four o'clock comes around, I doubt the department'll be paying me OT. What do you think?"

"Let me ask you this, Andrea. Are we still going to be here at four?"

"I don't know, Bo, I just don't know. I know you're not supposed to let me have any control and all that, but let me ask *you* something. What did they tell you? About me, and all of this, and everything?"

Pinter looks at the coach, who nods her head and indicates for him to go with it. She writes another note, then rips it from the pad, and he reads it as he answers her.

"Actually, I don't mind telling you. They said you figured out who Ben's shadow was, and killed him."

"What else?"

"That you shot Dolly, because she was going to get Ben fired." Pinter glances at me while he says this.

Pruitt comes up to me and whispers in my ear, "Hey Ben, I'm going to ask you to step out, but hang around for us, OK?"

I look him in the eye and say, "Sorry, Sam, but nope. I'm staying in here, and I'm going to listen to everything. Think of it this way. I might be able to tell you if she's lying about something. I might be able to help, and I won't be a problem. Just let me stay, OK?"

Capelko gives him a nod, much to my relief, and he says, "OK, but it really is better for your wife to leave. We can't have civilians in here, and she really should be with your daughter."

Sharon whispers that she was going to go out and find Leah anyway, and she gives me a kiss and quietly leaves. I am somewhat relieved, since I can see where the conversation with Andrea is about to go.

Andrea is saying to Pinter, "Well, they're right, I did shoot Dolly. I'm sorry for her family and all that, and for the heartache I've caused by it, but you have to understand two things. One, you don't turn on your brother officers. You just don't. End of story. And two, Ben didn't deserve to be fucked over for that scrote Joseph anyway. Pardon my French. He didn't do anything wrong. Look, Bo, let me level with you. Save you a whole lot of time, and from doing all your active listening HNT bullshit, OK? Like you said earlier, I'm not stupid. I know I'm not going to walk out of this room. I'm going to be carried out. I know this, and I think you do too. And everyone else who's monitoring your negotiations."

"Andrea, hang on. Nothing's written in concrete, and it ain't over 'til it's over. Nobody knows how—"

"You hang on, Bo. I'm going to die today. Real soon, in fact. So don't try to snow me, OK? That's already a given, so I don't mind telling you anything and everything, because I want the record to be straight before I check out."

"Andrea, don't talk like that. Let's wait to see how it ends before we make up our minds. Can we agree to that?"

"Whatever, Bo. Your version of what happened is pretty accurate, I'll give you that. But like Paul Harvey says, 'And now, the *rest* of the story.' Here goes—I love Ben. Period. End of story. We're supposed to be together. We were *always* supposed to have been together. The real reason I shot Dolly was because I love Ben. I got over thirteen million dollars in cash when I killed Karch, and I intended to use that money to make a life for Ben and me. I know he's there somewhere, and that you can have someone talk to him, so, ask him yourself.

"We were in love. We wanted to make a life together. But he already had a family, which he was willing to give up for me. We could have worked out the details with his daughter, but taking on LaMonjello really complicated things. Check this out with Ben; He'll tell you."

As she is saying this, another negotiator is busy writing on the overhead marker board which is starting to get covered with information. "Suicidal" and "Delusional" are the two newest entries. The coach shuffles through a series of laminated cheat sheets for abnormal psychological profiles, and pulls out the ones labeled "Suicidal" and "Narcissistic Personality." They are covered with personality indicators, and Pinter flips them over to glance at the reverse side, which lists suggested negotiating strategies for each. I am impressed at the amount of reference materials at hand for these guys. I have to admit that my respect level for what they do is changing. I had always just assumed they were geeks who like to talk on the phone. Now, I realize that LaMonjello's life is in their hands, and I silently send them my apologies and support.

"We can go over all that with Ben, and probably will, but first, I have to ask you about something else."

"Go ahead, Bo. I really do want to help."

"Thank you; I believe you. Anyway, we're pretty concerned about Robert Joelle. He was with you at the crime lab. Where can we find him? Is he OK?"

"He's fine. He's cuffed up in the trunk of my car, which is parked a couple streets over, on Fifth and Acacia. I was going to release him after I had gotten Ben's kids out of school."

The way that rolls off her tongue chills me to the bone. *After I had gotten Ben's kids out of school.* What then?

There is a flurry of activity as the SWAT liaison officer talks into a radio. Officers are already on their way to Andrea's car by the time Pinter starts talking again.

"OK, thanks," Pinter is saying. "Let's do this. Why don't you give me a second to tell Capelko where he is, and that way they can send someone over to get him, OK? Can I call you back in about five minutes?"

"I'm not going anywhere, Bo."

"OK. And Andrea?"

"Yeah?"

"I just wanted to tell you thanks. And that even after you come out of there, we all think you're a good cop. And on a personal note, I've always liked you. Everyone does."

"Thanks, Bo. Talk to you soon."

"Before we hang up, I want you to promise me something, OK? Promise me not to harm anyone, yourself included, all right? Can you promise me that?"

"Of course. Call me back in a few minutes."

The line goes dead, and Pinter presses a button on the cord of his headset to disconnect.

In the middle of debriefing the first conversation, which everyone agreed had gone very well, Pruitt gets back to us with the info that Joelle has been found alive and well in the trunk of Andrea's car wearing his own handcuffs. Andrea had taken his gun and radio, and detectives are interviewing him now. In the meantime, Pinter, his female coach, and several other members of HNT are deep into discussions about the negotiations.

"About the only hook I have is Ben here," Pinter is saying, referring to me as if I weren't present. "Even though this is obviously a crime gone bad, I don't see her making much in the way of typical demands, either expressive or substantive."

"Neither do I, which surprises me," the coach says.

"Any chance she's gonna want to negotiate her way out?" asks another negotiator.

"No way," Pruitt says. "She's going to want us to send Ben in."

"Suicide audience? Or murder-suicide?"

"I don't know. I can't decide."

"Let me go in," I offer. "I bet I can get her to release the kids in exchange."

"Uh-uh," says Pinter dismissively. "We don't do that. We're not going to reinforce any suicidal ideations by helping her enact a plan."

"We're also not going to reason her out of there," Pruitt tells him quietly.

"I know."

"Listen to me," I say. "Coming from the tactical side of things, they're not going to introduce gas, or do a dynamic entry with thirty children in there. You know that, right?"

Pinter says, "Yeah, I know that. That's why we're going to use the one weapon we have available to us."

"And, what's that?" I ask.

"Time. We got all the time in the world. Those kids are going to be crying, and getting hungry, and peeing all over themselves pretty soon, and it's going to wear her down. Maybe to the point to where she'll be willing to bargain a little."

"Yeah," I say, "but hear me out for a second, OK? If I offer to go in there in exchange for the kids, then it's just me and her. Maybe I can overpower her, or maybe SWAT can do a dynamic entry or something if it's just me and no kids."

"We're not going to do that, Ben."

"Bo," says Pruitt, "You'd better call her back. It's been five minutes since we got Joelle out of her trunk."

"OK," he says, dialing the keypad on the base unit. "When I get her back, I'm going to try to get her to let the kids go. Any suggestions on strategy?"

"She already told you she knows she's going to die. I'd say play on that," the coach says.

"How?"

"Just ask her to let them go. I mean, why not? She's not using them as bargaining chips, so maybe she'll just be willing to let most, or all, of them go. That way, there's no more chance of anyone else getting hurt. She already told you she doesn't want anyone getting hurt."

"Yeah, I suppose that might work. She's being nice and reasonable at this point."

"She's gonna want to talk a lot about her relationship with Ben. You going to go there?"

"Sure, but first we'll try to deal with the kids. At this point, I'm just going to play it by ear."

"OK, well, go ahead and call her."

Pinter dials her number, and Andrea gets it on the first ring. I can hear the kids crying in the background.

"Andrea, good news. Joelle is fine. I want to thank you for not hurting him."

"I don't want to hurt anyone, Bo. I never have."

"I know. Which kinda brings me to something else. You know there are a lot of really worried parents out here, and those kids in there are terrified. I can hear them crying in the background. Now, you're being nice and reasonable, and I can't tell you how much we all respect you for that. So, why don't you send those kids out here to their parents, OK?"

"Well, I've been thinking about that. I don't want them in here; I hate it that they're scared of me. I *love* kids, and these kids think I'm the bad guy. I guess I am. . . . I'll tell you what. I'll let them all go if you send Ben in here to talk to me. Alone, and unarmed."

This sparks a great deal of animated discussion between all the negotiators and brass present. Pinter continues talking as if he were alone in here.

"Look Andrea, I can't speak for Ben, but I can for the parents out here. You told me earlier that you weren't going to walk out of there. I'm pretty sure I know why you think that, but I'm not going there right now. Still, if that's the case, then why not send the kids out first, and then we can see if Ben would be willing to go in? From what you said earlier, it won't make a difference."

"Come on Bo, it *will* make a difference. It'll make a big difference. If I sent the kids out, what's to prevent SWAT from tossing in about a hundred flash-bangs and gas rounds? I don't want to kill anyone else, but I sure as hell am *not* going to jail. I don't mind dying; I know today's my day, but I'm going to do it on my own terms, and that means talking with Ben first. Face to face. So, I'm sorry, but the kids stay with me until then."

"Come on, Andrea, work with me. According to school records, you have thirty-two children in there. Work with us; give us some hope. Give their *parents* some hope. At least send the kids out. Then, we got nothing but time, and we can hash the rest out for as long as it takes."

"I'll tell you what. I got one girl that peed herself, and another boy who's thrown up all over the place. I'll send those two out."

Without missing a beat, Pinter says, "Of course we'll take them, but I'd love to see you get rid of say, thirty-one out of the thirty-two. What do you say? That'd still give you one."

I know that he's talking about leaving LaMonjello, and I hate him for that. I know also that what he's saying makes sense and is the smart thing to do. I bite my lip because I don't want to get kicked out of the negotiations van, but I am supremely glad that Sharon isn't here.

"Bo, I'll release those two. How do you want me to do it? I assume you have SWAT guys outside my door. Want me to just send them out?"

"Yeah. Have them open the door and walk out."

There is another flurry of activity in the back of the motor home as the tactical liaison officer gets on the tactical net and warns the team to prepare for an immediate hostage release of two children. I am aware of this, but I listen to the negotiations closely, hoping to hear of LaMonjello, and dreading it at the same time.

"Can you promise me that SWAT won't come busting in? I'll be in the middle of the kids, and I don't intend to harm a one of them. The last thing I want is an active shooter team coming in trying to take a surgical headshot on me before I'm ready and hitting some kid instead. So promise me no one's coming in. I'll take your word for it."

"I promise."

"Bo, like I said, I'm going to die in here today. I'm OK with that. I am *not* going to jail. So if you break your promise, I'll force the situation. I'll open fire, and your boys'll have no choice but to come in with guns blazing, and they'll shoot kids who'll be running all over the room. I won't have to do it. So don't let that happen."

"You have my word. It's one fifteen. Send them out in one minute, OK? That'll give me time to let the guys outside know what's happening."

"I'll give it two minutes. That way, you can let them know what'll happen if they get too eager. Call me back after you get the kids."

Bo starts to answer her, but she hangs up before he gets the chance.

Chapter 33

After Pinter hangs up, we all turn to the south doors of the building. Very shortly, two SWAT members come out leading a little boy and a little girl. Everyone breathes a sigh of relief. Score one for the good guys. They say that the first concession from a hostage taker is often the most difficult. If that is true, then the release of the two children is a good omen.

I am not among those expressing relief, for it is clear from the first glance that both the students she released are white. So far, no word has been mentioned about LaMonjello.

In desperation, I turn to the lead negotiator. "Bo, I'm willing to go in there, but she has to release LaMonjello first."

"No. She's suicidal. She wants you to go in there with her, so she can take you out with her. So you can 'be together' forever. You see that, don't you?"

"All I see is that there's still a bunch of kids left in that room. Every one of them is going to be a lot more scared than them," I say, pointing to the two who were just released. They are screaming their heads off outside the van. "Can you imagine what's going through their minds?"

"She's not gonna hurt them," says Pruitt.

"I don't care right now! Look at those two, and put yourself in the position of a six-year-old, for Christ's sake. How would you like it if *your* kid was in there?"

The coach says, "You see, Vince? That's what I meant. He shouldn't be in here."

"Cut it, Sonata," says Capelko sharply. "I said he can stay, so he can stay."

So that's her name, Sonata. I start to say something to her, but she pipes up, "I think you're wrong. We can't have him hear something and disrupt negotiations. Remember, his child *is* in there. He can't think straight, that's why he shouldn't be in here. Someone get him the hell out of here."

"Hey, fuck you, *Sonata*," I spit. "I'm not going anywhere. What the hell are you trying to say? Maybe I'm the *only* one thinking straight. I can get all those kids released. After that, I can either talk my way out of there with her, or overpower her, or talk her into killing herself without me, or whatever. If she gets me first, tough shit. At least she didn't get LaMonjello. But in the meantime, I can—"

"You know what, Ben? Fuck you right back! Look, I'm not the enemy here. I don't want to see anyone get killed in there. No kids, and no cops, not even you. She's suicidal, but there are conditions on her suicide. One seems to be that nobody else gets hurt. As long as she's not seriously threatening to kill kids if you don't go in there, I think we should to take our time and go slow. We might be able to talk her out *without* you going in there. And if she's starts making threats, then we can revisit the idea."

"That's bullshit! You go tell the parents of those kids that we can have their children out now, but we don't want to do that quite yet."

"It's not like that, and you know it."

"All right, that's enough," says Capelko. "You both have valid points. But Ben, one thing we don't want to do is rush things. Time is on our side. She's going to get tired, hungry, have to go to the bathroom, all sorts of stuff. As these things happen, she's going to be willing to make more concessions."

"I agree with Vince," says Pinter. "The statistics back that up too. Her releasing those first two is the best thing we've got going. It shows she's willing to deal. She doesn't *want* to hold the kids any longer than she has to. She certainly doesn't want to see any harm come to them."

"Christ, Vince, what the hell do you think is happening to them psychologically? You think they'll just forget about this tomorrow when it's cartoon time? There are thirty-two kids in there that are going to keep the counselors and psychiatrists rich for years to come already. Don't make them stay in there for hours and hours because you're unwilling to send me in. She said what she wants, what it will take to get them all released. Hell, send me in, and entry in thirty seconds after the last kid comes out if you want. I'll duck and take my chances, but the kids'll be *gone*. She wants to release them right now; who knows if she'll still want to in an hour, let alone sometime tonight or tomorrow morning!"

"Sorry Ben. Not now."

"Fuck you all! Will you at least ask her about my son? LaMonjello? He's the reason she's in that room."

"No way!" says Sonata. "Worst thing you could do."

Pinter raises his hand. "Sonata . . . " he turns to me and says, "Ben, we don't want to do that yet. I don't want to spark her interest in him specifically right now. For now, we're just dealing in generalities. I don't want to remind her that she's there to kidnap one kid in particular, and turn the spotlight back on him."

I sit back and stew, thinking that what he said makes sense. I hadn't thought of it like that. But damned if I'm going to say as much. Then, unable to remain silent any longer, I say, "Just enter it into your little log that at 1320, I volunteered to exchange myself for the hostages and you wouldn't let me. And I'll tell you this much. I will lead the pack in suing the shit out of this department if things don't go well. Just remember that."

Pinter writes something in the log and says, "It's noted, Ben. And don't worry, I understand, but knowing what I know about hostage-takers, it's too early to give in to her demands. If you acquiesce too early, they don't hold up their end of the bargain. That's been proven time and time again."

"This isn't some shitbag who bungled an armed robbery at 7-11, Bo. This is Andrea. She *wants* to let those kids go."

Capelko chimes in with, "We'll keep her offer, and yours, in mind, but for now, the answer's no. And that's the last word on it if you want to stay in here, Ben." I know him; he means it, so I shut up.

I'd sneak out of here and try to get inside on my own if I didn't know the team was right there staged outside the door to room two. But as it is, there's no way I'd ever get near the door, even if I did get inside the building. I'll just have to sit this out and see what happens.

Ultimately, I know I'm going to end up inside that room. I know Andrea. If she says that's what it'll take to release the kids, then that's what it'll take. She won't cave in just because she gets hungry or has to go potty. I just hope the delay doesn't cause too much psychological trauma to the kids.

It's what will happen after I'm in there that's beginning to gnaw at me.

Pruitt goes out to begin debriefing the children. Sonata turns to Capelko and says, "Vince, what's the tactical plan as far as rules of engagement go?"

"We've been at compromised authority for about half an hour now. Given the fact that she's not overtly threatening the kids or anyone else, I'm just going to leave it like that. One thing I don't want is some sniper to splash her all over a bunch of kindergarten kids."

Suddenly, Capelko seems to remember that one of those kindergarten kids has already undergone that exact thing, and he backs off his nonchalant tone. "Hell, Ben can tell you all about what that does to a kid. No, unless something drastic changes, we're not going past compromised authority."

I'm glad to hear it. The last thing LaMonjello needs is to see *another* person shot with a .308 right in front of him.

"I'm going to call her back," says Pinter. "Any suggestions on topics?"

"Just try to work on her conscience about the rest of the children is all," says Sonata.

He dials again, and Andrea gets it right away.

"Hello?"

"Andrea, it's Bo again. Hey, I just wanted to say thanks for releasing those two kids. Their parents are here, and they still haven't let go of them."

"Come on, Bo, I'll bet Sam Pruitt is giving them candy and debriefing them even as we speak. Right? 'How's she acting? Where's her gun? How are the rest of the kids? What's she saying?' I took your class, Bo, I know the drill."

"Actually, Pruitt's waiting in line," Pinter says, his wheels spinning. One thing he's known for is his ability to manipulate the bad guy on the phone, and he's about to do it now.

"The parents get them first, then they get a medical check to make sure you haven't hurt them, and *then* Pruitt gets 'em."

Sonata gives Pinter a thumbs up for a good spur-of-the-moment idea.

"Hurt them? *Hurt* them? Who's bullshit idea is that, that I would hurt them? Jesus Christ, what do they think this is, some kind of terrorist operation? *Hurt them?*"

"Hey, slow down, Andrea. Don't kill the messenger for the message. That's standard released-hostage treatment. You know that."

One of the negotiators whispers in my ear, "This is where Pinter really shines. Normally, you'd never use words like 'kill' or 'hostage,' but Pinter can think on his feet and evaluate a situation faster than anyone. See, he's got her on the defensive, showing her exactly what she's done by playing on her guilt. He'll parry it into another attempt to get her to let them go."

And that's exactly what Pinter is doing.

"You can't really call these kids hostages, Bo. I'd never harm them. I have no intention whatsoever of harming them, which is why it's so fucking pointless for you to give them a medical checkup."

"Andrea, *I* know that, because I know you personally, but Portland's SWAT brass doesn't know you from Adam. And Vince Capelko doesn't know you like I do. You know I'm not making the heavy decisions here, they are. And what are they supposed to consider those kids? Guests? I mean, shit, hostages is what they are."

"They're more like, I don't know, points of leverage. I want to talk to Ben. If I don't have some leverage, you won't let him come in here, even if he wants to."

"I know that, Andrea, and I've told everybody and their mother that, but still, you're holding thirty kids at gunpoint. You can't just overlook that."

"Christ, Bo. Nobody wants to see these kids get hurt. Why are you jerking me around? How about we say I'm just asking you to consider letting him come in here. If he wants to, of his own free will. Ben's choice. What do you say to that?"

"Send a cop into a room with a hostage-taker and thirty hostages? I don't think so."

"Bo, hostage-takers make demands. I'm not."

"Yes you are. Your demand is that Ben Geller be allowed to go in there."

"OK, fine. You want to clear things up? Good, let's clear it all up. Now it's not a demand. Now I'm simply asking you. So will that do it? Now will you send him in?"

Pinter frowns, then nods to himself, as if he's talked himself into something. "Andrea, no. Not just no, but hell no. Stop pissing in my hair and telling me it's raining. You *are* a hostage-taker. Christ, you're holding a room full of kindergarten kids! If you want to ask me for favors, ask me when you're not holding thirty hostage at gunpoint. Until then, you better realize something. You *are* the bad guy, and I'm not giving you shit. I'm especially not giving you Ben! So go ahead, do whatever it is you have to do. I don't care!" He sounds pissed, and I don't think he's faking it.

The entire HNT team stares at him in disbelief. There is nearly a minute of silence on the phone. He's offended her, challenged her, basically dared her to prove her strength. Even I can hear in her silence her incredulity that he would do such a thing; her consideration of shooting a hostage to show him exactly who the fuck *is* boss.

Apologize or something, I silently urge him. I don't know how Pinter can hold his tongue. I want to shout something out, but Pinter just sits comfortably back in his chair and waits her out.

I know what he's doing. Cops always do this—hold their silence, which all but forces the other party to make a statement, which generally turns out to be a very significant statement. But you don't play this game when there are kids' lives at stake. If Andrea is going to snap, or do something drastic just to prove him wrong, now's the time she would do it. I think Pinter's just made a horrible mistake.

Sweat literally breaks out on my forehead. In the background, we can hear muted kid sobs and coughs. The line is still open.

Finally, after a full minute of silence, Andrea says, "Fine, Bo. That's how you want to play it? Then let's see how you like *this*." And then she hangs up.

"I'm offline," Pinter says unnecessarily.

"What the fuck was that?" asks Sonata incredulously. I can't wait to hear his answer; I'd kind of like to know myself. You don't have to go to advanced hostage negotiations schools to know you don't talk to a hostage-taker like that.

"It, it just felt right," Pinter says, now obviously second-guessing himself. "Oh shit, I hope I didn't fuck things up."

"Bo," says another one of the HNT members, "Look, I think she's getting to you. No offense, man, but I think we ought to switch. I think we need to put Sonata on the phone now. Sorry, but you lost her, and we'll be lucky if this thing doesn't go south."

The liaison officer between SWAT and HNT is already on the radio briefing Capelko. Suddenly, he holds his hand up. "Hang on, something's happening," he says. He starts nodding triumphantly, then says, "Entry reports a bunch of kids are coming out!"

A range of expressions crosses Sonata's face, and then she gets a sheepish smile. "I don't know how you pull this crap and get away with it," she says, giving Pinter a high five. Hardly daring to hope, I step outside to see if LaMonjello is among the kids coming out.

I count twenty-four kids, all white and mostly boys. When they stop coming out, I feel almost sick with depression. A teacher gleefully checks names off a list and scurries away to give good news to their parents, and I go back into the HNT van.

"Twenty-four kids," I say. "Mine isn't one of them."

"I'm calling her back," says Pinter, dialing the HNT phone. It rings once, then Andrea picks it up and says, "You going to have medics check them out?"

"No, Andrea, I don't think so. Thank you for that."

"Look, Bo, I'm getting sick of all this. What more can I do to show you that I'm not some hostage-taker?"

"You've made a hell of a start, Andrea. Why don't you just release the rest of them? If you like, I can give you my word SWAT won't come in."

"The presumption being that I'll come out?" she asks.

"I don't know. Maybe you'll want to. You have a lot going for you, Andrea."

"I've killed five people, including a police officer. Are you really going to sit there and tell me how much I have going for me?"

"I mean your intelligence."

"I'm smart enough to know that you're not going to allow me to walk away from this, and I'm certainly not about to go to jail. That only leaves me one option, wouldn't you say?"

"There's always more than one option."

"Not for me there isn't. But I do have one request, and that's that you send Ben in. Send him in and I'll send out the rest of the kids."

"What do you want Ben for, Andrea? Because to be honest, I'm afraid you want to kill him. To take him with you."

"Don't worry about what I want Ben for. Just send him in."

"Andrea, before we go any further, let me make sure I have everything straight. I understand that these kids aren't hostages, but that you've got them more to ensure that we let Ben go in and talk to you, right?"

"Come on, Bo, I told you, don't pull your active listening crap on me. I know all about paraphrasing, monosyllabic responses, and open-ended questions, OK? Are you or are you not going to allow Ben to come in?"

"You know what my answer to that is. I gotta send that on up the food chain to Vince. He'll probably have to have to pass it on up to Moody, who will have some lengthy discussions with the City Attorney's office, who will want to talk to Ben and have him sign fifty release-of-liability forms. You know it's not my call, and you know it can't just happen like that," he said, snapping his fingers for effect.

"You're doing it again, Bo. Giving me your canned hostage negotiator bullshit. I just let twenty-four kids go, and now I'm asking you if you can send in Ben. Don't stall me with 'I'll send it up the chain.' I'll bet Vince, the Chief, and probably the city attorney are all in there right now, listening."

"They're not. They're pretty busy at this point, you know."

"Well, tell whoever is acting as the little runner boy between HNT and SWAT that he'd better get his ass in gear and get Capelko. I don't want to do this all day. Time may be on your side, but it sure as hell isn't in my immediate plans."

"What are you saying?"

"I'm saying I'm running out of patience. There are things I need to do, and I don't have all day. I want Ben to come in here. My reasons are my reasons, so don't ask me what I'm going to do, or tell me I gotta promise anything. Not ever again."

Her voice is building, and I can tell she's getting angrier and angrier. Her tone scares me. She's starting to sound like Coffee Shop Andrea again.

"I have five kids left in here," she continues, her tone building, her inflections becoming increasingly incendiary. "Coincidentally, that's just about enough to surround me with when the SWAT ninjas come busting in and I have to start throwing lead. So, unless you want these last little ones hurt or worse, you best get your shit together, and *send Ben the fuck in here*! Any other brilliant questions, Bo?"

She then hangs up the phone.

Chapter 34

"How much of this are we going to have to take before you let me go in there?" I ask, my frustration coming through loud and clear in my tone of voice. "One of those kids she's holding in there is mine."

"Wait," Sonata says, "Unless I miss my count, we're one kid off. She said she still has five left inside, right?"

"Yeah," says Pinter.

"But she only let twenty-four out. Combined with the other two that came out, that's twenty-six, plus the five she's got left inside, that's thirty-one. But there were twenty-eight kids in that kindergarten class, plus four that haven't been accounted for. That's thirty-two, so somewhere along the line, we're one kid off."

"Maybe some kid is home sick, maybe the count is off somewhere, or maybe one of the missing four is hiding somewhere in the building still."

"Probably."

The door opens and Capelko comes in. He's been made fully aware of what's going on.

"Screw the numbers," I say. "I want to know why I'm not allowed to go in there."

Pinter says, "Ben, we don't do hostage exchanges. Period. We just don't do them. Look how far we've come so far. We got twenty-six kids out of that room so far, and we haven't given her a thing. All she's done so far is make vague threats."

"Yeah, but what has she really done?" I point out. "She's gotten rid of all the excess baggage, and kept enough children to surround herself with so that we can't go in there with a dynamic entry. And now, she's threatening the ones that are left."

"Look Ben," Capelko says, "Pinter's right. We're doing fine so far, and there's no reason to assume that things won't continue like this. She doesn't want to hold hostages; she wants you to go in there so she can take you out with her. We're not going to do that. These guys are doing a hell of a job. Let them continue."

The phone rings, and Pinter picks it up.

"Bo, enough time. Are you going to let Ben come in? Because I know him, he wants to come in by now. You gonna let him?"

"Andrea, I'll level with you. He does want to, but the brass isn't letting him right now. They're still discussing all the ramifications. I really think—"

A gunshot, immediately followed by the chilling sounds of kids screaming in terror, cuts him off. The connection is then severed.

"Shit!" yells Pinter.

Capelko holds his earpiece to his ear, then says, "One gunshot, which looks like it went high through a window at ceiling level. It took down one of the blinds covering the windows. S/O Team One says they have a view into the room now. She was surrounded by kids, but when the blind came down, she moved the whole group to the back of the class, and now they're out of his sight."

"Ringing her now," says Pinter.

We all become silent as the phone rings and rings. She does not answer. He lets it go, and after the twentieth ring or so, it is answered and immediately hung up. Obviously, she doesn't want to talk right now.

Capelko holds his earpiece to his head, and then answers saying, "Capelko to S/O Team One, affirmative. Advance to shot of opportunity. All units copy? We are now at shot of opportunity."

Chief Moody's voice comes on the SWAT net. This is unprecedented. He may call the shots, but he never gets on the radio. "Belay that last order! We are *not* at shot of opportunity! Snipers, do you copy? Remain at compromised authority. Say again, negative on shot of opportunity. Acknowledge."

"S/O One, copy. Compromised authority."

The door to the HNT truck opens and Moody sticks his head in. "Get out here, Vince. Now."

"What the hell is he thinking?" Capelko says as he leaves the van.

We all stare at each other for a moment, then Sonata tells Pinter to get Andrea back on the line. He tries several more times, but she doesn't answer. Finally, fifteen minutes after the shot, the phone rings.

"I'm getting tired of this, Pinter. Tell Capelko things have changed. The kids are now hostages. Tell him I'm going to shoot one if Ben isn't in this classroom in ten minutes."

"Andrea, look, I know you're feeling pretty desperate. And I know that having Ben come in there's a really important thing to you. All I can tell you is that we're working on it as fast as we can, and that's *not* HNT bullshit. OK?"

"Don't presume you know how I feel, Bo. You have no *idea* how I feel. Ten minutes. And yes, that's a deadline. And yes, I said I will shoot a child if you don't meet it."

"Andrea . . ."

"Five kids at ten-minute intervals gives me fifty minutes, Bo. And then, I'm going to eat my barrel. You send Ben in here within ten minutes, or you're going to lose this one. Ask anyone. I'm crazy, and I know it. Ask Ben, he'll tell you. Ten minutes until—what's your name, buddy?"

I could hear a stifled sob in the background, and a little boy utter "Leonard."

"Until little Leonard gets one in the back of the head. Send him in. Now."

"*Andrea!*" But it was too late. She'd already hung up.

This was the Andrea I had gotten a glimpse of once before, in the coffee shop in Salmon Creek. This was the Andrea who scared me, who I felt was very capable of carrying out her threats of violence, and I tell Pinter that *this* Andrea *can* carry out her threats. Maybe not the other Andrea, but this one can.

Capelko re-enters the van and comes directly to me.

"We were listening to that last exchange in the command van. Ben, Moody's given me the authorization to make the decision, and I'm giving it to you. Nobody's saying you have to go in there, but you can if you want. You don't have to go. If you don't, nobody will say another word."

Which, in fact, means I'll be branded as a coward for the rest of my life, not that I give a shit about that. I *am* going in there, which is pretty much the antithesis of the way I've operated in the past. I've worked my entire career under the premise that I'd rather be a living coward than a dead hero. But that was before it was either me or LaMonjello.

I do *not* want to go in that classroom. I'm *afraid* to go into that classroom. There's no way I will be able to get the drop on her. I doubt I'll stand a chance. What's more, I know she means to kill me.

I think this is what Andrea had in mind when she went to the school in the first place. I think she wanted to take my kids and barter them for me; she just didn't plan on doing it in front of everyone at a SWAT callout. But this still works for her. The end result is still going to be the same.

The thought of going into that room makes my knees weak, but the image of LaMonjello, not to mention the other kids in there, makes me realize that I have to. I've already lived my life, and thank God I've already made my peace with Sharon. Like Andrea, I don't fear death, but I don't welcome it either. There's just so much more I want to do before I check out. I want to see Leah grow up. I want to see LaMonjello become a successful adult, with a family so very different from his sperm donor dad and crack whore mom. I selfishly want to be there and bask in success knowing that none of it would be possible if not for me.

But now, it appears that the only way I can make that all happen is to trade my life for his. I will do that, and I will do it with an air of bravado. But that doesn't mean that I have to be brave on the inside, where nobody else can see.

I steel myself, and then look at Capelko and say, "Screw what they would say. Screw the plan, and screw everything else. That's my child in there, and I'm not about to lose him, or anyone else's kid, either. Even if she intends to take me out, I still have a better chance than anyone in there. I'm going in."

"Ben, you know I can't guarantee your safety."

"I don't want any guarantees. I want this to be over. Look, Vince, I started all this by fucking her in the first place. I feel like it's my fault. Now, it's just poetic justice that I'm the only one who can do anything about it.

"I'm going to go talk to my wife and daughter. You call her back and find out how she wants to do the trade. She'll let the kids go. She *wants* to let the kids go. I know her, trust me."

He nods his head, as if it was his plan that I go in there all along. Terrified, I go out to find Sharon. She is approaching the trailer as I step out.

"Ben, I've been at the command post, and I heard what's going on. Oh, Ben! LaMonjello . . . What are you going to do?"

"Honey, I have to go in that classroom."

She fights hysterics, but begins to cry. "Oh baby, you can't . . . She's going to kill you, Ben!"

"Maybe she just wants me to watch her kill herself. I can do that. Maybe I can overpower her. Maybe once the kids are out of there, SWAT can come busting in. But without me going in there, I don't think we'll ever see LaMonjello again."

"Ben!"

I grab her and give her a kiss. Somehow, I am overcome with strength and resolve. I thought I would be a blubbery mess, but I'm as steady as a rock, which surprises me.

"I love you, Sharon. I was a shitty husband for a long time. I'm sorry about that, but I'm glad we've had a chance to get it together these last few months. Make sure to tell the kids how much I love them."

Sharon is a mess. Leah is now with her. I don't have much time to think about this. If I did, I would wonder if this is the last time I will ever speak with my wife and daughter, and I might not find my resolve as strong as it is right now. I hug her fiercely, then turn to Leah, whose tear-streaked face is scrunched in wrinkled agony.

"Daddy, where are you going?" she asks.

"Daddy's going to go into LaMonjello's room to bring him out," I say. I force myself to remain steady with her; I cannot break down now. It is much more difficult with Leah than it was for Sharon.

"Are you going to kill her?"

"No, honey. I'm just going to talk to her. I know her, and if I ask her real nice, she'll let LaMonjello and the other kids come out for me."

"But why is she's shooting her gun?"

"She's . . . Her mind is sick. It makes her do things she shouldn't. She doesn't mean to harm anyone. She really needs help, and we're going to make sure she gets it."

"Do you have to go in there? I don't want you to go!"

"Honey, Daddy knows her better than anyone. I can help her the most. I'll be fine, baby, and I'll bring LaMonjello out."

She jumps into my arms and locks her arms around my neck. "No, Daddy, I don't want you to go," she sobs into my ear.

"I'll be back real soon, sweetheart. I promise. And I'll bring LaMonjello with me too."

"I love you, Daddy . . ."

"I love you too, Princess. I always will. Now, you stay here with Mommy, and after I get LaMonjello, we'll all go out and get pizza. OK?"

"OK."

"I'll see you soon, honey."

"Goodbye, Daddy."

My resolve nearly breaks with the degree of finality with which she says this.

Chapter 35

I go back into the HNT van, where Pinter is again on the phone with Andrea. He's got her on the speaker, and she sounds angry.

"No, Bo, it's nonnegotiable. He comes in cuffed, no jacket, T-shirt tucked into pants with no belt. No guns, no keys. Backwards, with his hands open so I can see them."

"I got it. And what about the children?"

"I'll release them the instant Ben comes in. If anyone—you, the ninjas in the hall, even Ben—screws with this or tries anything at all I will take out hostages. I can do that; check with your psychological profiler gurus. I will be dead within the hour either way, so I won't have to feel guilty for too long."

"Andrea, there's no need to—"

"Just don't deviate. Pass the word. I do *not* want to harm or scare these kids any more than I already have. Now, I'm going to hang up, and then I want Ben to knock on my door. A child will open it at gunpoint. She will then be allowed to leave once Ben is inside. I'll check him out, then release the rest of the kids immediately."

"I got it."

"Do you agree? No tricks?"

"Do you agree not to hurt him?"

"That's not on the table. If you screw this up, if you try sending in the ninjas, I'll bet I can get at least one of them in the face. Check out my range scores. I've shot in the upper nineties since the day I was hired. I don't want to take out a SWAT guy, but I will if I have to. Now, I'm going to hang up. Have Geller at my door in two minutes."

She disconnects immediately, and there is a moment frozen in time. Then, in a frenzy of movement, I get my shirt and belt off. My black T-shirt is already tucked in, and Pruitt hands me a pair of cuffs.

"Here," he says, holding out a small handcuff key. "Stick it down your pants or something. At least give yourself a chance."

I take it, and drop it down the back of my pants.

"I'm putting them on loosely, and I'll leave them unlocked."

"OK."

I hate being handcuffed. We do it a lot in training, and I am not flexible. They are therefore extremely uncomfortable. I can't count the times I've told people don't worry, they'll stretch, but now it doesn't seem as funny as it always did.

Suddenly, I am terrified. I am afraid I might wet myself. I am going in that room, helpless, into the hands of one who has killed five people; of one whom knows I've taken her love for me and used it to double-cross her. Which has brought us directly to this point.

Pruitt ratchets the cuffs as loosely as he can, but there's no way I can get out of them. I also doubt I can get to the key, but at least I know it's there.

"OK," I say. "Let's go."

Pruitt leads me out of the trailer. Thankfully, Sharon and Leah are nowhere in sight. It is a short distance to the west doors of the school, but it feels like I'm walking the green mile. I can sense the telephoto lenses of the myriad of news vans and helicopters in the distance on my back as we quickly walk toward the doors.

Inside, there are SWAT members posted at intervals along the main hallway. Each mutters a brief word of encouragement. I mostly nod at them, afraid to use my voice lest it fail me. I am terrified, but I try not to show it on my face.

The entry team is lined up just outside the door to room two. One by one they reach out and pat me on the back. It reminds me of the spanking line we used to go through at summer camp when I was kid.

"Just keep your ass low when we come in," says the Portland point man at the head of the line.

"The thought's already occurred to me," I tell him.

"Take her out if you can, Ben. Good luck."

Pruitt lets go of me, and I walk the last two feet on my own. I turn around and face everyone. Their eyes are like steel, their faces like statues of hardened soldiers in combat. I nod, then knock on the door.

It opens behind me. From where the conga line is lined up around the corner, nobody can see the room. The openness of the room behind my back feels like the vacuum of outer space. I splay the fingers of both hands out and wiggle them around, to show that I'm not concealing anything.

"Back on in, Ben," says Andrea's voice, pretty far behind me. She must be at the other side of the room. "Rachel, you can leave now. Thank you, and please close the door behind you."

With a sob, a little blond-haired girl runs out of the room, slamming the door as she goes. She turns the corner and screeches in fear as she is grabbed by someone in the entry lineup.

"Walk backward to my voice," Andrea commands. The voice she uses is harder, steelier than I've heard before. I keep walking backwards. Suddenly, a hand grabs my cuffs and tightens them down painfully over each wrist. I also hear her lock the handcuffs down, which will make it much harder for me to get out of them if I get the chance and can find the key.

She searches me roughly without finding the key, then commands me to sit down on the corner of the teacher's heavy wooden desk. There is another pair of handcuffs attached to the frame of the desk, in a place where a drawer has been removed. I sit down, and she ratchets the open cuff to the center chain of the pair I am wearing.

My back is still to the room, and I cannot see the little group of hostages. I want to see LaMonjello's face, but I dare not turn around with Andrea being as unstable as she is. I would have expected him to cry out, or run up to me, and it bothers me that he has not.

I test the connection between the desk and me. I suppose if I wanted to, I could drag the desk around, but it would hurt like hell and I certainly couldn't go very far or very fast. I am indeed her prisoner now. To make matters worse, I feel the handcuff key sliding down the inside of my pant leg. I try to wiggle around so it might land on the top of my shoe, but instead it falls out the cuff of my pants and lands on the floor with a tiny metallic clink. Well, so much for the key. I couldn't retrieve it from the floor while cuffed like this no matter how much time I had to try.

"OK, guys, are you all ready to go home?" she says to the kids. She is answered by a sort of group whimper. I can take this no longer, and I turn my body as far as I can so that by twisting my neck until it hurts, I can see the kids.

I count four, all white, three girls and a boy. LaMonjello is not among them. My heart fails me for a moment. Andrea has not mentioned him specifically, and I first wonder if she has kept him apart for some nefarious reason. Then I remember that there was a discrepancy in the head count, and I wonder if it is possible that LaMonjello, using his inborn talent for sensing trouble, had somehow made it out of the room before Andrea had it all locked down. I hang onto this hope with all my heart.

"OK, kids, when I say go, everyone get up and walk out the door. Abigail, you go last, 'cause you're the biggest, and close the door behind you. Can you do that?"

"Y-yes, ma'am."

"Good girl. I'm sorry for all of this. You guys have been very brave. You should all be very proud of yourselves."

There is a muttered chorus of thank you from two or three of them, and Andrea says, "OK then. You can all go now. Bye-bye."

They make a beeline for the door and file out one by one. I know they are being grabbed and whisked away by the entry team the moment they take two steps out the door. Little Abigail, her face like an angel, dutifully stands by while the others go out before her. She looks at me for a moment before leaving. Her eyes are huge and brown, full of sorrow and compassion. I cannot express the volumes her expression tells me, but I will remember it for the rest of my life, however long that will be. Then, she disappears through the door and faithfully closes it behind her. Andrea turns a thumb latch, locking us in together, and we are alone.

I expect SWAT to throw in flash-bangs, or fire in a few 37-mm teargas rounds and come busting in, but nothing happens. It grows very quiet, and Andrea and I are alone.

I look around and take stock of my situation. The window in the door has been covered; I have already seen that. The bank of windows that face the playground is covered by four wide sections of blinds. One of them, the third one in, is lying on the floor from her gunshot, leaving a quarter of the windows uncovered. Andrea has situated the desk I'm sitting on out of the sniper's view from the outside.

She moved to the opposite side of the room from me when the last little girl left, and now, the uncovered section of windows is between us. To get back to me, she will first have to pass that portion of the window open to the outside, where a sniper is concealed behind a fence in an old man's garage some eighty yards away.

She addresses me from her side of the room. "What do you say, Ben? Together again at last, huh?"

I cling to the hope that LaMonjello has been spared all of this, and am able to find my voice. "I guess so. What happened to you, Andrea?"

"You screwed me over, Ben. After all I did for you, you found it in your heart to screw me over, like I meant nothing to you. How could you do that?"

"Andrea, we had an affair. We were never meant to be together. It was wrong of me, because I was married. How we felt about each other wasn't part of it. But just for you own information, I did love you. I really did. But that was before you changed."

"I changed? *I* changed? *You* changed, Ben. You changed, and you fucked me over. And, you're still doing it. I came to get your kids, to trade them for you, so we could be together. Forever. Do you understand what I mean?"

"Yeah."

"Forever. But you screwed me over even in that. Where is he, Ben? Is he home sick? Or did your slut wife manage to get him out before all this started?"

My mind is racing, and I can't think of an answer. Does it really mean LaMonjello's not here? Or is she screwing around with me, waiting for me to say the wrong thing?

I decide on a non-answer. "Does it really matter, Andrea?"

"No, I guess it doesn't. Not anymore."

"So, what's the plan?"

"I'm going to come to over there to you. And then we're going to . . . to go away. Just me and you, together. But to get to you, I have to pass that open window. And you know what? There's a sniper out there somewhere. When he sees me, he's probably going to take me out. If he does, then he's saved your life. If he doesn't, then you'll come with me, and we'll go away together."

"Andrea . . ."

Her voice softens, almost to a whisper. "Oh Ben, I—I love you. I always have." Tears run down her cheeks. "I'm sorry, Ben. I'm sorry it had to be like this."

Suddenly, I can feel the openness of the room around me. There is no one here, just Andrea and me. I want to tell her that when I came in here, we were at compromised authority, but I don't know if that's the right thing or the wrong thing to say. If we're not at shot of opportunity now, then I'm a dead man. A cold fear washes over me, and maybe for the first time, I realize that this is for keeps and I stand a very good chance of dying.

I really, truly do not want to die.

I want to say something, but now I'm afraid my voice will betray my fear. I don't want her to know how scared I am. What I want is for her to cross that open window, and I want to see her head dissolve, because then I'll live.

Hesitantly, she puts her foot out and takes a tentative step forward. She pauses briefly, and takes another step. Another one or two ought to put her within the sniper's view. "I only wanted to be with you, Ben. That's all I ever wanted."

I sit silently, willing her to take the next step. With greater resolve, she puts her other foot forward and moves into the area of unshaded window. She pauses for a moment, and then takes another step. Her eyes remain locked on mine, and I realize this is part of the game. In her heart, her love for me is so great that she doesn't want to kill me, but I know she will if she makes it across the open window. She is a tortured soul. I can see the hope on her face, the hope that the sniper will take her out. Her eyes are glued to mine; she wants to have eye contact with me when it happens. She wants my eyes to be the last thing that hers see.

I *will* the shot to come through the window. What the hell are they waiting for? She makes it about halfway across the open area, and then stops. She stares at me for a full ten seconds, then turns to face the window, and spends a moment gazing out. Without looking at me, she says, "They don't even care enough about you to order a shot of opportunity, do they, Ben? Here's their chance, and they're not taking it. What's that tell you?"

She's right. It tells me volumes. What's left of my will, my anger, and my courage all melt away when the shot doesn't come. The urge to pee is suddenly so powerful it takes everything I have just to hold it in. It's as good a time as any to become a believer in God, so I beg Him to kill Andrea before she kills me.

It does not happen. It seems He is moving in mysterious ways again.

She turns to face me. "I really didn't want it to be this way, Ben. I didn't want to have to take you with me, but I guess we were meant to be together, and we will be. We'll leave together, and no matter where we end up, we'll be together forever. Deep inside, it's what you want too."

"Andrea, please . . . " I say, my voice cracking. I'm now so scared I can't say anything else. I realize I am actually afraid of dying. I didn't think I was, but I had never been so close to it. It's amazing what you can learn about yourself when a little shit hits the fan.

"I'm going to give you a kiss, Ben. I want you to feel my love when we go. I'd like you to kiss me back, although I doubt you will. I'd like you to kiss me like you used to, when you meant it."

"Andrea, don't . . . Please . . . Oh God . . . " I'm about to beg, but I've been around long enough to know that it won't make any difference. In an unexpected moment of strength, I somehow silence myself. Better to go quietly than begging for my life. I hate myself for my cowardice, and I am supremely thankful there are no listening devices in this room. It comforts me that the last time anyone saw me, I was brave. Nobody will have to know the truth. Nobody will see me trembling so.

"While we're kissing, I'm going to shoot you in the head. And then I'm going to kill myself. But Ben, please, *please*, kiss me back, the way you used to. Please."

The expression on her face is one of peace. I realize that she hasn't wasted one word with me. Everything she has said is the truth to her, and she is going to do it. Tears sting the back of my eyes, and I squeeze my eyes closed.

One tear overflows, and tracks down the side of my face. One tear. I'm afraid of the flood that will follow. But then, rather than beg for my life, I am shocked to hear myself say, "You know what? Fuck you, Andrea."

I open my eyes, and now there are no more tears. She is momentarily caught off guard, and is just staring at me. Emboldened, I continue. "I never loved you. I never wanted to be with you. You were nothing more to me than a good piece of ass. Do you really think I'm going to kiss you? I wouldn't kiss you if you were the last woman on Earth. But know this. Before I came in here, I kissed Sharon."

I'm shocked as much as she is by anger and venom of my words. Shocked, but also buoyed. Suddenly, I feel good, and there's more I want to say. A lot more.

"I kissed Sharon like you want me to kiss you, Andrea. Not ten minutes ago. And I meant it. I love *her*. And *you're* the one that made me see just how much I love her. I could never love you. All the shit you've pulled since Karch? All of this? It only proves one thing. You're weak. You're a weak person, and you don't have the balls to kill me. So come on over here. Put your mouth on mine. I'll spit in it instead. *That's* how we'll go out."

Gone is the trembling. Gone is the fear. Gone is the weakness from my voice. In its place, I am steady, and I've never heard my voice so hard. The words I'm telling her are true, which is why they are so powerful. I don't care now. When she gets close enough and tries to kiss me, I will head-butt her with everything I have. If she doesn't try to kiss me, I'll kick her between the legs as soon as she's in range. And if she doesn't get close enough for that, she can shoot me. I just don't give a damn anymore.

Her expression turns from shock to a mask of rage. Coffee Shop Andrea is back, but I don't care. She pulls her service weapon from her waistband and strides purposefully toward me, staring hard into my eyes. I return the gaze unblinking, concentrating on Sharon, Leah and LaMonjello, and how much I love them.

Though she only has about ten feet to cover, it takes forever, because of the way the mind registers time in situations like this. It is as if I have hours for reflection as she approaches.

I tense, preparing myself to attack. I don't see Andrea Fellotino any more. All I see is a murderer, a cop killer. I can easily picture her killing Sharon, or Leah, or LaMonjello to get what she wants. I hate her, and I will fight her to the end, handcuffs or no.

When she is three feet away, she raises the gun, and as she is doing so, the closet in front of me erupts with a colorful barrage of jackets, lunch boxes, and papers. A screaming, compact, little black bomb of hatred explodes toward her like a missile.

It is LaMonjello, and his face is a mask of rage as he charges into her with the full force of his fury. She turns and directs the gun at him, but is a fraction of a second too late. LaMonjello is small, but he is determined, and he's seen enough to make him know how to hate. And tackling is his favorite part of football.

He catches her square in the solar plexus with more force than you'd think a kid his size could muster. Andrea is thrown violently backward against the uncovered window, her arms instinctively flailing out with her gun in hand. A wild shot, striking a fluorescent tube, makes my ears ring and my heart rattle. Thin glass shards and white powder rain down upon us.

Less than a second after her shot, the window shatters and her head dissolves at the same time. Andrea deflates like a popped balloon and crumples to the floor between a Star Wars lunch box and a tiny pink sneaker with an elephant on it. Multiple flash-bangs fly in through the shattered window, and as the spoons fly off, there is a quiet moment in which the only sound is the grenades landing on the floor.

A fraction of a second before they detonate, LaMonjello screams "Daaaaddddyyyy!" and leaps in my direction. I feel his arms locking around my neck as they go off, and my last cohesive thought is that the tears on his cheeks remind me of melting chocolate. And then deafening concussions and impossibly brilliant flashes of light scour my senses blank.

His words are lost as the room explodes around us. It is as if we are suspended in a towering thunderhead at the height of a raging storm. Even though I am prepared, I am still stunned to complete immobility by the sensory overload of the flash-bangs. I blink my eyes and see still-frame negatives of heavily armed men swarming into the room, like someone flipping through a homemade cartoon of images drawn on a pad of paper.

LaMonjello has welded himself to me with iron arms and legs, now wailing at full volume like he did during the Hicks callout. I close my eyes and try to bury my face into his, which is the closest I can come to hugging him back.

Epilogue

I've been placed on a two-week paid administrative leave. I've spent every moment at home with Sharon, Leah and LaMonjello. I do not think I can bring myself to return to work at the Stratton Police Department.

I had been twice forewarned that there are those "in high positions" who think I should not have been allowed to return after shooting Bob Slater to pieces two years ago. I've learned who some of these people are.

One of them is Russell Moody, our esteemed Chief of Police. Among the others are an outspoken member of city council, and the city attorney. I'm also told the mayor, unwilling to stand against the powers that be, had taken a stand against me. It seems Moody has had it in for me ever since the Slater shooting, but like the two-faced prick that he is, he hid behind a broad smile and a hearty, "Good job, son." Until, however, it was time to order a shot of opportunity. The order to remain at compromised authority after the children had all been exchanged for me had come directly from him.

I have spoken with Matthew Paulson, the Portland sniper who killed Andrea. He told me that when she stepped in front of the open window, he had a perfect shot. He said it appeared as if she were waiting to take the round; like she wanted it to come. Paulson got on the radio and made a desperate plea to be allowed to shoot, but Capelko said he'd been *ordered* by the chief to remain at compromised authority. Shortly after Andrea peered out the window, she walked toward me and left his sight. But then she was thrown backwards into his view again, and fired a shot, so he immediately took her out.

He never saw LaMonjello tackle Andrea, because it all happened past the open window. Paulson took her out without violating orders, and without ever knowing that LaMonjello was even there. He saved my life, thanks solely due to my son, who in fact *had* used his innate talent to smell trouble to get out of the picture, diving under a pile of jackets and clothing in the kindergarten room closet the moment the shooting started. Had he not tackled Andrea, she would have shot me in the head. There's not a doubt in my mind.

Since the end of the siege at Poway Valley School, Stratton detectives have been busy. In addition to their many other duties, they've executed a search at Andrea's apartment.

Among whatever trace evidence they found linking her to her various crimes, they also discovered underneath her bed a suitcase. In the suitcase were 13.2 million dollars, and change. In cash.

The money was initially impounded as evidence, but was ultimately returned to its original owner, an ex-Mafia guy named Pio Cantelli, now in his late seventies. Cantelli single-handedly built the Night Out chain of theater complexes spanning the country west of the Mississippi, originally as a front to launder mob money, but it became so successful, I'm told it is now a legitimate franchise.

Cantelli's daughter, actress Loretta Epstein, was the most notable hostage at Northwest Healing, and was the sole reason Bob Slater and Reginald Karch staged that siege in the first place. With his only daughter's life on the line, Cantelli ordered up the fifteen million in cash as easily as ordering *Carpaccio di Bue al Gorgonzola* from his favorite restaurant, and got it almost as fast, thereby ending the siege. But the suspect, Slater, disappeared with the money, and the rest is history.

Side note to that whole affair—Epstein finally got her Academy Award last year for Best Supporting Actress in the movie *Autumn Leaves*.

An FBI guy told me after Northwest Healing that the fibbies had been trying to nail Cantelli for years. All his businesses started out as fronts to launder dirty Mafia money, but they never were able to catch him at anything illegal. And now he gets his dirty money back. I love the irony.

As for my own immediate future, I don't know what I am going to do. My leave is up three days from now, and then I am supposed to go back to work. I don't want to ever go back, but I haven't been there long enough to retire, and I'm too old to start something else.

When the Andrea story went national, we began being hounded by major networks for interviews and appearances. It was not lost on the media that my family was held hostage two years ago, that lightning has again seemingly struck in the same place.

Contributions and donations have been pouring in. A fund was set up at Wells Fargo, where we bank, to accommodate the money. Several thousand dollars have come in so far, and that will likely continue for at least a few days, especially since we are slated to appear on *The Today Show* day after tomorrow. That money will help, but no matter how much comes in, it won't be enough to see us through all this if I quit my job. Also, I've been notified that the money used to pay off my mortgage and bills has been returned to Cantelli, leaving me back in deep in debt. I guess that's only fair; it was his to begin with regardless of how he obtained it.

Stratton Police has stationed an officer outside the house to keep the media and well-wishers away. I don't mind, since it seems to be the only way we can maintain any privacy.

After we left the school, two hours after Paulson took the shot that killed Andrea, I took my family to Giuseppe's for pizza. Since then, we have spent the entire time in the house, watching rented movies and just hanging out with each other. The Police Officer's Benevolent Group has delivered meals for us, and will continue until I go back to work.

Tomorrow morning, we are scheduled to hop a plane for New York City for our *Today Show* appearance. The kids are really looking forward to it, and spent this morning watching the show to see what it is all about.

LaMonjello knows perfectly well that he saved my life. He is proud of himself, and of me too, and he seems to feel no remorse about any of it. I have no idea how it will affect him in the future, and I'm sure that we will be keeping his therapists rich in the years to come. This will no doubt be the case for Leah as well, and I'd be lying by omission if I didn't include Sharon and myself too.

But I have to admit, I beamed when, the moment we were all reunited, he said, "Damn, Shair'n, you shoulda heard how Ben talked to dat woman. He tell her she don't mean *shit* to him. He say if she try to kiss on him, he gonna spit in her mouf. He say he love *you*, and that he be thinkin' 'bout *you* when he die, not her. He even say *f-you* to her!"

His bragging scores me more points with Sharon than all the romantic things I've ever done combined.

The kids are both sitting with me on the recliner as we watch the latest Disney animated movie. I'm having a great deal of trouble concentrating on the plot, because my mind is occupied with thoughts of what I will do. The last thing I want to do is go back to work for Moody, knowing what he did. My friends in the Stratton Police Officers Association are urging me to push for a stress retirement, but if I do that, I won't make more than a fraction of my current salary. Nevertheless, I suppose it's what I'll do, and maybe get a security guard job or something to augment my income.

As I think about the various ways the police department has screwed me the past few years, my Nextel buzzes. It has not done that since the hostage crisis ended and I am quick to answer it.

"Geller."

"Ben, it's David, outside your house. You have a visitor out here."

"So what? Send him packing."

"Uh, you might want to see this one."

"Who is it?"

"I don't know. But she's absolutely beautiful, and she arrived in a Hummer limo about four blocks long. She's . . . wait a sec, I *know* this chick. . . . Ben, you're not gonna believe this, but it's that actress who played Lorna in *Autumn Leaves*. Jesus Christ!"

Loretta Epstein. Wow. "Tell her I'm coming out, David."

"Cool. Let me know what happens."

Sharon and I go out to greet them. The driver opens the back door, and Loretta gets out, followed by a bent-over old guy with long strands of wispy gray hair. David, my bodyguard, unashamedly fawns over her, pulling his police notebook and getting her autograph before she takes a step toward the house.

She and her companion walk slowly up to the door, where she greets me by saying, quite unnecessarily, "Hello, Ben. I'm Loretta Epstein."

"I know. Hi. I'm Ben Geller, and this is my wife, Sharon. We, uh, really liked you in *Autumn Leaves*." I sound stupid, and I know it, but she is the first movie star I've ever met.

"Thanks. And I never got the chance to tell you two years ago, but thanks for what you did back at Northwest Healing. I really mean that, and uh, well, I'm sorry I never said it before."

"Hey, don't worry about it. I never knew you were this tall."

God that sounded stupid. OK, I admit it; I'm a little star-struck.

She smiles, and then says, "This is my father, Pio Cantelli." She helps the old man up the steps and into the house. "He wanted to come see you."

Whatever he may have been in his youth, Cantelli is nothing but an old man today.

"Mr. Cantelli," I say, nodding. "Please, come in."

We get inside, and Sharon pours coffee for everyone. Pio only wants hot water, which we give him.

He speaks in a raspy, old man's voice. "Geller . . . Ben. I'll get right to the point. I'm an old man. I've lived a what you might call an interesting life, and I've done very well by myself. I'm sure you know a little about me, about my ventures, etcetera. Most police do. I'm sure you've heard that I'm a feared Mafia don—you know, *Goodfellas*, *The Sopranos* and all that."

"I, uh . . . "

He waives a liver-spotted but well-manicured hand. "Ah, never mind. *Fugget about it,* right?" His laughter at his own joke dissolves to coughing. When he's done, he says, "Me, I always liked *The Godfather*. Anyway, you don't have to say anything."

"Anything" comes out "anyting," just like the movies, and I suppress a smile.

"I just wanted to tell you that I respect you. You've been through a lot. I know what you did to the bastard that held Loretta hostage two years ago, and I gotta say, I admire your work." This last line is delivered with a wink, and I don't know if he's joking or not.

"I wanted to thank you back then, but I was rather busy then. Anyway, I heard it almost cost you your family. And now, you've been put through all this. And with your family again too." He trails off, then says, "I'd like to meet your kids, Geller."

"Of course. Leah! LaMonjello! Come here, kids!" I shout.

They saunter in, and introductions are made.

"You're a very brave, handsome little boy," Cantelli says to LaMonjello, rubbing his now short-cut Afro. "And from what I hear, you're a pretty good football player too."

"I'm gonna be a Steeler when I grow up."

"Really? Then I got twenty Gs on them in your name for this year's Super Bowl."

"Say *what?*"

"Never mind. You're a good boy. I want you to remember that. And you, what a beautiful little girl you are."

Leah looks at the floor and smiles shyly. "Thank you," she whispers.

There is a brief moment of silence, and I tell them to go back and start the movie and I'll join them shortly. When they are gone, Cantelli says, "I love children. You have a wonderful family, Geller. Loretta here, she's my only family. I almost lost her two years ago. I credit you with saving her life."

"It wasn't just me, Mr. Cantelli. It was a team effort. I was just a small part of it."

He dismisses me with another wave. "Family is everything, Geller. I suspect you already know that. I also suspect that you're a man of principles. I am retired, but I'm still connected. I've been following politics in this town ever since that Northwest Healing business, and I don't mind saying we didn't put up with the kind of bullshit your police department pulls as a matter of policy. Not where I come from. Guys like your chief, Moody, well, they don't last long in our organization."

I don't know how to answer him. Before I can think of anything to say, he stands up to leave. Loretta gets up and tells us it was a pleasure meeting us.

He shuffles to the door, where the limo driver is waiting to help him out. Once he gets down the stairs to the sidewalk, he turns and says, "Russell Moody is a bad seed, and he won't last long. In fact, I was thinking of having him killed."

My mouth forms an "O," and Cantelli chuckles, but it quickly turns to another rasping cough. When he's done, he says, "I'm kidding, Geller. I can say things like that now, and no feds'll swoop down on me."

I give him an uncertain smile, and we shake hands, then he gets into the back of the limo. As the chauffeur walks around to the driver's side, the black window comes down, and Cantelli's hand motions me to come closer. He leans toward me, and says, "I'm giving you the money, Geller. Don't go back to your police job. You don't need that kind of trouble any more. Family, that's the ting. If anyone deserves that ransom money, you do. I got lawyers that will help you with taxes and investments. Don't worry about them, they work for you free. They'll take good care of you."

"Mr. Cantelli, I . . . "

He delivers what I assume to be his signature dismissive wave, and interrupts me. "You can call me Pio. You know, I think you're the first cop I ever liked. Seventy-eight years it takes me to meet a good cop. And now, you're not a cop any more. I like that."

"I . . ."

"You got a new account at your Wells Fargo. The bank manager and my people have everything set up. Go down there and talk to Mr. Lewis. Mark Lewis. He's the guy you'll be dealing with. Take the rest of your life off, and enjoy your family. No more police job for you. Take my advice, or you'll find yourself wearing concrete shoes."

He winks at me, and the window goes up, then the Hummer slowly drives away. Sharon looks at me and says, "You think it's true?"

"Of course it is," I say.

"What are we going to do, Ben?" She's starting to sound excited.

I look at my watch. It is ten to four, still business hours. I pluck my Nextel from my belt and dial a number from memory.

"City of Stratton. How may I direct your call?"

Looking into Sharon's eyes, I say, "Personnel Department, please."

For sales, editorial information, subsidiary rights information or a catalog, please write or phone or email

iBooks
1230 Park Avenue, 9a
New York, NY 10128, US
Sales: 1-800-68-BRICK
Tel: 212-427-7139
www.BrickTowerPress.com
email: bricktower@aol.com.

www.Ingram.com